WAYNE STINNETT

FALLEN PRIDE

USMC

A JESSE MCDERMITT NOVEL

Caribbean Adventure Series
Volume 4

2014

Published by DOWN ISLAND PRESS, 2014
Travelers Rest, SC

Library of Congress cataloging-in-publication Data
Stinnett, Wayne
Fallen Pride/Wayne Stinnett
p. cm. - (A Jesse McDermitt novel)
ISBN-13: 978-0615982915
ISBN-10: 0615982913

Graphics by Tim Ebaugh Photography and Design
Edited by Clio Editing Services
Proofreading by Donna Rich
Interior Design by Write.Dream.Repeat. Book Design

This is a work of fiction. Names, characters, and incidents are either the product of the author's imagination or are used fictitiously. Any resemblance to actual persons, living or dead, businesses, companies, events, or locales is entirely coincidental.

Most of the locations herein are also fictional, or are used fictitiously. However, I took great pains to depict the location and description of the many well-known islands, locales, beaches, reefs, bars, and restaurants in the Keys, to the best of my ability. The Rusty Anchor is not a real place, but if I were to open a bar in the Florida Keys, it would probably be a lot like depicted here. I've tried my best to convey the island attitude in this work.

FOREWORD

I'd like to thank the many people who encouraged me to write this third novel, especially my wife, Greta. Her love, encouragement, motivation, support, dreams for the future, and the many ideas she keeps coming up with have been a blessing. At times, I swear she was a Key West Wrecker in another life. Or maybe a Galley Wench, I'm not always sure. A special thanks to my youngest daughter, Jordy, for her many contributions and sometimes truly outlandish ideas. While only a twelve-year-old mind can conceive of some of the wacky ideas she has, many of them planted a seed in my mind that wound their way into the story. The title of this novel was her idea. I need to thank our other kids, Nicolette, Laura, and Richard, for their support and encouragement, but mostly for not laughing at a tired old truck driver thinking he could write yet another book during the downtime in the sleeper of his truck.

A very special thank-you to Nicole Godsey, of Nicole Godsey Photography for her outstanding cover photo. Also, thank you to her husband, Corey Godsey, and friend, Zack Bolter, two Wounded Warriors, who appear on the cover. You can see more of her work at www.nicolegodseyphotography.com

I also owe a special thanks to my old friend, Tim Ebaugh, of Tim Ebaugh Photography and Design, for the cover design. You can see more of his work at www.timebaughdesigns.com.

Lastly, where would any writer be without a great editor and proofreaders? While I can come up with a decent story line and characters, it's Eliza Dee of Clio Editing Services that puts the polishing touches on it all. Thanks also to beta readers Timothy Artus, Joe Lipshetz, Nicole Godsey, Debbie Kocol, Rob Pedrick, Mike Ramsey, Marcus Lowe, Alan Fader, and Bill Cooksey.

DEDICATION

To Greta.

My best friend, lover, motivator, inspirer, and wife.
To you, I promise all of my tomorrows.

"I've been followed and spied upon more than once in my life. An earlier life, anyway. I've spent a lot of time in Third World countries, jungle areas, the remaining dark places on this earth."
- **Marion "Doc" Ford**, *Everglades*, 2003

If you'd like to receive my twice a month newsletter for specials, book recommendations, and updates on coming books, please sign up on my website:

WWW.WAYNESTINNETT.COM

THE CHARITY STYLES CARIBBEAN THRILLER SERIES

Merciless Charity
Ruthless Charity (Summer, 2016)
Heartless Charity (Winter, 2017)

THE JESSE MCDERMITT
CARIBBEAN ADVENTURE SERIES

Fallen Out
Fallen Palm
Fallen Hunter
Fallen Pride
Fallen Mangrove
Fallen King
Fallen Honor
Fallen Tide
Fallen Angel
Fallen Hero (Fall, 2016)

The Gaspar's Revenge Ship's Store is now open. There you can purchase all kinds of swag related to my books.
WWW.GASPARS-REVENGE.COM

FALLEN PRIDE

MAPS

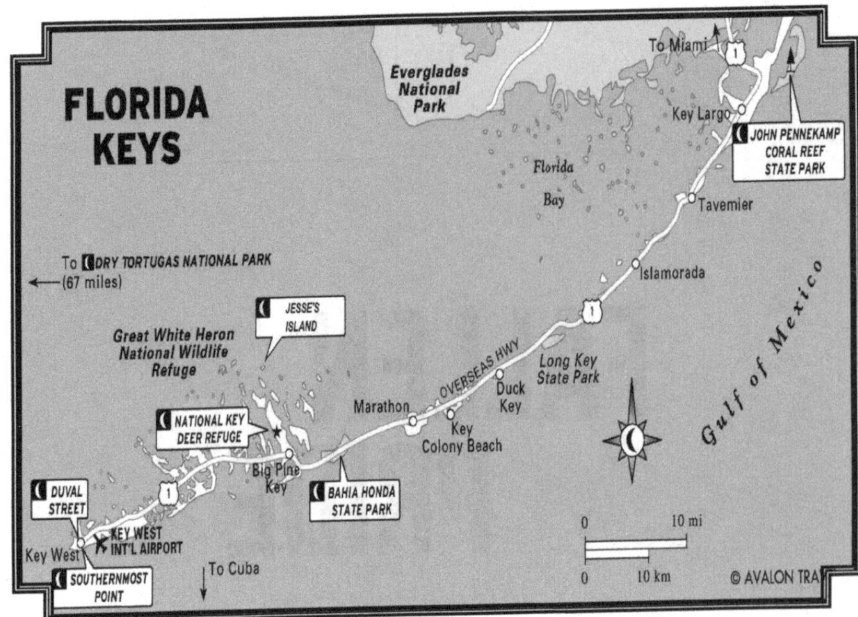

The Florida Keys

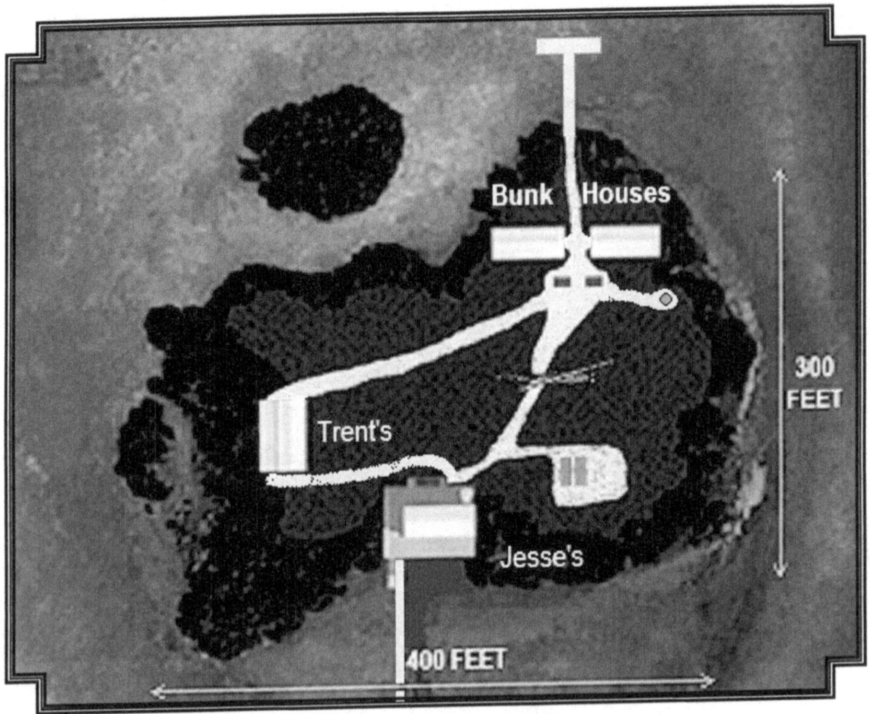

Jesse's Island

PROLOGUE

Two men lay among a cluster of large boulders. They'd been there over twenty-four hours, shivering through the still, cold night and sweating through the midday heat. Each man was covered with what's commonly called a ghillie suit, a heavy garment stitched with colored strips of free-hanging cloth meant to blend in with the surrounding elements. In this case, most of the surrounding element was rock and boulders, so there was a lot of gray in their covering. Indeed, they were nearly invisible from a distance. However, the ghillie suits were designed more for use in jungle and woodlands. Here on this desolate gray landscape they were quite visible if someone got within twenty or thirty feet.

Fortunately, there were few people in this part of Iraq and anyone that wandered within a hundred meters of where the two men lay waiting was visible to them. Behind them was an overhanging cliff about thirty feet high that kept them shadowed throughout the day. No

chance anyone would stumble on them from the rear. They'd chosen this particular location for just this reason. It offered ideal cover considering the options and was easily defended, should anyone from the small cluster of homes and shops below happen to come up into the hills.

One man had a high-powered spotting scope mounted on a short tripod and covered with the same cloth their ghillie suits were made from. As he looked through the scope, he spoke into a small microphone mounted on a boom in front of his mouth. "Alpha Six, Raptor has acquired the target. Looks like Nine of Diamonds, sending photo for confirmation."

Moments later, the image was received by analysts at Field Operating Base Grizzly in Camp Ashraf, Iraq. The FOB was where Alpha Company of the 1st Battalion, 9th Marine Regiment was based, attached to the 6th Marine Regiment. The image was scanned and facial recognition software only took a few seconds to confirm that the person the two men were watching was a high-value target by the name of Ahmed Qazir al Ramani, the Nine of Diamonds in the most wanted deck.

Over the headset, the man on the scope heard a voice reply, "Target is confirmed, Raptor. You're clear to engage."

"We have confirmation Jared," the man on the scope said to his partner. "You were right, it's Nine of Diamonds."

The second man lay motionless behind an M-40A3 rifle, loaded with Lapua .308 moly-coated boat tail ammunition. He spoke without moving his eye from the scope.

"It's a gift, Billy. Had it all my life. I see a face and can remember it forever. Range me."

Marine Sergeant William 'Billy' Cooper leaned into the scope, taking readings. "Range is nine hundred and five meters. Declination, minus ten degrees. Air is still and heavy." Billy was the spotter. Marine Scout/Sniper teams worked in pairs, almost always alone and far from the units they were assigned to, in this case Alpha, 1/9. The battalion had only recently been reactivated, having been stood down in 1994. In Vietnam the battalion earned the nickname 'Walking Dead' and they still carry it today.

The second man, Corporal Jared Williams, was an accomplished shooter long before enlisting in the Marine Corps after the terrorist attacks on 9/11. Born and raised in the mountains of eastern Kentucky, he'd won a number of shooting competitions starting at the age of twelve and all through his teenage years. He made a slight adjustment to the elevation of the rifle and said, "Target acquired."

Billy relayed the message to the FOB and waited. He didn't have to wait long before the voice in his headset replied, "You're clear to take the shot, Raptor. I repeat, shot cleared."

Billy took a slow breath. "You're clear to fire when ready, Jared. No change in conditions."

Jared hadn't moved a muscle in more than fifteen minutes. Only now did he make the tiniest of moves, as his right index finger, which had been alongside the trigger guard, moved imperceptibly to the trigger. He could see the target clearly through the U.S. Optics MST-100 scope. He was inside a small stucco-and-stone house a little

over half a mile away. He was sitting in a chair in front of a window, reading. Jared slowly took the slack out of the trigger after taking a long, slow breath and releasing it. It was an easy shot, conditions were ideal and the target was unmoving. He had twelve prior confirmed kills, all of them more difficult than this one. Eight on his previous tour in Iraq, and four in the last three months since joining 1/9 and arriving back in country.

The pressure slowly increased on the trigger as the image in the scope moved up and down a fraction of a millimeter at regular intervals, caused by the beating of Jared's own heart. He knew exactly the pressure required to release the firing pin and send the round downrange, and he timed it so that it occurred when the image rose with the beat of his heart and the crosshairs fell on the bridge of the man's nose. The report of the rifle echoed off the granite cliff behind them, dispersing and seeming to come from all directions at once. Another reason they had chosen this site.

At half a mile, it took slightly more than a second for the round to traverse the distance from the muzzle to the target. A second that would change the young shooter's life, permanently. It all seemed to happen in slow motion as he continued to watch through the scope to confirm the kill. In the first half a second, a slight shadow passed over the man's face as he was reading. In the next half a second, his eyes came up slightly over his reading glasses and a smile came to his face. In the following millisecond, which seemed to take hours, someone stepped in front of the man in the chair. His eight-year-old daughter. In the next few milliseconds a hole appeared in the glass of the window and cracks radiated out from it like

a spider's web. In the last millisecond a pink mist emanated from the girl's head, spreading over the man in the chair as the girl fell forward into her father's lap, dead.

CHAPTER ONE:

Present Day Key West

Jared Williams bolted upright, shaking and drenched in a cold sweat. The image of the dead girl in her father's lap and the man looking right at him through the hole in the glass was still fresh in his mind. As it always did, it took a few seconds to take stock and realize he'd had the nightmare again. He was in his bed, in his small apartment above a garage. The garage sat on a small corner lot in Old Town Key West with a two-story Conch house next to it. It was owned by a wealthy Canadian, who was only in residence for a few months in the winter. Jared took care of the property and grounds in exchange for free rent.

He had experienced the same recurring nightmare hundreds of times since that day two years earlier. His gift of remembering faces was now a curse. After the incident, he and Billy had made their way around the cliffs and up into the mountains for helicopter extraction two days later. While Jared was being debriefed by an un-

identified agent with Central Intelligence, the man had insinuated that he had killed the girl intentionally. Jared had come unglued and lunged across the table in a fit of rage, nearly beating the man to death before Billy could pull him off. He had spent the following month in the brig, before being flown back to Camp Lejeune, North Carolina, for a quiet court-martial. He was sentenced to time already served and forfeiture of all pay and allowances, reduced in rank to Private, and dishonorably discharged. The pride of the Marine Corps couldn't handle any more bad press about its Marines killing innocent civilians.

His next two months were spent in an alcohol-induced stupor when he returned to his home in Kentucky. His brother had followed him into the Marine Corps and was currently stationed at Camp Lejeune, though Jared hadn't gotten a chance to see him before leaving. His mom and dad, now empty nesters, had pulled up stakes and headed south to get away from the cold mountain winters. But Kentucky was his home and where his friends were, so that's where he went. It didn't take long for him to find that his old friends from high school were no longer the same. Many had left the hills and taken jobs in the surrounding cities, or headed off to college. Those that remained in the small town of Sassafras, near the Virginia border, seemed different from him somehow. A few years older, but they seemed to be perpetually stuck in high school. Unable to find a job, he was soon almost out of money. He sold his 1985 Ford pickup to a friend, bought a Greyhound ticket to Key West, and called his dad to ask if he had room to put him up for a week or two, until he could find work.

Arriving in Key West was like entering a different dimension. The verdant green hills and mountains of Kentucky were replaced with the flat blue of the tropical ocean. The regimented military lifestyle was replaced with the wild abandon of this centuries-old pirate town.

His dad had taken a job on a shrimp trawler as a mechanic a year earlier. His reputation had quickly grown in the small island community as a man with a knack for understanding and being able to fix all sorts of mechanical problems. In a place with almost as many boats as people, he'd found plenty of work on his days off, repairing boats, cars, and trucks, and even doing some mechanical work on private planes. He'd saved up, got his private pilot's license, and bought an old float plane, with the idea of taking tourists and fishermen around the island chain to places you couldn't get to by car, and getting them there faster than by boat.

Jared's folks didn't really have room in their small mobile home on Stock Island, but let him stay on the couch anyway. His dad made it clear that it was temporary and gave him a month. David Williams hadn't raised his boys to be slackers, and they weren't. Less than a week after Jared's arrival, his dad made the arrangement for the garage apartment with a fly fisherman from Canada he'd met earlier that winter and taken up in his plane several times. A few days later, a friend of his mom told her about a job opening at a restaurant and bar just off of Duval Street, where most of Key West's hot spots were located. Arriving at the Blue Heaven and meeting the manager, he learned that the opening was for a bouncer/bar back. Being just over six feet tall, two hundred pounds, and muscular gave him an edge and the fact that he had

served in the Marines got him the job. He didn't mention that he'd been dishonorably discharged and the manager never asked.

He worked hard for two years, making friends around the island and at the restaurant, a popular place with locals and tourists alike. The job suited him. He quickly found that his training on the battlefield gave him the ability to read people better than most, and usually he could stop an altercation before it even started, simply by imposing himself on the occasional rowdy drunk. This was something his boss liked. He looked after the waitresses and bartenders like they were his little sisters and soon they looked up to him as their big brother, even the ones that were a little older than him. During his time off, he worked out a lot. The Canadian had a complete weight set in the garage, and the work around the property could be hard at times, especially after a storm. He would cut up the many branches that fell from the oak and elm trees, using an old bucksaw he'd picked up at a yard sale. He soon added fifteen pounds of hard muscle to his already powerful physique.

The nightmares didn't go away, though. One of the regulars at the bar was an old guy named Jackson Wainwright that everyone just called Pop. He seemed like a harmless guy most of the time. On the smallish side, maybe five foot eight and a wiry hundred and sixty-five pounds, with long gray hair and beard, he was usually barefoot or wore flip-flops, but always dressed in baggy shorts, and a worn-out tee shirt. One night, a year after Jared arrived in Key West, Pop went completely nuts and started a fight with two Vietnamese tourists. Jared had to break it up and kick him out. That's when he learned

that Pop was a Vietnam veteran. Once he got the old man outside, struggling all the way, Pop collapsed at the curb, sobbing incoherently. Not knowing what to do, Jared sat on the curb next to the old man, and within a few minutes each realized they were kindred spirits. He sought out Pop many times after that night, when the tension and nightmares came. It seemed to help them both, just to sit and talk about their experiences and fears. Still, the nightmares didn't go away.

CHAPTER TWO:

There's Gold in Them Thar... Waters.

We were anchored at the GPS coordinates that my old Platoon Sergeant, Russ Livingston, had last dove on and where he'd been murdered. In the last six months we'd learned a lot about the Confederate blockade runner *Lynx*. Some of it through research done by Chyrel Koshinski, a former CIA technical analyst, and some from a man named Jackson McCormick. He was the great-grandson of Lieutenant Colonel Abner McCormick, Commanding Officer of the 2nd Florida Cavalry during the Civil War. When the *Lynx* was sunk coming out of Fort Pierce, Colonel McCormick was aboard with twelve gold bars weighing a combined hundred and twenty pounds. He was in charge of taking the gold to a Colonel Harrison of the 1st Florida Battalion in Saint Augustine. The gold was a gift from the French government to help fund the Confederacy and had been melted down into Confederate gold bars at the mint in New Orleans.

Deuce and I had visited Mister McCormick several weeks ago. Deuce was Russ Livingston's son and had become one of my closest friends in the last year. He's a Navy SEAL, but is now attached to the Department of Homeland Security. Last fall, he'd roped me into helping them and I'd sort of become a part of the team he was in charge of, searching out and eradicating terrorist threats in the Caribbean.

It was during that time that a woman I'd known a year earlier, Alex DuBois, had come back to the Keys and we'd quickly fallen in love. Actually, we were already in love but never realized it. She was kidnapped on our wedding day by the people Deuce was investigating and murdered that night. Since then, I'd pretty much given up on life and only found purpose in helping Deuce's team on another assignment.

While we were visiting Mister McCormick, he had shown us the letters his great-grandfather had written to his wife. This was Russ's first clue to what the *Lynx* was carrying. In those letters, Colonel McCormick had written that he had a French passenger that he was escorting to Saint Augustine, who would help finance the Confederate cause. The French passenger's name, he'd written, was Douzaine Lingots Dior. Few people in Florida at that time spoke French, but the Colonel and his wife did. It was a rudimentary code telling her that he was taking a dozen gold bars to Saint Augustine. With just a glance, Deuce and I agreed that if we could find it, we'd cut Mister McCormick in. My old friend, Rusty Thurman, had a salvage license, so we'd enlisted his help. Rusty owns the *Rusty Anchor Bar and Grill* in Marathon and Deuce was engaged to his daughter, Julie.

We'd been looking for four days, with no luck. Sometimes we would spend eight hours a day under the surface of the shallow waters off Fort Pierce. We were taking a lunch break when Deuce said what all three of us were thinking: "Maybe Lester came back and found the rest, but didn't tell Sonny about it."

Elijah 'Sonny' Beech was a loan shark and smuggler in West Palm Beach and Lester was one of his crew. It was Lester that had killed Deuce's dad and two other of Sonny's crew had killed my wife. All three murderers were now dead and Sonny was enjoying the sunshine in Gitmo, due to the fact that he'd attempted to smuggle terrorists into the country.

The more I thought about it, the less likely it seemed. "I don't think so," I finally said. "Lester had everything on him that he'd stolen from your dad and not pawned." I found Lester more than a week after he'd knocked me off my own skiff and escaped into the mangrove covered keys, north of Big Pine Key. He'd gotten lost, run out of gas, and been nearly dead from hunger and dehydration on a small island near Raccoon Key when I'd found him. I'm sure he died eventually, but not by my hand. "If we don't find anything today," I continued, "we'll have to either give up or start again next week." Deuce's fiancée, Julie, was currently undergoing training with the Coast Guard at their Maritime Enforcement facility at Marine Corps Base, Camp Lejeune, North Carolina, and would graduate in three days. All three of us planned to be there when she did.

Rusty checked the onboard compressor and said, "Tanks are full. Let's get back down there."

We put our gear back on and stepped off the dive platform at the stern of my boat, *Gaspar's Revenge*. She's a forty-five-foot Rampage convertible that I use for fishing and diving charters, though lately I wasn't doing much of either. I'd bought the *Revenge*, along with my tiny island in the Content Keys, six years ago when I retired from the Marine Corps. This past winter, I'd learned that my late wife had left me an inheritance, most of which I'd donated to causes that were important to us both. I had my military pension and was under an agreement with Deuce's former boss to make myself available to move his men and equipment around on the *Revenge* whenever the need arose, so I really didn't need to take out charters very often.

We descended to the bottom and once more split up, using underwater metal detectors to sweep the ocean floor. We'd moved the boat several times over the last four days, but never more than a few hundred feet from the coordinates that were on Russ's GPS, and we restricted our searches to an area no more than fifty feet from the boat. As I swam along a small ridge, my detector pinged. We'd had dozens of false readings, but this one was strong. I pulled a small gardening shovel from my belt and started probing the bottom where the detection was strongest. Almost immediately, I hit something large and hard. I dug away the sand to reveal what looked to be a large, heavily encrusted anchor chain. I uncovered more and more of the chain, until I could see a good ten feet of it. Each link was about six inches long and three inches wide, with the rings being at least three-quarters of an inch thick. As I pondered the chain's significance, I looked over at the ridge we'd been following. Suddenly,

it struck me. I was looking at the remnants of a boat, the lines still clearly visible in my mind's eye.

I reached back, pulled on a plastic ball that was bungeed to my tank, and released it. It made a loud clanging sound that traveled a long way underwater. A few minutes later, Deuce and Rusty swam over the ridge and down to where I rested on my knees on the ocean floor. I pointed out the chain and Deuce swam to it and examined it closer. He looked up and nodded, thinking the same thing I was. Could this be the anchor chain of the *Lynx*? All three of us had studied the shipbuilder's drawings and read everything Chyrel had found on the subject, and the chain was the perfect size based on all the references we found to it.

Then I pointed to the ridge itself. At first, Deuce and Rusty didn't see it and looked back at me with a shrug. I cupped my hands, with the outside edges of my palms together, the signal for 'boat'. They looked back at the low wall and I watched both their heads turn as they studied the length of it. Together we swam toward it, then up to the top. I used the gardening shovel to move some of the sand away from the edge and soon found what looked like a large ship's rib just below the sand. Moving exactly two feet along the top of the ridge, I did the same thing and found another. Rusty moved the opposite way and found a third one. He then pointed away from the ledge, where the bottom fell away about twenty feet from where we were. I kicked toward the surface until I could hover about ten feet above the others to get a bird's eye view. Rusty and Deuce joined me and I could tell from the look in their eyes they could see it also. There, on the bottom, was the outline of a broken ship, over two hun-

dred feet in length. However, unless you were looking for a ship, it appeared to be just two ledges that ran parallel, then came together at both ends. We knew the *Lynx* was steel-hulled, but underlaid with wooden stringers. It was the stringers that had caught my attention, seeming to be too symmetrical. The steel hull had long since rusted away to nothing.

I looked up at the position of the *Revenge* and noted she was nearly on top of us. I needed to move her straight forward of the current position about fifty feet, slightly more than a boat length. Then we could use the mailbox I'd bought to clear some of the sand away. A mailbox is a large tube that turns at a ninety-degree angle and fits over the propeller of a boat to force water straight down. In its raised position, the opening pointed aft, it looked like a mailbox.

I motioned to Rusty and pointed at the center of the ship below us, then pointed to Deuce and myself and up to the *Revenge*. Rusty and I had probably made a thousand dives together and he knew instantly what I wanted him to do. He swam down to the bottom, positioning himself right in the middle of the old ship.

Deuce and I swam to the surface and I climbed aboard, telling Deuce to hang on the swim platform and tell me when to stop. I climbed up to the bridge and engaged the anchor windlass. Fortunately we'd let out a lot of anchor rode. Slowly the *Revenge* crept forward, pulling the anchor line aboard. After a few minutes Deuce called up to me, "Hold it there. I'm directly over Rusty."

A minute later, Rusty was aboard and we put two large Danforth anchors in the small rowing dinghy we were towing. Deuce climbed into the dinghy and rowed astern

at a thirty-degree angle until the hundred-foot anchor lines were fully paid out. He dropped the anchor overboard and Rusty hauled on it until the line was tight, then lashed it to the port cleat while Deuce rowed in an arc to another position thirty degrees out from the stern in the opposite direction. There, he dropped the second anchor. Rusty hauled on that line and tied it off to the starboard cleat once it was taut.

Now we were anchored solidly above the wreck. Rusty and I lowered the mailbox, which I'd rigged without having to drill holes in the transom by attaching it to the swim platform itself. It wasn't perfect, but should work if I didn't rev the starboard engine too high. As Deuce was rowing back to the boat, I noticed a Florida Marine Patrol boat approaching. It came alongside as Deuce was climbing back aboard. There were two FMP Officers aboard, a Lieutenant and a Sergeant, the Sergeant at the helm.

"Good afternoon, Lieutenant," I said while climbing down from the bridge.

"Good afternoon, sir," he said. "I'm Lieutenant Briggs. Can I ask what you think you're doing?"

"You could," Deuce said. "But we know what we're doing."

The Lieutenant looked from me to Deuce. "It appears to me that you're doing some kind of salvage work here. You have to be a licensed salvor to do that and this doesn't look like a salvage boat."

Rusty had already gone to his bag to get his salvor's license, knowing the FMP Officer would want to see it. Handing it to the man he said, "You mean like this one, Eltee?"

The Lieutenant studied the document and looked at Rusty, then at the two of us. "I'll need to see some ID. From all of you."

Deuce stepped closer to the gunwale and stared down at the Lieutenant. He'd retrieved his wallet from his pants pocket, lying on the cleaning table by the salon hatch, and he opened it and showed the Lieutenant his DHS credentials. "No, you won't. I'm an agent with Homeland Security. You can leave now."

"Mister," the Lieutenant said, "I don't care if you're James Bond himself. These waters are my juris—"

Deuce cut him off midsentence. "Lieutenant Briggs, you work for the State of Florida and I just identified myself as an agent for the Department of Homeland Security, a federal agency. Our papers are in order and you're dismissed. Or, if you like, I can have Captain McDermitt here contact your boss and he can tell you you're dismissed. Both ways, you're gone and we're in the water in less than five minutes. Your call."

The Lieutenant looked at his Sergeant, then handed Rusty the license back. "No wonder nobody likes you Feds," he said as he motioned for the Sergeant to shove off.

Once they were well away, Deuce turned to Rusty and grinned. Rusty said, "You really get your rocks off doing that, don't you?"

"Absolutely." Then he looked over at me and added, "Let's blow some sand away, Jesse."

I climbed back up to the bridge and started the starboard engine, while Rusty and Deuce looked over the transom on either side. I put the engine in forward and brought the rpms up to one thousand. The mailbox

would probably hold at fifteen hundred, but the water was only twenty feet deep and the big props on the *Revenge* move a lot of water. I held it there for about four minutes, then backed it down, put the transmission in neutral, and shut off the engine.

"Can't see shit," Rusty said. "You sure blew up a lot of sand."

We had to wait about ten minutes more while the compressor refilled the three tanks yet again. By then, the current had carried away most of the sand and we could see the outline of the ship clearly. We put our gear back on and headed back down to the bottom. We only had a couple of hours of daylight left.

Before we even got close to the bottom, Rusty pointed and we all saw it. The unmistakable glint of gold. Even after more than a hundred and forty years buried in the sand, it gleamed like the day it had been removed from the molds. Gold is too dense for anything to attach to it. Scattered in a small area were eleven gold bars, and we each picked one up. I looked over at Deuce and Rusty. They were both having a hard time breathing, grinning around their regulators as they were. We carried the bars up to the boat, and I climbed up on the swim platform while they went back down four more times. I stacked the gold bars in one of the fish boxes built into the deck as they brought them up.

Once we had them in the fish box, we each leaned against the railing and looked down at them. "I can't believe it," Deuce said. "We actually found it."

"That there's one hundred and ten pounds of pure gold, man. I thought they'd be bigger," Rusty said with a

grin. "Just the melt value alone, that's worth over a million bucks."

"Historic value," I said, "twice that and then some. Since it's the property of a nation that no longer exists, the government will have a hard time proving ownership."

"Think there's anything else down there of value, Jesse?" Deuce asked.

"I doubt it. You read the information Chyrel gathered. The *Lynx* already unloaded here in Fort Pierce and was commandeered by Colonel McCormick at the last minute. All the crew made it ashore except him."

"No reason to hang around," Rusty said. "I know a guy with the Florida Historical Society. I'm sure he'd be interested in buying it. We're gonna have to get the state and federal governments involved too, since we're inside the twelve-mile limit."

"I doubt Washington would even send anyone down," Deuce said. "Not over a paltry couple of million dollars."

We started getting ready to return to the Keys. Deuce rowed out to where the stern anchors were set, taking a long coil of rope. He free dove down to each and used the rope to hoist them up to the dinghy, and then I used the windlass to hoist the bow anchor. Within fifteen minutes we were ready to get underway.

Just as the sun was starting to set, I pushed the throttles forward and the twin 1015-horse Cats responded instantly, lifting the bow and bringing the big boat up onto plane. I never get tired of that feeling. It was two hundred and fifty miles back to Marathon, so we set the autopilot and took shifts on the bridge for the ten-hour run.

CHAPTER THREE:

Red Right Returning

We pushed a little faster than normal cruising speed. What the hell? We had over a million dollars in gold. Burning a little more fuel wasn't about to break us. We arrived at Rusty's home and place of business, the *Rusty Anchor Bar and Grill*, at zero three hundred to a less-than-millionaire welcome.

Tying off to the dock, we noticed that there were no lights on in either the liveaboards tied at the docks, or the bar. Not really unusual, as closing time was zero two hundred or whenever Rusty chose. Since the Florida State tax official and the appraiser from the Historical Society weren't due to arrive until zero eight hundred, we moved the gold to the forward stateroom. I have a digitally controlled lock that allows the bunk to be raised and a large storage chest under it with a combination padlock, along with several other smaller boxes and cases. The chest had plenty of room for the gold and with it being inside a

locked chest, under a locked bunk, inside a locked cabin, with a security system, we agreed it was safe.

The three of us decided a drink was in order to celebrate our newfound fortune. Walking to the bar, I heard a dog bark and my big Portuguese water dog came bounding around the corner from the backyard.

"Pescador! How ya doing, buddy?"

He was excited that I was home, obviously. His heavy tail was nearly wagging him as he jumped from one of us to the other, accepting ear scratches.

Rusty unlocked the door and we went inside. He'd left his old Jamaican cook, Rufus, in charge and hired my former first mate, Jimmy, to help out behind the bar. The place looked just as clean and spotless as it had when we'd left.

Rusty walked behind the bar and pulled a bottle out from one of the lower cabinets, along with three highball glasses. "Pusser's?"

"Absolutely," I replied. "Admiral Nelson's best."

He poured two fingers in each glass and we sat down at the end of the bar. Pescador lay down by the door, as he usually did.

"What do you think the appraiser's gonna say, Jesse?" Rusty asked.

I thought about it for a moment. I was no expert on lost treasure, but Deuce's dad and I had found some years ago. We'd sold it to a less-than-reputable dealer for the melt value to avoid the taxes. Afterward, we'd learned that sometimes the intrinsic value was high enough that paying the taxes yielded more return. However, that was only for treasure found outside the territorial waters. "I'm not a hundred percent certain about the amount,

but this being Civil War treasure it's bound to be quite a bit more than the melt value, even after taxes. I'd guess about two million. He's going to try to lowball us, though. The tax man will help us get the best price."

"Yeah," Deuce said, laughing. "So the State can get a bigger share of it."

Rusty put the bottle back in the cabinet and said, "We better get a little rest. It's gonna be a long day."

Deuce and I headed down to the docks while Rusty locked up and walked to his little Conch house next to the bar. Julie had been trying to talk Deuce into buying a boat for several months. She wanted a little houseboat they could dock here at the marina. Deuce had decided on a forty-two-foot Whitby cutter-rigged ketch, though. I had to admit it was a nice little blue water cruiser. My first mate, Doc Talbot and I had helped crew her when Deuce flew to Bimini and bought her. Julie still didn't know about it. They were getting married in two weeks and he was going to take her cruising to the Lesser Antilles for a month-long honeymoon.

As we walked along the docks he asked, "How should this be split up, Jesse? I really don't need or want any of it."

"You have more than yourself to think of, old son. Julie's a sensible girl and doesn't need much, but one day you're going to have kids and they'll need to go to college. Besides, it was your dad's find. I propose a five-way split after the state takes its share. Twenty percent each to the three of us, another twenty percent to Mister McCormick, and twenty percent to Russ. I'm sure he'd have wanted his share going to his grandkids' education."

"But it was your boat, Jesse. You should get a bigger share. Plus, you had all the expense."

I stopped and turned to him at the gangplank to his sailboat. "Deuce, I have way more money than I'll need in two lifetimes and you know my needs are few. I'm giving a chunk of my share to Chyrel and the rest is going into maintaining the island for a few years."

"Dad always put a lot of stock in education. He and Mom lived on base most of the time and he put away every penny he could so my sister and I could go to college. I guess I'll do the same." Then he grinned and added, "Julie ever tell you she wants a bunch of kids?"

Then he turned, went down the gangplank to his cockpit, and disappeared into the aft cabin. Pescador and I continued to the end of the long dock to the *Revenge* and turned in. I set the coffeemaker up to start at zero seven hundred and turned in for a short nap.

The aroma of Colombia's greatest export roused me three hours later. The sun was streaming in through the overhead porthole. I poured a cup into a heavy mug that had the Marine Recon emblem on it, a winged skull with a regulator in its mouth and crossed oars behind it, and then poured the rest into a large thermos. Carrying both and an extra mug up to the bridge, I sat down and watched the early-morning activity in the marina. Mornings are my favorite time of day. Enjoying a cup of coffee while watching the sun slowly climb into the sky seems to recharge me, regardless of how little sleep I might have had the night before.

Rusty had done a lot of work over the last year and it showed. Just over a year ago, this was nothing more than a shallow canal, accessible only by skiff, a type of shallow

water boat that's very common in the Keys. He'd dredged it to ten feet and enlarged the end to make a turning basin large enough for a sixty-footer to comfortably turn around. He'd had concrete poured along both sides down to the waterline, with built-in rubber fenders, and added water and electric hookups every thirty feet. The result was a slow influx of permanent and semipermanent liveaboards.

Across the canal from me was a beautiful blue-and-white wooden sailboat. It belonged to my old friend, Dan Sullivan. He spent nearly as much time taking care of his boat as he did playing his guitar, which was considerable. She was over one hundred years old, a gaff-rigged Friendship, built in Maine at the turn of the last century.

Next to him was a big, slow-moving thirty-six-foot Monk trawler, owned by a young couple from South Carolina. They'd arrived in Marathon a few months ago and I hadn't met them yet. Of course, I spend most of my time on my island up in the Content Keys.

Further north from the Monk were two smaller sloops. Nobody lived on them and I had no idea who owned them.

Astern the *Revenge* was an old, sedate thirty-foot Pearson cabin cruiser. She was owned by a middle-aged man by the name of Hank Cooper. He'd arrived in Marathon devastated and nearly broke after a divorce, and the Pearson was apparently the only thing his ex-wife hadn't gotten. He seemed intelligent and educated, but had taken the first job he could find as an overnight cab driver for the island's largest cab company, Cheapo Taxi.

Aft the Pearson was the small-boat dockage, with an assortment of ten or twelve skiffs and open fishing boats,

depending on the season. Rusty had installed a fuel dock at the end next to his big flat-topped barge and offered both gas and diesel fuel. The lower rates he charged for dockage attracted the small boat owners and offset a slightly higher gas price than surrounding marinas.

"Jesse!" The familiar voice came from across the canal. Dan was in the cockpit of his sloop. "When did you guys get back?"

"A few hours ago, Dan. How's things been here this week?"

"Nothing exciting," he called back. "You up for a morning run?"

Dan and I worked out on occasion. He preferred running and I preferred swimming, but we had a mutual interest in martial arts. "Can't this morning," I said. "We have a meeting in an hour."

He gave me a questioning look, but I didn't elaborate. "Well, it's Saturday, so you know where I'll be this afternoon. I'll buy you a beer later."

I replied by lifting my coffee mug and nodding as he trotted off through the tree line on a path that would take him over to Sombrero Beach Road. Dan is a singer and song writer and played weekends on the deck behind Rusty's bar. It was probably the most profitable addition Rusty had made this year. The deck was quite large, with seating for almost a hundred people, and a small stage in the corner.

Deuce stepped down from his sloop, walked over, and joined me on the bridge. I poured coffee into the extra mug and handed it to him. He sat down on the bench seat to port and asked, "Think they'll be on time?"

"I'd bet my life on the tax man being punctual."

"No doubt," he said.

"The Florida Historical Society guy sounded mighty interested, too," Rusty said as he stepped aboard.

"Grab a mug from the galley, Rusty," I said.

He disappeared into the salon, then climbed up to the bridge, and pouring himself a cup as he asked, "What'd the Feds say?"

"Not interested," Deuce replied. "They knew it'd cost them more in attorney fees to prove ownership. But they will expect a ten ninety-nine from the Historical Society."

The sound of tires on the crushed-shell driveway interrupted our conversation as the three of us turned around to look. I smiled when I saw the Jaguar sedan pull into the little parking lot.

Rusty noticed my smile. "Nice lady there. She ain't gonna wait forever, brother."

"Shut up, ya damn Jarhead," I said. Rusty and I had gone through boot camp and served together in a few places early in my career. Deuce's dad was our Platoon Sergeant when we were stationed together in Okinawa, Japan. Rusty had left the Corps after just four years because his wife was pregnant. She died giving birth to Julie and it's only been the two of them for the last twenty-seven years.

The door to the car opened and a woman got out. She had a huge mane of dark red hair, which caught the sunlight filtering through the trees and gave the appearance of a Phoenix. She was dressed in dark blue Capri shorts, a light blue short-sleeved blouse, and navy topsiders. She walked toward the boat in a casual way that was born of a self-assurance few women possessed.

"Permission to come aboard, Captain?"

"Like he's got the cojones to tell you no," Rusty said.

Jackie Burdick stepped lightly down to the deck and was up the ladder to the bridge in seconds. "He's got 'em, Rusty. I've seen them myself. He's just afraid I might cut 'em off next time he's on my table."

Rusty and Deuce both roared with laughter, scaring a pelican off the end of the dock into the water. Lieutenant Commander Burdick had been the doctor on duty at the Navy hospital a few months ago when I'd had to undergo emergency surgery to remove a bullet lodged near my spine. A few weeks later she'd stepped in front of another bullet meant for me and spent a week recovering in her own hospital.

"Good to see ya again, Jackie," I said.

She sat down in the only remaining seat, the second chair next to me. "Thanks for inviting me, Jesse. You actually found it?"

"It's stored below," I said.

"I'd love to see it."

"You guys wait here and yell down if our guests arrive." Jackie and I went below, through the salon into the forward stateroom.

"You know," she said with a seductive smile, "not many guys would use a million dollars in gold to lure a lady into their bedroom."

I'd gotten used to her quick, frank, and flirtatious ways over the last few months. No denying she was very attractive, but we were only friends. I bent over to key in the code to open the bunk. "Not many ladies are worth a million bucks."

"Flattery will get you anywhere."

The bunk raised up and I bent again to haul the big chest out. "Push the bunk back down, would ya?"

I set the chest on the bunk and spun the combination lock. Sunlight was coming in through the top hatch as I opened the trunk. It struck the gold bars inside, which reflected the golden light back up and throughout the stateroom.

She clutched both hands to her throat. "Oh my!"

"Go ahead. Pick one up."

She looked up at me and grinned. Then she reached into the chest and started to lift one out. I could tell it was heavier than she thought. A ten-pound gold bar isn't very big, only seven inches long, two inches wide, and an inch thick. Not much bigger than a candy bar. She finally got one in each hand and asked, "How much are these two worth?"

"You're holding about a quarter million dollars."

"That's more than I'll earn in three years in the Navy! And you just picked it up off the bottom of the ocean?"

"Well, it took us a couple of months of research and a week of diving, but yeah."

She gently placed them back in the chest. Then she turned and looked around the stateroom, stopping for a moment at a couple of mementos from the Corps that hung on the bulkhead. "What are these coins?"

"They're called 'challenge coins'. High-ranking officers have them made and give them out to subordinates. In a military bar, if one person challenges another to a drink, the one who produces the higher-ranking officer's coin drinks free."

"You have a lot of them," she said, stepping closer to read the names. "This one on top, PX Kelley, who's he?"

"Means I drink free anywhere. He was the Commandant of the Marine Corps, when I was in Beirut."

Tossing her hair over her shoulder, she appraised me with those bright green eyes. Then she walked around the bunk, her eyes not missing anything.

"We got company," came Deuce's voice over the intercom.

I took one of the bars out and placed it on the shelf. "Mind lifting the bunk for me?"

I put the chest back under the bunk, closed it, and took the single gold bar into the salon, where I placed it on the middle of the settee. Jackie and I stepped down into the cockpit as two men in suits got out of near-identical blue sedans, probably rentals. Both men were carrying briefcases. The shorter of the two reached into the backseat and took out a larger, square case. The two men looked around and then started walking toward Rusty's house.

In my experience, landlubbers are very predictable. To them, people can only live where roads go to and you can only find people inside of houses. A loud whistle came from the bridge, stopping the two men. When they looked our way, I motioned for them to come over.

Rusty and Deuce climbed down from the bridge and the four of us waited in the cockpit for the suits. "Are you Mister McDermitt?" the taller man asked.

"Yeah," I replied, and nodding to the others, I added, "This is Doctor Jackie Burdick, Deuce Livingston, and Rusty Thurman. Come aboard, we can talk in the salon."

"I'm Chase Conner, Mister McDermitt," the tall man said. "I'm with the Florida Department of Revenue and will also be representing the IRS." Even at zero eight hundred the temperature was already above eighty-five de-

grees and quite humid, but he was impeccably dressed in a dark blue three-piece suit.

"I'm Owen Bradbury," the other man said, "of the Florida Historical Society. Thank you for inviting me. I'm surprised the federal government isn't here to challenge ownership." He too was wearing a business suit, but it was probably a couple of years old and off the rack. Both men were wearing the bane of my existence, hard-soled black oxfords.

"Challenge ownership of gold that belonged to a foreign country that no longer exists?" Rusty asked. "It'd be too expensive a court battle."

"Take your shoes off before boarding. Hard black soles damage the deck." Before either man could protest, I opened the hatch and stepped up into the salon, followed by my friends.

The two men entered the salon in bare white feet, having chosen to remove their socks also. They stopped suddenly when their eyes found the gold bar, gleaming in the sun coming through the portholes.

Rusty and Deuce sat down on the couch to port and Jackie went behind the counter in the galley. "Mind if I get a bottle of water, Jesse?"

"Help yourself, Doc. Would you guys like a cup of coffee or anything?"

Bradbury ignored the question and went to the far side of the settee. He set his large case on the deck, sat down, and opened his briefcase. Conner still stood at the hatch, staring at the gold bar. His fixation was broken when Bradbury picked it up and began studying it with a magnifying glass he'd pulled from his case.

"I thought it'd be bigger," Conner said. "You said it was a hundred and ten pounds."

"There's another ten just like it," Deuce said.

Conner looked at Deuce, then quickly crossed the salon, set his briefcase on the settee, and slid over next to Bradbury. "Ten more like this?"

"We're guessing the weight at ten pounds each," I said. "Maybe Mister Bradbury could tell us better."

Bradbury looked up, set his magnifying glass aside, pulled out a small electronic scale, and set it on the table. He turned it on, waited a few seconds, and pushed a button on the front of it, holding it for a moment. When he released it, the numbers flashed all zeroes three times and he gently placed the gold bar on it. "It's precisely one hundred and fifty troy ounces. That's a little under ten point three pounds. It certainly looks genuine and that's the precise weight of the lost Confederate gold. I'll have to run tests on all eleven to be sure." Then he looked up at me. "There were reported to be twelve in the lost shipment. Did you not find them all?"

"My father found one," Deuce said. "He was killed for it and the murderer sold it to a pawnbroker who probably had it melted."

"That's a shame." He reached down and picked up his larger case and opened it. Inside was an electronic device with small windows on two sides and a hinged top. "Do you have electricity?"

I took the offered cord and plugged it into a receptacle inside the cabinet behind him. He turned the device on and explained, "This is the latest in portable precious metal analyzers. It can tell us within one one-thousandth of a percentage point the purity of the gold. Sto-

ries about Confederate gold go back to the end of the war. Most finds are found to be forgeries. This one has the correct stamp and a date of 1864. Most of the bogus finds are convincing enough, in that they have the correct markings. Most, however, are gold-plated lead. One case I read about was indeed real gold, but the incorrect purity. The forger used highly refined gold, like what is struck today. In 1864, the purity of Confederate bullion was point nine nine eight five, that is ninety-nine point eight five percent pure gold. Today, bullion has a purity of point nine nine nine nine, something no smelter of the nineteenth century could produce."

He opened the hinged top, which revealed a small round window and some kind of electronics in the lid. He placed the gold bar over the little window and closed it. Then he removed a small laptop computer and plugged it into the device and turned both of them on. After tapping a few keys, he looked up. "Are you ready?"

We all nodded and he tapped a few more keys and looked at the laptop display. When he looked up, he was grinning. "Congratulations, gentlemen. This bar is indeed ninety-nine point eight five percent pure gold, not plated. More important are the trace elements." Looking down at the laptop display he continued, "We're showing point zero three percent zinc, point zero four percent copper, and point zero eight percent silver. These are the exact trace elements found in gold coins and bullion struck by mints in France in the 1860s. You have most certainly found a shipment of lost Confederate gold."

Deuce and Rusty high-fived each other and Rusty exclaimed, "Hot damn!"

"What would you appraise its worth, Mister Bradbury?" Conner asked.

Pulling a calculator from his briefcase he said, "This bar, at one hundred and fifty troy ounces, is worth one hundred and five thousand, three hundred and eighteen dollars. Assuming the other ten are the exact same weight, the total value would be one million, one hundred and fifty-eight thousand, five hundred and two dollars."

"That'd be the melt value, right?" Rusty asked.

"Yes, the historical value would be quite a bit more. Although not as much as if the entire shipment had been found together. I think I can say without equivocation that the Museum of Florida History would be willing to pay one point five million dollars to have these on display."

"Two million," I said, which caused Conner to smile.

"No, I don't think the museum would go that high. I could probably talk them into going as high as one point eight million."

"Seems to me," Deuce said, "the Civil War Museum in New Orleans might be willing to pay a lot more. Seeing as how the bars were struck there."

This brought a frown to both men's faces. Conner, because he knew if the sale was in Louisiana, Florida would have a court battle to prove the location of the find was in Florida waters. Bradbury, because he really wanted them at his museum.

"You know anyone in New Orleans, Deuce?" I asked.

"I do," Jackie said. "It just so happens that my college roommate from my undergrad years is the curator of

that museum. I have her number on my rolodex in the office. Want me to call my Chief?"

"No need for that," Bradbury said, taking out his cell phone. "Is there somewhere I can make a call?"

"Down that ladder well," I said, pointing forward. "First hatch to port is the crew cabin."

Bradbury stepped down into the small companionway, looked left and right, and then turned right into the head. A moment later he stepped out and crossed the companionway into the crew cabin.

It only took two or three minutes and he rejoined us. "Yes, Mister McDermitt, the museum will be glad to offer you two million dollars. I'll have the necessary documents overnighted to me and we can settle the transaction tomorrow. I'll arrange for an armed security detail until then and they will transport the bars to Tallahassee."

"Transport any way you like, but no armed security detail is going to be aboard my boat, unless I know them."

"I wish you'd reconsider, Mister McDermitt. If word gets out about this, there could be trouble."

"Captain McDermitt is no stranger to trouble, gentlemen," Jackie said. "I removed a bullet from his spine just a few months ago. My guess is the man that did it is no longer among the living."

"If you insist," Bradbury said.

I knew Conner was waiting for his turn to speak and he did. "Since the find was inside the state's three-mile limit and the sale of this gold is going to take place in the state of Florida, the state will receive twenty-five percent of the proceeds. I will also have the requisite paper-

work drawn up and overnighted if you have agreed on the price."

"Two million is a good price," I said. "You have a deal, Mister Bradbury." I extended my hand and he took it, sealing the bargain.

"I'll have a cashier's check drawn up. Who shall I make it payable to?"

"Better make it to Rusty," I said. "He holds the salvage license."

The two men left and I put the gold bar back with the others, under the bunk. Coming back into the salon, Jackie asked, "Who's up for breakfast? My treat."

"Not me," Deuce replied. "I had a bite to eat a couple of hours ago."

"I have to go to the bank and set up an account," Rusty said with a sly grin.

Jackie turned to me and smiled. "That just leaves you and me and I don't see any dirty dishes in your sink."

"Wooden Spoon?" I asked.

"Good choice. We can take my car."

"I don't fit into those sporty cars very well, Doc. Mind if we take mine?"

My car isn't really a car. It's called *The Beast*. It's a beat-up 1973 International Travelall 4x4. Not long ago, my friends did some work on it for me while I was in the hospital, swapping the worn-out gas engine for a big, powerful, brand new diesel engine, transmission, transfer case, axles, interior, and a host of electronics. They presented it to me the day I was discharged. That was when Jackie stepped in front of a bullet meant for me.

"Do you have a ladder so I can get in it?" she asked.

We said goodbye to Deuce and Rusty on the dock and I couldn't help feeling the two of them were dodging breakfast on purpose to try to get Jackie and me together. The two of us walked around to the far side of the property where *The Beast* was parked. She didn't need a ladder, though it was a bit of a climb.

After a late breakfast, we talked over coffee for an hour and then I drove Jackie back to the *Anchor*. She had some patients she needed to check on and headed back down to Boca Chica Naval Hospital. I walked down to the *Revenge* and saw that Pescador was in his usual spot in a corner of the cockpit. He lifted his head and looked at me expectantly. I pulled a bag from my pocket and tossed him half a T-bone. He caught it in the air and held it while he looked at me, waiting.

"Go ahead," I said. He sat down and started tearing big chunks off the bone and swallowing them whole. "Stay here, I'll be back in a little while." I walked to the bar and went inside. Deuce and Rusty were eating an early lunch.

"Not hungry, eh, Deuce?"

"Well, it was real early when I had breakfast."

"How'd it go with the Doc?" Rusty asked.

I straddled a chair at the table. "We're friends. That's all."

"Hey, it was her idea, man," Rusty said. "You need to move on that. She ain't gonna wait forever."

"How'd it go at the bank?"

Rusty swallowed a bite of his fish sandwich before answering. "Everything's all set. As soon as the deposit's made, Pam'll send a cashier's check to Mister McCormick by courier and make the transfers to yours and Deuce's accounts."

"I still don't like it, me getting a double share," Deuce said. "It's not right."

"Sure it is. Look, me and Jesse knew your old man when you were just a kid. I can't count how many times he said he wanted you, and every Livingston after you, to get a college education. You got no say here, son."

So, we agreed to split it five ways, three hundred thousand, each to me, Jackson McCormick, Rusty, and Deuce, and the last share to Russ. His share would go into a trust fund for the education of his future grandchildren. Deuce tried to protest again, but neither Rusty nor I would have it any other way.

Deuce rolled his eyes and said, "Damn stubborn Jarheads. What are you guys going to do with the money?"

Rusty thought for a minute and said, "I think I'm going to use half of it to spruce things up around here. Then maybe I'll fly to the Philippines and find me one of those mail-order brides."

Deuce grinned and looked at me. "What about you, Jesse?"

"It's going into the same trust that I put Alex's money into. I met with a lawyer last month and had a will made up. If anything happens to me, five million goes to that school she started out in Oregon, with her friend Cindy Saturday as the executor. The rest stays local."

We spent the rest of the day drinking beer and listening to Dan play on the back deck, then turned in early. Tomorrow was going to be a hectic day.

The Old Home Town Looks the Same

Conner and Bradbury arrived the next morning, much as they had the previous day. Except for the armored car. The big truck had to pull forward and back up three times to get turned around. The two men had all the paperwork and Bradbury had two cashier's checks, one for five hundred thousand dollars and one for one point five million. Rusty signed all the paperwork, and Bradbury gave the smaller check, which covered the taxes, to Conner, who had more paperwork for Rusty to sign. Then Bradbury handed another check for one point five million to Rusty. The armored car was loaded and the suits left.

We had to meet David Williams at the airport at eleven hundred, so we started packing. Williams used to be the Engineer on a shrimp trawler out of Key West. For a couple weeks I was helping a friend who owned the boat, by the name of Carl Trent. He and several others in Key West were being threatened into running drugs for a

big-time Cuban smuggler. After the smuggler retired to Gitmo, along with a terrorist named Syed Qazi Al Fayyad, Trent sold his shrimping business and came to work for me, as caretaker of my island. Williams came to work for me also, along with Trent's First Mate, Bob "Doc" Talbot, a former Navy Corpsman. Both of them were on kind of a part-time basis. Williams was a pilot and his son had recently been transferred to Camp Lejeune, so he'd volunteered to fly me, Rusty and Deuce up there for Julie's graduation.

At eleven hundred we were at Key West Seaplane Adventures, at the Key West airport, where Williams kept his vintage 1953 de Havilland Beaver. We were only planning to stay overnight and fly back the next day, so everyone was traveling light. Williams was already there when we walked out onto the ramp, performing his preflight check.

"Hey, guys, beautiful day for flying." Nodding toward my dog, he added, "Pescador going with us?"

"Thought we could drop him at the island so he could play with the kids for a couple of days."

Handshakes and greetings were made and we stowed our gear in the back of the plane. "Ride up front, Jesse," Williams said. "You can spell me on the controls, if I get tired. I've already done the preflight."

"Don't have to ask me twice," I said, climbing up into the copilot's seat.

Minutes later, we were all aboard, strapped in and ready to go. "I filed a flight plan from here to Jacksonville, Florida. We can refuel there and make it to Jacksonville, North Carolina, well before sunset."

He reached down beside his seat and wobbled the fuel primer, then toggled the master switch, turning on the batteries, lights, and gauges. I'd flown in all kinds of airplanes and even had some flight time in helicopters, but an antique with a big radial engine was a new experience.

Talking more to himself than anyone else he said, "Lights on, batteries good, gauges working." He pushed the far right of three levers full forward and moved the left lever back and forth a few times, returning it to the original position. Then he checked a large switch, making sure it was off, and continued, "Mixture rich, magnetos off." He slid the little side window open and yelled out, "Clear propellers!"

He pushed a button on the dash and the starter began winding up, slowly turning the big engine over. It sounded more like a big wood chipper, with a centrifugal flywheel, whining louder and louder.

"Shouldn't the magnetos be on?" I asked.

"Walking the props," he said. "In these old radial engines, oil builds up in the lower cylinders when she sits for a while. Counting twelve props ensures that all nine cylinders go through four revolutions to pump the oil out."

He went through the procedure again with the magnetos turned on. The engine caught on the first revolution, a bunch of blue smoke blew out, and at first the engine only seemed to be running on one or two cylinders. After a moment it leveled out to a nice smooth idle.

After five minutes at high idle, he picked up the mic and said, "Key West ground, this is Beaver one three eight

five, holding at the passenger terminal, ready to taxi. Requesting a VFR departure to the northeast."

We were all wearing headsets to allow us to talk over the loud engine through the intercom, but we could also hear the answer from the ground controller over them. "Beaver one three eight five, Key West ground. You're cleared for VFR at ninety-five hundred feet. Taxi via Bravo, hold short runway nine."

Williams repeated and confirmed the instructions and said, "Key West ground, Beaver one three eight five with request. Be advised, slight change to our flight plan. We'll make a water landing in the Content Keys to discharge one canine passenger."

"Key West ground, roger. Upon landing, give Carl and the family my best."

I looked questioningly at Williams. He toggled the intercom switch, shrugged, and said, "It's a small island."

Williams taxied the plane to the west end of the single runway and set the brakes. Then he pushed the throttle forward and the airplane shuddered against the brakes.

Throttling back, he switched the radio frequency and said, "Beaver one three eight five is holding short of runway nine at Bravo."

A new voice came over the radio. "Beaver one three eight five, Key West Tower, roger. Traffic niner miles inbound is a Cessna. Runway niner, wind one hundred and twenty at eight, cleared for takeoff, report clear to the northeast. Have a safe flight."

He again repeated and confirmed the instructions then released the brakes before pushing the throttle forward again. We pulled onto the runway and turned into the wind as he pulled the flaps lever back. We slowly ac-

celerated down the runway and at sixty-five knots, lifted off the ground only half way down the airstrip. He climbed to fifteen hundred feet, reported he was clear of the field, and headed northeast toward my island home.

We were only going to be there for half an hour. I'd been away for over a week and Trent was busy building a little house for his family. He was also building an aquaculture system to raise crawfish and vegetables and I wanted to check on his progress. We'd originally planned to raise tilapia and catfish, but changed our minds to crawfish. He has a friend in Belize that raises fresh water shrimp and he wanted to mimic his system as much as we could. Besides, I love Cajun crawfish.

The wind was out of the east, as usual in early summer. We came in low over the tiny island just northwest of mine and settled into the shallow channel north of my home. We turned and came back to the long pier on the north end of the island. As we approached, I saw Trent coming between the two small buildings, which I'd added last winter, and out onto the pier.

Deuce opened the port-side door and stepped out onto the pontoon. As we neared the end of the pier, Williams cut the power and Deuce stepped off onto it, holding the wing strut and easing the bird against the rubber fenders. He quickly tied the pontoon off to two cleats on the pier and the rest of us climbed out.

Pescador took off down the pier at a full run, shooting past Trent, and only stopped to lift his leg on a mangrove at the water line. Then he took off again, looking for the kids.

"Welcome home, Jesse. I thought you guys were going up to North Carolina today." Then nodding to Deuce, he added, "Good to see you again, Deuce."

"I thought Pescador might like to see the kids while we're gone. And I wanted to see how things were coming along here, too."

"Hey, Carl," Rusty said as he struggled through the small hatch. Rusty's not very tall, only about five foot six, but a portly, albeit solid, three hundred pounds.

"Come on," Trent said, "I've got quite a bit done this past week."

"I need to make a call," Williams said.

"Best place is up on the front deck of the main house," I said. "Really about the only place you can get a cell signal."

The five of us walked toward shore, where Trent's wife, Charlie, was waiting. Williams said hi and kept on going across the clearing toward the main house. The rest of us talked for a moment at the end of the pier and then walked to the west side of the island, where Trent was building his little house. He had gotten a lot of work done. When I left to go treasure hunting, he'd only had the concrete piers poured. Since there wasn't anyone currently staying in the bunkhouses, they'd remained living in the western one, while working on the aquaculture system. Two weeks ago, we had done as much on it as we could, while waiting for the generator and pumps to be delivered and I had helped him dig the holes for the piers and pour the concrete footings for their house.

Since then, he'd built the raised floor, framed the walls, built the trusses, and decked the roof, and now he looked

to be in the process of hanging the exterior siding. Opening the door, Charlie proudly said, "Come on in."

We stepped inside and she flipped a switch next to the door and an overhead light came on. "The generator came in two days ago," Trent said. "I poured a mounting pad on the east side of the pier among the banyan trees. It's mounted about eight feet off the ground. Between here and the bunkhouses, I built a small shed among the gumbo limbos. That's where the batteries are. The main house is still on solar and wind with its own batteries, but the bunkhouses, this house, and the pumps will run off of thirty deep-cycle twelve-volt marine batteries. The generator will come on automatically if the voltage drops below eleven volts, but you can't hear it unless you're real close to it."

"Damn, you have been busy," Rusty said. "I didn't see any wires, though."

"Everything's underground, in two-inch PVC conduit."

"You missed your true calling, Trent," I said as I looked more closely at the details of the structure.

"Thanks, Jesse. I really don't know much about carpentry, though. I just looked at what you'd done on the bunkhouses and did about the same. Should have it livable in another week. So long as the storms hold off."

It wasn't a big house. I guessed it to be about the size of the bunkhouses, maybe thirty feet square. The front faced the interior of the island and consisted of a single room, with plumbing for a small kitchen at one side. To the rear were two small bedrooms and plumbing for a head between them. I could see that he'd framed two large openings at the back of the bedrooms and walked toward the one on the left.

"A deck?" I asked. "With French doors?" They looked out over a beautiful view of the only real beach on the island, with coconut palms on both sides and the sandbar just beyond it. The decking was already complete with full-width steps down to the sand. There were four rustic-looking handmade rockers already there, two of them very small.

"Yeah," Charlie said. "The view at sunset is beautiful."

"Looks real homey," Rusty said.

"It certainly is," she sighed.

I looked at Trent and said, "I'm glad y'all like it here. Miss the open ocean much?"

"Not a bit. Truth is I'd been thinking 'bout getting off the blue for several years."

"How's the aquaculture system coming?"

"Just waiting on the pumps. I finished plumbing the tanks last week, just after you left. Pumps are supposed to arrive at the *Rusty Anchor* tomorrow. I'll pick them up tomorrow evening, when we make a run into town for groceries."

"Looks like you have a handle on everything. We need to get back in the air if we're going to make North Carolina by dark. Anything you need?"

"Well, I wanted to finish the roofing, but there's not enough corrugated tin left."

"Order what you need from Home Depot and tell them to deliver it to the *Anchor*. I already added you to my account there. While you're there, Charlie can pick out fixtures and appliances for the head and galley." Turning to Charlie, I added, "And think big. Remember, there'll be times when we'll need to feed a lot of people here. The grill works for cooking some things, but a big oven for

baking would be great. And don't let him get chintzy on things. A nice big tub, water heater, the whole bit. The new water maker will be delivered here by barge in a week. After that, no more water rationing."

"A hot bath," she said, smiling, and then kissed me on the cheek. "You sure know how to spoil a lady."

"We'll be back tomorrow, but I'll probably stay on Marathon until the next day."

We walked back to the pier and found Williams already at the plane. He seemed anxious and fidgety. I assumed he just wanted to get back into the air. As we were saying goodbye to the Trents, their two kids, Carl Junior and Patty, came running up with Pescador. They were each carrying small buckets, each one half-full of clams. I told Pescador to stay with the kids and we boarded the plane.

We taxied away from the pier, headed west. Williams then turned into the wind, lowered the flaps, and pushed the throttle forward. Seconds later, we bounced lightly on the water once and became airborne.

"I could get used to that," I said. "From a boat to a plane."

Williams nodded but didn't say anything. We crossed the southeast corner of the Gulf of Mexico, glistening below us, in less than thirty minutes. Below and to port was Marco Island, the playground of rich Florida transplants. To starboard lay the vast expanse of the Everglades. Further ahead and to starboard were the clear blue waters of Lake Okeechobee. Deuce and Rusty were talking in the back about bass fishing in the lake, but Williams was intent on flying, seemingly lost in thought.

Forty-five minutes later, we crossed Highway 70, north of Lake Okeechobee, and Williams still hadn't contact-

ed Orlando air traffic control. I didn't know a lot about flying, but if it was anything like driving in the Orlando area, we were headed into a lot of traffic.

I tapped Williams on the shoulder. "You okay?"

He seemed to snap out of whatever trance he was in and said, "Yeah, um, I'm fine. Just things on my mind, sorry."

"It's just that we're well past Lake Okeechobee. Looks like Lake Wales coming up."

"Oh shit," he muttered and reached up to change the channel on the radio. Grabbing the mic off the dash, he spoke into it. "Orlando Control, this is Beaver one three eight five."

The response was immediate, "Beaver one three eight five, Orlando Control. Climb to seventy-five hundred feet, turn left to three hundred and fifty degrees."

Williams banked the plane sharply, added throttle, and pulled back on the yoke. In modern private planes there are two separate wheels, each mounted to the dash. In this plane each wheel is mounted to a Y-shaped yoke that is mounted to the floor. We leveled off at seventy-five hundred feet at the correct heading.

"Something bothering you, David?" I asked.

"It's my kid, my oldest. Remember I told you I had two Marine sons, Jared and Luke? The oldest lives in Key West now. He got out about a year ago and moved down here. He was in and out of trouble, both in the Corps and since then. Took a job at the Blue Heaven when he got here. I've been trying to get hold of him, but he hasn't answered the phone in a couple of weeks. I stopped by his place a couple of times. Once he told me through the door to go away and the second time he wouldn't even come to the

door. I don't know if he's drinking, on drugs, or what. He just hasn't been the same since he came back from his third tour in Iraq and got out."

"He works at the Blue Heaven, you said? About six feet tall and a solid two twenty?"

"You know him?"

"Met him once, briefly. It was a few months back, just before Cuba."

"He's a good kid, Jesse. Something went real bad wrong when he was with Sixth Marines in Iraq and it changed him."

A lot of things go 'real bad wrong' in combat. In my twenty years in the Corps, I only lost two men killed in action, and both times, something went real bad wrong. After the first Gulf War, I lost three to suicide, and dozens of others left a promising career. "He never told you what it was?"

"No," he replied.

The radio interrupted our conversation, "Beaver one three eight five, Orlando Control."

Williams picked up the mic and said, "Beaver one three eight five."

"Orlando Control, Beaver one three eight five, turn right to ten degrees and descend to fifty-five hundred feet."

I looked out the window on my side and could see the city of Orlando, as the plane banked to starboard and the nose dropped. A moment later, we leveled off with Lake Apopka just ahead and to starboard.

"I asked him about it," Williams continued. "He was in his last year of a four-year hitch. He'd talked about reenlisting, but suddenly he was out. He never told me why,

or what happened. That was a year ago. He went home to Kentucky, but after a month called and asked if he could bunk with us. I found him a place in Key West, he got a job, and everything seemed okay. I heard from others that he got a little crazy once or twice and was arrested once. I just don't know what to do, or how I can help."

Deuce's voice came over the intercom. "You might not be able to. If something real bad happened, it might be psychological. Has he tried to get help from the VA?"

"That's just it, Deuce. I don't know. He won't talk to me about it."

Orlando interrupted again. "Beaver one three eight five, Orlando Control."

Williams picked up the mic again and said, "Beaver one three eight five."

"Beaver one three eight five, turn left to heading zero degrees. Maintain five thousand feet. Contact Jacksonville Control when you're over Lake George. Have a nice flight."

Williams banked the plane and picked up the old heading. Apparently Orlando didn't want our old plane anywhere near their bustling airspace. We flew on in silence for another fifteen minutes. I could see the concern in Williams's face and one look at Deuce and Rusty told me they both were thinking the same thing I was. Something bad happened. That's what combat is. Bad. Without knowing what his son did in the Marines, I could only guess. So I asked.

"What was Jared's MOS?"

Williams looked confused for a second and then replied, "His job? He started out in infantry. He was always

real good with a rifle as a kid and they sent him from there to Scout/Sniper school."

A sniper. That opened up a lot of possibilities. I was a Marine sniper for a while, myself. Had Jared been a few years older, I might have trained him.

"Maybe when we get back," I said, "I can go down and talk to him. Meantime, how about letting me take the controls for a while?"

Rusty's voice came over my headset. "This ain't no whirly bird, you know."

That brought Williams out of his funk and he laughed along with Deuce and Rusty. Williams raised both hands and said, "Off stick."

I took the wheel in front of me and, taking his cue, replied, "On stick. Now, where's the collective?"

Williams changed from a troubled dad to a flight instructor instantly. "Controlling a fixed wing isn't a lot different than a chopper, Jesse. The foot pedals control the rudder, the same way they control the tail rotor in a chopper. Push the right one and the plane will turn right, but you have to combine that with ailerons to bank the plane, using the wheel. Pushing or pulling on the yoke will move the elevator to climb or dive. Go ahead and try an easy right turn, then come back to the same heading."

I did as he said and banked the plane, making an easy turn to starboard, then banked left and came back on course. I noticed the altimeter showed we'd descended nearly a hundred feet and pointed it out.

"When banking, the plane will slide a little and lose altitude. Compensate for it, while turning, by pulling back slightly on the yoke to maintain the same altitude. Try it again to the left this time."

I banked slightly left, added a little left pedal, and pulled back on the yoke just a little. Then I did the same thing to the right and brought us back on course. We'd actually gained a little altitude.

"The balance comes with lots of practice. Different planes react differently. The Beaver's a pretty heavy plane for a single-engine. She can carry six people, with luggage, or up to two thousand pounds of gear. They're used a lot up in Canada and Alaska by bush pilots."

The old plane didn't have an autopilot, so I stayed on the controls until we were over Lake George. Williams took the controls back as he switched the radio to the right frequency for Jacksonville.

He picked up the mic and spoke into it. "Jacksonville Control, Beaver one three eight five."

"Beaver one three eight five, Jacksonville Control," came the response.

"Beaver one three eight five, requesting landing instructions to refuel before heading on to Jacksonville, North Carolina."

"Beaver one three eight five, ceiling is ten thousand feet and scattered, visibility is ten miles, wind is out of the east at five knots. Turn left, heading three hundred and fifty degrees."

As we neared Jacksonville, the instructions came faster, "Beaver one three eight five, turn right to heading fifteen degrees. Traffic six miles out and above, heading east, is a triple seven heavy."

Williams acknowledged the controller and I asked, "What did he just say?"

Williams pointed ahead and slightly up until I spotted it. "It's a Boeing 777 on approach. We'll follow him in."

The controller's voice came over my headset again. "Beaver one three eight five, turn right to ninety degrees. Maintain five miles to triple seven heavy. You're clear for VFR approach to runway twenty-six. Call on one eighteen point three, when down."

He again acknowledged the controller and I said, "Five miles is only a couple of minutes behind him, right?"

"Yeah, but the 777 will be going faster than us. By the time we touch down, he'll be taxiing."

We landed without incident and Williams switched the radio frequency for taxi instructions and directions to the fuel pumps. Thirty minutes later we were back in the air, with instructions to contact Charleston, South Carolina, when we were forty miles away from there. Leaving Florida behind us, we climbed to seventy-five hundred feet and headed out over the Atlantic on a heading of forty-five degrees. All but the last seventy-five miles or so would be over water.

We made it through Charleston approaches without having to change course, but they did have us drop down to thirty-five hundred feet. The sun was still well above the horizon as we crossed back over land southwest of Wilmington, North Carolina. We were vectored around the west side of the city at seventy-five hundred feet and we made our approach to Albert J. Ellis Airport, near Camp Lejeune, thirty minutes later.

We unloaded the gear from the plane and helped Williams get her refueled and tied down on the tarmac near the hangars of Jacksonville Flying Service. Deuce had made arrangements for a car to be waiting for us. Of course, his car of choice was a black Expedition, with

dark tinted windows. The keys had been left at the incoming flights desk at the JFS office.

We carried our baggage out to the parking lot. Rusty looked at the behemoth and then at Deuce. "Don't you Feds ever drive anything low profile?"

"Have you seen what's available at Hertz these days, Rusty? They call a Corolla a midsized car. I was only thinking of you when I had the company send this over."

"Where'd they send it from?" I asked.

"FBI residential office in Wilmington."

"You can do that?" asked Williams. "I thought you worked for Homeland Security."

"All the agencies work together, or we're supposed to. Sometimes, we get good cooperation, sometimes we don't."

We loaded the gear in the back of the big SUV and climbed inside. Deuce immediately pushed all four buttons to send the windows down, as it was over one hundred degrees inside the car. He started it up and cranked the A/C up to high. By the time we got to the airport exit, the stifling air had been blown out the windows, so he closed them.

Sitting up front with Deuce, Williams asked, "Which way?"

"Surprised you ain't got satellite imaging in this tub," Rusty said from the back.

"Head east and turn right on Catherine Lake Road," I replied. "Should be at the end of the road we're on."

"Should be?" he asked.

"I haven't been here in eight years. But we'll find it. Just head in the direction the other cars are coming from."

"Yep," Rusty said. "That'll get us to Swoop Circle."

"Swoop Circle?" Williams asked.

"Yeah," Rusty said. "It's a gathering spot for Marines after liberty is sounded on Friday. Guys with cars pick up guys without cars and head home for the weekend, splitting the gas. It's called swooping."

We turned onto Highway 111 toward Jacksonville and passed Lake Catherine a few minutes later. I used to live on the north side of the lake. It seemed like a lifetime ago.

"Remember when you used to live up there?" Rusty said reading my mind.

"Ancient history, Rusty."

"When's the last time you talked to them?" He was referring to my two daughters from my first marriage. She divorced me in 1990, when I volunteered for an advance unit going into Saudi Arabia before the run-up to Desert Shield.

"Fourteen years ago," I replied. I didn't even know if they still lived in the area. I still sent them cards on their birthdays and at Christmas. The checks inside were never cashed.

"Maybe while we're here, you could—" Rusty started to say. I cut him off as we approached Highway 24.

"Take a right up here, Deuce. We're staying at the Fairfield on the other side of town. Around the next curve, stay left on 178."

After a few stoplights, we crossed the bridge over New River. I knew Rusty would remember this area, as it had been the off-duty gathering spot for Marines stationed at Camp Lejeune for many years.

“Hey,” Rusty said as if on cue. “Wanna head down to Court Street? We could check out Birdland and have a cold one at Sam’s pool hall.”

“Not there anymore, Rusty.”

Rusty was craning his neck to look down Court Street, angling away behind us on the right. “Which one?”

“All of them,” I said. “The city was in the process of cleaning things up last time I was stationed here. I bet there’s not a single beer to be found on Court Street now.”

“You’re kiddin’. Where do Marines go to blow off steam?”

“There’s still plenty of bars around, but most of the junior Marines aren’t even old enough to get in one.” Then to Deuce I said, “About a mile ahead, turn left on Western Boulevard.”

“Town’s sure changed a lot,” Rusty said.

“Still a Marine town, though,” I said. We pulled into the parking lot at the Fairfield and found a spot away from the main entrance. I’d reserved four suites and the front desk got us registered in quick time.

As we were turning to go to the elevator, I heard a familiar voice say, “I heard you were going to be in town, McDermitt.”

I turned toward the man who had spoken. He was a tall black man, with broad shoulders and a shaved head. He was dressed in the Marine Corps Charlie uniform, khaki short-sleeved shirt and olive-green trousers. He wore a Colonel’s eagles on his lapels and a chestful of ‘been there, done that’ ribbons. Tom Broderick, the Commanding Officer of Force Recon Company, Second Recon Battalion. Or he used to be, when he was a Captain.

"Damn, they'll let anyone stay at this dive," he said as he walked towards us, smiling.

I took his outstretched hand. "Yeah, and I guess the Corps has lowered its standards for Field Grade Officers. How the hell are ya, Tom?"

He laughed and said, "Doing well, Jesse. Sergeant Major Latimore told me you'd be staying here. Just had to come into town and welcome you home."

I turned to the others and said, "Guys, this is Tom Broderick. He was a wet-behind-the-ears butter bar when we first met." Then to Tom I said, "Tom, this big guy, believe it or not, is former Recon Sergeant, Rusty Thurman. We're here for his daughter's graduation from the Coast Guard Maritime Enforcement School. This is Dave Williams, our pilot. His son's stationed here."

Tom shook hands with both of them but kept glancing at Deuce. Finally, he stuck out his hand and said, "You look familiar. Have we met?"

Before Deuce could answer, I said, "Yeah, you have. But he was a pimple-faced kid at the time. This is Lieutenant Commander Russell Livingston, Junior, Navy SEAL. We call him Deuce."

Tom looked at me, then at Deuce. "Staff Sergeant Russ Livingston's kid?"

Deuce took his hand firmly and said, "Guilty as charged, Colonel."

"Just Tom, Deuce. Your dad was one of the best noncoms I ever met. How's he doing?"

"He died last fall, sir," Deuce replied. "Murdered."

"Damn sorry to hear that. Hope they caught the bastard."

"We did," Deuce said.

He looked seriously at Deuce for a second and then glanced at me. "Yeah, I just bet you did." Then, changing the subject, he asked me, "How long you in town for?"

"Just for the night. Julie graduates in the morning, then we're flying back to the Keys."

"Aw, hell. Well, at least let me treat you guys to supper."

"That'd be great," I said. "Can Tex join us?" Tex was what we used to call Mike Latimore, back in the day.

"If not, I'll order him to. One of the perks of command. Logan's at twenty-one hundred?"

"Perfect."

"We'll see you then. Nice meeting you gentlemen." He turned and headed toward the exit as the elevator opened and two middle-aged couples got off.

We boarded the elevator and went up to the third floor. We had the four suites at the north end of the hallway, two on either side, and agreed to meet in my room at twenty thirty. Logan's Steakhouse was just around the corner and we'd walk over from the hotel.

I was showered and ready in twenty minutes, so had a good half hour to kill. I used to have a lot of friends in 6th Marines, so I called the base operator and asked to be connected to Headquarters Battalion. I got a young female Lance Corporal on the phone and dropped a half dozen names, until finally she recognized one. Master Gunnery Sergeant Owen Tankersley. He was one of my range coaches, when I was with 2nd Recon. She told me to hold and after a minute, Tank's voice came over the phone.

"Gunny McDermitt, as I live and breathe. How the hell are ya?"

"Hey, Tank. Making my way in the First CivDiv. How've you been?"

We reminisced for a few minutes, then he asked, "So, why you calling me after, what, nine years?"

"Eight, but who's counting? I was wondering if you could give me some intel on a shooter. He's the son of a buddy of mine and he's having some trouble back home."

"I will if I can. What's his name?"

"Jared Williams," I replied.

There was a few seconds of silence and I asked, "You still there, Tank?"

"Yeah, Jesse. I know about Williams. He was with the Walking Dead in Iraq. Alpha 1/9 was attached to us, after they spooled back up in late 2003. Four confirmed kills while he was with us and eight on his previous deployment. That Marine was an artist with the long gun. Anyway, we deployed to the sandbox that spring. He and his spotter found a high-value target up in Indian Country, north of Ashraf. He was given the green light to take the target out. According to him and his spotter, the target's eight-year-old daughter stepped in front of him at the crucial second. A CIA spook debriefed them both and made some sort of accusation that he'd killed the girl on purpose. Williams came unhinged and nearly killed the spook with his fists. He got sent stateside riki tik, court-martialed, and sent home with a DD. Raw deal, but apparently the spook had connections in high places."

"Thanks, Tank. Any idea where the spotter's at today?"

"Arlington," Tank replied. "Found not culpable in either the shooting or the assault on the spook. He was reassigned to Charlie 1/6 and KIA in Fallujah the following November. Earned a posthumous Silver Star."

"Damn," I said.

"Yeah, it was bad. Sure could have used you there, Gunny."

"Thanks for the intel, Tank. Look, I'm in town until tomorrow. Going to the Coast Guard Maritime Enforcement School graduation in the morning with some friends. One of them is Williams's dad. He flew us up so he could visit his other son, who's stationed here. Think you can meet us for lunch tomorrow and talk to him about Jared?"

"Luke Williams?"

"Yeah, you know him?"

"He's in Bravo, 1/6. Just picked up Corporal."

"Can you bring him with you for lunch?"

"Absolutely. When and where?"

"You tell me. But no mess halls."

He laughed and said, "Eleven hundred at Gourmet Grill, best cheeseburgers on base. Main Circle, go one block north to the corner of G Street. You can't miss it. You'll see a lot of brass. I'll shake Williams loose for the day, so he can go with you to that Coastie grad and have some time with his Pop."

I thanked him again and hung up, just as I heard a knock on the door. It was Deuce, early as usual. I let him in and told him what I'd learned from Tank about Dave's son.

"Thing like that could really haunt a guy," Deuce said. "Especially when you toss in another twelve faces."

"It affects different people in different ways," I said, pondering my own demons.

There was another knock on the door. It was Rusty and before I closed the door, Williams came out of his suite

across the hall. "Hope you don't mind, Jesse. I called Luke and he's going to join us. He's on duty tomorrow and I won't have any other chance to see him."

"The more the merrier. But he's coming with us in the morning. I pulled a few strings. Come on in for a minute, before we go down."

Deuce and Rusty were sitting in the two chairs at the table, so Williams and I sat on the sofa. "The strings I pulled are with an old buddy that served with Jared in Iraq. He gave me the skinny on what happened over there. He's meeting us for lunch tomorrow and he'll give you the details if you want. Long story short, Jared killed a noncombatant by accident, was accused of doing it on purpose by a VIP, and nearly killed the man with his bare hands. The reason he can't get help from the VA is because he was dishonorably discharged."

"Dishonorably discharged? But the Corps was his life. He wanted to make a career of it."

"Tank'll have more information tomorrow," I said. "Jared's spotter was killed in action a few months later."

"What's that mean, a 'noncombatant'?"

"His target was supposed to be a high-value terrorist. I don't know what he might have told you, but your son had twelve previous confirmed kills. Apparently, the target's eight-year-old daughter stepped into his line of fire at the last second."

Williams head dropped into his hands and his whole body shook. When he looked up, his eyes were red. "Jared killed a little girl?"

"The way Tank talked about it, I'm certain it was accidental," I said. "Things like that happen in combat." He

was taking it pretty hard, harder than I would have figured. But he was a civilian.

Williams looked at me, then to Deuce and Rusty. Finally, he looked back at me and in a halting voice he said, "I had three kids, Jesse. Jared's the oldest and Luke is three years younger. When Jared was five, we had a daughter. She was killed when she was eight years old. A drunk driver hit us and we went over a ravine. Jared was only thirteen. My wife and I were both out cold. Jared and Luke managed to get us out of the car. Mary drowned. Jared knew CPR and tried to revive her, but it was too late. He's always blamed himself for her death."

"Damn," Rusty said. "I don't know what to say."

"It sure explains why he's been having trouble," Deuce added. "But with that DD, the VA won't touch him. The man needs help, though. Maybe we can get him in to see the right kind of shrink."

"He can't afford it," Williams said. "I'd help, but I know he's too proud to accept it."

Rusty walked across the room and sat down on the sofa next to Williams. "Deuce said 'we,' Dave. Not you. We'll get him some help and he'll accept it. We take care of our own."

Williams excused himself and went to the head. When he came out, his head was up and his eyes were clear. "Thanks, guys. Let's go eat some beef. I'm anxious for y'all to meet Luke."

We walked out of the hotel lobby and across the parking lot to the restaurant. Williams spotted his son waiting by the door and trotted ahead, embracing the young man. When he released him and turned back to us, he was smiling broadly.

"Guys, this is my son, Luke. Luke, these are the guys I told you about, Jesse, Deuce, and Rusty."

I stepped forward and took the hand he offered. "Pleased to meet you, Corporal."

He shook hands with Rusty and Deuce, then turned back to his dad and said, "I wanted to surprise you, but I guess you already found out."

Williams looked puzzled. "Go ahead and surprise him, Luke. I'm the only one that knows."

Now the younger Marine looked puzzled, but he turned to his dad and said, "I got promoted to Corporal just yesterday."

Rusty grinned and said, "Guess you know what that means, young Corporal." Then to me he said, "You ready, Gunny?"

"Absolutely, Sergeant," I said as I took the younger Williams by the arm and spun him between the two of us.

Luke suddenly realized what was happening. I'm sure his arms were already aching from the previous day. It's Marine Corps tradition for senior Marines to 'pin' the stripes on junior Marines when they're promoted. Rusty and I held Luke by both elbows with our left hands. I held my right hand up behind his back and showed Rusty two fingers. We each drew our fists back and brought them forward suddenly, stopping just short of the Marine's shoulders. Then we drew them back again and 'pinned' his stripes with a solid punch to each shoulder.

Luke winced from the pain, but grinned and turned to each of us and exclaimed, "Oohrah!"

"Semper Fi, Corporal!" Rusty and I shouted together.

"Did I just witness a couple of civilians assault you, Marine?" came a voice behind us.

Luke instantly went ramrod straight, as Tom walked up between two parked cars, dressed in Alphas. His eyes went wide, seeing the silver eagles on his lapels and shoulders, indicating a Marine Colonel was talking to him. "Good evening, sir," he said. "No sir, these men are friends. I was promoted yesterday, sir."

"At ease, Corporal Williams," Tom said. Then he turned to me and said, "Sorry I'm late, Jesse. Something came up and I didn't even have time to change."

"We just got here ourselves, Tom," I said. "Luke, this is Colonel Tom Broderick. Tom, meet the newest Corporal in your battalion, Luke Williams."

Tom smiled and extended his hand. "Congratulations, Marine." Then he leaned in closer and said, "I'm the SOB that approved your promotion."

"You've already met Rusty, Deuce, and Dave this afternoon. Dave is Luke's dad."

Tom shook Williams's hand again and said, "You raised a fine young Marine here, Dave."

"Where's Tex?" I asked.

"He'll be here shortly. Same thing that held me up is holding him up, but shit rolls downhill."

We walked inside and the hostess escorted us to a corner table in the back large enough for fifteen people, but with only seven chairs, five against the wall and one at each end. Tom and I took the end seats and the others sat down against the wall, leaving the seat next to me empty. Not the best seating arrangement for comfort, but it afforded a clear view of the rest of the room and both exits. No doubt arranged by Tom.

Luke looked uncomfortable sitting next to a full-bird Colonel. Tom leaned over and said, "We're both off duty,

son. Call me Tom. Hell, that arrogant bastard at the other end of the table used to call me by my first name when he was a Sergeant. Did it in front of his squad once, if I recall."

Just then, Mike Lattimore walked in, also dressed in Alphas. Most of the patrons of the restaurant were young Marines and their families. Seeing a Sergeant Major walk through the door, everyone between the door and our table parted. Tex was a Sergeant when I'd first met him as a young PFC. Tall and broad shouldered, he was now over thirty years in the Corps and had the seven service stripes on his lower sleeves to prove it.

I stood up and met him with a firm handshake. Nearing fifty years old, he still looked much younger. "Damn, Jesse, you need a frigging haircut."

"Good to see ya again too, Tex."

He nodded at the others and said, "Thanks for inviting me, Tom." Then he took the chair I'd been sitting in and looked up at me. "Well, sit your ass down, boy."

The others laughed as I grinned and said, "You're still an asshole." Then I took the seat to his left. I introduced him to the others. He looked at Deuce and said, "I bet you don't remember me. Me and your pap was real tight back in the day. Real sorry to hear about what happened."

Two waitresses arrived, one carrying a tray with four pitchers of beer, the other with a tray of mugs, shot glasses, and a bottle of Pusser's Navy Rum. "How old are you, Luke?" Tom asked.

"Just turned twenty-two, sir," he replied.

"Good enough, but cut the 'sir' shit, okay?" Then to Tex he said, "Sergeant Major, peel your blouse." Both men stood up and removed their blouses, leaving only

the long-sleeved dress shirt and tie on. While the shirts also had the rank insignia on their collars and sleeves, it was slightly less imposing to the young Marine and he seemed to relax a little.

The waitress, having overheard Tom's question and knowing a Junior Enlisted Marine wouldn't dare lie to a Senior Officer, didn't embarrass Luke by asking for his ID and poured two fingers of rum in each of the glasses, as the other waitress filled the mugs. Tom looked at the first waitress, a young brunette, and said, "Your biggest ribeyes all around, baked potatoes, and whatever green stuff you have that's fresh."

When she walked away, Tex stood up, lifted his shot glass, and said in a booming voice, "Gentlemen."

The rest of us stood and offered our glasses. Marines sitting nearby also stood, facing us at the position of attention, as Tex continued, "Lift yer grog, mates. To the late Russell Livingston, a warrior's warrior and my friend. And to all the others we've lost over the years." Then nodding to Luke and Dave, he added, "And to those who keep coming to fill their ranks and the mothers and fathers who raised real men. Semper Fidelis!"

A chorus of raucous "Oohrah!" and "Semper Fi!" filled the restaurant, as we clinked our glasses and tossed down the fifteen-year-old rum. I suddenly felt more at home than I had in years, and was struck by a sudden melancholy that I'd left it behind.

For the next hour we ate, caught up on what we were doing, reminisced about old times, remembered other Marines and where they were currently serving or had retired to, and told many great 'sea stories'.

Tex asked Luke, "What's your MOS?"

"I'm oh three eleven, with Bravo, 1/6."

"Good outfit. Let me give you some advice. Don't let them move you, and try to avoid getting promoted too high. Right now, you're surrounded with buddies that will cover your ass. Any Marine above Gunny is starting to play too much politics. Present company excluded. You planning on a career?"

"Shipping over in two months, Sergeant Major, er, Tex."

Tom clapped him on the shoulder and said, "That's what I like to hear. Good leaders are hard to find and even harder to keep. Like Jesse and Tex over there. You do like they did and your men will follow you right into hell, carrying jerry cans full of avgas."

CHAPTER FIVE:

To All Who Shall See These Presents, Greeting

I woke with a rum-and-beer-induced headache at zero six hundred. We'd eaten, drank, and shared what was going on in our lives until nearly midnight. Not a real good idea, when we were planning to fly back in the afternoon. At least Williams had the presence of mind to limit his intake to just a single shot and two beers. I showered and got dressed in my best jeans, a light blue guayabera shirt, and topsiders. I was just booting up my laptop when there was a knock on the door.

"Figured you'd be up early," Deuce said when I opened the door. "You get the email?"

"Just opened it up. What email?"

"I'll save you having to stress those three brain cells. I forwarded it to you. It's from the new Assistant Deputy Director. Wants me to arrange a fishing charter with you, to take out some VIPs. I told you about him, right?"

"Army Colonel, yeah. So who's the VIPs he wants me to get seasick?"

"He didn't say. Just said to set it up with you as soon as possible. This week. Two VIPs and six security, besides myself. He said we'd need two boats minimum."

"Six security for just two guys? He wants me to take the Vice President fishing or something?"

Deuce put on his serious face for a moment. "Might be, but I don't think the old guy's heart could handle it. He wants us both to video call him at zero seven hundred."

I checked my Citizen Eco dive watch and said, "Better not keep him waiting."

We sat down on the sofa and I spun the laptop in front of Deuce. He clicked the 'Soft Jazz' icon that his tech genius, Chyrel Koshinski, set up for the secure video link. His face appeared in a small screen at the top right of the screen and seconds later her face appeared on full screen.

"Hi, boss," she said and Deuce turned the laptop slightly toward me. "Hiya, Jesse. Long time no see."

"Good to see you again, Chyrel," I said.

"I guess since you're in your office, you got the email also?" Deuce asked.

"I have the link to Quantico already set up. The ADD's secretary is standing by. She said he's extremely punctual. I'll patch the link in."

"Airborne Colonel," I muttered. "Of course he is."

A little telephone receiver started blinking in the top right corner. It was the old-style corded telephone handset, like we used in the '70s. Kind of ridiculous for a modern, encrypted satellite video call. The blinking receiver switched to a small screen, where a young woman was looking into the camera.

Chyrel's image and the young woman's switched places and Chyrel said, "Hi again, Teresa. I have Mister Livingston and Captain McDermitt on the line, whenever the Director is ready."

The young woman, Teresa, looked at her watch and said, "Right on time. I'll patch you through." A moment later, her image was replaced by a man in his early fifties, with a tanned, fit-looking face. His hair was in a crew cut, gray at the temples.

"Good morning, Commander," he said. "That must be Captain McDermitt with you?"

"Yes sir," Deuce said as he pushed the laptop a few inches away, so that we were both in the smaller picture.

"Good to meet you face to face, sort of, Captain."

"Just Jesse's fine, when I'm not on the boat."

"Fine, then. Jesse, my name's Travis Stockwell. I assume Deuce has told you about me and my request?"

"Only that you want to arrange a fishing charter, Travis." Hell, if he didn't want me to call him by his first name, he shouldn't have given it. At least he wasn't on my boat, uninvited, like his predecessor had been.

"This will be a charter for two very important people. I've read your jacket and feel extremely comfortable with arranging this meeting. Can you be available, with two boats, for a day of fishing Sunday?"

"Today's Friday," I said. "Kind of short notice, but as it happens I have a pretty open schedule this weekend."

"Good. Are you familiar with the marina on the west side of NAS Boca Chica?"

"I know where it's at, yes."

"Good. I'm flying in Saturday evening and will meet you at the docks at oh five thirty hours. Air Force One

will land at oh six hundred hours. The President and Secretary Chertoff will arrive at the marina at oh six fifteen and the three of us, along with two Secret Service agents, will go with you on the boat, total party of five. The second boat is needed to carry the rest of the Secret Service detail, another four agents. Do you have someone to pilot the second boat? Someone with a security clearance?"

"The President?" I said. "Of the United States?"

"I thought you told me he was bright for a Jarhead, Deuce," Stockwell said. Then he grinned and said, "Yeah, the President of the United States, Jesse."

"We have just the person to pilot the second boat," Deuce said, unflustered. "One of my team is a local. Grew up in the Keys and just finished Maritime Enforcement training for the Coast Guard. Knows boats and the local waters better than anyone I know."

"Perfect," Stockwell said. "Will there be any problem having two boats there?"

I finally got over the shock and said, "No, no problem. I have two boats that will be perfect."

"What about crew? Any crewmembers outside the two of you will need secret clearance and to be vetted by the Secret Service."

"Coast Guard Petty Officer Third Class Juliet Thurman will pilot the second boat and I'll be her crew," Deuce said. "She has a secret clearance."

"I'll pilot the boat with the VIPs on board," I said. "My First Mate is Navy Petty Officer Second Class Robert Talbot, a part of Deuce's team, and my Second Mate will be Navy Lieutenant Commander Jacqueline Burdick, MD."

"A doctor is your Second Mate?" he asked. Then without waiting for an answer he said, "I'll submit all your

names to Secret Service for vetting. You will all need to be in uniform. Will that be a problem?"

"No sir," replied Deuce before I could object. I don't like leather-soled shoes on my deck.

"I don't need to remind either of you that this is completely classified. The Secretary wants to talk to the three of us, face to face, and the President wants to meet you both personally."

I was about to ask why, when Stockwell said, "The President expects to spend the morning fishing and has already been assured of a good catch. So, get your reels oiled up. We're goin' fishin'."

The screen went blank. Deuce and I looked at each other. "The President?" we both said in unison.

"In uniform?" I said. "I don't even know if I still have a uniform."

"You know what this means, don't you?"

"Yeah," I replied. "I'll have to salute your ass." A knock on the door kept us from talking about it anymore.

I opened the door and both Rusty and Williams came in. "We better get a move on," Rusty said. "You two won't have a problem getting on base, but me and Dave will need to stop at the PMO for a visitor pass."

"They're issued at the gate now," I said. "I already called ahead and the guards at the gate will have them waiting. But yeah, we better get going."

"What were you doing on the computer?" Rusty asked.

"Playing solitaire," Deuce said.

"Yeah, whatever."

"Rusty, are my old uniforms still hanging in your guest closet?"

"Yeah," he said with a puzzled look. "Yours and mine both. But I don't think mine fits anymore. Why?"

"Jackie and I have something to go to and I'll need my Charlie uniform."

We left the suite, got in the big Expedition, and pulled out onto Western Boulevard. "Just stay on Western. It's about three miles to Highway 24 and turn left."

"Where's Luke going to meet us, Dave?" Rusty asked.

"He's got his own car. Said he'd meet us at SNTC on Snead's Ferry Road, wherever that is."

"SMTC," I corrected him. "Stands for Special Missions Training Center. It's on the east side of the base, at Courthouse Bay."

We turned onto Highway 24 and I said, "The main gate is about two miles on the right. When you pull into the gate, get over in the left lane and roll your window down."

At the gate, I showed the young Lance Corporal on duty my retired ID card. Deuce flashed his DHS ID and asked the young Marine if he had two visitors passes for Rusty and Williams. Once they showed their drivers licenses, the guard went into the building and came back out with their passes.

We continued onto the base and I said to Deuce, "A little over three miles, bear left at a Y intersection. That's Snead's Ferry Road. From there, Courthouse Bay is about fifteen miles."

"Fifteen miles?" Williams asked. "How big is this base?"

"Altogether, it covers about two hundred and fifty square miles," Rusty said. "Some of the best fishing on the coast."

We got to the Coast Guard facility a little after zero eight hundred. The graduation ceremony was supposed to start at zero eight thirty. We found a place to park and within a few minutes Williams located his son. I asked a Coast Guardsman where the graduation was to take place and he pointed out the building. It appeared to be a small auditorium. There were only a handful of guests, as the class only had twenty people in it. Julie was one of only two women in the class.

We found seats in the small section of bleachers set aside for guests and within minutes a Coast Guard Captain came to the podium and the ceremony began. After a few brief words, a Chief Petty Officer led a group of fourteen people into the small auditorium. Julie was the only woman among them and she looked real sharp in her dress white uniform.

The Captain described the training the fourteen had undergone and praised them on their fortitude. At the end, he pointed out that one graduate stood out among the others and would receive the Honor Graduate recognition and be promoted meritoriously.

"This Seaman," the Captain said, "exemplifies the character traits and leadership qualities the Coast Guard is looking for in its noncommissioned officers. Not only did this Seaman qualify in the upper percentile of nearly all training assignments, but she was voted by her peers as an outstanding leader. Seaman Juliet Thurman, front and center!"

Rusty couldn't contain himself and let out a loud whoop. I turned to him and said, "Can you maintain?"

Julie stood and marched smartly to the front of the podium and the Captain continued. "Seaman Thurman is

the first female to graduate this school and has set an example for others to follow. Her knowledge of small craft and safe water practices has been exemplary, as was her performance on the shooting range." Then he picked up a sheet of paper that I knew to be Julie's promotion warrant, or whatever Coasties call it.

He walked around the podium and stood in front of Julie, and in a loud voice he said the words that we who have served could recite without reading: "To all who shall see these presents, greeting. Know ye that reposing special trust and confidence in the fidelity and abilities of this Seaman, I do hereby appoint Juliet Thurman a Petty Officer Third Class in the United States Coast Guard. To rank as such from this second day of June, 2006." He continued, charging Julie to carry out the duties of her rank and charging others of lower rank to obey her orders. But I didn't hear all that. I was as proud of her as I would be if she were my own daughter.

The ceremony ended with the traditional tossing of head gear, then the graduates were dismissed. Julie came running toward us as we stepped down off the bleachers. She went straight into Deuce's arms and gave him a long kiss. Stepping back, she said, "I've missed you so much, Russell." Julie wasn't real big on calling him by his nickname.

Then she gave Rusty a big hug and he was beaming as he said, "I'm so proud of you, baby."

The Captain walked up with one of Julie's classmates as we were congratulating her and said, "Petty Officer, all the others have received their orders already. I was told your orders were supposed to arrive by special courier

today at graduation, but they haven't arrived yet. Is one of these gentlemen your father?"

"Captain Osgood, this is my dad, Rusty, my 'adopted dad,' Jesse, and my fiancé, Russell."

He shook hands with each of us and I introduced Williams and his son.

Deuce introduced me to Petty Officer Third Class Jeremy Dawson. He was the other on Deuce's team undergoing Maritime Enforcement training.

"I understand Julie learned her boating skills from the two of you," the Captain said. "You raised quite a daughter."

"Thanks, Skipper," Rusty said.

"I'm your courier, Captain," Deuce said. "Commander Russell Livingston, currently assigned to DHS." He opened his briefcase and took out a legal envelope. "These orders transfer Petty Officer Thurman to active duty and reassign her to the Department of Homeland Security, Caribbean Counterterrorism Command. If you'll look them over, sir, all that's required is your signature."

The Captain shuffled through the papers. When he was satisfied, Deuce produced a pen from his briefcase and closed it for the Captain to sign the orders on. When he finished, he handed them back to Deuce, who put them away in his briefcase.

"Does this mean I have to salute you now?" she asked Deuce with a grin.

"Absolutely, babe," he replied with a laugh.

The others in the class stopped by to congratulate her and a few minutes later, we were back in the parking lot. At the Expedition, I told Deuce, "Why don't the three of you head back to the hotel, so Julie can get changed? The

three of us are meeting a friend for lunch and Luke will give us a ride back in an hour or so."

We split up and I got in the small backseat of Luke's black Mustang. Williams ratcheted the front seat as far forward as it would go to give me some leg room, but it was still pretty cramped.

"You know where the Gourmet Grill is, Luke?"

"That's officer country," he replied. "Not officially, but not many enlisted Marines go there."

"First time for everything," I said. "Besides, the friend we're meeting is saltier than any officer aboard the base."

Twenty minutes later, we pulled into the parking lot and Tank had been right. Nearly every car in the lot had a blue sticker on the windshield, indicating it was owned by an officer. It was ten forty-five, but Tank was already there, standing by the door in his Alpha uniform. Tank should have retired long ago. He was in his midfifties, but looked much younger. He'd been in the Corps since Vietnam, where he'd received the Medal of Honor. He always said he only stayed in because he got a kick out of officers saluting him, and the Corps allowed it because they weren't about to push retirement on an MOH recipient.

A young Marine Captain was walking ahead of us as we approached him. Tank made for quite an imposing figure in the Alpha uniform, with eight rows of ribbons, topped with the pale blue Medal of Honor ribbon, the dive helmet and wings of Recon, and nine 'hash marks' from his elbow to his sleeve denoting more than thirty-six years of service. The young Captain approached him, expecting to be saluted, and Tank just stood there. The Captain was about to say something when he no-

ticed the ribbon on top of Tank's rack and quickly saluted him.

After the Captain went through the doors I said, "Never gets old, does it?"

He gripped my extended hand and said, "Hell no, only thing I hang around for anymore. Damn good to see you again, Jesse."

"Same here, Tank. Meet a couple of friends of mine, Dave Williams and his son, Corporal Luke Williams. Dave, Luke, this is Master Gunnery Sergeant Owen Tankersley."

He shook hands with both of them and opened the door for us. "Just a high-ranked doorman these days. Hell, the Corps doesn't even give me anything to do anymore."

We went inside and the talking among the Marines in the restaurant came to a near complete silence as all heads turned toward the two enlisted men and the two civilians. Tank paid them little attention as he nodded to the hostess, who quickly escorted us to a rear table, away from the others.

"Have a seat, men," Tank said. "I asked the manager to set up a table back here just for us."

We sat down in a semicircle around the table and a waitress appeared and quickly took our orders. Tank, as usual, cut straight to the chase. "So, you want to know what happened to your son in Iraq?"

"I just want to help him," Williams replied.

"It was pretty bad," Tank began. "Jared was part of the lead element when 1/9 was spooled back up, and he was assigned to Sixth Marines when we deployed. Three months into our deployment, he and his spotter locat-

ed a high-value target in a house north of Ashraf. They'd been in position for two days, watching and waiting for a chance to take out one of Al-Qaeda's top people. Once he was cleared to engage the target, he took the shot. But the target's daughter stepped in front of the window and she was killed. Jared was debriefed by a CIA spook, who made out like he'd killed the girl on purpose. I didn't blame the kid one bit when he flipped and started beating the shit outta the spook. Anyway, the CIA guy had connections, both political and financial. He took the beating kind of personal and railroaded your son, had him court-martialed and dishonorably discharged. I know Jared. He was a good Marine and had a real future in the Corps. Personally, I'd like to meet that spook, Jason Smith, in a dark alley one day."

I was stunned at first. "Jason Smith?"

"You know him?"

CHAPTER SIX:

Smith Revealed

Three hours later, we were flying over the ocean again, south of Myrtle Beach, South Carolina. I'd been lost in thought ever since lunch with Tank. Jason Smith was Deuce's, and therefore my, old boss, the former Assistant Director of the Caribbean Counterterrorism Command for DHS. Deuce hadn't told me any of the details about why he was no longer there, or why he'd been transferred to Djibouti, in the Horn of Africa. I'd been there once, not a pleasant assignment and a wonderful place for him to be sent. To say I didn't like the man would be putting it mildly.

"Jesse!" Williams said.

"Yeah, huh?"

"I said, do you wanna take the controls for a while?"

Deuce, Rusty, and Julie had been talking away in back. Deuce told her about Sunday's plans with the President and the role she was going to play. They were now quiet, looking forward to where I sat in the copilot's seat.

"Sorry, I must have dozed off. How about Julie and I switch seats? Maybe she'd like to fly some."

I started unbuckling my seat belt and looked back at Julie. "Me?" she asked. "Fly an airplane? This is only the fourth time I've ever been in one and the first three were airliners."

Deuce saw that I'd been troubled since we got back to the hotel and said, "Go ahead, babe. Just like driving a boat."

I climbed back, sat down in the seat opposite Rusty as Julie climbed forward, took the copilot's seat, and put on the headset. Once she was settled in and Williams was busy telling her what to do, I motioned to Deuce. He took off his headset, leaned forward, and in a low voice asked, "What's on your mind, Jesse?"

Rusty leaned across the narrow space between the seats and pulled off his headset. "I need to know more about how and why Smith got transferred," I said.

"It's a bit of a long story," Deuce replied. "Can it wait?"

"Smith was responsible for Williams's son getting a DD. He was the one that debriefed him in Iraq two years ago."

"Long story short, he was pissed about our sudden takedown of the camp in Cuba and his not calling the shots."

"I thought he was in the loop the whole time," Rusty said.

"No, I should have let him make the call, but I knew he wouldn't go for it and would screw around till Tony was killed." Tony Jacobs was one of Deuce's operators that came with him to DHS from the SEALs, a wiry black guy with a great sense of humor. I'd grown to not just

like him, but respect his sense of service. Several months ago, we'd dropped him and another team member, Art Newman, off near the coast of Cuba to swim ashore and get intel on a terrorist camp that was stockpiling weapons for an attack on civilian targets in Miami. Tony had been captured and Deuce and I, along with a few other operators, had gone in and gotten him out, along with the leader of the terrorist cell and the arms supplier.

"So, he complained to the Secretary?" I asked.

"The DHS Secretary, SecNav and the CNO," he said, meaning the Secretary of the Navy and the Chief of Naval Operations. "He tried to get both you and me ousted for being insubordinate, but he'd been a thorn in the side of all three for some time. He was only appointed ADD due to some political ties. Chertoff, Winter, and Admiral Mullen conference-called me and I told them exactly what happened and about my concern for Tony being left behind. Smith's a civilian and didn't understand our creed of not leaving a man on the battlefield. Apparently they agreed, because the next thing I knew, he was gone and Stockwell took over."

I thought it over a moment. "I wonder if there's any grounds that might be used to get Williams's son's DD overturned."

"It's happened before. A lot of guys in the last couple of years have been dishonorably discharged for things that weren't quite right. Poor leadership in most cases. Want me to look into it?"

"Yeah," I said. "I've only met the kid once, but he seemed to be a pretty decent guy and my friend Owen Tankersley vouched for him at lunch today."

"Owen Tankersley of 'they thought I knew where the mines were' fame?"

"One and the same," I replied.

"He's still active duty? That was what, 1969?"

"It was 1970. Yeah, he's still active. He's a Master Gunnery Sergeant, with Ninth Marines."

Deuce thought about it for a minute and said, "But would he stick his neck out for a junior Marine who was dishonorably discharged?"

"I think he would," Rusty said. "Met him once in Oki. He was a good Marine then, always looked after his troops. Hard to believe he's still active after thirty-seven years."

"Good PR for the Corps to have a salty old noncom with a Medal of Honor around his neck," I said, then added with a grin, "Plus he likes having officers salute him."

"I'll do a little background investigation tomorrow," Deuce said. "Maybe I can have a word with Stockwell on Sunday about it. Give me Tankersley's contact information when we land and I'll give him a call, too."

We sat back and put our headsets back on. Williams was still coaching Julie and when I looked forward, she was on the controls, grinning from ear to ear.

We refueled in Jacksonville, Florida, had a quick bite to eat, visited the head, and were back in the air in forty minutes. Less than three hours later, we touched down at NAS Boca Chica. I called Jackie while we were on approach and asked her when she would get off work. She was just ending her shift, so I asked if she'd like to have dinner and give me a ride back to Marathon. I had something important to talk to her about.

We sat in the back of the Runway Grill. A few months ago, Jackie had brought me here while I was recovering

in the base hospital. "So, is this a date date, or do you just have something to tell me?"

We'd just ordered our steaks, so I simply posed the question bluntly. "Do you have a security clearance?"

"Ah, not a date, then." She looked a bit disappointed. Jackie is a beautiful woman, with long auburn hair and chiseled features like fine china, and even under her doctor's smock, it was obvious she took great care of her body. "But, to answer your question, these days all Naval officers receive a secret clearance, regardless of whether they're a medical doctor or a secret squirrel infantry officer. Why?"

"Would you like to go on a date?" I said with a grin.

"I need a security clearance to go on a date with you?"

"Kind of a group date," I said, still grinning.

"What gives, Jesse? Stop beating around the bush."

"Okay," I said, getting serious. "What I'm going to tell you goes no further than this table." She nodded, so I continued. "Remember that phone call you got, while I was still in the hospital here? The 'highest-ranking government official' that ever called you?"

"DHS Secretary Chertoff? Yes, I remember."

"He said he wanted me to take him and a guy from Texas out fishing. Remember that?"

"There's nothing wrong with my memory, Jesse. Would you just get on with it?"

I grinned again and said, "I need someone in uniform, with a security clearance, to be second mate on Sunday, when I take the Secretary and the President on a fishing trip."

"You're kidding!"

"Nope, just got the call this morning. You game?"

She thought it over for about a half second and said, "I'll get to meet the President? In person?"

"I already submitted your name to the Secret Service," I said, grinning ear to ear. "Hope that's not too presumptuous of me."

"It's a date, then! What do I wear?"

"How about a string bikini?"

She reached across the table and punched me in the shoulder. "Or whatever the Navy equivalent of the Marine Charlie uniform is." I chuckled.

"That's the khaki short sleeves, with green pants?"

"Trousers, but yeah."

"I'll wear the service khaki uniform, then. Will I really get to meet him?"

"It's a small boat," I said. "You might bump into him from time to time."

"But I can't tell anyone?"

"Not until after he leaves. I'll make sure there's pictures."

Our food arrived then and we ate. She asked me how my back was and if I had any more problems. I'd been her patient last winter, when I took a bullet in the back in Cuba. It had torn a hole in my right lung and lodged in my spine, just millimeters from my spinal cord. She'd operated for three hours to remove it and put me in a medically induced coma for two weeks.

"I'm right as rain, thanks to you," I said.

"Probably more to do with your physique than my skill," she said with a wicked grin. Probably remembering when she'd bet me a steak dinner that I couldn't stand up the day after I came out of the coma. When I did it, I was totally naked. But the effort got me outside

that evening to watch the sunset and she was true to her word and bought both me and my first mate, Doc Talbot, a steak dinner. Doc had been a Navy corpsman in Afghanistan. When I met him, he was Trent's mate on the shrimp trawler. I managed to get him a spot on Deuce's team, as they were in need of a corpsman or medic. He probably saved my life that night in Cuba.

After dinner she drove me up US-1 to Marathon. We stopped at a little parking lot on the east side of the Seven Mile Bridge to watch the sun go down. It's a spectacle I try to enjoy every day I can. The sky was cloudy as the sun sank toward Mother Ocean and disappeared behind a cloud bank. A moment later, the lower part began to emerge below the clouds and soon turned the far away cloud bank a pale orange before it slipped below the horizon.

We got back in Jackie's Jaguar and drove to the *Anchor*, where my boat was still docked and a full-blown 'wetdown' celebration was taking place. It's an old Naval tradition, usually for newly promoted officers, where he or she throws a party and spends the difference in pay between their old rank and their new one to pay the bar tab. Since Rusty and Julie owned the bar, this could turn out to be a wild one.

Jackie and I walked into the crowded bar amid a chorus of shouts and whistles, as everyone tossed down a shot of rum. "Welcome aboard, mates!" shouted Rusty over the din. "You've missed the first toast, but belly up, there's sure to be more."

"Have you ever been to a wetdown?" I asked Jackie as we stepped up to the bar. Rufus was behind it with Rusty,

and he placed two shot glasses in front of us and poured a finger of Pusser's in each.

"Actually, no," she replied. "I always thought they were a bit too formal."

"Marines don't stand much on formality," Rusty said. Then he turned to the crowd and lifted his glass. "Mister Vice, a toast."

Julie and Deuce were seated at the head of the bar and Julie stood up. "Ladies and gentlemen. To the Commandant of the United States Coast Guard, Admiral Thad Allen!"

Jackie started to stand up, but I touched her arm and shook my head. A roar went up from the seated crowd, "United States Coast Guard." Everyone, Jackie and I included, tossed down the rum.

"It's tradition to remain seated during the toasts," I explained. "This is kind of a mix between a wetdown and dining in."

Rufus and Rusty quickly poured another finger in the dozens of glasses that appeared on the bar. When everyone was again seated, Rusty called on Julie for another toast.

"Why does he call Julie 'Mister Vice'?" Jackie asked.

"You really need to get out among your Naval friends more," I said. "Preferably the enlisted. Nobody parties like we do. Mister Vice is the traditional name given to the lowest ranking member, and is the one that proposes the toasts."

Julie stood up, lifted her glass and said, "Ladies and gentlemen. To the Commandant of the United States Marine Corps, General Michael Hagee!"

Jackie caught on quickly and lifted her glass with the others and shouted, "United States Marine Corps!"

The toasts continued to the other branches, until finally Rusty poured a full two fingers in every glass and Deuce stood up, turned to Julie, and solemnly said, "Mister Vice, one last toast."

Julie stood and turned to the crowd and in a hushed voice said, "Ladies and gentlemen, will you please stand?"

With the scratching of chairs on the hardwood floor, everyone stood up. Julie turned to the corner of the bar to the left of the door, and I noticed for the first time the Missing Man table. Everyone turned toward it.

"Ladies and gentlemen," she began, raising her glass. "A toast to all the warriors who preceded us but never came home. We knew them, we'll remember them, and they will not be forgotten. To our fallen comrades!"

"Our fallen comrades!" everyone shouted and tossed down the fifteen-year-old rum.

Rusty rang the ship's bell behind the bar, and immediately the back door opened and four men carried huge trays to the main table set up in the center. Each tray was loaded with the bounty of the sea, lobster, stone crab claws, clams, oysters, and fish of all kinds.

"Everyone dig in!" Rusty shouted as he tried to hide wiping a tear from the corner of his eye. For his size, thick red beard, and general gruff attitude, the guy was actually pretty emotional at times. I couldn't help but be moved by Julie's toast myself.

Jackie stepped away from the bar and started toward the Missing Man table. I followed her and came up beside her in front of the arrangement. "I've heard of this,

but have never seen one. I assume everything has some significance?"

Doc Talbot, his wife, Nikki, and a few others stood around the table with us, and they all looked to me for an explanation. I'd explained the meaning at many Marine Corps functions in the past and remembered it all. I slowly raised my glass in salute and tossed down another shot.

"The table is round," I began, "to show our never-ending concern for our fallen comrades. The tablecloth is white, symbolizing the purity of their motives when answering the call to duty. The single red rose in the vase reminds us of the life of each of them, and the loved ones and friends who keep the faith. The vase is tied with a red ribbon, a symbol of our continued determination to remember them. A slice of lemon, or in this case a Key lime, on the bread plate is to remind us of the bitter fate of those who will never return. A pinch of salt symbolizes the tears endured by the families of those who have given the last full measure of devotion. The Bible represents the strength, gained through faith, to sustain those lost. The glass is upside down because they can't toast with us. The chair is empty because they are no longer with us."

She turned toward me, reached up, and wiped a single tear from the corner of my eye. "Damned eyeball sweat," I said. "Come on, let's get some of those stone crab claws."

We partied well into the night. I caught up to Doc about midnight and explained our charter on Sunday. A guy I didn't recognize seemed to be trying to listen in so I didn't give any details other than we had a VIP charter. "Do you have a serviceable uniform?" I asked.

"What the hell for?" he asked, choking on his beer.

"The client's a Navy man, likes to see uniforms."

"You don't think that's kinda weird?"

"I prefer eccentric," I said. "Hey, it's a good-paying charter and you know me, anything to please the client."

Doc quickly picked up that I was being evasive for a reason. He's been out with me enough to know I really didn't like clients and left that completely up to him.

"Got a Charlie, wrapped in plastic. Should still fit."

"Perfect," I said. "I won't be the only one in green. I'll be at the marina on the west side of NAS Boca Chica tomorrow night. The clients arrive at zero six hundred, so I'll need you aboard no later than zero five thirty."

Deuce joined us at the bar and said, "When are you heading out tomorrow?"

The guy that was eavesdropping seemed to listen just a bit more intently, but he was trying hard not to show it. He was sitting on the stool behind me, but I could see him in the mirror over the bar. With my left hand I reached up and tugged on my ear. Being a former SEAL and current spook, Deuce was instantly aware and glanced over my shoulder at the guy.

"I'm gonna leave early," I said. "About zero seven hundred. Want to stop by the house and check on some things."

"We'll be ready," he said. Then he turned on his heel and walked over to the end of the bar where Jackie, Julie and Rusty sat. Minutes later the eavesdropper left the bar, without finishing even half his beer.

Doc said he and Nikki had to get back down to Key West, she had to work in the morning. We said goodbye

and I walked over to where Deuce and Julie were sitting. "Rusty and Julie said they never saw the guy before. You?"

"Me neither. He seemed a little too interested in our itinerary on Sunday."

"You didn't say anything to tip anyone off?" I looked at him with an arched brow. "No, I didn't think so. This charter is so hush hush, even the clients' wives don't know anything about it. What do you make of the guy?"

"Might just be someone interested in fishing, I really don't know. Let's just keep our eyes and ears open."

He thought that over for a moment and said, "Yeah, that's probably all it is."

"So, Jules," I said, "you like your new place?"

"It's just freaking awesome! Deuce told me you helped crew it back here from Bimini."

"Yeah, for a Sailor, he's not much of a sailor. Somebody had to go along to show him the difference between standing rigging and running rigging."

"He's taking me to the Antilles for our honeymoon."

Jackie walked up then and caught what Julie said. "You'll love it there. Some of the most beautiful islands in the Caribbean."

Later, since we'd had so much to drink, I invited Jackie to stay aboard the *Revenge*. "Are you asking me to spend the night with you? Because it sure sounds like you're asking me to spend the night with you."

"I'm just saying it would be a bad idea to drive back to Key West after four shots of rum and three beers. Useless-One has been known to put people to sleep late at night. You'll find the guest cabin in my boat to be very comfortable."

"Guest cabin?" She pouted.

"Guest cabin."

The bar was nearly empty as we said good night to everyone an hour later. When I glanced back from the door, Rusty and Deuce both gave me a sly wink. I just rolled my eyes at them.

CHAPTER SEVEN:

Red Sky in Morn, Sailor Be Warned

I woke up early Saturday morning to rain beating down on the cabin roof. I grabbed a quick shower, put on a pair of fisherman's shorts and a tee shirt, and went up to the galley, where the smell of fresh coffee was coming from. I'd set the timer for zero six hundred. A quick glance out the starboard porthole told me all I needed to know. The rain was coming down in sheets and the palm trees on the west side of the canal were whipping their fronds in what looked to be a twenty-knot southwest wind.

Before heading down to Boca Chica, we needed to go up to my island to pick up our other boat, a thirty-foot Winter center console called *El Cazador*. It had been confiscated last winter in a drug bust and, as is Deuce's team's custom, they added it to our growing fleet to use against the bad guys. The former ADD didn't want to pay to dock it up in Homestead where the team's based, so we brought it down to my island.

I opened my laptop to check the weather radar, when I heard the guest cabin door open and close. Jackie came up into the salon wearing one of my tee shirts, her lion's mane of hair disheveled from sleep. On her it looked good.

"I need to keep an emergency bag in my car," she said. "My teeth feel nasty."

"Guest head, across from your cabin, top drawer to the left of the sink. Should be four or five new toothbrushes and several kinds of toothpaste."

"Is that coffee I smell and rain I hear?"

"Go brush, I'll have a mug ready when you get back."

"Mmpf."

Either she wasn't a morning person or didn't drink much, I thought. Or maybe both. A minute later, I heard the shower come on, so I held off on pouring her coffee and checked the weather on the laptop.

The radar image showed a slow-moving band of heavy rain, stretching from north to south and moving east. I switched on the NOAA weather radio, which confirmed that and said that seas on the ocean side were six to ten feet, with three to five in the Gulf. I checked the laptop for tomorrow, and it predicted sunny skies and calm seas, again confirmed by the monotone mechanical voice on NOAA. Getting from the *Anchor* to Moser Channel and under the Seven Mile Bridge was going to be a wet ride, with quartering seas at first and full abeam before the turn under the bridge. Nothing the *Revenge* couldn't handle, and as far as getting wet went, as Russ always used to say, "If it ain't rainin', you ain't trainin'." I learned early on that unless you stood on your head, the

human body was waterproof. I wasn't too sure about my guest, though.

Just then, Jackie came up into the salon, with a huge towel wrapped around her head and another around her body. *Oh shit*, I thought. *You're in trouble now, McDermitt.* I handed her a mug of steaming coffee, which she gratefully took in both hands, not bothering with the sugar and cream I had set out on the settee.

"I don't suppose you have a blow dryer aboard, do you?"

"Equipped for anything and everything," I replied. "Middle drawer of the dresser in the guest cabin. You'll find some clothes in the hanging closet that should fit you. I need to head up to my island today and check on things, before going down to Boca Chica. Thought maybe you'd like to tag along. We'll be back here before sunset on Sunday."

"You're taking the boat out in this storm?"

"It's not that bad. We've been through a lot worse."

"Okay," she said without hesitation. "What time will we get to the base?"

"Midafternoon, easy. Plenty of time to starch your uniform before meeting the President in the morning."

"Oh my! I'd almost forgotten that." She finished her coffee, set the mug in the sink, and headed down to the cabin. I heard the blow dryer and started making breakfast.

"Omelets okay with you?" I shouted.

"Whites only, if you can," she shouted back.

How do you separate the yolk from the white? I wondered. I put two small pans on the stove and cracked two eggs in each. Using the shell, I managed to keep the yolks out of the pan and, rather than toss away good food, I

added them to the other pan. I chopped some onion and green pepper, sliced some tomato, added some chives and cheddar cheese, then turned on the two burners.

Jackie came up to the salon wearing a pair of cutoff jeans and a short-sleeved denim shirt a girlfriend had left aboard last winter. She had the tail of the shirt pulled up and tied in front.

"I like the Daisy Duke look on you, Doctor Burdick."

"These aren't new, are they?"

"No, but they're clean. Washer and dryer in the forward stateroom."

"Belong to your girlfriend?"

"You know I don't have a girlfriend. A charter passenger left them," I lied. I've learned over time that women can be particular about wearing an old girlfriend's clothes.

"Your boat is really beautiful, Jesse. I thought you said it was a work boat?"

"Out that hatch," I said, pointing astern, "and up on the bridge, it's all business. In here, well, even the most diehard fisherman wants to relax in style."

"Hello, the boat!" came a shout from the dock, which gave Jackie a start.

I got up and opened the hatch. Deuce and Julie came rushing in, wearing yellow slickers. "We're just finishing breakfast," I said. "You want me to whip you up an omelet?"

"We've had breakfast, thanks," Julie said. "I brought your uniform. Dad said he checked it over and everything's there and all squared away."

"Thanks, Jules." It was inside a weatherproof garment bag, still wrapped in plastic from a dry cleaner in Jack-

sonville, North Carolina. I took it and hung it up in the hanging locker by the hatch. Jackie and I ate quickly and I cleaned up, while Julie and Jackie talked excitedly about meeting the President. I went back over to the hanging closet by the hatch and pulled out my rain slicker. "When y'all are ready, there's a thermos in the top right cabinet. How about filling that and bring a couple mugs up to the bridge? We're going out to start the engines and cast off."

Deuce and I stepped quickly through the hatch. While I climbed up to the bridge, he went up on the dock and untied the lines. Both engines sprang to life instantly and settled into a low rumble. The wind held us stationary against the fenders until I was ready to pull away, so Deuce climbed up to join me.

"I told Stockwell about the guy listening in last night."

"What'd he have to say?" I asked.

"Pretty much the same as you. As long as nobody here has said anything, and I assured him nobody had, he figures it was either someone just interested in fishing, or maybe a charter competitor, looking to pick up some local intel."

Jackie and Julie came through the hatch and handed up the mugs and thermos. Jackie was wearing a slicker, with the hood pulled up over her head, but Julie was just wearing a slicker top with no hood. She'd weathered her share of rainy weather on the water and was used to it. The bridge isn't fully enclosed, but open astern. I always unroll the clear side curtains when I leave the boat, because rain comes up quick here. With the wind blowing off the starboard bow, it was dry. For now.

Jackie started to take her slicker off and I said, "We probably won't stay dry. In about ten minutes, we'll be turning north and the wind will come from behind us."

"I'll keep it on, then. Is it supposed to rain all day?" she asked as she sat in the second seat next to me and Deuce and Julie sat on the bench seat to port, Deuce to the rear.

I switched on the radar, sonar, VHF, and NOAA radio and said, "Forecast says it'll move through in an hour or two and should be sunny and calming by fifteen hundred."

Another boat had taken up residence in front of me in the last day or two and he'd docked a little too close. I nudged the starboard engine into reverse and gunned it for a second, swinging the bow away from the dock. Then I shifted the port engine into forward as the bow cleared the other boat and shifted the starboard engine to forward. We slowly idled down the long canal to the open ocean.

The *Rusty Anchor* is on the ocean side of US-1, sitting between two residential areas. Rusty's family had owned the land for over a century. His dad had built the bar and dredged a shallow canal in the '60s. In the last two years, Rusty had improved the bar, dredged the canal deeper, built docks and dredged a wide turning basin at the end of the canal. He was well on his way to running a full-fledged marina, complete with a fueling dock.

"Better find something to hang on to," I said as we neared the end of the canal. I could already see white caps in the shallows and big rollers further out.

"Are you sure this boat can handle that?" Jackie asked.

"Just watch and see," I replied. Passing the end of the jetty, I knew without looking we had over ten feet of wa-

ter under the keel, so I pushed the throttles forward to thirteen hundred rpm and the *Revenge* dropped down at the stern as the big four-bladed props displaced the water under her. The bow rose slightly and she surged up on plane, just as the first waves started to smack the wide Carolina flare of the bow. The second wave sent up a spray that flew back and over the foredeck. I switched on the windshield wipers.

Within a minute, we were out of the choppy water of the shallows. I turned into the wind, heading southwest, and pushed the throttles a bit further. Williams had done some work on the engines, mostly computer stuff, and bumped the horsepower up from 1015 to over 1030. I had a top speed of forty-eight knots, in calm seas with a tail wind. At fourteen hundred rpm, we were making about twenty-five knots, plowing head on into the oncoming waves. The bow was knocking the tops off and we were coming down off the crest a little too hard, so I backed it down to thirteen hundred rpm.

In my opinion, there's a time and place for speed. Too many boaters will run wide open everywhere they go, just for the adrenaline rush of velocity, I guess. Jet skis are the worst, built for no other reason than to go fast. I have no attraction to them at all. More than once, I've had idiots jumping my wake on the damn things. Never being in any kind of hurry, I'd simply drop down off plane and idle along until they left.

"Those are some really big waves," Jackie said.

"You should have been aboard during Hurricane Wilma," Deuce said, and from the look on his face I could tell he regretted it. It was the day my late wife, Alex, had returned to the Keys. A whirlwind romance had culminat-

ed in our getting married days after the storm and she was murdered that night.

"You were out on the boat during a hurricane?" Jackie asked.

"Just moved it from Dockside to the *Anchor.* Before the storm actually hit." Changing the subject, I added, "Would you pour me another cup of coffee, Jackie? Just a half cup, or it'll be all over me."

She poured the cup and handed it to me. I drank it down quickly and started a slow turn that would take us across Pigeon Key Banks, toward Moser Channel. "It's gonna get rough ahead," I said. "Pigeon Key Banks coming up. Find something to hang on to."

Coming down off the last wave before the shallows, I pushed the throttles up to sixteen hundred rpm and the *Revenge* surged forward into the choppy water. The waves were only about four feet, but they were coming at all angles to the bow, so spray and foam were flying in all directions. We entered the channel and I turned due north, toward the high span of the Seven Mile Bridge.

Clear of the Banks, we had a following sea and the rollers were moving pretty fast. We were barely outrunning the wind, so I pushed the throttles further to eighteen hundred rpm, the knot meter bouncing around thirty-five knots. We climbed the big rollers in the channel and came down gently over the crests, gaining speed as we surfed down the far side. Minutes later we passed under the bridge and between the pilings of the old bridge.

In the lee of the bridges, the sea calmed a little, but it was still pretty heavy, by Gulf standards. I dropped the throttles down a little to reduce the pounding. We were barely outrunning the wind now as we headed north. I

turned slightly west, picking up the markers for East Bahia Honda Channel.

"That was kind of exciting," Jackie said. "More coffee, anyone?"

I nodded as Deuce handed his mug across and Julie shook her head. "None for me, thanks."

Jackie filled our mugs and handed them back. "Want to take her for a while, Petty Officer Jules?" I asked.

Julie looked at me, surprised. "Sure."

We swapped seats and she said, "Monkey to Bullfrog to Turtlecrawl, right?"

"Works for me," I replied.

"What's all that mean?" Jackie asked, puzzled.

"Place names," Julie replied. "Monkey Banks is straight ahead about ten miles, then we'll turn west toward the light at Bullfrog Banks and straight ahead to the light at Turtlecrawl Banks. There we'll turn a little left into Harbor Channel to Jesse's house. It's a lot shorter in a flats skiff."

A chirping sound came from between me and Deuce. I said, "Must be you, I don't even know where mine is."

He pulled out his cell phone and answered it. After a moment he said, "He's right here with me, sir. Along with Commander Burdick and Petty Officer Thurman. Can I put you on speaker?"

After a second he punched a button and Stockwell's voice came over the speaker. "I'm headed down to Homestead. From there I'm going to take a chopper to Boca Chica. Jesse, will you be there early tomorrow or tonight?"

"We're on our way to my island now," I replied, "to pick up the other boat. We'll have both of them at the mari-

na before sunset. Deuce and Julie will stay aboard the *Revenge* with me tonight."

"How long will you be at your island?"

"A few hours. I need to check on some things and touch base with my caretaker."

"With your permission, I'd like to stop there on the way. Deuce's description has me intrigued. I could be there by thirteen hundred hours, or shortly after."

I looked at Deuce and grinned. "Sure thing, Colonel, please do."

"I have two guests with me. Hope it's not a problem."

A familiar voice came over the speaker, "Hey, boss. Hey, Jesse and Julie. How are y'all doin'?"

"Is that you, Tony?" Julie yelled.

"In the flesh," he replied. "The Colonel was kind enough to ask me and Dawson to come along. Not going out fishing with you guys, though. Thought maybe we could hang on your little island paradise for some R&R, Jesse."

"Any time, brother," I said.

Stockwell's voice came on the speaker again. "Good. Look forward to meeting you all. See you at thirteen hundred."

Deuce closed the phone and I said, "I like him better than Smith. Why do you suppose he wants to see us before morning?"

"No idea," Deuce replied. "He's real easy to get along with, but a real stickler for details. Maybe he wants to inspect your uniform."

A few minutes later, Julie started a slow turn to the west. She knew these waters like the back of her hand and was actually navigating mostly by the bottom contour shown on the sonar. As we came out of the turn and

were heading due west, the rain suddenly stopped completely and we could see Bullfrog light dead ahead of us. The sky was blue to the west, as the clouds from the storm moved east.

"I could live here forever," Jackie said, "and I don't think I'd ever get used to how sudden the rain starts and stops."

I got up and walked in front of the helm to the starboard side, unsnapped the side dodger and started rolling it up. Deuce did the same on the port side. Ten minutes later, Julie pulled back on the throttles and dropped the big boat down off the step, and she settled into the water with a throaty burbling from the exhaust. She steered us into Harbor Channel and said, "You better take over, Jesse. I'm not real comfortable backing in." We switched seats as we approached my island.

"That's your house?" Jackie asked, standing up for a better view.

"That's home," I replied as I pushed the button to sound the twin air horns on the roof. I turned south and brought both engines into reverse. Standing up and putting the wheel on the small of my back, I took the key fob from my pocket and pushed the unlock button on it. A catch released in the docking area under the house and the big door slowly started to open on giant hinge springs.

Actually, my house isn't more than a shack on stilts. Just over a thousand square feet, with a large combination living room, dining room, and kitchen in front and a bedroom and head in back. When I'd retired six years ago, I'd used up nearly all of my savings, which I'd scraped together over twenty years in the Corps, and add-

ed my inheritance from my grandfather to buy my boat and this tiny island. It's about two acres in size at low tide and the only beach is on the west side. It took me a whole winter and spring to dig the small channel from Harbor Channel, just deep enough for my little skiff to get to it. I'd carved a hunk out of the island and spent all summer building my stilt house above the channel.

Last winter, I'd enlarged the channel and done a lot of work on the island, adding two bunkhouses and enclosing the dock area under the house. I'd gone up to the commercial docks in Miami during that first summer and scrounged through the piles of discarded pallets and lumber. There were lots of South American hardwoods there and I managed to find plenty of mahogany planks and quite a few discarded lignum vitae posts, rare in the States, but plentiful down there. The exterior siding is mostly mahogany. The roof is corrugated steel I'd scrounged from NAS Key West when they'd torn down some of the old Quonset huts. The floor beams are fourteen feet above the channel at high spring tide, just enough room for the *Revenge*. The floors, studs and beams are solid lignum vitae. My little house could withstand anything Mother Nature could conjure up.

"It's beautiful," Jackie said. "Like something from *Swiss Family Robinson*. Why did you blow the horn?"

I nodded toward the long dock I'd recently built on the spoils of the channel as Pescador came trotting out to the end. "Just letting my dog know I was home." Using the throttles behind me and moving the wheel with my back, I maneuvered the boat into the channel and tucked it alongside the Cigarette under the house. Deuce climbed down to tie us off as Trent came down the steps

from the deck. I gently nudged the fenders on the dock and clicked the lock button on the fob. A battery-powered motor activated and slowly pulled the big doors closed as I shut down the engines.

"Welcome home, Jesse," Trent said. "Good to see you again, Deuce. I understand congratulations are in order, Julie?"

"Thanks, Carl," Julie said. "How'd you find out?"

"Coconut telegraph," he responded.

As Jackie and I climbed down, I said, "Carl, this is Commander Jackie Burdick. Jackie, meet Carl Trent, former slayer of shrimp."

"So, you're the one that fixed Jesse up, huh?"

"I just patched up a little damage," she replied. "He'd probably have recovered with or without my help."

Pescador came over and sat down on the dock in front of me. I reached down and scratched his ears and said, "Jackie, meet Pescador. Say hi to the nice lady, boy." He looked up at her and barked once while wagging his heavy tail.

"We're only here a few hours, Carl," I said. "We'll be leaving this afternoon with the *Revenge* and the *Cazador* for an early charter tomorrow down in Key West. I just wanted to stop and see how things were going and if you needed anything when we come back on Monday."

"Come on," he said excitedly. "Wait till you see it."

I assumed he was excited about the progress he'd made on his house, but once we reached the deck, it looked like he'd only gotten the metal on the roof and not much else. We went down the back stairs and he headed to the east side of the clearing. There was a lot of construction debris near the edge of the tree line. When we got closer,

I saw what it was. He had the tanks built for the aquaculture system, the pump and filters installed and everything plumbed.

"It's nearly full now. The new water maker arrived yesterday, so I ran a hose from the cistern to get enough water in it to start the pump. Then I ran a one-inch line out into the bay to pick up seawater and tied it into the water maker, which is now refilling the cistern. Should be full in another two days. Put a float switch in so it'll come on automatically when the water level in the cistern drops below half-full."

I checked out the two long tanks he'd built. The one we were going to raise the crawfish in looked to be about twenty feet long, eight wide and three feet deep. It sat close to the tree line to be shaded throughout the morning and had an awning to block the sun in the afternoon. The other tank was the same length and width, but only about half as tall. It was out away from the tree line and sat on a platform, so that the tops of both tanks were level with one another.

Jackie stood next to me, looking it over. She turned to Trent and said, "You have the filters wrong."

"You know about aquaculture?" I asked.

"What's aquaculture?"

I stared at her for a moment. "If you don't know what it is, how can you say the filters are wrong?"

"I have an aquarium and know a little about biology," she said with a smile.

"Go on, Doc," Trent said.

"I'm guessing you're going to raise fish in one and plants in the other?"

"Crawfish," I said. "But yeah."

"Whatever. The idea is to use the waste from the fish, er, crawfish, to provide nutrients to the plants and the plants to provide clean, oxygenated water to the animals, right?"

We both nodded and she continued, "Fish waste is ammonia. That will kill plants and fish, if allowed to get too high. I use a wet/dry filter in my aquarium, a lot smaller than the one you have here," she said, pointing to the last filter in the loop. "Aerobic bacteria in the wet/dry break the ammonia down into nitrite, also dangerous, but less so. Anaerobic bacteria in the sand filter will break the nitrites down into nitrates, which the plants will thrive on. The wet/dry should be first. Pump the water from the plant tank and let it gravity feed the filters, with a skimmer at the surface."

"I got more plumbing to do," Trent said. "Thanks, Doc."

"How many gallons is it?" Julie asked Trent.

"Once everything's up and running, about fifty-five hundred gallons. But, you see the drain on the vegetable tank? We can connect it to another tank to expand it. From what I've read, we should be able to raise maybe four or five thousand crawfish and harvest maybe a thousand a month. The crawfish tank will have mesh dividers of varying size openings, so the little ones can move to the far end away from the others. With each spawning, I'll harvest the biggest ones from the end and move each group up one divide to make room for the new babies."

"Really ingenious. Anything you need?" I asked.

"How about cable Internet?" he said with a laugh. "Running back and forth to the library in Marathon to look stuff up takes a lot of time."

"I think I can hook you up with something," Deuce said. "I'll have Chyrel send down a laptop with a satellite modem."

"What do you think we should grow?" I asked.

"Charlie's in charge of that. She says stuff she can either freeze or can and stuff that she can pick a little at a time. We can probably grow tomatoes year round. Green beans, lettuce, cabbage, basil, cucumber, maybe okra and corn, but we'd have to build something that will hold them up as they grow taller."

"Let's start with tomatoes and lettuce. She can experiment with what grows best. Where are Charlie and the kids, by the way?"

"Fishing. Took the Grady out on the Gulf at sunrise."

Jackie turned to me and said, "So, are you going to give me the nickel tour?"

We left the others and walked across the wide clearing toward the bunkhouses, Pescador trotting ahead. The Trents were still living in one of the bunkhouses. I'd built them to house Deuce's team whenever they needed a place to train or stage for a mission. We walked out on the long pier beyond the bunkhouses and sat down on the end of the pier. I had the floating pier built off island and barged up from Big Pine Key.

"Where are you from originally?" she asked.

"I was born and raised up in the Fort Myers area."

"Ah, that explains the name on your boat. He was a pirate up there, right?"

"So the story goes."

She turned toward me and I could feel it coming like a freight train. The inevitable questions about past relationships. But she started further back than that. "So,

you weren't always a Marine. What was your childhood like?"

"Normal, I guess. I was actually raised by my grandparents, though."

"What happened to your mom and dad?" she asked. Then her eyes changed to a serious look. "I'm sorry. You don't have to talk about it, if you don't want to."

"It's okay," I said. "My folks died when I was little. Dad was a Marine, a Sergeant on his second tour in Vietnam during the Tet Offensive. He was killed in action. Me and my mom moved in with his parents. She was the youngest of four kids, born late in her parents' lives, and they passed away about the time I was born. Mom had a hard time coping with Dad's death. She took her own life when I was eight."

"Oh my," she gasped. "That must have been really hard for you."

"Pap, that's what I called my grandfather, did his best to explain it. Said she couldn't bear to be without Dad and went to be with him, knowing that Pap and Mam, my grandmother, would take real good care of me. Pap taught me everything I know about the water and fishing. Mam taught me how to live a simple and frugal life. They didn't have to, but they lived through the Depression, so it was second nature for them, I guess. Mam passed away in ninety-three, while I was in Somalia. She was cremated, and Pap waited till I got home so the two of us could spread her ashes on the Peace River. Pap died four years later."

"What kind of man was he?"

"A big, robust, fun-loving guy. He loved playing practical jokes on his friends. He was a Marine, too. Served in

the South Pacific during World War Two. When he came home, he went to college on the GI Bill and became an architect. Owned his own firm until he sold it and retired young, to sail and fish."

"He must have been a very successful man."

"Yeah, he gave a lot to charities. When he died, he left everything to me, his only heir. I used it to buy the *Revenge* and this island."

"What's the name of this island, anyway?"

I shrugged. "Doesn't really have a name. None that I know of, anyway. Just one of the Content Keys."

She stared off over the water, watching an osprey circling over a school of baitfish. Then she turned to me again and said, "I've all but thrown myself at you, Jesse. What's a woman got to do to get your attention?"

I looked at her for a moment, then gazed out across the water. "Jackie, I've been married three times. Two divorces."

"I know about Alex, Jesse. It's been almost eight months. Do you think she'd want you to be a hermit?"

I laughed. "No, I know she wouldn't and I'm far from being a hermit."

"So what, then? You don't like me? You think I'm ugly? You don't like redheads?"

"I like you fine and you're a damned beautiful woman. Which I'm sure you're aware of." We sat in silence for a minute. Trent had told me once that the only way to make a relationship work, whether it's a friend or a lover, was total honesty. "I was involved with someone last winter. Probably too soon after Alex died. She split when she realized how dangerous my life was. I don't know

that it's fair to put someone through that. It's what cost me three marriages."

She thought about it a moment. "My ex was a jet jockey. He was deployed three of our five years together. I know a little about what your ex-wives went through. It can drive a person crazy not knowing. But I think I have kind of a unique perspective on your lifestyle."

She had a point there. Over a week in the hospital recovering from the bullet wound meant for me.

"What I do now goes beyond that a little," I said. "One day, I could just not show up for a dinner date and not be heard from for days. Maybe never. No explanation, no note, no call. Nothing. I like you, Jackie. But you wouldn't want to live like that."

"So you just want to be friends? Is that it?"

I wanted a hell of lot more than that, but the rational side of my brain took over. "Yeah, friends."

She gave me a sultry look and smiled. "Friends with benefits?"

You could have knocked me over with the proverbial feather and I guess it registered in my expression.

"What? Women don't have needs?"

"Yeah, I mean no, I mean, well, I just never thought about it."

"It's a new century, Jesse," she said with a smile as she stood up and tossed her hair over her shoulder. "You should join it."

She turned and started walking toward shore with my dog as I sat there dumbstruck, then scrambled to my feet and trotted after her. I showed her the rest of the island, which didn't take very long. Trent had done more work on his house than I'd thought earlier. Besides hav-

ing the roof on, the interior walls were complete. Rather than drywall, he'd used tongue-and-groove heart of pine. It looked to be reclaimed wood, so I asked him about it.

"Yeah," he said. "A friend, who's a builder, tore down an old bar up in Tavernier to build a new house and I heard through the coconut telegraph that he'd pay five hundred dollars to have it carted away. Borrowed a flatbed from another friend and hauled it up to that sawmill in Homestead. They charged me four hundred dollars to mill it all flat and straight, with tongues and grooves. The other hundred about covered the gas in the truck."

"Looks real cozy," Jackie said.

"Charlie did like you said, Jesse. Ordering the appliances. It wasn't cheap."

"Didn't think it would be. You get what you pay for right?"

"They'll have them at the Home Depot on Tuesday."

"Give Skeeter a call on Big Pine," I suggested. "He'll let you use his little salvage barge to bring everything up in one trip. This is looking really nice, man."

He thanked me and I took Jackie on up to the house to show her around. Deuce and Julie were sitting at the table in the galley. Deuce was just ending a call on the phone. "How'd you get a signal in here?" I asked. "Out on the front deck is the only place I've ever got one."

"Yeah, right," Deuce said. "When's the last time you even made a phone call from out here?"

I had to think about it a moment. I couldn't remember. I don't use phones very often.

"Jesse, that phone I gave you back in January is the same as this one, a satphone. You can get a signal any-

where. That was the Colonel. They'll be here in twenty minutes."

We walked out and crossed the clearing to the two large tables Trent had built and within minutes the sound of a helicopter could be heard. A quick glance at the flagpole told me the wind was coming out of the east and very light, meaning the pilot would probably fly over, turn, then come in over Trent's house.

While the others waited at the table, I walked over to the east side of the clearing. The pilot flew over a moment later at a slow speed, turned and lined up to land. I guided him down with arm signals and he landed gently in the center of the clearing. Both the pilot and copilot climbed out the front doors of the Air Force TH-1 Iroquois training helicopter. The port-side door slid back and Tony and Dawson climbed out, both carrying packs. Since nobody else got out, I assumed the copilot was Stockwell, but the copilot remained with the chopper. The pilot removed his flight helmet and handed it to the copilot. He then joined Tony and Dawson and walked toward the tables, where I'd already joined the others.

Removing his sunglasses, Stockwell extended his hand and said, "Nice to finally meet you in person, Jesse. I'm Travis." I shook his hand and he continued, "Thanks for allowing me to stop here. I've been wanting to see this place since Deuce told me about it."

I liked him right away. He was a little shorter than me, maybe five eleven or so and lean. His hair was once dark, but now had a touch of gray mostly at the temples and was closely cropped. His eyes were dark blue and danced constantly, taking in everything around him.

"Pleased to meet you, Colonel," I said, using his former rank, which surprised Deuce judging by the look on his face.

"Call me Travis," he said. "I imagine we'll be working together in the future and I like to get to know people I work with."

I introduced him and Dawson to Jackie and Trent. Then Deuce introduced him to Julie. "Congratulations on your promotion, Julie. That's one of the reasons I wanted to stop here and to bring Jeremy. Mind if we sit down?"

"Would you like a bottle of water, or maybe a beer?" I asked.

He glanced at his watch and said, "Sure. A cold beer would hit the spot right now. I can always let the Zoomie fly the next leg."

I handed him a cold Red Stripe from the cooler we kept stocked and sitting under the table and Trent said he had some work to attend to and walked toward the tanks. "Nice landing, by the way," I said. "Deuce didn't mention you were a chopper pilot."

"I'm not," he said. "Not primarily, anyway. Took some flight training with the Seventh when I was a young Lieutenant."

"What'd you come to see us about?" Deuce asked.

"Commander Burdick, I read your jacket and saw that you do indeed have a secret clearance. For that reason, you can remain, but everything we discuss is classified."

"All officers in the Navy have a secret clearance," she said. "But if you want, I can go help Carl."

"No reason," he said with a smile. "If the Secret Service trusts you to be close to the President, I guess I can trust you on this."

He looked at Julie and Dawson and continued, "First off, our team cross-trains one another, as I'm sure Deuce has already told you. The skills you two learned in Maritime Enforcement are greatly needed by the rest of the team. Julie, I want you to put together a two-week training course for the whole team on small-boat boarding tactics. Get with Deuce and learn everyone's strong and weak points and utilize that in the training. Jeremy will assist you in the actual implementation of the course and the Coast Guard will provide the boats."

"Aye aye, sir," Julie said.

"Wouldn't it be better if they trained on the boats here?" I asked. "I mean, if a scenario were to come up where they'd need to use that training, would they have to wait for the Coast Guard to provide familiar boats?"

"Hmm," he said, thinking. "Good point. Make it a three-week course and include every available type of small craft you can lay hands on, including those from the Coast Guard."

"When do you want to start the training?" Deuce asked.

"No set timetable, just whenever she can arrange it. That brings me to the second reason for my visit. I'd like to take a page from Jesse's playbook and get everyone in the team into some kind of local job as cover. Not a real nine-to-five job, but kind of an entrepreneurial thing, where they could take time away suddenly without raising suspicion or getting fired. The two Scotts and Jeremiah, for instance, could open a private scuba-diving school. Charity could open a small martial arts school. Chyrel, a computer repair store. Things like that. What do you think?"

"Great idea," Deuce said. "Something that will make them not stand out so much as outsiders and fill a lot of their free time."

"Exactly," Stockwell said. "The next thing I wanted to talk to you about goes right along with that. The team needs to be more covert in their dealings with the public in general. As local citizens, that'll go a long way with helping each of them maintain a low profile. But their appearance, particularly yours, Deuce, just reeks of military. Let your hair grow out some, and cut back on the daily shaving to maybe once a week before church."

"We're still active duty, even though we're attached to DHS," Deuce said.

"You mean to tell me you never let your hair and beard grow out when you were with the SEALs?"

"Well, yeah. But only when we were going undercover and it would sell the cover."

Stockwell cocked his head, arched an eyebrow and looked at Deuce with a lopsided grin.

"Point taken," Deuce said.

"Now, on the subject you emailed me about, Deuce. Upgrading a dishonorable discharge? Where'd this come from?"

"Personal friend of mine, Travis," I said. "A young Marine who was railroaded by your predecessor."

Stockwell nodded. "Smith. Deuce explained your suspicions and it doesn't surprise me."

"He was debriefing a Marine sniper team in Ashraf, Iraq, two years ago. They'd been involved in the accidental death of a noncombatant. Apparently Smith accused the shooter of killing the girl on purpose and the Marine gave him a beating. Smith, using his political and fi-

nancial connections, had the Marine dishonorably discharged. That Marine is the son of a friend of mine."

Stockwell looked at me and said, "Marines take care of their own, I get it." Then he looked at Deuce and continued, "I contacted Tankersley for the details, per your request, Deuce. He had his report already filled out and faxed it to me. I put together a DD form 293, filled in the required sections, and sent it to Tankersley, who completed his required sections and faxed it back. Then I called SecNav and explained yours and Tankersley's suspicions about Smith. He wasn't well liked by SecNav, I take it?"

"You could say that," Deuce said.

"He asked me to send him the forms and when he saw who was requesting the upgrade on Williams's behalf, he called me back. An active-duty recipient of the Medal of Honor can throw a lot of weight around Washington without any political baggage. The SecNav will consider it personally, under one condition. That Williams accepts the honorable discharge, without seeking back pay. Is that what he's after?"

"No sir," I said. "He's not even aware of this. His dad is my mechanic and wanted me to find out what could be done to help Williams out with some psychological problems he's having."

"How soon can he be in Washington?" Stockwell asked.

"I'll go see him Sunday after the fishing trip. He lives in Key West."

"If he agrees to not seek back pay, I see no reason why it won't be upgraded to honorable, with all the rights and privileges that go with it."

"Including the opportunity to reenlist?" I asked.

Stockwell looked at me and grinned. "Is that what he's really after?"

"He'd planned on making the Corps his career and Tank thought him to be a very good leader."

"Yes," Stockwell said. "If he gets the upgrade, he'd be eligible to reenlist. Sounds like he'd not only be a credit to the Corps, but he'd be among his peers, which would be better for him than seeing some VA shrink."

"I'll talk to him Sunday," I said. "Thanks."

"Lastly, the details for tomorrow. I've already contacted the base Commanding Officer and he's arranged for the whole dock in front of the main building at the marina to be cleared. Dock your boats facing the sea, with the escort boat to the rear. The Dockmaster will have the names of both boats and if anyone asks anything, you don't know who the VIPs are. The President's motorcade will pull up next to the dock and they'll board within minutes, so have the engines running. You and your crew members should be standing at the docks to receive the President. He'll do a quick meet and greet there, like he always does, then board and cast off immediately. Any questions?"

"None that I can think of, Colonel."

"That's about all I had, then. Thanks again for letting me stop here, Jesse. Now is someone going to tell me what the hell that contraption is Carl's working on?"

"It's an aquaculture system," I said. "We're going to raise crawfish and vegetables right here on the island."

"Crawfish?" he said. "And vegetables? Why?"

"Jesse wants to be a hermit," Jackie said with a smile. "Completely off the grid."

"A hermit?" Stockwell asked.

"Just a crazy idea I had. We get most of our food from the sea. When I first cleared this area, I wanted to grow some vegetables, but the soil's all wrong. Trent suggested aquaculture and I was curious. Besides, I love Cajun crawfish."

Deuce and I showed Stockwell around the island. He was impressed with the bunkhouses, the new electrical station, the water maker, and especially the remote location. "How long do you think you could support an eight-person team out here?"

"Eight?" I asked. "As long as they like seafood, pretty much indefinitely. Why?"

"I like the location for intense training. This will be perfect for Julie's small-craft boarding training. No distractions and no outside interference or monitoring. And I like your idea of using it as a base of operations for missions. Can I see your boats?"

We walked over to the house and up to the deck. The sixteen-foot-wide deck surrounds my house on three sides, all but the east side, and is completely enclosed below, where the docks are located. Originally, I'd only planned on docking the *Revenge* and my eighteen-foot Maverick Mirage skiff under the house, but with a little extra work and planning, we were able to get all six boats docked below.

Stockwell turned to us at the steps down to the docks and said, "Can Jesse and I have a moment alone?"

"Yes sir," Deuce said and turned to Jackie. "Come on inside, Doc, we'll show you the house."

Stockwell and I walked down the steps toward the front of the house and I opened the door to the dock area.

Charlie was just coming out, carrying a cooler with what I guessed was tonight's supper.

"Have any luck?" I asked.

"Got a few grouper and snapper," she said as the kids ran up the steps.

"This is Travis Stockwell," I said. "Travis, meet Charlie Trent."

"Pleased to meet you, ma'am. Can I help you with that cooler?"

"Thanks, but it wasn't a big catch. I can handle it," she replied. "Nice to meet you."

Stockwell stepped through and let out a low whistle. The *Revenge* was docked in the first slip and a three-foot-wide dock went from the door to the rear of the house. The dock continued along the rear wall and back to the front along the east wall, with another dock extending down the middle. There are small storage closets at the end of each dock, at the front of the house.

He walked down the dock and around the stern of the *Revenge*. The Cigarette was docked in the next slip, with barely a foot between them. Beyond it, the Grady was docked in front of Alex's skiff against the center dock, with my skiff tied off to hers. Against the far dock lay the Winter center console, *El Cazador*.

"Not a lot of room left down here," Stockwell said.

Joining him at the stern of the *Cazador*, I said, "This is the boat Julie will pilot with the Secret Service detachment aboard."

"*Cazador*? That's Spanish for hunter, isn't it?"

"Yeah, we sort of adopted her when drug smugglers didn't want her anymore."

"How fast are these two?" he asked.

"The *Revenge* has a top speed of forty-six knots and *Cazador,* about forty knots."

He glanced at me, surprised. "Not your average fishing boats, huh?"

I laughed and said, "No, they were both built specifically for the drug trade."

He nodded toward the Cigarette, "What about the go-fast boat?"

"Not much for fishing," I replied. "But she'll get you there really quick, over a hundred knots. She came with the *Cazador.*"

"Very impressive," he said. "Everything."

"Was there something you wanted to talk to me about?"

"Yes," he said. "I wanted to talk to you about the woman killed in the boat accident last winter, Isabella Espinosa."

"With all due respect, I think we both know that wasn't her real name."

He eyed me sharply. "Afia Qazi, daughter of Syed Qazi Al Fayyad and a known terrorist. Deuce gave me his report, including the single shot fired that ignited the fuel tank. I then shredded his report. The investigation has been closed, and the Monroe Sherriff's Office and the Florida Marine Patrol have officially called it a boating accident involving an illegal Cuban national."

I gave that some thought. "So, you're telling me I'm not a suspect in the killing of a known terrorist?"

"What terrorist?" he said with a sly grin. "A Cuban national, in the country illegally, with ties to a drug smuggler. I also did some more in-depth reading in your service record book. I was particularly impressed with a single day in Mogadishu."

“Ancient history, Colonel,” I said.

“Are you saying you’re no longer able to make a shot like that? Not many people can make a twelve-hundred-meter kill shot.”

“If need be, I probably could.”

“Deuce also told me how you handled a situation with his two long gun shooters. Think you could work with them some? Maybe make them a little less spooky?”

He was talking about the Australian, Donnie Hinkle, and his spotter, Glenn Mitchel. They had been a SEAL sniper team before coming to DHS to join Deuce’s team. Before the Cuba operation, the rest of the team sort of steered clear of them. I had a few words with the two men and made them see the error of their ways.

“Sure,” I said. “Hinkle and Mitchel are good men, just a little aloof.”

Back in the clearing, we joined the others. “One last thing,” Stockwell said. “If we’re going to use this place for training and staging, we need to know the name of the island.”

“It doesn’t have a name,” Jackie said. “Just one of many little islands in the Content Keys.”

“So what do you call it, Jesse?” he asked.

“Never called it anything. Just ‘the island’.”

“Guess that’s good enough, then,” he said. “We’ll just call it The Island.”

He and the pilot climbed back in the Huey, Stockwell in the copilot’s seat. Minutes later, they lifted off and headed southwest. The sun was heading toward the horizon and I wanted to get to Boca Chica well before sunset. “We have about fifty miles to go to get to the marina,” I told

the others. "If we're going to make it and still have time to eat, we better get going."

We said goodbye to Trents and I once again had to tell Pescador to stay here. He didn't look very happy about it. We untied the two boats, boarded and started the engines. I yelled across the Cigarette to Julie, "On the key fob, push the unlock button to open your door." She nodded and pushed the button, as I pushed the same button on mine, and the two doors slowly began to swing outward.

When the door was fully open, I put the engines in forward and idled out from under the house. Once clear, Julie slowly pulled out behind me and I pointed the key fob aft and pushed the lock button. The electric motor started pulling the door closed and I saw that Julie had done the same thing, closing the east door.

At the end of my channel, I turned northeast into Harbor Channel and brought the big boat up on plane. Looking back, I saw that Julie was up on plane as well, maintaining a safe distance.

"Isn't Boca Chica the other way?" Jackie asked from the second seat.

"Water's too shallow for a straight shot. We have to get out in the Gulf, turn west and circle around the end of Key West." I switched on the radar, sonar and VHF radio.

The sky was a deep cobalt blue after the morning's rain. I turned north following the channel into the deep blue water of the Gulf of Mexico. The seas had flattened out and I pushed the throttles up until the knot meter showed our speed to be twenty-five knots. Glancing back, I saw that Julie was moving out of my wake and coming

alongside, about thirty yards off the port side. She throttled back, matching my speed.

"Want to take her for a while?" I asked.

"Jesse, I've never driven a powerboat."

"You're in the Navy and you're never piloted a boat?"

"Sailboat, yeah. I wouldn't have the first idea what to do, going this fast."

I stood up and moved to the port-side bench. "Just like driving a car, except there's no brakes."

She grabbed the wheel from the second seat and said, "Are you crazy? What if I hit someone? And what do you mean no brakes? How do you stop?"

"Just slide over and take the helm. There's nobody out here to hit."

She slid over and looked at me. "Hey, I'm driving! But how do I stop? You never told me that."

"If we need to stop, you just pull back on the throttles."

"How do I know which way to go?"

"Just follow the sun."

"Seriously? That's it?"

I laughed and said, "For now, yeah. If you're gonna earn your keep tomorrow, you gotta get your feet wet. It's a big ocean. If you take us a mile or two further out into the Gulf it won't make any difference. The sonar is set to alert us if we have water ahead that's shallower than ten feet. If you hear it beeping, just turn right a little. I'll be back in a minute, need to find my cell phone."

I went down to my stateroom and found it in a drawer, but the battery was dead. I took it and the charger back up to the bridge and plugged it in. I turned it on and pulled up the number for Lawrence Lovett, an Andro-

sian friend and taxi driver in Key West. He answered on the first ring.

"Hi, Lawrence, this is Jesse," I said. We talked for a minute and I asked him if he could meet us at the Boca Chica Field Marina in an hour. He promised he'd be there and I ended the call.

"I'm sure you'll want to go home and change before dinner," I said to Jackie.

"Oh? Are you asking me out on a second date?"

"Actually, if you count today's boat ride, it'll be the third date," I said with a grin.

"Where are you taking me?"

"Well, since your car's still in Marathon, I thought we could walk over to the Runway. When Lawrence drops you at your house, just tell him what time you'll be ready and he'll be there at exactly that time to bring you back to the marina. Where do you live, anyway?"

"I share a house in Old Town with one of the nurses. She works nights and I work days, so we rarely see one another."

Jackie piloted all the way to Northwest Channel, where I took over. Julie fell back and got in line behind us as I turned south into the channel and dropped the speed to twenty knots. Fifteen minutes later, we crossed the main ship channel and turned east at Whitehead Spit, and I bumped the throttles back up to twenty-five knots. There were a few other boats on the water, but all the cruise ships were either docked or still far out to sea. Fifteen minutes later, we picked up the lights for Boca Chica Channel and turned northeast.

I picked up the mic and said, "Coming down off of plane, Jules."

I waited until I heard her respond, "Roger, Jesse," and then slowly pulled back on the throttles. The big boat settled into the water and we idled into the marina. There was no fuel dock at the marina, but the *Cazador* had already been topped off and the tanks on the *Revenge* held more than enough for tomorrow's trip. We idled into the turning basin and I maneuvered the *Revenge* to the center of the long dock, in clear view of the main building. The *Cazador* having only a single engine, Julie swung it in a sweeping turn and lightly kissed the dock fifteen feet astern of the *Revenge.* The Dockmaster and another man came out of the building and helped make both boats fast.

"You must be Captain McDermitt," the Dockmaster said.

"Yes, I am," I said. "The other boat is skippered by Captain Thurman. You were expecting us?"

"Yes sir. The CO said you were picking up some VIP clients here in the morning for a day of fishing. He also said not to ask who, so I won't."

"Wouldn't matter," I lied. "You probably know better than I do who they might be. All we've been told was to pick them up here."

The man shrugged and left. I added two more lines to secure the boat to the dock and watched as Julie did the same. Jackie had disappeared into the salon to gather her things and stepped down to the dock just as Deuce and Julie walked up.

"I need to call a cab," Deuce said. "We're going to stay at the Double Tree."

I glanced up the road from the dock and could see Lawrence's black Crown Vic heading our way. "I already

called one, Deuce. He can drop y'all on the way to take Jackie home." Turning to Jackie, I added, "Call me when you're on the way back."

I walked them out to where Lawrence was standing by the front of his cab. He hurried around the car before we got there and opened all the doors.

"Be gud ta see yuh gin, Cap'n," he said with a big grin.

I took his extended hand. "Good to see you again, Lawrence. These are my friends Jackie, Julie and Deuce. They're going over to Key West and Jackie will need a ride back later."

"Be muh pleasuh, sar," he said. He reached out and took Julie's small bag and uniform bag before she even realized it, and carried them to the trunk. "Mistuh Deuce, yuh can ride up in di front, if ya want."

Before Lawrence got back behind the wheel, I slipped thirty dollars in his hand. He got in the cab and they drove off, so I went back aboard the *Revenge*, opened the hanging locker by the salon hatch and took the uniform out that Julie had brought. I carried it into the stateroom and tore the plastic off so I could inspect it myself.

My weight hadn't changed since I left the Corps, so I knew the fit wouldn't be a problem. I checked my shoes first. They looked like they could use a shine, but a quick buffing would do alright. I took the trousers off the clips holding them in place and checked all the seams for loose threads and found none. I took the hanger with the blouse and hung it on the drape rod over the hatch. I only found one loose thread on the left sleeve and snipped it off with a fingernail clipper.

The six rows of ribbons were in the right order with the stars and oak leaf clusters for multiple awards in the

right places, and everything was correctly aligned. Shooting badges were also properly aligned, as were the scuba badge and jump wings. The brass on the belt just needed a little buffing with a towel, as well as the eagle, globe and anchor on the cover. Overall, everything looked just like I'd left it nearly seven years ago.

I carried the blouse and trousers into the stateroom and put them in the hanging closet, leaving the shoes, cover, and belt in the salon to touch up later. I grabbed a decent pair of jeans and a pale blue guayabera shirt and went into the head. Looking in the mirror, I suddenly realized I needed a haircut if I was going to wear the uniform.

For five years after I left the Corps, I'd maintained a regulation haircut, but in the last two years, I'd let it go. I hadn't had a haircut in several months and it was well past my ears.

I pulled my phone out and called Jackie. "Do you know if the base barber shop is open on Saturday?"

She started laughing. "I was beginning to wonder if you'd even notice. Don't worry, I planned to bring my scissors and clippers on our date."

"You can cut hair? To Marine regulations?"

"I cut my ex's hair. Of course, doing a crew cut might be a little more difficult than a Navy hairstyle."

"Thanks, Jackie," I said. "See you soon."

After I disconnected, I stripped down and had a long, hot shower and shave. Lately, I only shaved once every few days, sometimes as long as a week. I'd have to do it again in the morning, too.

Once I was dressed, I grabbed a beer from the galley, set the alarm, locked the salon hatch and went up to the

bridge, making sure to bring my phone. The sun was almost to the horizon and starting to turn the water in the marina a soft golden color. There wasn't a cloud in the sky.

After I finished my beer, my phone chirped. Jackie said she was on her way back, but wanted to go somewhere off base. She said that Lawrence was happy to take us anywhere.

Five minutes later, Lawrence pulled up, got out and opened the back door. When Jackie stepped out, as I was climbing up to the dock, the sight of her almost caused me to fall in the water. She was wearing a short black dress with thin straps and black high-heel shoes. Her hair spilled over her shoulders and seemed to snatch the light right away from the setting sun.

"Wow," I said. "You look beautiful."

"This old thing," she said. "Just a rag I pulled out of the closet. Do you like jazz?"

I stopped dead in my tracks and grinned. "Yeah, as a matter of fact."

"Great. There's a place called Virgilio's. You know it?"

"I've heard of it before. Didn't know they had music."

"Just recently the owner added a small stage and there's a great little soft jazz band that's been playing there for the last few weeks."

I held the door for her as she got in the car and said, "Sounds like a plan to me. Virgilio's, Lawrence. With a stop at White Street Pier."

"White Street Pier?" Jackie asked as Lawrence pulled out of the parking lot.

"So we can say good night to El Sol."

We crossed the bridge onto Stock Island then drove on across to Key West and turned south on Roosevelt. When we got to the pier, Lawrence pulled into the parking lot, got out and opened the door for us.

I slipped him a twenty and asked him to wait, and we walked out onto the pier. Most of the action at sunset was down at Mallory Docks, but there were a few people on the pier, several fishermen and three couples, dressed for the evening. Jackie took my arm as we walked out to the middle of the pier. The sun was just beginning to touch the far horizon and we leaned on the railing to watch.

Slowly, the giant red orb slipped further and further into the water, flattening out as it did so. Jackie was standing upwind and I could smell the shampoo she used. It reminded me of night blooming jasmine, with just a hint of orange blossom. As the sun disappeared below the horizon, I was watching her reaction. As the last of it disappeared, her breath seemed to catch in her throat.

"Beautiful," she said.

Looking at her profile, I said, "Absolutely."

She turned to me and said, "Flattery will get you anything, mister. But not until you feed me. I'm starved."

We walked back to the cab, got in and Lawrence pulled out of the lot, heading north on White Street. "How's things been in town since I last saw you, Lawrence?"

"Much bettah sar, now dat Santiago be gone. Whole heap a people heah owe you fer dat."

Jackie looked at me questioningly and I just shrugged. "You wouldn't happen to know Jared Williams? He works at Blue Heaven."

"Ya sar, met him a time or two. Nice young mon, most di time. Got in a bit a trouble last week wit di police."

"Does he work Sunday night?"

"Ya sar," he said as he turned left onto Southard Street. "Works der ever night, cept Monday."

"What'd he get in trouble with the police about?"

"Was lass Monday, his night off. Whut I heah, he bout tore up Hog's Breath. Police let him go ness day. He jist been drinkin' too much."

Lawrence crossed Duval Street and pulled over to the curb at the corner. He got out, moved quickly around to the passenger side and opened the door for Jackie. He even held her hand as she stepped out of the car. "Have a good evenin', Mizz Jackie." He nodded to me and said, "Have di manager call me when you ready to head back to di boat, Cap'n. He have my number."

"Thanks, Lawrence," Jackie said.

We walked around the corner and into the small restaurant. The hostess took us to a table in the back that had a good view of the small stage. The band really was very good and the food was excellent. After dinner we listened to the band for a while and had a couple of glasses of wine. At twenty-two hundred I suggested we'd better call it a night since we were going to have to get up well before sunrise. I asked the waitress if she could call Lawrence for me and she hurried off to do so.

We finished our wine then walked outside to wait. Lawrence was just pulling up to the curb. I opened the door for Jackie and we got in the backseat of the big sedan.

"We'll drop you off at home, then Lawrence can take me back to the boat."

Jackie laughed and said, “Take us to di boat, mon!”

As Lawrence pulled away from the curb, I said, “Are you forgetting something? You have to be in uniform at zero five thirty.”

“Her bags be in di trunk, Cap’n,” Lawrence said with a conspiratorial laugh.

Jackie turned to me and smiled seductively. “Friends. With benefits.”

Fifteen minutes later, Lawrence pulled into the marina. He opened the trunk and took out Jackie’s bags. Three of them. “Are you planning on a cruise?” I asked.

“Never know,” was all she said.

Before boarding, she was nice enough to take her heels off. I unlocked the hatch and disabled the alarm.

“Where do you want to do it?” Jackie asked as she stepped up into the salon.

My face must have registered my surprise. “The haircut, mister. I know where we’re going to make love.”

CHAPTER EIGHT:

Gone Fishin'

I woke to the smell of coffee coming from the galley, reached over and turned off the alarm I'd dug out of a drawer last night, before it started squawking. My watch showed zero three fifty-seven. I always set the coffee maker to brew ten minutes before the time I wanted to wake up and the smell was usually all it took. But, we were up pretty late, so I'd set the alarm. Jackie was curled up next to me in the big bunk, snoring.

I quietly got out of bed, put on a pair of shorts and went into the galley. I poured a cup of coffee and a moment later I heard the shower come on in the guest head so I held off pouring Jackie a cup. Since we only had an hour to get ready, I finished my coffee and went into the forward head and had a quick shave and shower myself.

When I stepped out I noticed the door to the guest cabin was closed and light was coming from under the door. I could hear a blow dryer going so I went into the forward stateroom and got dressed. It'd been almost seven years

since I'd worn the uniform, but it still felt like a second skin, completely comfortable. I went back into the head and checked everything once more in the full-length mirror. Jackie had done a great job on the haircut. I had a few gray hairs around the temple, but cut in a high and tight, they were gone. *I could easily pass for an active-duty Marine*, I thought.

I walked in socked feet into the salon with a chrome-polishing chamois and heard the blow dryer switch off as I walked past the guest cabin. It only took a couple of minutes to bring the brass on my belt back to a bright gleam. I wet a clean dish towel and worked on my shoes for another couple of minutes, until the shine came back.

Now fully dressed, I poured another cup for me and one for Jackie. A moment later I heard the door to the guest cabin open and close, then Jackie stepped up into the galley, in uniform also. Unfortunately, her wild mane of hair was pulled back and wrapped into a tight, though sizable bun. I snapped to attention and said, "Good morning, ma'am. Care for a cup of coffee?" She smiled and looked me over from head to toe, pausing for a moment at my ribbon rack and badges.

"At ease, Marine," she said. Then she took two quick steps into my arms and stretched up on her toes to lightly kiss me on the lips. "You look good enough to eat."

I heard two car doors close outside and the car drive off, then a tap on the side of the bulkhead, and a voice said, "Ahoy, the boat."

"That'll be Deuce and Julie," I said. "We have about thirty minutes before Stockwell arrives. Omelet okay?"

"Get the door, I'll cook this time."

"Aye aye, ma'am." I was probably enjoying this too much.

I disabled the alarm and opened the hatch. Deuce and Julie were standing in the cockpit. Deuce was wearing his Navy service khakis and Julie was wearing the tropical blue service uniform of the Coast Guard. He said, "Damn, he's uncovered."

Julie laughed as she came in and said, "He's been looking forward to you saluting him, Jesse. I told him Marines don't salute indoors, or uncovered. Good morning, Commander, you look nice."

"Thank you, Julie," Jackie said.

"I see you have your new stripes sewn on," I said.

"Yeah, I was up pretty late doing it."

"Have you guys eaten yet?" I asked.

"We stopped at the Huddle House on the way," Deuce said. "But thanks."

Jackie whipped up two omelets and we ate quickly. At zero four fifty-five, I heard a car pull up outside and a door close. "We better get outside," Deuce said.

I grabbed my cover and held the hatch open for the three of them. "Let's get this over with," I said, then followed them through the hatch. I covered my head, closed the door and turned around. "Your dad would roll over in his grave if he saw me do this." I came to attention and gave both Deuce and Jackie my best salute, which they returned quickly.

"Yeah, he would," Deuce said with a crooked grin.

The four of us stepped up to the dock and fell in according to rank by the cockpit, Deuce, Jackie, me, and Julie.

"Attention on deck!" Deuce commanded.

Stockwell stepped off the curb to the dock and stopped in front of the four of us. He was dressed in the Army service uniform, with a tan Ranger beret on his head. The four of us saluted him as one and he returned it. "At ease. Fall out," he said. "And except when the President arrives, that's the end of military formality. Thanks for putting that on, Jesse."

We relaxed and I said, "There's coffee in the galley, care for a cup?"

"Absolutely. I know you Jarheads like it strong enough to stand a horseshoe up in."

I turned at the rumbling sound of a motorcycle pulling into the parking lot. Doc parked the bike, got off and put on his piss cutter and strode toward us. He saluted the Colonel as he stepped onto the dock and said, "Good morning, sir."

Stockwell returned his salute. "You must be Doc Talbot."

"Yes sir, sorry I'm late."

"You're right on time, Doc. Like I just told the others, until the VIPs arrive, we'll dispense with military customs. You, Jesse, and I are civilians now. I'm Travis Stockwell. Please call me Travis." He extended his hand and Doc took it firmly.

"Pleased to meet you, Travis."

"Can't see much of it in the dark, but it sounds nice. Harley?" Stockwell asked.

"Indian Chief," Doc responded.

"Really? I have a Road King up in DC. Don't get much chance to ride it, though."

We went into the salon and Julie poured four cups for us and got a bottle of water for herself. Stockwell took

a seat on the aft section of the L-shaped sofa. "This is a beautiful boat. I didn't expect such luxury in a fishing boat."

"Thanks, Colonel," I said as I sat down next to Jackie at the settee. I noted the blue-and-tan UN Somalia service ribbon on his chest. "I see we chewed some of the same sand."

I saw him glance at my ribbons. "1/7 or 1/9?"

"1/7 then, but I spent some time with 1/9 as well. Third of the Seventy-fifth?"

He nodded and just like that we connected even more. Julie looked puzzled and said, "I'm sorry, sir, I'm new at this. What are y'all talking about?"

"Jesse and I served together in ninety-two," Stockwell said. "In Somalia. With time you'll get better at it. Ribbons and badges are more than just decoration. They tell the story of a military person's life. Some are awarded to all branches, while others are branch-specific. For instance, Jackie, Deuce and Jesse wear sea service ribbons. Nothing unusual for a Sailor, but it tells me that Jesse served aboard a naval vessel at some time. I can also tell that Doc here was wounded in action and Jesse was wounded in action twice. And since few naval vessels are co-ed, and with Jackie being a doctor, I would guess she served on either a hospital ship or an aircraft carrier."

Jackie nodded. "The Big E."

"You were wounded twice?" Julie asked. "You never told me that."

"I never told you a lot of things, Jules," I said with a laugh.

"I can also see that you're out of uniform, Julie," Stockwell said.

She looked down at her uniform, then looked back up, puzzled.

Stockwell stood up and walked over to where she stood by the counter. "You didn't read your transfer papers very carefully, did you?" he said with a crooked grin.

She looked at him, then at Deuce, who was also grinning. "No sir, Deuce took them from Captain Osgood when I graduated Maritime Enforcement."

Stockwell reached into his pocket and pulled out a small black case. Opening it, he showed her a medal with a matching ribbon. He removed the ribbon and handed it to Deuce. Then he handed the small case to Julie and said, "Put this in your pocket for now."

"I don't understand, Colonel," she said.

Deuce stepped over and removed the backing clutches on the ribbon. He pushed the pins through her shirt and reattached the backing locks.

"You're the first woman to wear that, you know," said Stockwell. "In fact, only twenty-seven men wear it. It's the Coast Guard Special Operations Service Medal. Your transfer orders say that you're authorized to wear it. Congratulations."

She looked over at me, then up at Deuce. "You two knew about this?"

I'd learned a long time ago not to hide anything from Julie. *And Deuce had better learn it quick*, I thought. She hates surprises. Raising my hands in defense, I said, "I didn't know anything about this."

A loud whine came from outside, the sound of a large jet flying low, approaching the marina from the west. "We'll talk about this later, Commander," Julie said.

The five of us went out onto the dock, just in time to see Air Force One fly over.

"Holy shit," Doc said. "The VIP is the President?"

Stockwell laughed heartily and looked at me. "You didn't tell him?"

"Never really got the chance."

"Okay, they'll be here in fifteen minutes," Stockwell said. "The advance team from the Secret Service will be here in ten. You've all been vetted, so there shouldn't be any problems. Get the engines started."

Julie ran to the *Cazador* and I boarded the *Revenge*. Within seconds the engines were quietly burbling and we joined the others on the dock.

The advance team arrived five minutes later and there was a problem. Two agents got out of a black sedan and the lead agent identified himself as Paul Bender. He spoke directly to Stockwell. "Colonel Stockwell, good to see you again, sir."

"Same here, Agent Bender. Allow me to introduce you to Commander Livingston, Lieutenant Commander Burdick, Gunnery Sergeant McDermitt, and Petty Officers Talbot and Thurman."

"Nice to meet you all," he said. "You've all been checked and cleared. The President is looking forward to meeting you and enjoying a day on the water. Are any of you armed?"

I looked at Deuce as Stockwell assured Bender that we weren't. Deuce nodded imperceptibly and I said, "That's not exactly true, Colonel." Agent Bender looked at me with raised eyebrows, so I continued. "I have a small assortment of weapons on board. Locked in a chest, which is locked securely under the forward bunk."

"That's a problem, Gunnery Sergeant," he said. "We'll need to remove them."

Stockwell stepped forward and looked Bender straight in the face. "Agent Bender, Gunny McDermitt is a highly decorated Marine, whom I personally vouched for. It's his boat and his charter."

"Doesn't matter, Colonel."

I stepped forward, towering over both Bender and Stockwell. Looking down on the Secret Service agent, I said, "Understand this, Bender, and understand it good. I don't go out on the water without protection and backup. Take it up with the Secretary and the President, or the charter is canceled."

"Colonel," Bender said, "you need to get your troops in line."

I took a half step closer and leaned forward so that my face was inches from Bender's. "I'm a civilian, Bender. Have been for almost seven years. Before that, I was chewing sand and taking out bad guys when you were popping zits and chasing little girls on the playground. On my boat, I make the rules. Neither the Colonel, you, nor even the President himself, is going to change that."

That's when the motorcade pulled up. Three more agents climbed out of the first car and a fourth from the passenger side of the second car. All four took up positions on the four corners of the second car, scanning the area intently. These guys were consummate professionals.

Bender turned and walked over to the passenger-side rear window and it came down a few inches. He spoke to someone inside for a moment and the window went back up. A few seconds later the door opened and Secre-

tary Chertoff himself got out and walked toward us. I expected him to be dressed in a suit, but he was in fishing shorts and a golf shirt. I'd only seen him in pictures, but he looked older somehow.

"May I speak to you privately, Mister McDermitt? In your cabin?"

I led him aboard the *Revenge*. "What's this about personal arms on this boat?"

"Mister Secretary, I work these waters every day. I never go out on the blue without being armed."

"Show me."

I took him forward, lifted the bedspread on the bunk and pointed out the digital lock. "Only Deuce and I know the combination." I punched in the code and pulled the release. The bunk lifted up on hydraulic pistons and I pointed out the large chest. "And we're the only ones who know the combination to that box."

"Open it."

"No sir," I said. "With all due respect sir, what's in that box is my business and nobody else's."

"What's in it?"

"Well, it ain't no BB gun. I've had need to arm several men in a hurry in the past year and if need be, I can arm every one of those agents outside, better than they're carrying now."

"I doubt that, McDermitt."

"All six of them are carrying Sig P229s chambered for three fifty-seven magnum cartridges. Three of them are carrying Belgian FN P90s under their suit coats." The P90 is an ugly-looking bullpup-type submachine gun. But with a fifty-round magazine and the ability to fire nine hundred rounds per minute, it's extremely effective and

can be carried on a shoulder sling under a coat, so it's hardly noticeable. He looked surprised, so I grinned and added, "If the President would like, I can up-arm all six of them."

"You brought an arsenal to take the President fishing?"

"No sir. Like I said, this chest is always on board. Everything in it is cleaned and ready for use. That's one of the reasons Deuce and I are still alive to take you guys fishing."

"So I've heard. That little trip into Cuba was armed by you?"

"Yes sir. We didn't have time to wait for armament."

He looked at me a moment and at the cluster of ribbons and badges on my chest. "Wait outside with the others. I'll talk to the President."

On the dock, he walked back to the car and got in. Stockwell looked at me and raised an eyebrow. "Just a few toys," Deuce said. "Nothing to get too excited over."

The five of us were standing in a loose line, with Stockwell standing at an angle next to Deuce at the end. Bender lifted his hand to his mouth and spoke into his sleeve, just like they do in the movies. I made a mental note to tell Chertoff that I could upgrade their communications, too. Bender said something to the four agents at the corners of the car and the rear passenger door opened again.

Chertoff and the President climbed out of the car and started walking toward us. The President was wearing jeans and a well-worn long-sleeved work shirt. On his head was a long-billed fisherman's hat that had the Texas Lone Star flag on it. I noticed the jeans and hat were well worn, also.

"Attention!" shouted Stockwell. The five of us immediately aligned ourselves and snapped to attention.

Instead of the usual hand salute command, Stockwell said, "Present Arms!" I couldn't help but grin just a little.

As the President walked toward us, he snapped a return salute and Stockwell said, "Two!"

The President stopped a few feet in front of Stockwell and with a slight Texas drawl said, "Good to see you again, Travis. Mike tells me y'all might be prepared to go to war?" Before he could answer the President looked right at me and said, "I suppose a Texican should be able to trust a Silver Star recipient. If a big ole shark comes at me, you be sure to shoot him for me, Gunny."

I grinned and said, "Aye aye, sir."

With the ice broken and apparent permission to keep the weapons on board given, he stepped forward and shook hands with Stockwell.

"Mister President, this is Commander Russell Thurman, my team leader. We call him Deuce."

"Nice to meet you, Deuce. How 'bout you introduce me to the rest of your crew here."

"My pleasure, Mister President," Deuce said. "This is Lieutenant Commander Jackie Burdick, MD. She's the second mate on the boat you'll be on, sir."

The President shook Jackie's hand and said, "A Navy Doctor as second mate?"

"It's an honor to meet you, sir. Actually, I think I was only invited so I could meet you. I'm a friend of Jesse's."

"You were the doctor that treated these two guys?"

"Yes sir, I was."

"I read the report from Admiral Arthur. He had nothing but high praise for your quick action and skill."

"Thank you, sir," Jackie said with a slight coloring of her cheeks.

Deuce said, "This is Gunnery Sergeant Jesse McDermitt, retired. He's the Captain of the boat you'll be on."

I took his offered hand and said, "Truly an honor to have you aboard, sir."

"The honor's mine, Jesse. Mike told me about what you did in Cuba a few months back. If you were active duty and the mission could be talked about, you'd be wearing a little bronze star on that top ribbon."

"Thank you, sir."

Going down the line, Deuce said, "This is Petty Officer Second Class, Robert Talbot. He's my team's Corpsman and will be first mate on your boat."

"Good to meet you, Doc. That is what those Jarheads call you guys, right?"

"Yes sir. Very honored to have you aboard, sir."

"I read the after-action on your part in the mission. Very good job, son. Ever think about reenlisting? The Navy needs men like you that can keep their head in battle."

"Thought about it many times, sir. Thank you."

"Lastly, Mister President, is Coast Guard Petty Officer Third Class Julie Thurman. She's the most recent person to join our team, just graduated from the Maritime Enforcement School. She'll be the Captain on the escort boat and I'll be her First Mate."

"It's an honor to meet you, sir," Julie said, taking his hand.

"First woman to graduate that school, right?"

"Yes sir, it was a tough school."

"What I heard, you could have been one of the Instructors. I understand you're getting married next week?"

Julie looked surprised and glanced at Deuce quickly.

"Yes sir," Deuce said. "She has agreed to allow me to be her first mate permanently."

"Congratulations to you both," the President said with a chuckle. "Now, I hope y'all aren't planning on staying in those uniforms the whole day, are you? I thought we were gonna slay some denizens from the deep."

"No sir," Stockwell said. "We can change while we're underway."

Before we split up to the two boats, the President surprised me. "Paul, make sure your men step lightly. Those hard-soled shoes play hell on fiberglass and teak." I glanced down and saw he was wearing topsiders. Also well worn.

"Of course, Mister President," he said and relayed the order to his men over his sleeve mic. Four of the Secret Service agents joined Deuce and Julie. Bender and the agent that drove his car, along with Stockwell, Chertoff and the President, joined us on the *Revenge*. Julie and Deuce had a change of clothes on the *Cazador* and could change in the small head in the engine room, under the console.

The agents went into the salon ahead of the President, Secretary, and Stockwell. A moment later, the two agents came out and took up positions on either side of the bridge, facing aft. Jackie and I climbed up to the helm and I shouted down to Doc and back to Julie, "Cast off!"

Doc had the lines loose in seconds and, looking back, I could see that Deuce had done likewise. Julie was using the bow thruster to swing the bow away from the dock.

The agents on her boat were standing fore and aft the console, much like they had around the President's car. Julie nudged the throttle and idled past me and into the channel. I followed about twenty yards behind. Once we cleared the outer markers, Julie's voice came over the radio. "Going up on plane, Jesse."

"Roger," I said and nudged both throttles up to thirteen hundred rpm, both boats lifting up on plane simultaneously. "Switching to alternate com, Jules." Deuce and I had already planned on using encrypted earwigs for communication once we were away from the dock. Both he and Julie had one and I had two, one for me and another for Doc.

Julie and I had already discussed many options on where to fish yesterday, but I suddenly realized I hadn't even asked what they wanted to fish for. I was well stocked on bait for anything they might want to catch, so I turned to Jackie and said, "Why don't you go down and ask our guests what they'd like to catch? Then you can let me know over the intercom in the forward stateroom while you get changed."

"Aye aye, Captain," she said and climbed down to the cockpit.

As she disappeared through the hatch, I called down to Doc, who was busy setting up fishing tackle. "Hey, Doc, go get changed. Then you can spell me up here, so I can get out of this monkey suit." I put the earwig in my right ear and turned it on. Speaking low, I said, "Com check."

"Loud and clear," came Deuce's voice in a slight whisper.

"Same here," Julie piped in.

"Roger on both of you. I'll give Doc his when he gets changed."

Jackie's voice came over the intercom, the light showing she was talking from the forward stateroom. "The President said that what the First Lady misses most living in DC is she can't get fresh dorado. What's that?"

I pressed the button on the intercom for the forward stateroom and said, "Thanks, Jackie. Dorado is Texican for dolphin. Everyone riding okay down there?"

"The Colonel and the Secretary look a little green, but the President is having a great time. Bender won't allow him out of the cabin until we're well offshore."

"Looks like we're hunting mahi, Jules. I owe you twenty dollars."

"She's below changing," Deuce replied. "I'll let her know."

"Let's open 'em up. Make your heading one hundred and thirty degrees. We're headed for the Stream."

I watched as the big center console surged forward to thirty knots. I pressed the button on the intercom to the whole boat and said, "Increasing speed, Mister President. We're taking y'all out to the Gulf Stream. We always catch mahi along the weed lines out there. We'll arrive in about an hour. If you need anything, just ask Commander Burdick. Agent Bender, we're two miles offshore now."

Doc climbed up to the bridge and took the helm so I could go down and change. He was wearing a long-sleeved denim shirt and jeans, with boat shoes. I gave him the earwig and he put it in his ear, without comment. Turning it on, he said, "Com check."

"Good here," I said. Julie and Deuce both responded that they could hear him too.

"I'll be back in a minute," I said. "We're going to the weed line for mahi."

"Ya know," Doc said. "It felt kinda good being in uniform again. Even if it was just a dog-and-pony show."

"Yeah, me too. Just a little."

I climbed down to the cockpit, where Bender and the other agent were still standing on either side, scanning the water behind us.

"I apologize about back there, McDermitt," Bender said. "Just doing my job."

"No worries, Paul. Just doing mine."

"Say, tell me something. In a pinch how fast can this boat go?"

"On flat seas, with a following wind, about forty-seven knots."

He thought for a minute and responded, "Fifty-five miles per hour? That's pretty damned fast. Hope we don't need it, but it's good to know."

I grinned and said, "The other boat can make forty knots. We wouldn't want to run off and leave your auto guns." Then I disappeared through the hatch, leaving him wondering. Jackie was right. Both Chertoff and Stockwell didn't look real well. The President, on the other hand, seemed to be enjoying the ride. I guess if you can do barrel rolls in a fighter jet, a little rocking on the water won't bother you. Jackie was still in the forward stateroom and I headed that way. As I passed Stockwell, leaning on the galley counter, I said, "Dramamine, top drawer right side."

"Thanks," he said and reached for the drawer as I started down the steps. "Commander Burdick is still down there changing, Jesse."

"I know," I said and saw him grin as he opened the top on the pill bottle, swallow one and pass it to Chertoff.

Jackie had on a pair of jeans and a long-sleeve red cotton shirt. She was tying her hair in a loose ponytail when I walked in.

"Why exactly am I here, Jesse?"

"I kinda like having you around," I said, slipping my arms around her from behind. "Plus the duties of second mate include being galley wench."

She spun around inside my arms and punched me hard in the shoulder. "Galley wench, huh?"

"Well, it's a step up from swab."

"Seriously," she said, "why did you ask me to come along?"

"You were the one that took the call from Chertoff, when I was still in the hospital, remember? I just thought you'd get a kick out of meeting him and the president."

"That's it, then?" she said as she withdrew from my embrace.

"And the galley wench part," I said with a grin. "Doc and I will be pretty busy. Maybe you could offer refreshments? Make sandwiches? Usually, I tell my clients they're on their own for drinks and food. Didn't think that would be appropriate for these clients."

She smiled and said, "Yeah, I can handle that. How do I look?"

"Good enough to eat," I said and started to take my uniform blouse off. "Chertoff and Stockwell just took some

Dramamine. They didn't look too well. President Bush seems to be right at home, though."

"I'll head on up and see if they need anything, then."

She left and I changed quickly. Taking off my trousers, I heard Julie in my earwig. "You do realize you forgot to turn your com off, right, Jesse?"

"Shit," I said. "Sorry."

"Had a hard time not laughing," Doc said. "Galley wench?"

"Hardy har, guys." I dressed quickly in fishing shorts, topsiders and a *Gaspar's Revenge Fishing Charters* tee shirt. Since I'd be on the bridge most of the time, leaving the cockpit to Doc, I wasn't concerned about getting too much sun.

When I stepped back up into the salon, the President was gone. Chertoff and Stockwell were sitting at the settee and Jackie was cutting up fruit and putting it into a bowl. Both men looked a little less green, but it would take at least a half hour for the medicine to have full effect.

"At some point during the day," Chertoff said, "the President would like to sit down with both you and Mister Talbot."

"On the way out would be fine. Jackie here can take the helm for a few minutes." She looked up at me, alarmed. I grinned at her and said, "The boat has autopilot, so you'd only have to keep an eye on things."

"Very good," Chertoff said. "About fifteen minutes before we get to where we're going would be fine."

I nodded and continued out to the cockpit, expecting to find the President in the fighting chair, but he was

up on the bridge with Doc. I climbed up and Doc shifted over to the second seat.

"I was just complimenting Doc here, on what a fine boat you have, Jesse."

"Thank you, sir."

"Did Mike talk to you about having a few minutes of your time?"

"Yes sir, he did."

"We really don't need him and the Colonel. We can have our little pow wow right here and now, if it's okay with you."

"Certainly, sir," I said as Doc started to get up.

"I wanted to talk to you, too, Doc." He sat back down, looking puzzled.

"There's a couple of things I wanted to get straight from you two and something I'd like to ask you."

"Yes sir?" Doc and I said together.

"I read Deuce's report on what happened down south of here a few months back. Me and Mike talked about it at length. Deuce is a special agent for DHS and the two of you are more or less civilian contractors? Is that about right?"

"Yes sir. That's the arrangement we had with Jason Smith, Colonel Stockwell's predecessor."

"He's one of the things I wanted to talk to you about, but we'll get to that later." He uncrossed his legs and leaned forward with his elbows on his knees. "One of Deuce's men, Anthony Jacobs, was captured while on a fact-finding mission, and Deuce decided, without Smith's approval, to go in and extract him. Is that about the way it happened?"

“Mister President, you’re a former military man and the current Commander in Chief. I’d be insulting you if I reminded you of the unwritten rule on leaving a man behind.”

He sat back and laughed. “I like you, Jesse. Not many men can be insulting, while saying they’re not. You’d have made a good Texican. You’re right. That’s not where I’m going, though. You obviously know Deuce very well?”

“Since he was about five years old. His dad was my platoon sergeant in Okinawa and a good friend.”

“How well do you know Smith?”

“I only met him a few times, sir. I wasn’t impressed. I thought him to be conniving and bent on furthering his career at any cost.”

“An opinion shared by others, Jesse. Had Deuce waited for him to decide what to do, what do you think the outcome would have been?”

I thought it over for a minute. “I’ve commanded men in combat, sir. I know the cut of a coward’s jib. If we hadn’t decided on going in, Tony would be dead and odds are, a lot of Cuban exiles in Miami would have died the following week.”

He considered this, looking out over the bow. “I’m inclined to agree, Jesse. I don’t usually get in the way of the people I put in charge of doing things for the security of our country. Had I been in Smith’s place, or Deuce’s for that matter, I’d like to think I’d have done exactly what you men did that night. But, since this involved the illegal entry into a sovereign nation, even though it was a Communist nation, I had to come down here and get the word straight from the horse’s mouth, so to speak.”

"Mister President," I said, "I've followed every military decision you've made since 9/11 and I can say without hesitation, you'd have made the same decision that night."

"Thanks, Jesse. Now to the meat of the matter. We're hearing more and more terrorist chatter throughout the Caribbean. Tell me something, how hard would it be to come into our country by boat down here?"

"How hard? Sir, you know yourself how porous the southern border is. Imagine if there were tens of thousands of people running all up and down the Texas border in dune buggies hunting quail every day. How hard would it be for bad guys to cross that border in a dune buggy?"

"I see your point. Just since leaving the marina, I've counted a dozen other fishing boats out here, both coming and going."

"Exactly, sir. On any given day there are tens of thousands of boats out here on the water. And that's just from Key West to Miami. Thousands more on the Gulf side."

"That brings me to my question. Secretary Chertoff wants to expand Deuce's team down here, bring in more men and equipment and enlarge the Coast Guard presence throughout south Florida and the Caribbean. The ability for terrorists to reach our shores here is a great threat to our national security. I agree with him. After reading the reports on your mission, my first recommendation to him was that you, and Doc here, both be attached permanently to DHS as special agents. What do you say?"

"I can't speak for Doc, sir," I said. "But I have no need of a badge and like things pretty much as they are." I looked over at Doc and nodded to him.

"Mister President," Doc began. "As I said earlier, I've given a lot of thought to reenlisting in the Navy. The only thing that's stopped me has been my new wife. We're planning a family, you see. A part of me says yeah, go for it. But, like Jesse says, I like it pretty much the way it is, where I can assess each mission and decide on whether I want to be part of it or not."

The President grinned and said, "That's pretty much what Deuce told Mike last week. I don't blame either of you. I'll tell Mike to continue to honor the deal you both made with Smith." Rubbing his hands together, he added, "Now, how about we get to fishing? Laura has been wantin' some fresh dorado for years. She doesn't even know I'm down here. Gonna surprise her."

With that, he stood up and climbed down to the cockpit, where Bender and the other agent were waiting. "Better get down there, Doc, and get the outriggers set up," I said. "We're only a few miles from the weed line."

Ten minutes later Doc was shouting, "Fish on!" The President was in the fighting chair and I pulled the throttles back to an idle. A good-sized bull dolphin hit the ballyhoo on the starboard outrigger. Doc pulled the rod from the holder and handed it to the President. It took him twenty minutes to get the big fish alongside, where Doc could gaff it and haul it aboard. The President didn't need any coaching from Doc at all. It was obvious he'd fought many game fish. After a couple of pictures, Doc scaled it and said, "Forty-nine pounds, Mister President. Great job!"

Over the next two hours, the President, Chertoff, Stockwell, and even Bender took turns fighting dolphin, wahoo, king mackerel and even a small yellowfin tuna. We released everything except the five biggest dolphin and a half dozen good-sized mackerel.

At noon, we stopped for lunch and just let the two boats drift near each other. Deuce came aboard the *Revenge* and I let Jackie keep an eye on the helm. The President and Chertoff wanted to see us both in the salon. "What do I do?" she asked.

"Probably nothing," I said. "Julie will keep the *Cazador* off of us. The radar is set to alert if anything comes within five miles, so just enjoy the view." I climbed down and went into the salon.

"You sure kept your word, Jesse," the President said. "This has been a hell of a lot of fun."

The President and Chertoff were sitting on the settee and Stockwell was seated on the couch on the opposite side of the salon. Deuce and Doc were behind the counter in the galley.

"Thank you, sir," I said.

"Have a seat. Mike here has a proposition for you."

I glanced at Deuce, who nodded imperceptibly and sat down at the far end of the settee, facing aft.

"Like I told you, Jesse, Mike wants to expand operations down here. I told him you and Doc wanted to maintain the status quo and he's come up with an idea I think you'll like."

He nodded at Chertoff, who looked at me and said, "Colonel Stockwell told me about your little island and how you and he plan to use it for training and as a jump-off point for future missions. I want to duplicate this idea

a little further up the Keys, maybe on the northern tip of Key Largo. We'd like you and Commander Livingston to locate the right kind of place and maybe even find another charter Captain up that way, with a similar background to your own. The Colonel is already in the process of recruiting a second team, to complement Commander Livingston's. His team, along with you and Petty Officer Talbot, will continue to work and train just as you have been, no changes. But we'd really like your help in finding the right person and the right boat for transporting the new team. Think you could help us out with that?"

"I don't see why not," I said just as a loud beeping noise started. It was the radar alarm.

Julie's voice came over my earwig. "We have company. A small craft headed our way, about five miles northwest."

Deuce heard her also and was already heading to the hatch. "Get the engines started, Jesse."

Julie had already come alongside and Deuce stepped easily over. As I climbed to the bridge I said to Bender, "Probably nothing, but there's a small boat headed our way from the northwest."

Jackie slid over to the second seat and I sat down and started the engines. "What's going on?" she asked.

"Probably nothing," I said. I switched the radar to a five-mile radius and saw what appeared to be a small fishing boat on the outer edge. I took the binoculars from the cabinet on the left side of the console and scanned the water to the northwest even though I knew the boat was small and too far away to see. "The radar's alarm is set to five miles and a small boat is heading our way."

Stockwell figured out the intercom and I heard his voice over the speaker. "Give me a sitrep, Jesse."

"Nothing yet, Colonel. A small boat is heading towards us, about four miles out to the northwest right now. Probably just a sports fisherman."

I reached up and turned off the alarm, then checked the radar again. The boat was still coming straight towards us at about twenty knots. Over my earwig, I heard Deuce say, "Let me know when you can see him, Jesse."

I scanned the horizon in the direction I knew the boat to be approaching from and finally spotted it. "Got him, Deuce. It's a small cuddy cabin, maybe twenty-three feet." I switched the intercom to the whole boat and repeated the information.

Bender climbed up to the bridge with his own binoculars. "Where is it?" he asked.

I pointed in the general direction. "Still too far away to make out any detail."

We were broadside to the approaching boat and Julie was hanging off the stern, bow toward it. I checked the radar again and it was now within two miles and still coming straight at us. I turned on the VHF radio and checked that it was on channel sixteen. "This is *M/V Gaspar's Revenge* calling the twenty-three-foot cuddy cabin approaching our port side. Do you copy?"

There was no response, so I repeated the call. Still nothing. "I have him now, Jesse," Julie said over the earwig. I looked back and saw she had drifted a little and was about thirty yards astern. She was standing to the port side of the center console, training her own binoculars on the approaching boat. The four agents with her

were all up in the bow now and Deuce was standing on the starboard side.

Glancing at the radar, I could see that the boat was slowing and turning slightly east, now only a mile away. I was busy watching the radar screen when I heard Julie say, "It looks like the guy from the bar, Jesse. He's stopping."

Beside me, Bender was looking through the binoculars and suddenly yelled, "RPG!"

A sudden roar from behind us sounded as Julie nailed the throttle and turned the *Cazador* hard over on its chines, bringing it alongside, then shifting to reverse, bringing the big open fisherman to a sudden stop.

Everything seemed to happen in slow motion. I looked across the *Cazador* toward the boat, which was broadside to us, just as a flash of white smoke came from it. In that same instant, the three men in the bow who were carrying the FN P90 machine guns opened up, firing toward the boat. He was way beyond their range. I heard a popping sound as Julie fired a flare gun into the air. The incoming rocket-propelled grenade suddenly turned skyward and exploded directly over the *Cazador*.

I slammed both throttles to the stops, turned the wheel to starboard and yelled, "Doc, get the President to the engine room!"

As we launched forward onto plane, headed away from the attacking boat, I looked back and saw Julie turning and accelerating toward it. Deuce had joined the four agents in the bow. He must have borrowed a Sig from one of the agents with the FNs and all five of them were firing at the boat.

Bender was now standing by the ladder, yelling at the other agent in the cockpit, as Doc was hurrying the President and Chertoff into the engine room. "He's reloading!" Bender yelled while looking aft through his binoculars.

The agents on the *Cazador* must have found the range, because there was a thunderous explosion as the attacking boat's gas tank exploded. I looked back and saw a giant mushroom of orange fire and black smoke rolling up into the clear blue sky. In seconds it was all over and I pulled back on the throttles to an idle.

Bender was speaking into his sleeve, "Trailblazer is safe. Head immediately for Angel." Then he turned to me and said, "Turn around, and head back to the marina as fast as possible."

I pushed the throttles forward again and turned to port. In the distance, I could see that Julie was well past the smoldering remains of the boat and headed northwest as fast as the *Cazador* could go. "Julie, Deuce, keep the throttle wide open. We'll catch up."

"How are you communicating?" Bender asked.

"Earwigs," I said.

"What other communications do you have aboard?"

"VHF."

"Where?"

I switched it on and he changed the frequency, then spoke into the mic. "VFA-106, Trailblazer is under attack. Launch countermeasures immediately." Then he looked at me and asked, "What's our exact position?"

I pointed at the GPS's latitude and longitude display. "Give them these numbers. Our heading is two hundred and ninety degrees."

He relayed the information, then added, "Scramble Coast Guard recovery helo. We splashed one tango at our current position. A small fishing boat."

Five minutes later, I'd caught up to the *Cazador* and slowed down to match their speed. Suddenly, two FA-18 Super Hornets roared overhead only fifty feet off the water. The two attack aircraft climbed vertically and turned, then leveled off at about two thousand feet, slowed and began to circle us.

Even at full throttle, it was going to take at least a half hour to get back to the marina. I called down to the cockpit, "Doc, think you can get those fish cleaned before we make the dock?" He gave me a thumbs up and opened the fish cooler.

Bender turned to me and said. "You know, if it hadn't been for the other Captain's quick thinking, we might all be dead. All of you performed perfectly."

"Think it's safe for the President to come out of the engine room? It gets pretty hot down there."

Speaking into his sleeve he said, "All clear up here. Take Trailblazer inside the cabin."

A moment later, Stockwell joined us on the bridge. Jackie was still in the second seat. "Commander Burdick, would you see if our guests need anything?"

She'd been completely quiet throughout the ordeal, maybe in shock. She shook it off and said, "Right away, Colonel. Was anyone hurt?"

"Minor injuries on the other boat, but Commander Livingston has taken care of them. The Secretary has a slight burn on his hand."

"I'll take care of it," she said as she left the bridge.

Stockwell sat down in the second seat. "How could anyone know the President was aboard?" he asked, looking right at me. I thought about it for a minute and said, "Just before he fired, Julie said it looked like that guy from the bar that Deuce told you about."

"What guy? What bar?" Bender asked.

So I told him all about the wetdown party and the guy that had seemed too interested in what we were talking about.

"Weren't you told how sensitive this visit was?" Bender demanded.

"Look Bender," I said with equal force. "There was no mention of the President at any time. If it was the guy from the *Anchor*, he didn't learn about the President being here from any of us."

"There will be an investigation," Bender said with a scowl. "By the FBI."

"We'll be investigating also," Stockwell said. "But I can assure you there was no leak on our end."

CHAPTER NINE:

Key West Connection

Thirty minutes later, we came roaring into the channel to the Boca Chica Marina. Navy Shore Patrol had secured the docks and forced everyone in the marina away from the area. Air Force One was at the west end of the runway, with the engines running. We circled the turning basin and came up to the docks as Bender and the second agent came out of the salon with the President and Chertoff. Doc barely had time to tie a line to one of the dock cleats and set the cooler on the dock before the four agents from the *Cazador* swarmed the dock and more agents came out of the two waiting cars. They were no longer hiding their weapons, but displayed them openly.

In seconds, the President and Chertoff were whisked away in the two cars, Bender carrying the cooler. In another few minutes, we could hear the roar of Air Force One's engines as it took off down the runway.

Deuce and Julie joined us as we climbed up to the dock. Julie had a bandage on her left arm, just above the elbow, and there was blood on her shirtsleeve.

"Are you alright, Julie?" Stockwell asked.

"Yes sir. Just a scratch."

"How did you know it was a heat-seeking rocket?" he asked.

"I didn't really," she said. "I guess some part of my brain told me there wasn't any way a regular RPG rocket could be aimed from a pitching boat at another pitching boat. It was just instinct to fire the flare gun, I guess."

"Whatever it was," Stockwell said, "you reacted quick enough to save the President. There's going to be an investigation. All of you are to cooperate with the FBI on it. I think we should all sit down tomorrow and go over every aspect of what led up to this. At the island? About noon?"

"Yes sir," Deuce said. "Think we might be able to find out what the Coast Guard chopper finds out there?"

"We will," he replied. "It might take a day or two, though."

"Deuce," I said, "you and Julie take the *Cazador* to the island. You can stay in the house. I'll be up there in the morning. I still have to go into Key West and meet with Williams."

"I'd forgotten about that," Stockwell said. Then he turned to Jackie and said, "Can I drop you somewhere, Commander?"

"Thanks, Colonel," she said. "But I live in Key West, Jesse can drop me off."

"Very well," Stockwell said. "I'll see the five of you tomorrow." Then he turned and walked to his car at the end of the dock.

Jackie turned to me and said, "I still need to get to Marathon and get my car."

"I'll have Lawrence take you up there after you get off work tomorrow," I said. "I called him just before we came into the marina. He's going to meet me over on Stock Island."

"You staying at Oceanside?" Doc asked.

"Yeah, I want to leave there about zero eight hundred, if you want to ride along."

"I'll see ya then," he said as he started toward his motorcycle.

By now people were coming back into the marina and the Dockmaster walked toward us. Deuce said, "We're outta here. See you at noon, Jesse."

"Go ahead and get aboard, Jackie. Start up the engines and I'll cast off."

She was on the bridge and had the engines burbling as I tossed off the last line and the Dockmaster came up to me. "What the hell happened out there? That was the President's plane, wasn't it?"

"Just another VIP client," I said as I stepped across the gunwale and down into the cockpit. "Gotta run."

Minutes later, we idled out of the channel, turned west and made the short run to the channel into Stock Island and Oceanside Marina. Jackie was quiet all the way and I didn't bother her. She'd bring it up when she was ready.

"I never even got a picture," she finally said.

"Doc got one of you and the President, while he was holding up a mackerel. He's going to email it to me to send to you."

"Really?" she said with a smile. "That's good. I was afraid nobody would believe me when I told them what happened. Wow, what an exciting day."

"You can't tell anyone about the attempt on the President's life," I said. "The fishing, sure. Stockwell hitting on you, sure. But, not about the attack."

"Stockwell hitting on me? What are you talking about?"

"Oh, come on. Don't try to tell me you didn't notice. You probably have bruises."

"He wasn't hitting on me, Jesse. Do I detect a little jealousy?"

Now there was a loaded question, if ever there was one. No good way to answer that one. "Doc showed me the picture," I said, changing the subject. "Very flattering. It'll make a nice blowup you can frame and put on your wall."

We arrived at Oceanside and I went in to make arrangements for an overnight slip at the private dock. Once we were tied up and the engines shut down, we went down to the galley for a quick bite to eat. As I was washing the dishes Jackie said, "I'll be in the shower." Then she started down the steps to the forward stateroom. On the last step she turned her head, flipping her hair over her shoulder and said, "Don't be long."

An hour later, while we were sitting on the bridge, Lawrence pulled into the marina and over to the private dock area. I locked up the cabin and we went out to his

cab. "Did yuh see di President's plane dis mornin'?" he asked. "Flew right over di island."

"He was our charter," I said. "Nice guy."

"Yuh took di President out fishin'?"

"Along with a couple other VIPs," Jackie said.

"I'll be," he exclaimed. "Where to, Cap'n?"

"We're dropping Jackie at her house, then I'm going to Blue Heaven, to see Jared Williams."

"He won't be dere, Cap'n. I jus drop him off at di cemetery."

"The cemetery?" I asked.

"Ya mon, his friend Pop kill hisself yestuhday. Funeral's tuhday."

I thought that over and told Lawrence to drop me at the cemetery after we dropped Jackie off at her house. Ten minutes later, I walked Jackie to the door and then climbed into the front seat with Lawrence. "Who was Pop?" I asked.

"He a old timer on di island, name of Jackson Wainwright. Was in Vietnam a long time 'go. Not right in di head ever since. No kin, but young Jared was close to him and paid for his plot."

It was only a couple of minutes to the cemetery. I told Lawrence to wait and handed him a twenty. I walked through the gate toward the statue of the Lone Oarsman, a memorial to the men killed on the *USS Maine* in Havana Harbor in 1898. A woman I once dated said the Oarsman and I were kindred spirits. The cemetery is pretty large, but I figured it shouldn't be too hard to find an ongoing funeral. On the far side of the cemetery I spotted a canopy with a large group of people around it and started that way. As I got close I could see that most of the

mourners were young people, and a middle-aged couple in the next of kin seats was crying. There were a lot of teenage kids, but I didn't see Jared anywhere. I looked around and way in the corner of the cemetery, I spotted him. Hard not to see him, in fact. He was wearing Marine Corps dress blues.

I walked that way and as I got closer I could see the casket, draped with an American flag. Jared and one other man were standing there. The workmen who were waiting to cover the grave were at a respectable distance. The other man wore tattered clothes and had a scraggly beard and hair. A sharp contrast to Jared, who was in a heated discussion with the vagrant.

Jared turned toward me when I walked up and there was fire in his eyes. I was wearing a fisherman's cap, jeans and a denim shirt with the Marine Corps logo on the breast pocket, with the sleeves rolled up to the elbow. He saw the eagle, globe, and anchor before his eyes turned to my face. He recognized me and said, "You're a Marine, McDermitt?"

"Retired," I said. "Sorry for your loss, Jared. Lawrence just told me you were close."

His eyes moistened a little. "Yeah, we helped each other out. He was a good man. Would you give me a hand folding his flag?"

"Be honored to, Jared."

He turned to the vagrant and hissed, "Get lost."

The man muttered something unintelligible and stomped off toward the gate. I took the position at the head of the casket, to allow Jared to do the folding for his friend. He stood ramrod straight at the foot of the casket and slowly raised his right hand in final salute. To-

gether, we lifted the flag and sidestepped away from the casket. I'd performed this ritual too many times in the past and it was apparent that Jared had also. Our movements were sharp and crisp and his folding of the flag was done with reverence and precision. A moment later, he made the last fold, I folded the corner of the union as he opened the slot created, and I tucked it inside. He took the now folded flag and creased the edges, stuffing the corner of the union tighter and straightening it into a perfect triangle before he cradled it to his chest.

He turned smartly to the right and stepped away from the grave a few paces to where the next of kin would be seated, if there were any. There was no one else there and this really tugged at my heartstrings. He stood there motionless for a moment, his head bowed as though he were speaking to someone seated, his lips moving in silent recitation.

After a moment he turned toward me, eyes red and moist. "Why'd he have to do this?" he asked.

"I don't know, son. We all carry demons and for some, they just get too strong."

He looked at me and noticed the Recon tattoo on my forearm for the first time. "You're a Recon Marine? See any action?"

"Yeah," I said. "Second Force Recon. No action like you guys today. I served through twenty years of fairly peaceful times. Minor skirmishes in Lebanon, Somalia, and Grenada."

"When were you in Lebanon?" he asked. All Marines know about Beirut. His eyes seemed hollow and as I thought back, I was sure mine matched his.

"The day we lost two hundred and twenty Marines," I said solemnly and stared off toward the Lone Oarsman. I don't like to talk much about that day, but Jared also knew the horrors of war and he'd just lost the one person he could talk to about it. "I was with BLT, 1/8. My squad was on mounted patrol and we'd left the barracks at zero six hundred. We went up the coast road, then west on the loop around the city, heading to our assignment area. When we got to the west side of Beirut, we heard an explosion to the south. It wasn't unusual to hear explosions, but I felt something churn in my gut. A couple of minutes later, we heard the report over the radio that the barracks was under attack. Then all hell broke loose. We had to fight our way back to the barracks and set up a perimeter around the damaged gate when we got there. To this day, I can still remember the smell."

"I killed a little girl," he blurted out. "I didn't mean to. I didn't even know she was in the house. She stepped in front of the bullet, a second after I fired." His eyes started to brim with moisture. Eyeball sweat.

"I know. We have some friends in common." Then to change the subject, I asked, "Was Pop a Marine?"

"No, he was Army Special Forces. Did three tours in Nam, then got booted out."

"A piece of paper doesn't change a man's honor," I said. "Your being here proves that."

"What friends?" he asked.

"Owen Tankersley."

Jared nodded and said, "He believed me."

"I know that too. I just saw him a few days ago. That's why I'm here. Want to go get a drink and talk?"

We walked back to Lawrence's cab in silence. As we approached the car, Lawrence got out and opened both back doors for us, then stood by the passenger side with his head bowed, holding his hat in his hands in front of him.

We got in the back of the car and I told Lawrence to take us to Don's Place, on the other side of the cemetery on Truman Street. When we got there, I told Lawrence I'd call him later and slipped him another twenty. He handed it back and said, "Dis ride be on me, Cap'n." Then he turned to Jared and said, "Man nuh dead, nuh call him duppy." Then he turned, got in the car and drove away.

Jared looked at me, puzzled, and said, "Known that old guy for two years and some of the things he says just make me scratch my head."

"It's an old Jamaican saying. It means 'As long as someone's alive, don't dismiss their potential.' I've come to realize that Lawrence is a very wise man."

We walked into the bar and took a seat at a table in the corner. There were only a handful of people in the bar, but it was still early. A waitress came over and I asked her to bring us a couple of Red Stripes and two double shots of Pusser's Navy Rum. Jared laid the folded flag on the table between us and placed his cover on top of it. The waitress recognized we weren't there for fun and hurried to the bar to fill our order.

"You saw Tank the other day?" Jared asked.

"Yeah, I was at Lejeune with your dad. He flew me and some friends up there for the graduation of my buddy's daughter from Coast Guard Maritime Enforcement training."

"You know my dad?"

"He does some mechanical work for me from time to time. We had lunch with Tank and your brother."

"How's he doing?"

"David, Luke, or Tank?"

"All three, I guess. I haven't seen Tank in a couple years and Luke in almost a year."

"Your dad's worried about you. Luke just got promoted. And Tank? Well, he's still Tank."

"Probably still wearing his Alpha uniform to get officers to salute him, I bet."

"Yeah," I said with a laugh as the waitress set the cold beers and shots on the table. "Some things never change."

I lifted my glass and looked him in the eye. "To Jackson Wainwright, a hero."

Jared lifted his and said, "To Pop."

We tossed down the rum and followed it with a long pull on the cold beer bottles.

"I want to ask you a personal question, Jared."

He looked at me and said, "Fire away."

"If you could change anything, what is it you'd like to do more than anything else in this world?"

"To serve my country," he replied without thought. "But, since you seem to know the details of what happened, you probably know that ain't gonna happen."

"I wouldn't be too sure," I said with a grin.

"What do you mean?"

"I know a few people. A few people in places of power."

He leaned across the table and said, "Marine or no, you jerk my chain and I'll kick your ass."

I looked him straight in the eye and said, "I'm not jerking your chain. The paperwork has already been pro-

cessed. Tank initiated it. It's sitting on the SecNav's desk as we speak. Wanna go to DC?"

He sat back in his chair and I could see he was thinking about it. "There's just one catch," I said. "The SecNav will sign the paperwork changing your discharge to honorable, restoring your rank and removing all mention of the incident outside Ashraf, but only if you don't pursue back pay. Once it's changed, you have all the rights that go with it." Then I leaned forward and added, "Including reenlistment."

He looked up sharply at that. "And all I have to do is agree to that, come up with the money to go to DC and sit down with the freaking Secretary of the Navy? I just spent every nickel I had to bury Pop."

"All expenses are covered to get you up there and then on to Camp Lejeune. Do you know Colonel Tom Broderick?"

"I've heard of him. Never met him, though."

"He's an old friend of mine and Tank's. Currently the CO of Second Marines. His Regimental Sergeant Major, Mike Latimore, is another old friend of mine and Tank's. If you agree to the SecNav's conditions, you can reenlist right then and there. As a favor to me and Tank, Tom will request you be assigned to Wounded Warrior Barracks at Camp Lejeune to undergo a psych evaluation and maybe work with some of the other guys who've been injured. Tank works there and has made it his mission to create a Wounded Warrior Regiment, so injured guys that want to stay on active duty can. Within a month, he'll have you reassigned to Second Force Recon Company at your old rank if that's what you want."

"How's this possible?" Jared asked. "And why're you doing it?"

"It's a long story, Jared. But, the short of it is, the guy who railroaded you was a thorn in the side of his higher-ups and it's come to light that he used undue influence in having you discharged. As to why? That's easy, Marine." I lifted my beer bottle and said, "Semper Fi."

He raised his and clinked the bottles together. "Always faithful."

"To God, country, and Corps. But, mostly to each other."

We talked a while longer and had another shot. Then Jared asked, "What did you mean by all expenses are covered?"

"I created a trust fund several months ago, to help out injured vets. I think this qualifies. You can pay me back by picking up Sergeant in the next two years and being the leader that Tank seems to think you are."

He extended his hand across the table and said, "Deal."

We agreed that the sooner the better and planned to go to DC the following weekend, so he could give a week's notice at his work. Then we ordered another beer and I called Lawrence to pick us up. He was just pulling to the curb when we walked out. Once we got into the cab I told Jared, "Call your dad, okay? Let him know what's going on. I'll arrange the flight for next Saturday." I gave him my satphone number and told him to call me anytime.

After dropping Jared at his house, Lawrence took me back to the marina. When I unlocked the salon I saw a light on my phone flashing. It was where I'd left it on the settee. I checked it and saw that I had a text message from

Deuce, telling me to call him as soon as I could. I called him and he picked up on the first ring.

"The Coast Guard chopper recovered a body," he said.

"Did you get any details?"

"White male, about thirty, just under six feet tall and about a hundred and eighty pounds. Dark hair and eyes. Sounds like it fits the guy at the *Anchor*."

"And about ten million others. I'll trust what Julie said, though. She's always had an eye for faces."

"Jesse, they got fingerprints and IAFIS got a hit almost immediately."

"I thought those super computers took hours," I said. "Who was he?"

"Ex-CIA, left the Clandestine Service three years ago. Name's Richard Stolski."

"CIA? I don't get it. Why would a CIA spook, ex or not, want to kill the President?"

"Feebs are working on that," he said, meaning the FBI. "Apparently it was a rental boat. They found his car at Garrison Bight Marina, where he rented a twenty-three-foot Sea Fox. Paid cash for four days. That was on Friday."

"Damn," I said. "When we left the *Anchor* early Saturday morning, remember the boat that was docked close to the bow? I'm pretty sure it was a Sea Fox."

"What are you getting at?"

"Maybe the President wasn't the target," I said.

There was silence on the other end for a moment. Finally Deuce said, "Ex-CIA? Shadowing you, me, or both of us? I don't like where that takes us."

"What else did the Coastie investigators tell you?"

"Actually, they didn't tell me anything. Julie got all the information. The car was a rental, too. Rented in Miami

using a cloned credit card. They said it looked like more than one person had been in the car. Half-full drinks of different kinds in two cup holders."

I gave that a few seconds' thought and said, "He had a partner. And he's still out there. We need to find this guy, Deuce. Most riki tik."

"There's absolutely nothing to go on. Either the car and everything in it was wiped down, or they wore gloves the whole time they were in it."

"Anything else?" I asked.

"That's it for now. The Feebs are collecting background data on the guy. Colonel Stockwell says they agreed to share whatever they come up with, but with the guy being ex-CIA, that agreement has probably already sailed."

"Yeah," I said, "you're probably right. I'm guessing you already have Chyrel working on it?"

"Good guess. Actually, we're here at the *Anchor* waiting for her. When she gets here, we're taking her and all her equipment up to the island. She's going to set up shop in one of the bunkhouses. Hope you don't mind."

"No," I said. "Good idea, in fact. Is there anything she needs?"

"I doubt it. She's coming down in the van and bringing a ton of equipment."

I thought for a moment and came to a decision. "I was going to stay here tonight, but the *Revenge* is just too big a target. I'll be up there in a couple of hours."

I ended the call and headed up to the bridge. I started both engines and waited until they quieted to an even, low burble. Then I climbed down to the dock to cast off the lines. A few minutes later, I was idling out of the marina and into the channel. This whole thing had me kind

of rattled. Why would an ex-spook be after us? Or was he really after the President? How could he have known the President was going to be aboard? Right now, we had more questions than answers.

That's where Chyrel Koshinski would come in. As a former CIA computer analyst, she had no equal. As a hacker she didn't even have any close competition. She was able to not only hack into secure computer systems that had security protocols, she could do it without being detected. If anyone could dig up anything on Stolski, she could.

I turned on the radar, sonar and VHF radio. Then, being certain there were no other boats ahead, I pushed the throttles forward. The big boat responded as always, settling low in the stern and the bow lifting slightly. A few seconds later, she was up on plane and I turned west, toward the setting sun. There were storm clouds out there and the sun was just disappearing behind them. It looked like we would probably get a little rain tonight.

Before I made the turn at Whitehead Spit, at the western tip of Key West, I scanned the channel, checked behind me and double-checked the radar. There were no ships in the channel, but there was a boat heading west about two miles behind me. Not one to take chances, I pushed both throttles to the stops and increased speed to forty-five knots as I shot across the shipping channel and turned north toward Northwest Channel. I kept the throttles wide open all the way north to Middle Ground, then on northwest until I was off Calda Banks. I turned due north there, out of the channel, between the Banks and the Northwest Channel jetty, knowing that there

was at least seven to twelve feet of water all the way to the open Gulf.

Once past the five-fathom line, I turned northeast toward home, but kept the engines at full throttle. Half an hour later, the Harbor Key Bank light was in view and I made straight for it. There were no boats behind me, so I brought the speed back down to twenty-five knots. It was nearly low tide, so I couldn't take the shorter route through the narrow gap between Upper Harbor Key and the Content Keys. I kept going to the entrance to Harbor Channel, where I brought the *Revenge* down off plane and idled the short distance home in the gathering darkness.

When I clicked the key fob to open the door, I was pleasantly surprised to see a low-wattage light come on inside. I'd been planning to add one, wired to the release mechanism. As usual, Carl had been a step ahead of me. Once the boat was backed up under the house and the door closed, I shut down the engines and was greeted by Pescador on the narrow dock. "Hey, buddy," I said as he sat down on the dock, wagging his huge tail. "Did you miss me?" He barked once, which I took as a yes. I always imagined he could understand everything I said.

The *Cazador* was docked on the far side, so I knew Deuce, Julie, and Chyrel would be here. The Grady-White was gone, though. I assumed Trent or his wife were out fishing. Deuce and Julie met us at the top of the steps up to the deck.

"We just got here fifteen minutes ago," Deuce said. "Weren't expecting you for another half hour."

"Guess I'm getting paranoid in my old age. A boat was tailing me south of Key West about a mile behind me,

so I hammered the throttles all the way to Sawyer Keys. Where's Chyrel and the Trents?"

"Setting up her equipment in the east bunkhouse. Carl's going to partition off part of it later, so she doesn't have to sleep on your boat again. Dawson and Tony are helping him plant right now and his wife and kids are staying in town tonight."

"Plant?"

"Yeah, the system is ready and he picked up some tomato plants to start things off. He has a thousand baby crawfish on order and they should arrive tomorrow. That's why Charlie and the kids are down in Marathon. They're planting ten tomato plants now."

"Let's go check it out," I said. As we started walking toward the rear steps I asked Julie, "Anything new from your contact at the Coast Guard?"

"No, nothing at all. Seems they've suddenly become tight-lipped. How'd things go in Key West, with David's son?"

"Really well. He's a sharp kid. He agreed to go to DC, but has to give notice at his job first."

Reaching the bottom of the steps, I saw Tony, Dawson, and Trent working on the aquaculture system. It was easy to see that Tony had taken charge. He grinned as I walked up and said, "Hey, Jesse. How's it hanging?"

"Good, Tony. You must have a green thumb all the way up to your elbow."

"Grew up on a farm in North Carolina, man. Couldn't wait to get away from there. That's why I joined the Navy. Can't get much further from a farm than out on the ocean. Now, it's all I can do to keep from thinking about growing stuff. How weird is that?"

"What about you, Jeremy?" I asked.

"City boy," he said. Then he grinned and added, "But I always liked playing in dirt."

"We got everything running, Jesse," Trent said. "Tony's come up with some great ideas. We went ahead and bought some dissolvable nitrate and added it to the water, to jump-start the tomatoes. All the pumps and filters are working perfect. Gonna put some baby crawfish in here tomorrow."

"How long does it take them to mature?" Tony asked.

"About four months in the wild," Trent said. "Found that out at the library. We might be able to shorten that to two or three months here on the island. I'll know more when Chyrel gets me hooked up to the interweb and I can do some more research."

"So, we could have a Cajun boil by the end of summer?" I asked.

"In theory, yeah. We have a little more work to do before we can start breeding them. They burrow when the females lay eggs. I'll have to get some Louisiana clay for the bottom of the brooding area. I figure after the first hatching, we can harvest about half of them and leave a few hundred for brood stock."

"Sounds good," I said. "Speaking of Chyrel, I need to see her. You guys should knock off for the night."

"Just want to get these plants in," Tony said. "Chyrel's in the east bunkhouse."

I left them and walked across the clearing toward the two bunkhouses. Pescador trotted ahead and disappeared between the bunkhouses, headed for the pier. Things were finally coming together here on my little island. I reached the bunkhouse and knocked on the door.

"Come in," Chyrel said. I opened the door and was amazed at all the electronic equipment she'd brought. She was dressed in baggy shorts and a tank top, with an unbuttoned work shirt over it and her glasses pushed up on her forehead. She was behind a makeshift table, loaded with computers, monitors, and probably ten miles of wire and cable.

"Hey, Jesse, how've you been?"

"Good, thanks. Wow, how did you get all this stuff here?"

"It looks like a lot, but it's not. I had it all boxed up and Deuce brought it out on the boat. I should have everything ready to go in an hour. Thanks for letting me come out here to work. I really like it out here."

"Anything that helps to find the other guy and who was behind the attack. Hey, I want to give you something," I said as I reached into my pocket. I handed her a cashier's check made out to her, for twenty-five thousand dollars. "This is for your help in finding the wreck."

She looked at it and said, "I can't take this. What I did was nothing." She started to hand it back, but I shoved my hands in my pockets.

"It's yours. Deuce told me you did all the research on your own time. You deserve it."

She looked at it again, then looked back at me and smiled. "Well, I would like to buy a little boat. Something like that little blue one of yours."

"A flats skiff? I didn't even know you fished."

"Whatever it's called," she said. "It just looks cool and goes really fast."

"Okay," I said. "Then you should go see a guy on Big Pine, by the name of Skeeter. Trent can take you. Tell him I sent you and he'll fix you up right."

"I'll do that," she said as she put the check in her pocket. "Now, get out of here so I can work."

I left her to her work and joined Deuce, Julie, and Tony at the table outside. I could hear Trent behind the bunkhouse, hammering. The partition would be nothing more than a twenty-foot-by-seven-foot wall. He must have been building it outside so as not to disturb Chyrel.

Julie had a laptop, a notepad, and several file folders she was reading by the light of a kerosene lantern hung on a rod above the table. Now and then she made a note on the pad. Night had fallen and there was little sound, except the gentle lapping of the small waves against the mangrove roots to the east. Tony and Deuce were sitting backwards at the other table, leaning against the table top and staring up into the star-filled sky.

"Working on your class, Jules?" I asked.

"Yeah, I have an outline about ready to present to the Colonel. I'm trying to make it so it's not only useful information and practical implementation, but fun also."

"Good idea. Having a good time while training always seemed to make the training stick for me."

I sat down next to Deuce and Tony and followed their gaze toward the heavens. "You know," Tony pondered, "being out on the water like this, seeing so much more of what's out there, really makes a person feel pretty insignificant."

"That it does," Deuce responded.

"You think Chyrel will be able to dig something up?" I asked.

Deuce chuckled. "All her equipment has battery backups. When she fires everything up, it'll put a drain on the island's main battery system almost immediately as it all goes into recharge mode and the generator will kick on. I predict that fifteen minutes after that, she'll come out here with some news."

Just then, as if on cue, we could just make out the sound of the generator starting through the trees. I glanced back to the bunkhouse and saw the unmistakable blue glow of computer monitors. I noted the time on my watch to check Deuce's prediction.

CHAPTER TEN:

Second Attempt

Deuce was close. Chyrel came out with two folders after only ten minutes. "You guys aren't going to believe this." She handed Deuce and me a folder. "I made two copies."

We all walked over to the other table, where the light was better, and sat down. I opened the folder and looked at the first sheet, with Tony looking over my shoulder. It was background on Stolski. He'd been an agent with the CIA for nearly ten years, moving from one country to another every year or two. When he left the Clandestine Service, he apparently did some work as a mercenary, even a few contracts for the Agency itself.

The second page was a list of known accomplices and other agents he was close to that had also left the Agency. Each one had a picture and a short bio. The one at the top, Kyle Parker, stood out, as he had left the Agency at the same time as Stolski. Parker had also worked with Stols-

ki in four different countries over a span of three years with the Agency.

"Parker," Deuce said.

"He'd be my guess, too," I agreed.

I flipped to the next page. Apparently, Chyrel had become adept at reading Deuce's mind. It was Parker's full bio. I glanced up at her and she grinned. Parker had also been hired as a freelance operator by the Agency a number of times. He had a strong background in explosives, too. Something else struck me then. I flipped back to Stolski's bio and put them side by side.

I looked up at Chyrel and said, "Can you get anything more on the last time both Stolski and Parker were hired by the Agency to do freelance work? Both did five or six jobs for them the first year after leaving, but neither in the last two years. Did they screw something up?"

"I'll get right on it," she said and started to turn.

"Chyrel," Deuce said, stopping her. "How hard would it be for you to follow their money?"

She cocked her head and grinned. "Oh, please."

"Sorry. Let me know when you find something."

I went back to the file. The next page contained evidence photos of the boat Stolski had rented. Besides finding the body, the Coast Guard had found his weapons. He'd been armed with a 9mm Glock 17, and the rocket launcher was actually a Russian-made SA-18, which explained its heat-seeking ability. Next were several photos of a number of pieces of identification, with matching credit cards. In all, Stolski had passports, driver's licenses, and credit cards for three different aliases. They looked like excellent forgeries.

"Get to the next page," Deuce said.

I flipped the last of the pictures over and looked at the last sheet. It was a letter of commendation from the Station Chief in Karachi, Pakistan. I didn't get what Deuce thought was significant, until I saw the name of the Station Chief at the bottom, Jason Smith.

"Smith?" I asked.

"Could just be a coincidence," he responded.

"But, then again, it might not be."

"If it's not," he said, "I don't like where this takes us even more than before."

"Yeah, it means Smith still has Parker out there, or someone else, but my money's on him. And he's after you, or more than likely you and me. We should have someone on watch."

"I'll take the first watch," Tony said.

"I got second," Dawson piped in.

"Third." Deuce raised his hand. "Then I'll wake you, Jesse."

"You won't need to wake him," Julie said with a laugh. "His coffeemaker will."

Moments later Chyrel came out of the bunkhouse with another folder. She placed it in front of Deuce and said, "You're really not going to like this."

He opened the folder and studied the three sheets of paper inside. "Help me out here, Chyrel. Financial reports aren't my strong suit."

"Using the debit card numbers from the pictures, I checked for recent activity. Stolski made three cash withdrawals from an ATM here in the Keys in the last three days. That gave me the routing number to his bank in Miami, which I hacked into. Last Thursday he made a substantial transfer into that account from another bank in

New York. Like you said, I just followed the money. He transferred money from one bank to another to get it to the New York bank and then to Miami. It comes originally from a numbered account in the Caymans. That took a few minutes, but I managed to access the data. Two weeks ago, fifty thousand dollars was wired to that account from a numbered Swiss account. It took another few minutes to access that one. It's owned by a shell company, which is in turn owned by another shell company. That one is owned by Downeger Industries. The CFO of Downeger Industries is listed as Charlotte Downeger Smith. In 1997, our old boss, Jason Smith, married a woman by the name of Charlotte Downeger, sole heir to the substantial liquid, stock, and land holdings of Downeger Industries in upstate New York. She was murdered by a mugger in Manhattan almost three years ago, less than a year after she inherited the estate."

"Damn," Julie exclaimed.

"Damn is right, babe," Deuce muttered.

Suddenly, I could see the connection. "Chyrel, find out two more things, then you can call it a night. First, check the background of Charlotte Smith's father. Specifically, was he in the military? Second, is it possible to check bank records from 2003? Did Stolski receive a large sum of money about that time?"

"I'll get right on it. Is there a specific time frame for Stolski receiving the money?"

"Yeah, look at the month prior to and just after Charlotte Smith's murder."

"You're kidding, right?" Deuce said. "I knew the guy for a year. He could be a prick, but he's no murderer."

"That's what they said about Jeffrey Dahmer, Deuce. Just check it, will ya, Chyrel?" Deuce nodded to her and she went back to the bunkhouse.

"I'm surprised you haven't made the connection, Deuce. Think about it. Downeger?"

He looked off toward the pier, between the bunkhouses for a moment. Suddenly, he turned back to me and said, "Master Chief Archer Downeger!"

"Who's he?" Julie asked.

"One of the originals!" Tony exclaimed. "He was the first Instructor at the Amphibious Scout and Raider School, in Fort Pierce, during the early months of World War Two. They were the forerunners of the modern day Navy SEALs."

"It's a pretty long reach," Deuce said.

A moment later Chyrel returned and plopped yet another folder in front of us. "Master Chief Petty Officer Arthur Downeger, United States Navy, Retired. Is that what you were looking for, Jesse?"

"Depends on what else you found," I replied as Deuce picked up the file and started looking through it.

"Two weeks before Charlotte Smith was murdered, Stolski made a single deposit of seventy-five thousand dollars into his primary bank account in Washington. He was working at the CIA office in New York at the time."

"Not so much of a reach now, is it?" I said, looking at Deuce, who was still reading the papers in the folder.

He frowned and all he could say was, "All that time."

"We need to get this information to the FBI," Julie said.

"No," Deuce finally muttered. "No, we need to get this information to the Colonel."

Deuce, Chyrel and I went to the bunkhouse. She activated the encrypted video connection on her laptop. A moment later, Colonel Stockwell's face appeared on the monitor.

"I was just about to call you, Deuce. What's up?"

"Chyrel is sending you a secure fax, sir. We figured out who Stolski's accomplice might be. Another former CIA operative by the name of Kyle Parker. And they weren't after the President. They were after me."

"Stand by a second, the fax is coming in now."

He turned away from the monitor and picked up a bunch of papers from a fax machine right behind him. He put on a pair of reading glasses as he shuffled through the papers.

Deuce continued, "Stolski and Parker were paid by none other than Jason Smith, sir. And we uncovered more. It looks like Smith paid Stolski seventy-five thousand dollars in 2003 to murder his wife so that he could inherit her money. Money that she'd inherited from her father, one of the original Navy SEALs."

"That part's purely circumstantial," he said, setting the papers aside. "But I agree it's very likely he was responsible for this morning's attack. Contact Kumar Sayef. Get him and another team member on the next plane to Djibouti. I want to have a word with Mister Smith, before the FBI does. That's what I was about to call you about. The Feebs want you and Jesse in DC for a debriefing with the Secret Service. It's set up for next Saturday. They wanted it earlier, but the President himself intervened. He wants to meet with you, Jesse, Julie, Doc Talbot, and Doctor Burdick. He's making a surprise visit to the

troops on Tuesday in Afghanistan and asked if you could make it Saturday."

"Not a problem, Colonel," Deuce said.

"Are you sure, Commander?" Stockwell said with a grin.

Behind us Julie said, "We're getting married Sunday."

Deuce cringed, but recovered quickly. "We'll just have to get there and back in one day, sir."

"I'll arrange a Gulfstream," Stockwell said. "Consider it a wedding gift."

Then the screen went blank as he disconnected. "You think he'd mind an extra passenger?" I said.

"Who?" asked Julie.

"Jared Williams. I promised him I'd take him to DC on Saturday."

"Shouldn't be a problem," Deuce said. Then he turned to Chyrel and said, "Get Kumar on there. Then you can turn in. I promise."

With just a few quick keystrokes, Kumar's face appeared on the screen. Kumar Sayef was one of Deuce's first team members. He's in his late thirties, but could easily pass for fifteen years younger. He's a Sergeant First Class and was serving with the Army's 1st Special Forces Operational Detachment-Delta, commonly referred to as Delta Force, when he was recruited by DHS. Born in the Upper Midwest to Pakistani parents, he's fluent in several Arabic dialects, as well as French, Spanish, and Italian. More than fluent, in fact. Many Middle Eastern languages have subtle regional accents, which he's also mastered.

"Hiya, Deuce," he said with a decidedly Midwestern accent. "What's up?"

"Colonel Stockwell has a mission for you, Kumar. Chyrel's making the arrangements as we speak and will send instructions to you in a few minutes. How's your French and Ta'izzi Adeni Arabic?"

"Aw, man. There's a reason they call Djibouti the 'Armpit of Africa,' ya know."

"In and out. Two days at the most. I promise."

"What's the objective?" Kumar sighed.

"Locate and capture Jason Smith, then bring him to see the Colonel." The bewilderment on Kumar's face was apparent, so Deuce added, "We have proof he was directly involved in this morning's attempt to kill Jesse and me."

Kumar's face turned hard. He was a team player and fiercely loyal to Deuce. "My go bag's by the door. I'll grab a bite to eat while I wait for Chyrel's instructions."

"Thanks, Kumar. Call Art, he's going with you. Let me know when you land." Art Newman has been on Deuce's team from the start. Before that, he was on Deuce's SEAL team.

"Roger that, boss."

The screen went blank and Chyrel said, "I have a Gulfstream 5 available out of Miami, taking a group of oil executives to Yemen. Leaves in an hour and lands in Aden, Yemen at nineteen hundred local time. I've already added Kumar's name to the flight manifest, as a French envoy from the Seychelles, in Miami on business. Art's his Executive Assistant. They already have cover ID and background that'll stand close scrutiny."

"Perfect," Deuce said. "Send Kumar the information."

"On its way," she said. "I also arranged a helicopter from Aden to Djibouti, through the French Embassy. They'll be in the city shortly after nightfall."

"Okay, let's all get some rest," Deuce said. "The ball's in motion and we won't know anything until tomorrow evening."

"I have a little more work to do here," Chyrel said. "Do you have a cot I can set up in here for tonight?"

"Better than that," I replied. "There's a real comfortable hammock over by the casuarinas, strung between two palm trees. I'll get it and have Trent put a couple of hooks in the walls to hang it in here. He's already working on a partition to separate this end of the bunkhouse. Deuce, you and Julie can take the main house and I'll bunk under the stars."

"No," Julie said. "We can sleep on the boat. You shouldn't have to sleep on the ground."

"Jules, I've probably slept more nights on the ground than not. Besides, it'll be easier for Dawson to get to Deuce in the house. I'll get a couple things out of the boat before everyone turns in."

I left the bunkhouse and went straight to Trent's little house and told him what I wanted him to do with the hammock. He was busy cutting two-by-fours for the partition in the bunkhouse. Then I went to the *Revenge* and raised the bunk in the forward stateroom. I took out three small boxes and one of the fly rod cases, which I left on the table in the house. From the hanging closet in the bedroom, I grabbed a bedroll and blanket before returning to the group. Trent was in the bunkhouse with Chyrel, getting the hammock strung up.

I placed the three boxes on the table and opened the first one. I removed my Pulsar Edge night vision optics headset and handed it to Tony. Then I opened the other two boxes and passed out three Sig Sauer P226 nine-milli-

meter semiautomatic pistols and three magazines loaded with Parabellums to Tony, Jeremy, and Deuce, keeping the fourth for myself. They were standard issue for SEALs, so I knew Tony and Deuce would be more than familiar with them. Dawson, being Coast Guard, was more used to the Beretta M9, I figured.

"You familiar with the Sig, Jeremy?" I asked.

"Very much so. I own two."

"What about me?" Julie asked.

"Deuce told me you've been practicing with the rifle. If anything happens, I want you up on the roof. My M-40A3 sniper rifle is on the table in the house. There's a ladder next to the cistern and a small platform in the center of the roof. From there, you can see the whole island and every approach through the night optics on it."

"Why not Russell? He *is* a SEAL sniper."

"Deuce is also about twice your weight. Nothing personal, Deuce. But my roof is all that keeps the rain off me."

"None taken," he said. "Jesse's right. You can get up there a lot quicker than me and if something happens during my watch, you could get there that much faster."

I checked my watch and saw that it was after twenty-two hundred. "Alright, everyone turn in. It's late."

As Julie and Deuce headed for the house, Dawson went to the western bunkhouse. Trent had finished the wall with only one side paneled and Dawson helped him muscle it through the door at the west end. A few minutes later, they had it in place and Trent nailed it to the exterior walls. He said he'd put the paneling on the other side tomorrow.

"You think he'll try something here tonight?" Tony asked as I rolled my bedroll out on the ground by the table.

"I doubt it. But forewarned is forearmed."

As he started toward the tree line he said, "See you in the morning." It'd been a long day and I was asleep before my head hit the bedroll, Pescador already asleep lying next to me.

The smell of coffee woke me. Deuce was kneeling beside me with two cups and extended one to me as I sat up. "Thanks," I said. I took a swallow and looked around. It was dark and very quiet. Pescador looked at me, ears up.

"Go ahead," I said to the dog. He ran silently between the bunkhouses and lifted his leg on a rock by the pier.

"Nothing," Deuce said. "But we'll keep a watch at night until he's found anyway."

"You don't like waiting any more than me, do you?"

"No, proactive is my nature."

"Me too," I said as I rolled my bedroll and blanket, then sat down at the table. Deuce sat down across from me. "You're not going back to bed?"

"Nah, sun'll be up in an hour. Besides, I snoozed a little on the way here yesterday."

We both heard a twig snap and were instantly down behind the table, guns drawn. Pescador had returned and was on full alert, the hair on his neck sticking up. He instinctively never made a sound, knowing that we'd heard the noise, also. Deuce pulled the Pulsar night optics down in front of his eyes and scanned the area to the east where the sound had come from.

My eyes were accustomed to the dark, but I still couldn't see what he could. He held one finger up and then two

fingers down, wiggling them and pointing right to left, letting me know it was one person on foot and they were headed toward the north end of the island.

He pointed to me and then to the gap between the bunkhouses, made a gun firing signal with his left hand and moved his hand in a pushing motion, pointing toward the east side of the island.

I nodded and moved quickly toward the gap, Pescador trotting silently beside me. I knew that Deuce would be able to cross the clearing unobserved with the night vision. He would then be in position to intercept whoever it was after I got around ahead of him and started shooting, driving him back the way he came, toward Deuce.

I made it between the bunkhouses and moved quickly between the pier and the casuarinas that surrounded this end of the island. From there I moved more cautiously, staying low and taking advantage of the cover. Pescador followed close behind me, like a dark, silent shadow.

From where we heard the sound to where I was now moving was about a hundred yards. I figured if he was moving stealthily, he'd be at least fifty yards in front of me now. But I had no idea if he was equipped with night vision or not. I trusted that Pescador would alert me if he heard him getting too close.

I moved another ten yards to a gumbo limbo tree with some low, thick branches. By now Deuce would be in position, so I motioned Pescador to stop, aimed toward the edge of the tree line along the water and started firing. I fired four shots in quick succession and heard someone crashing through the brush at the water line just twenty yards ahead of me. I came out from behind the tree and fired twice more, rushing forward as noisily as I could.

Pescador ran just ahead of me, barking twice. His voice is a deep, menacing sound and carried through the darkness well. Whoever the guy was, he now knew he had an armed pursuer and a big dog chasing him.

It was all on Deuce now. Shouts were coming from the bunkhouse, responding to the gunshots. I heard a door slam in the direction of the main house. Then I heard a loud thump and a moan.

"Tango down!" I heard Deuce yell. I pulled a powerful penlight from my pocket and started toward him. More flashlights were sweeping the area.

Not wanting to be taken for an intruder, I shouted loud enough to be heard at the main house, "Tango down! Hold your fire! Deuce has him down on the east side of the island!"

By the time I got to Deuce, Dawson and Pescador were already there. The guy was on the ground facedown and Deuce had him pinned at the back of his neck with one knee, while the other was across his right forearm. Pescador had him by the sleeve of his left hand and it was stretched out away from his body. A scoped hunting rifle lay next to him, which I picked up. A moment later, Tony came running up with a length of quarter-inch twisted sisal rope. He dropped down on the opposite side of the guy, next to Pescador, and tied his left hand. Pescador released his sleeve and moved to the guy's head, his hot, rumbling breath inches from the guy's face. Tony brought his left hand up to the small of his back and when he grabbed the guy's right wrist, Deuce lifted his knee. Tony quickly brought it up to his other hand and tied them together. Only then did Deuce stand up, still wearing the night vision goggles.

Julie, Chyrel, and Trent came running up, adding more flashlights to the scene, so Deuce removed his night vision. Tony and Dawson grabbed the guy by the upper arms and lifted him to his feet. He had a gash on the side of his head, and blood was running down his left cheek, but there was no mistaking that it was Kyle Parker.

"Jules, get the lamp lit," I said. "Bring him over to the table." Julie ran ahead of Tony and Dawson, half dragging Parker.

"What the hell happened?" Trent asked. "Who is that guy?"

"He's a hired killer," I replied. "But, he's out of business now."

"I don't get it. What's he doing here? Did you guys know he was coming here?"

Deuce turned to Trent and said, "Calm down, Carl. We only figured out what was going on late last night." As we walked toward the now lit area around the table, Deuce continued in a calming voice. "Yesterday morning, someone tried to kill Jesse and me, but he ended up being the one getting killed. Late last night, we found out he had an accomplice, so we kept watch all night in case he tried again. Everything's okay now. Think you and Chyrel can rustle up some breakfast?"

"Breakfast?" he said, looking confused. "Yeah. Yeah, sure. Pancakes okay?"

"That'd be great. Thanks. And don't worry, there were only two of them."

Trent headed off to the western bunkhouse and Chyrel followed, trying to keep him calm and answer his questions as best she could.

"Sit him on the bench, facing away from the table," Deuce ordered. "Near the end, and tie his hands and feet to the legs of the bench and table. It's time to get some information from our guest."

Tony pulled another length of quarter-inch twisted sisal rope from the pocket of his cargo pants and removed Parker's shoes and socks before tying his feet together and pulling them back to the legs of the bench. He did the same thing with the tailing of the first rope, tying his hands to the legs of the table. He wasn't gentle. Sisal rope is made from the fiber of the agave plant and is widely used in baling hay and for many marine uses. It's a very coarse, rough fiber and when used to tie someone's hands, it's extremely uncomfortable.

After securing him to the table, Tony went through his pockets, producing a throwaway cell phone and keys that apparently went to a rental boat, but nothing more.

"I'm not going to tell you anything," Parker spat out.

"Sure you will, Parker," Deuce growled. "But not until after we eat." Parker jerked his head up, surprised that Deuce knew who he was. "Oh yeah, we know who and what you are. And we know you were working with Stolski. What we don't know..." He kind of trailed off there. "Well, what we don't know, we have ways of finding out, don't we, Gunny?"

"Oh yeah," I said. "But you're right. No hurry. Stolski's dead and this turd fondler will pray to join him soon enough. You want another cup of java, Commander?"

Julie caught on quick and said, "Come on, Gunny. Can't we just slap him around a little before chow?"

"You'll get your chance, Petty Officer," I said. "But let's have some coffee and pancakes first."

"Alright," she hissed. "I'll get it. But don't start without me."

She headed toward the main house and I looked over at Deuce and whispered, "Better not leave her alone with this guy. You remember last time?"

"The Cuban?" Deuce asked. "Or the Iraqi?"

"The Iraqi." I winced as we walked over to the other table. "Poor sonofabitch had to eat his own pecker."

Tony stood there staring at Parker, his arms crossed and his feet apart. Pescador stood next to him with the hair on his neck and back standing up, a low, menacing rumble coming from deep in his chest. Tony was in bare feet, wearing only a pair of cargo shorts, the muscles in his chest and abdomen flexing with every slight move and his dark ebony skin glistening with sweat. Apparently, he and Deuce had played this game before. He shouted unintelligible gibberish that sounded like some strange African dialect with clicking sounds, never taking his eyes from Parker. Parker looked up at the strange sounds with a look of fear and dread.

"No," Dawson shouted as he turned around. Then very slowly, as if speaking to a child, he added, "You may not eat him."

Tony's face became even harder if that were possible, his nostrils flaring as he bent his head slightly, looking at Parker with dark, hooded eyes and mumbling more gibberish.

Deuce, Dawson and I sat down at the far end of the other table. Soon Julie joined us with three mugs, a thermos and two large bottles of water. She whistled and tossed one to Tony. He caught it backhanded, never taking his eyes off Parker. Tony opened it and took a couple of swal-

lows, then pulled a towel from one of his cargo pockets and set the towel and the water bottle next to Parker on the table. The former CIA agent knew full well the meaning of the towel and water. Tony left him sitting there and joined us.

A few minutes later, Chyrel brought a plate full of pancakes out, stacked on top of several more plates, and set them on the table, with a bottle of syrup and several forks. Apparently she was privy to the game, too. She never said a word, just took the throwaway phone Deuce had picked up from the table and went back to the bunkhouse. I passed out the plates and forks and we all dug into the pancakes.

After a minute, Deuce whispered to Julie in a voice low enough that Parker couldn't hear, "Maybe you should join Chyrel."

Julie surprised me with the sternness in her whispered voice. "The other one tried to kill us. This one came here to kill you and Jesse. I'm okay with whatever you plan to do, so long as you don't actually kill him."

Deuce poured another cup of coffee, picked up the file on Parker and walked around to stand directly behind him. Parker tried to crane his neck around, but finally gave up. "You won't get anything out of me," Parker said. "I've been waterboarded before." But his voice belied his bravado.

Deuce set the heavy mug down on the table, causing Parker to involuntarily jump. Again, he tried to twist around to see what Deuce was doing. Deuce opened the file and started to read some of the highlights of Parker's short career with the CIA out loud.

The look on Parker's face said it all. Most of what was in the file should have been redacted and he knew it. "Not much of a career," Deuce said. "And no reference to having been captured or undergone waterboard training. The Gunny here has, though, haven't you, Gunny?"

"Yes sir, many times. Died twice, had to have CPR to bring me back."

"Care to show our guest here what the real thing's like?"

I caught on instantly to what Deuce was doing. He knew I could hold my breath for almost two full minutes. He wanted me to mimic drowning through waterboarding.

I got up and moved over to the bench next to Parker. Deuce quickly snatched up the towel and put it around my face, pulling my head back on the table, while Tony stepped in front of me and pinned my arms. I'd seen men waterboarded before and knew exactly how they acted.

Slowly he started pouring the water onto the towel. After about thirty seconds, I started making a show of struggling and puffed a little air out. Then I started struggling and puffing harder. At the one-minute mark, I was fighting really hard against Tony, but not so hard that I could break free. Finally, Deuce released the towel and Tony let go of my arms. I managed to get a mouthful of water and made a great show of choking, coughing, and spitting up water as I fell to my hands and knees, gasping for air.

"Anyone can survive this once and not talk," Deuce said. "Imagine how many times a professional, such as myself, can bring someone that tried to kill me to the very brink of death and not actually kill them, when I

can do it so easily to one of my own men. You'll tell me what I want to know, Parker. You'll tell me more than I want to know."

Chyrel came back and handed Deuce a file folder and two more large water bottles. He placed the water on the table just beside Parker's head. By now, it was obvious the man was very afraid. Around him was an apparent African tribesman who wanted to eat him, a woman that wanted to feed him his own genitalia and a madman that would torture one of his own.

Dawson walked over and stood in front of Parker. He squatted down so that he was eye level with the man and in a calm, soothing voice said, "I know you're scared, Parker. You reek of it. It's in your eyes and the way your voice cracks. You don't have to go through this. Just tell the Commander what he wants to know, okay?"

Parker looked up at Tony, standing behind Dawson, then at me, struggling to get to my feet, and finally at Julie, standing at the end of the table with a menacing look on her face. "You c-c-can do anything you w-want. I'm not g-gonna talk!"

Dawson smiled reassuringly at the man and, in a lightning-fast move, brought his fist up and hammered it down between the man's thighs, smashing him so hard in the groin, I winced.

Parker howled in pain, but only for a second. Deuce quickly grabbed the wet towel and covered his face, yanking his head back hard on the table. Tony grabbed a bottle, twisted the cap off and slowly started pouring it over the towel. Parker began to struggle immediately and within seconds, he was sucking in water and cough-

ing it back into the towel. It lasted only about fifteen seconds and Deuce released the towel.

Parker's head tilted forward as he coughed up huge mouthfuls of water. A few seconds later, Deuce grabbed him by the hair and jerked his head back, shouting, "You called Jason Smith yesterday at nineteen hundred! The call lasted two minutes! What did you ask him?"

Between racking fits of coughs, Parker managed to get out that he'd called Smith to say he lost me, he'd asked if Smith knew where I was headed, and Smith had told him about this island. It only took another ten minutes and Deuce had every bit of information about Smith that Parker knew.

It was Stolski that had been contracted to murder Smith's wife three years ago. That was his first contract after leaving the Agency. Stolski had brought Parker in and cut him in for a fourth of the contract. In fact, it was the reason he'd left. During the first year, both men had received several contracts from the Agency, mostly through Smith. But, when Smith had left the Agency himself, to pursue his political ambitions, the contracts nearly dried up. So, both men had jumped on the chance to get a good-paying contract from Smith. He'd first contacted Stolski just two weeks after being transferred to Djibouti. Stolski said it would have to be a two-man job and wanted more than what Smith had offered. They brought Parker in and they agreed on a price of two hundred thousand dollars, half upfront and half when the job was completed. With Stolski out of the picture, Parker saw a chance to increase his pay and contacted Smith to renegotiate. Besides the fifty thousand dollars he'd already received, Smith wired another fifty thousand to

Parker and agreed to pay him that much again when he finished the contract.

Just after sunrise, we were sitting in what was now Chyrel's satellite office in the bunkhouse. "Just because you're paranoid doesn't necessarily mean nobody's not out to get you," Deuce said as we waited for Chyrel to get Stockwell on the encrypted video call.

"Let's hope Kumar is able to nab Smith," I said. "Otherwise, we'll be looking over our shoulder for a while. What time is it in Djibouti?"

"Just after fifteen hundred, eight hours ahead of us," Chyrel said. "Connection being made."

Stockwell's face appeared on the screen. The guy must never sleep. It seemed no matter what time Deuce called, he was in his office. "We captured Parker early this morning, Colonel. He's confessed to being contracted by Jason Smith, along with Stolski, to kill both Jesse and me. He also admitted to being a part of the murder of Charlotte Downeger Smith and said that Jason Smith paid them a hundred thousand dollars to murder her."

"I don't suppose these confessions will hold up in court, will they?"

"No sir, they won't," Deuce readily admitted.

"I can probably make the case to the AG that a hired mercenary taking a contract on a federal agent could be construed as an act of terrorism. Considering that the President was also threatened, I'd say Mister Parker will be enjoying the sunset in Gitmo by the end of the day."

"Have you heard from Kumar, Colonel?"

"Not yet. His bird isn't scheduled to land in Yemen for another two hours."

"What should we do with Parker?"

Stockwell thought for a moment and then said, "Get him ready to be delivered to a Navy chopper at sea. It shouldn't take me more than an hour to get the paperwork pushed through. I'll call you with a rendezvous point once I know it'll go through. Good job, all of you."

The screen went blank. "I sure wouldn't want to be Parker," Chyrel said.

"What do you mean?" Julie asked. "Prisoners in Gitmo live in luxury."

"Yeah, luxury behind barbed wire fences for the rest of your life. I couldn't take that."

"You do have a point," Julie said. "But it's still better than he deserves."

The three of us left the bunkhouse and joined Tony and Dawson standing guard over Parker, not that he was going anywhere. He was still tied to the table, head hanging down, crusted blood on his cheek from where Deuce had clobbered him with a dead branch from a lignum vitae tree. Even a dead branch from one of those trees is as hard as tempered steel. His wrists and ankles were chafed and bleeding also, from struggling against the coarse ropes, and he'd soiled his pants.

"He's not going on my boat like that," I said. "Take him up to the deck, strip him down and put him under the shower. In the hanging closet by the front door you'll find a go bag that has some flex cuffs in the side pocket. Should be an old pair of fishing shorts and a tee shirt on the shelf there, too. We're leaving in about half an hour."

Tony had put on a shirt and shoes along with a shoulder holster that had a knife sheath on the front. He pulled out his Ka-Bar and sliced the ropes securing Parker to the table with a single swipe, and another pass be-

tween his ankles freed his feet. The two men lifted him and half dragged him toward the main house, Pescador leading the way.

Half an hour later, we were idling out into Harbor Channel in the *Cazador*. I brought her up onto plane headed due south. The coordinates Stockwell had given us were at the edge of the Gulf Stream thirty miles almost due south of Bahia Honda. Since we only had two hours to get there, I decided to take the smaller boat because it only needs three feet of water and we wouldn't have to go way east to pick up the main channel. We were meeting a Navy MH-60 helicopter that was coming out of NAS Jacksonville on a routine long-range training flight to Guantanamo Bay, Cuba. It would be stopping to refuel in Miami and would meet us at the coordinates Stockwell had provided at exactly zero nine thirty. It would only have ten minutes on station at the most.

It was just me, Deuce, and Dawson aboard and we had Parker tied up in the little head below the console. Deuce took his phone out, pulled up the text message from Stockwell and punched the coordinates into the Simrad chart plotter. "It's twenty-eight nautical miles almost due south of the Bahia Honda Channel Bridge. Total distance is about thirty-seven nautical miles and we have ninety-three minutes to get there."

I ran the calculation in my head and said, "That's twenty-five knots average speed. It's almost like he knows the most economical speed of this boat." I turned hard to port, entering the unmarked narrow channel through Cutoe Banks, and slowed down just a little to weave and thread my way through the Banks. Then I headed northeast towards Marker 52, just north of Big Spanish Key. A

couple minutes later we were clear of the Banks and I turned south toward Big Spanish Channel and pushed the speed up to thirty knots. "But, I'd rather be early than late."

"You know these waters well," Dawson shouted from where he was seated on the port gunwale. "That little cut couldn't have been more than three or four feet deep and not much wider."

Deuce was leaning back against the seat, as I was, deep in thought. We were now in deep water headed southeast between Crawl Key and Annette Key. "What's on your mind, Deuce?"

"All of it, man. Sometimes, like this morning, I wonder if I'm doing the right thing bringing Julie into all this."

"She's a really independent woman," I said. "I don't think anyone could get her to do something she didn't want to do."

"What if I wasn't involved in all this? Think she'd want to become involved on her own?"

"No. That I'm sure of. Look, she's a woman in love and she's going to go where her heart takes her. And you are involved, there's no getting around that, unless you want to quit. Quitting's not in your nature."

"Sometimes," he said, "I'm just not so sure now."

We passed under the bridge at Bahia Hondo into the open Atlantic and I switched on the Simrad radar. All the electronics on board were Simrad. Good equipment, but not the best. The more I used this boat, the more I liked it, though. The sweeping Carolina flare of the bow allowed it to run at a good speed, even when seas were a little rough. Today, we had a southeast wind, blowing at about ten knots, and the rollers were only a few feet

and widely spaced. She rode up the crest, tilted slightly and rolled down the other side with no spray at all. The big 480-horse Cummins diesel engine, which David had tweaked to about 500 horsepower, ran quietly and smoothly.

When we were five miles out, I told Dawson he could bring Parker up on deck. I didn't want him throwing up in the head. Dawson opened the small hatch and pulled him out, squinting in the bright sunlight. He was drenched in sweat and not just from the heat down there. I think fear had a lot to do with it.

It took another forty minutes to reach the rendezvous point and we were ten minutes early. Parker was sitting on the small bench seat in front of the helm. We hadn't told him where we were taking him. Neither Deuce nor I felt he deserved to be told.

I pulled back on the throttle and we dropped down off plane, idling toward the weed line, where the Gulf Stream starts. I checked the radar and there were no other boats within ten miles.

"What are you going to do to me?" Parker asked.

"Shut up," I replied. "Or I'll feed you to the sharks."

"I can pay you. I have lots of money."

"Not anymore, you don't," Deuce said. "It's been seized by the government. Now shut up."

A blip appeared on the radar, moving fast straight toward us. A minute later we could hear the approaching helicopter. I could tell from the sound that it was slowing down, without having to look at the radar. Stockwell had given Deuce the VHF radio frequency and he switched the radio on and adjusted it. Then he spoke into the mic.

"Seahawk, this is motor vessel *Cazador*. We have you approaching two miles out."

"*Cazador*, we have you in sight. We understand you have a guest that will be staying with us for the foreseeable future?"

"Affirmative, compliments of Homeland Security."

"We'll come in and hover to lower a man down. Have your passenger ready."

I shifted to neutral and shut off the engine as the big chopper approached, getting lower and lower. "Where are they going to take me?" Parker shouted. "I'm an American citizen. I have rights. You haven't read me my rights."

Deuce moved forward and knelt beside the man. "No, you don't have any rights. You and Stolski plotted to kill the President of the United States and you were captured attacking federal agents with the intent to kill. You don't have the right to an attorney and you don't have the right to a speedy trial. Now if you don't shut your mouth, I'll break your jaw and ensure that you do, in fact, remain silent. You're a terrorist and you're going to Gitmo."

By now, the chopper had come in and was hovering about forty feet above us. The side door opened and a man leaned out and grabbed the lowering cable and attached it to his harness. A few minutes later, he was standing in the forward cockpit. I went forward and he shook hands with the three of us. He had a second harness already attached to his and we helped him get it on Parker, who was babbling about not knowing anything about an attack on the President.

Once the harness was on him, the Petty Officer clipped it to the cable and signaled the chopper to lift them. He

saluted Deuce and up the two men went. The chopper didn't even wait until they were inside, but turned southeast and started moving away. We watched until both men were inside and closed the door, then the chopper began to climb and increase speed.

"Only one person left to send down there," I said.

"Kumar should be landing in Yemen about now," Deuce said. "By the time we get back, he'll be in Djibouti."

"Then we better get going."

CHAPTER ELEVEN:

Gone Like a Puff of Smoke

It was nearly noon before we got back to the island. After docking the boat, we hurried up to the deck, down the back steps and across the clearing to the bunkhouses. Tony and Trent were sitting at one of the tables.

"Any word from Kumar and Art?" Deuce asked.

"Nothing yet," Tony replied. "But they should be landing any minute. How'd it go with Parker?"

"He whined and cried, but by now he's meeting some of Jesse's buddies in Gitmo," Deuce replied as he headed into the bunkhouse.

Tony had the hunting rifle that Parker had been carrying disassembled on the table and was cleaning it. "What ya got there, Tony?" I asked.

"Nice of him to leave it, huh? It's not in bad shape, but really needed cleaning and could use a few things that're worn out. Winchester model 70, chambered for three oh eight. Same rifle White Feather used, wasn't it?"

He was referring to one of the greatest Marine snipers of all time, Carlos Hathcock. "Yeah, it is. A little outdated compared to what we can get our hands on today. What were you planning to do with it?"

"I have one exactly like it, back home on the farm. Same scope and everything. Called my dad this morning and asked him to ship it to me. I was thinking the pair would make a pretty cool wedding present for Deuce and Julie."

"Yeah," I said. "They'd like that. A couple that plays together, stays together, huh?"

"Thank you! She's been doing some shooting on the range up at Homestead. The lady's got skills. Hey, is there a good gun shop around here?"

"Jig's Bait and Tackle, down on Big Pine. It's on US-1, easy to find."

"A bait shop? Really?"

"Just about every business down here sells bait and just about every bait shop does something else on the side. What is it you need?" I asked as I sat down.

He picked up a long, thin spring. "This firing pin spring is pretty worn. I'd like to replace it and the pin. Might as well replace the trigger spring too."

"The trigger spring, Jig's might have in stock. Anything he doesn't have in stock, he can get in two days. I get all my parts through there." I picked up the barrel and examined it, then set it down and picked up the trigger assembly. "This trigger assembly and guard is aftermarket. If yours is still original, I'd replace this too." Picking up another part, I looked closely at it. "There's been a lot of rounds through that barrel. Might as well replace this extractor too."

"Thanks, Gunny. Maybe I can borrow a boat and go into town in the morning."

"We're going to pick up some appliances and materials at the Home Depot in the morning. Ride with us and you can run over to Jig's while we're loading their delivery truck and meet us back at the dock."

The three of us looked up at the sound of an outboard approaching from the south. "That'll be Charlie," Trent said, "with the baby crawfish and supplies. We don't have to tell her what happened this morning, do we?"

"A lie of omission, Carl?"

He looked at me and grinned. "Yeah, I know. Look, what happened this morning rattled me a little. You guys are used to it, but I don't mind tellin' you, I was scared shitless when the shooting started. I know you and the other guys can handle things like that, but how about keeping me in the loop, okay? Then I can decide whether to take Charlie and the kids away. But, this once, I don't think it'll hurt anything if she doesn't know."

As we got up and left Tony to his cleaning, I said, "That's a deal, Carl."

When we opened the door to the dock area, Charlie had already swung the Grady around and was backing up to the dock in front of my skiff.

"Hey, Jesse," she said with a smile. "The crawfish arrived this morning. They're up in the bow with some groceries. Kids, give Jesse and Daddy a hand, ya hear."

Little Carl and Patty scrambled to do Charlie's bidding. Mostly Carl. He lifted the boxes of groceries up to the dock and Trent stepped down to help him with the heavier sealed coolers of crawfish. "Crawfish have an

exoskeleton. They shed it, like a locust. I learned that at the library."

It suddenly dawned on me. In a couple of months Carl was going to be starting kindergarten. "Where are you going to go to school this fall, Carl?"

"I dunno," he answered.

"We really haven't thought about that," Charlie said as she climbed up to the dock and handed me the keys to the Grady.

I didn't even give it a second thought and handed them back to her. "She's yours. You'll need something reliable to ferry him ashore in the mornings and pick him up."

"We can't accept that, Jesse. You've done so much already."

I picked up the two coolers and said, "Nonsense. You two have done a lot more for me. You deserve it. Next time you go down to Big Pine, stop and see Skeeter and tell him to order a wraparound screen for the Bimini top. Can't have little Carl going to school all wet when it rains."

Before she or Trent could say anything, I turned and walked around the dock to the door. I carried the crawfish containers over to the aquaculture system and set them down in the shade of a sea grape bush. As I passed Charlie on the way back down the front steps to the docks she quietly said, "Thank you, Jesse." Then after she'd gone a few steps further up she stopped and said, "Oh, Jesse, I almost forgot. While I was at the *Rusty Anchor* a woman came in asking for you. She said she was a friend of Alex's. Her name is Cindy Saturday. I told her I'd probably be seeing you and would let you know."

"Thanks, Charlie," I said, heading on down to the docks. Several months ago, the lawyer that came all the way from Oregon to transfer Alex's estate had told me about Ms. Saturday. She was a partner in a school Alex had started to teach troubled teens how to fly fish. I'd donated a good portion of Alex's estate to the school and agreed to help fund a similar school here in the Keys.

I went aboard the *Revenge* to look for my cell phone and found it after a brief search. It was in the refrigerator. When I tried to turn it on, it flashed the low battery warning and turned back off. After another few minutes of searching, I found the charger and plugged it in. Once it powered up, I saw that I had fourteen missed calls, three voice messages, and two text messages. The two text messages were from Ms. Saturday and Rusty, both saying the same thing. She was in town and would like to meet with me. Two of the voice messages were from her also. She had a pleasant-sounding voice. The third voice message was from Home Depot, saying that my appliances had arrived.

I called Home Depot and told them I'd arrange to have the appliances picked up in the morning. Then I called Skeeter. He owns a boat sales and repair shop on Big Pine Key. I asked if Trent had talked to him about using his barge and he said he had and we could stop by and pick it up any time. I ended the call and punched in the number Ms. Saturday had left. She answered on the second ring.

"Hi, Mizz. Saturday. This is Jesse McDermitt. Sorry I missed your call. You're in town?"

"That's alright, I sometimes go days without a cell signal when I'm on the river. And please, just call me Cindy. Yes, I arrived yesterday. I had no idea how beautiful it is

down here. No wonder Alex loved it so much. You have my deepest condolences, Jesse. She talked about you all the time, when she came back to take care of her brother."

"Thanks, Cindy. I suppose you want to get together and talk about the school?"

"That too, but it can wait. What I'd really like to do is go fishing. Alex would talk for hours about the great fishing down here. I rented a skiff, but need a guide. Think I can hire you for a day?"

"I'm not really a flats guide," I said. "And my fly casting is abysmal. I mostly charter offshore. But I'd be glad to show you around some. Where are you now?"

She laughed and said, "Yeah, she mentioned that in her last email. I'm staying at a place in Marathon called Blue Water Resort. Do you know it?"

"I'm only fifteen miles by water from there. If I give you GPS coordinates, do you think you can find your way up here? I have some things I'm taking care of and can't get away for a little while."

She hesitated and I added, "I'm on my island with a number of friends. Julie, the daughter of the short, round guy you met at the *Rusty Anchor*, is one of them, and her fiancé. She's probably the best to talk to about flats fishing around here. Plus Charlie, who gave me the message that you were trying to contact me, her family and a few other friends. We could put two or three boats in the water and make a fishing party. We actually need to restock the freezer anyway."

"Okay," she said without further thought. "I can be there in about an hour."

"Perfect. I can get things wrapped up here and turn the rest over to my caretaker."

I gave her the GPS coordinates and told her the easiest way to get here and we said goodbye. I ended the call, stuck the phone in my pocket and went down to the cockpit. The others had already left the dock area, so I went up to the deck. Tony and Trent were at the aquaculture system and I went over to join them.

"You wanna do the honors?" Trent asked.

We opened the coolers and looked inside. Each one held about three gallons of water and hundreds of tiny crawfish. "That's a thousand?" Tony asked. "Man, I'd hate to have the job of counting those little things out."

"The female carries the eggs under her tail like a lobster," Trent said. "When they first hatch, they cling to her swimmers for the first week or so. These are about three weeks old."

I picked up the first cooler and slowly poured them into the far end of the huge tank. They disappeared instantly. "Go ahead, Carl. Dump the others in." Trent picked up the second cooler and slowly poured the contents in.

"Right now they have full run of the tank," he said. "The mesh between the sections is small enough for them to go anywhere and the cage over the skimmer to the filters is so fine they can't get sucked in. As they get bigger, they won't be able to get through to this end. We'll have to move a few that get stuck on the wrong side so when we have babies later on, they'll be safe from cannibalism."

Julie and Deuce came over and Julie looked into the tank. "I don't see any."

"They're barely an eighth of an inch long," I said. "They disappeared as soon as they hit the water. Either of you have plans for the day?"

"Why?" Deuce asked.

"That lady from the school Alex started is in town and wants to do some flats fishing. Thought we could have some fun and stock up our fresh fish supply. She's on her way up here now."

"Sounds like fun," Julie said. "A couple of the guides were talking about how reds and snook were being taken in the flats over around Raccoon Key."

"Yeah, it does," Deuce said. "We probably won't have any news on Smith until this evening, anyway."

We spent the next thirty minutes getting my two skiffs out and tied off to the pier in front of the house, stocking the coolers with drinks, checking rods and reels, and putting together some lunch. Tony and Dawson said they'd stay and do some more planting. Charlie had brought back seeds for a number of different herbs, plus spinach, lettuce, green beans, and broccoli.

Deuce and I walked to the bunkhouse to check with Chyrel. Along the way, we stopped at the Trents'. Carl was busy installing windows on the west side of the little house while Charlie was on the porch, watching the kids gather clams in the shallows and getting splashed by Pescador. Those two kids were becoming great little providers.

"Carl, you and Charlie want to go fishing?" I asked. "Tony, Jeremy and Chyrel are staying, along with Pescador. The kids'll be fine."

Charlie perked up at the idea of going fishing, but Carl looked a little apprehensive so I added, “The kids can help Tony plant. He’ll keep a sharp eye on them.”

“Okay,” he said. “The freezer’s running low. Who all’s going?”

“The two of you in one skiff, Deuce and Julie in another and a guest will be arriving shortly and I’ll join her in the third. We should be able to fill the freezer in a few hours.”

My thinking was that since Deuce and I weren’t very good at fly casting, and Charlie preferred bait casting, that’d put one fly rod and one bait rod in each boat.

“We’ll shove off in about thirty minutes,” I said. “The boats are loaded and ready.”

Deuce and I walked over to the bunkhouse to see Chyrel. She said that Kumar had emailed minutes earlier, saying that they were on the ground in Yemen, waiting for the chopper. He said they should be in Djibouti in four hours and would send another email upon arrival. We told her we were going out to catch some fish to stock the freezer and should be back by midafternoon.

“Make sure to take your satphone,” she told Deuce.

Walking back across the clearing, we heard an approaching outboard. That reminded me of something, “Hey, how did Parker get here?” I asked.

“A small inflatable, with an electric trolling motor,” he replied. “I’m sure there’s a powerboat stashed on an island somewhere around here. Probably a rental.”

We got to the dock, where Julie was helping Cindy tie off her rental skiff. It was one of Skeeter’s Mavericks. Cindy looked to be in her early thirties, not much older than Julie. She had shoulder-length brown hair, streaked by

the sun. She was shorter than I thought she'd be somehow. About five foot four inches tall and a hundred and thirty pounds.

She stepped to the dock and said, "You must be Jesse," extending her hand.

"I am," I said, taking her firm grip. "This is Julie and Deuce. Another couple that live here will be joining us in a few minutes."

"Alex emailed me and told me about this place, just before she died. She said she looked forward to showing it to me one day."

"We have a few minutes," I said. "Come on up to the deck and I'll give you the bird's-eye tour."

We went up to the rear deck and I pointed out all the features that could be seen from there, which was pretty much the whole island.

"I didn't expect a whole community. Alex said it was very secluded and you lived here alone."

"I did. After losing Alex, I needed people around," I lied.

The Trents came up the steps, with the kids, Tony, Dawson, and Pescador, and I introduced them all to Cindy. Charlie told the kids to be good and help Mister Tony. They started down the back steps, holding hands. As we started to leave Pescador barked once.

"No," I said. "You can go next time. Stay here and keep an eye on the kids." He turned and trotted after the kids.

"Alex mentioned him in her emails, too. She said he was the smartest dog she'd ever encountered."

"Sometimes I think he's an alien from a far more advanced planet," I said as we started down the front steps.

Five minutes later, all three boats idled out the channel and headed south. I led the way, piloting Cindy's rent-

al, and turned west between the Water Keys, with Julie at the helm of Alex's skiff and Trent following behind in my skiff. Before the north end of Raccoon Key, I turned south to avoid the shallows on the north end of the island and circled around it, into a natural channel, and headed northwest. A few minutes later, we approached Crane Key and I slowed down. The channel spread out wide here and just ahead were the shallows known as Crane Key Mangrove.

I brought the skiff down off plane and shifted to neutral as the other two boats drifted up on either side. Cindy looked over the gunwale and said, "How deep is it here?"

Her boat didn't have a depth sounder. "It's probably ten feet," I replied. "A few holes might be fifteen."

"Really? I've never seen water so clear. I can make out every detail on the bottom."

"We'll spread out here," I said. "To the north where those mangroves are is a shelf where the bottom rises from seven or eight feet to less than a foot. There'll be snapper, grunts, and a few grouper and snook." Pointing toward the mangroves, I added, "Up on those flats, Cindy, we might be able to put you on some bonefish. No good to eat, but a real challenge to catch."

"We'll go west to the channel markers," Charlie said. "I got some good-sized grouper there last week."

I pointed to the northeast and said, "Over there's another dropoff, Julie, north and east of Crane Key there. You and Deuce can wade the sandbar between the two dropoffs and you're sure to get snapper and maybe even a snook or two."

The other two boats started up and headed off in both directions. In the stillness, Cindy opened her fly rod case

and said, "Alex told me about catching bonefish and how difficult they were. She called them gray ghosts and said they were real easy to spook."

"They are, but that's not the challenging part. They have a bony palate, so a barbed hook is useless. Once you hook one, you have to constantly keep pressure on them to keep them from throwing the hook out. Want to give it a shot?"

"Yeah, sounds like fun."

"Go on up to the casting deck. I'll pole us toward that little bay area ahead. They scavenge on the bottom in just a few inches of water. You can usually see their dorsal and tail fins sticking out."

I got the pole from its mount on the starboard gunwale and stepped up to the poling platform above the outboard. A few pushes had us up on the shallows and I scanned the area ahead, but didn't see anything.

I pushed a couple more times with the pole, heading deeper into the little bay. Cindy pointed toward the mangroves on the left, and sure enough there were three bonefish tailing in the shadows.

I whispered just loud enough for her to hear, "Tease them with a couple of light rolls a few feet ahead of them."

She stripped line from the reel and started her cast. Her form reminded me of Alex. She'd tried several times to teach me her technique, but I never could get it. I'd practiced after she was killed and got better, but nowhere near as good as her. After a couple of casts, not letting the fly touch the water, she had the distance and gently let the fly fall into the water about three feet ahead of the lead bonefish. Before the line settled into the water, she

whipped the rod back to her side, the line arcing behind her and then whipped it forward again, the fly touching the water less than a foot in front of the fish.

The lead bonefish exploded on the fly and the fight was on. It didn't last long, though. The fish charged to the left, stripping line, then turned and came straight toward the boat, threw the hook and disappeared.

"Amazing," Cindy whispered, not the least bit disappointed. "Very strong and smart fish." She reeled in her line and I poled slowly to the east, knowing that those three were long gone. I spotted another one near the other side of the bay and pointed toward it.

"He's likely to do the same thing," I whispered. "Be ready for the charge."

Again, she stripped out line and started her cast. When the distance was right, she let the fly barely touch the water a foot ahead of the big fish, before whipping it back up again. She did the same thing again, teasing it. On the third cast, the bonefish took the fly just as it touched the water. This time, she was ready and when the fish charged, she stripped line furiously, while lifting the rod tip. It turned and charged the opposite way, taking a good thirty feet of line before turning toward the boat again. Cindy learned fast and within five minutes had tired the fish and brought it alongside.

"There's a camera in my fly rod case. Would you mind?"

As she lifted the fish from the water, I got her camera out and took two pictures of her with her first bonefish. She got down on her knees and gently lowered the fish into the water. Holding it under the belly, she faced it into the light current to allow water into its mouth and

across its gills. A moment later, with a shake of its tail, it was gone.

Cindy stood up, wiped her hands on her pants and said, "I'm going to send that to my fiancé. He works overseas. Now I see why Alex loved this place. I just know a school here will be successful."

"You knew her long?" I asked.

"We grew up together. She was a country girl and I was a city girl. We met one weekend when my parents took us camping on the Columbia River and hit it off right away even though she was a couple years older than me. She taught me to fish and just about everything I know about the outdoors, I learned a lot from her. I was sad to see her leave, but now I can see why she did."

"Want to catch another one?" I asked.

"We're supposed to be filling your freezer," she replied. "What exactly is a grunt?"

I laughed and said, "I'll let you figure that out yourself. They're not very big and eat just about anything you throw in front of them. But nothing's better in a pan."

For the next hour we fished for grunts and caught about thirty, along with three red snappers, a marbled grouper and a good-sized pompano. She was amazed at the fight the pompano put up for its size. When Cindy landed the first grunt, it started making its usual grunting noise, grinding its teeth. She laughed and said, "Yeah, now I get it. Not much of a fighter, though."

"That's why we like 'em. That and they're really tasty."

To the east, I heard the familiar sound of Alex's skiff starting up. She'd bought it a few days before we got married and it had a huge 300-horse Mercury outboard on it. I debated selling it, but decided to keep it and swapped

the engine with the 250-horsepower Yamaha that was on the Grady-White.

When I looked to the east, I saw the skiff leap up onto plane and come roaring toward us. A minute later, Julie pulled back on the throttle and turned broadside. Julie and Deuce both had anxious looks on their faces.

"Chyrel called. We need to get back to the island," Deuce said.

"What happened?"

"Smith disappeared," he replied.

"Y'all go ahead. I'll go over and let the Trents know we're leaving." Julie mashed the throttle and the little Maverick jumped up on plane again, heading south.

"Who is Smith?" Cindy asked.

"I'm sorry, Cindy. I can't tell you that. And I'm doubly sorry that we have to cut this short."

I sat down and started the outboard as she broke down her rod and put it in the case. When she was seated I put the boat in gear, brought it up on plane and headed southwest, toward Cudjoe Channel, where the Trents were anchored up. I came up slowly and cut the engine before I got close.

"I have to get back, Carl," I said when we were still twenty feet away. "Deuce and Julie already left. Something's come up."

Trent nodded and said, "We'll stay a little longer unless you need me. The fish box is nearly full."

"Nothing for you to do," I said. "Head back when you're ready." I let the skiff drift southward with the current until we were fifty yards away, then restarted the outboard and headed back.

"In Alex's last email, she mentioned you might be going to work with a government agency. Deuce too?"

I looked at her and said, "He's kind of my boss, but I really shouldn't say anything more."

"I understand," she said. "My fiancé, Hans, works for the government and can't talk about a lot of what he does, even though he's only a low-level clerk at an embassy in northern Africa. Thanks for bringing me out here. You were wrong about one thing, though."

"What's that?"

"A good guide doesn't necessarily have to be a good fly fisherman. You know the water and you know the fish. You're a great flats guide." I smiled and thanked her.

A few minutes later, we passed through the Water Keys into Harbor Channel and made the turn up to my house. I brought the skiff down off plane and idled up to the pier. Cindy tied off the bow line and I reached over and tied off the stern line.

"You're welcome to stay for supper," I said as we climbed out of the boat. "Charlie is used to cooking for a lot of people."

"Thanks," she replied. "But the sun's getting low. I should head back before it gets dark."

"There's plenty of room here if you want to stay the night. You can stay in the guest cabin of my boat. Plenty of fishing in the morning." Why I wanted her to stay, I couldn't say. Maybe it was just the connection to Alex.

"Well, if you're sure I won't be in the way."

"Some of us might be a little busy, but by sunset things should cool down. There's a shower and a washer and dryer aboard and I'm sure we can come up with some clean clothes."

"I always bring a change of clothes when I go out on a boat, along with anything else that I might need if I get stuck overnight."

"Smart thing to do," I said. "Just go through that door at the bottom of the steps. You'll find the *Revenge* is pretty comfortable and it's unlocked. Guest cabin is to port, through the salon and the head is across the companionway. I hate to be rude, but I need to check on some things. There's two tables at the far side of the clearing. That's where we usually congregate. See you shortly."

I left her to get her gear out of the skiff and trotted to the bunkhouse. I saw Tony and Pescador with the kids near the aquaculture tanks and stopped to tell him we had a guest. He said that Dawson had gone snorkeling for stone crab and slipper lobster. It's not as common in the Keys as the spiny lobster, but there's no season, so they can be caught year round.

When I got to the bunkhouse, Deuce was in a video conference with both Kumar and Stockwell. Kumar was explaining that when they'd arrived in Djibouti, they'd gone straight to the CIA station house, but the agent on duty had said that Smith had left at noon and hadn't come back. He was supposed to meet with two other field operatives and had failed to cancel the meet. His cell phone was on his desk. "From what the Assistant Station Chief said, he just vanished into thin air," Kumar said.

"That's not good," Stockwell said. "Djibouti can be a dangerous place. But leaving his cell phone probably means he found out that his hit men failed and he's running."

"Deuce," Chyrel said, sitting at another keyboard. "Sorry, but I just found something important. I placed a sur-

veillance code on Smith's Swiss account and just got a hit. But, it's an hour old. He transferred two point five million dollars."

"Transferred it where?" Deuce and Stockwell asked at the same time.

"I'm still trying to trace it, but not having very much luck. He apparently had a sophisticated transfer program written that moved it from one account to another all over the world. It appeared and disappeared in more than forty accounts in a matter of microseconds and then it just disappeared. No way to tell which one it's currently in, without manually hacking each one to see. Wherever it is, he can make a phone call and transfer it securely."

"And that happened an hour ago?" Deuce asked.

"Exactly when we landed here in Djibouti," Kumar said. "What do you want us to do here?"

"Somehow he found out and he's got a big head start," Stockwell said. "He's not in the country anymore. Deuce, make arrangements to get them back home. I'm going to send a few more of the team members down there."

"Roger that," Deuce said and Stockwell's screen went blank. "Kumar, Chyrel will send you instructions for extraction shortly."

"Make it a few hours from now, at least," came Art's voice over the feed. "It's after midnight here and we haven't slept in sixteen hours."

"Get some rest, then," Deuce said and the screen went blank. Deuce turned to Chyrel and said, "Find a flight out of Djibouti for them around local sunrise."

Deuce and I walked out to the tables in front of the bunkhouses and sat down. I reached over and pulled a

cold Red Stripe from the cooler. "Beer?" I asked. He took it and I grabbed another.

"I'm going to have to postpone the wedding," Deuce sighed.

I looked at him, surprised. "Like hell you will. Jules doesn't want anything fancy, but I can tell you for sure she's already made a lot of arrangements that can't be undone. You're getting married in less than a week, man."

He looked over at me and said, "With Smith on the loose, it's not a good idea."

"Deuce, describe the guest list that will be sitting on the groom's side."

He thought for a moment and grinned. "I see your point. A bunch of fishermen and divers on one side, door kickers and snake eaters on the other."

I held up my beer and he clinked the neck with his. "If it makes you feel better, we'll all come armed. What caliber do you think will go best with my eighties leisure suit?"

He chuckled at that as Julie and Cindy came across the clearing. "I think we'll stay here a few days."

"Now you're talking," I said. "Jeremy and Tony are getting tired of each other. Maybe Stockwell will send Hinkle and Mitchel down to spice things up a bit."

He laughed again as we stood up, and said, "Now I'm thinking you were serious about the leisure suit."

As the sun began its descent to the horizon, Trent lit the grill in the big stone fireplace. Charlie brought out a huge platter of fish fillets, and Dawson returned with eight good-sized slipper lobster and a bucket half-full of stone crab claws. Trent had set three traps for stone crabs in the shallows west of the pier a few days earlier. We sat

down to a nice supper and sat around talking about fishing as the sun began to set.

Just before dark, I heard my phone chirp. I'd completely forgotten I still had it in my pocket. When I pulled it out, I saw that it was a Keys number and answered it.

"Jesse, this is Jared. Sorry to bother you so late."

"No bother. Just sitting around telling sea stories with some friends. What's up?"

"I got canned. Went in this evening to tell the boss that next Friday would be my last day and he fired me."

"That sucks. You have enough to hold you over until next week?"

"Barely," he said. I could tell there was something else bothering him. I didn't say anything, just let him get to it in his own time. "I also got tossed from my apartment. The owner came into town unexpectedly and said he'd sold the place. He's moving all his stuff out now. It's a furnished apartment over the garage and everything I own will fit in a sea bag, with room to spare. I guess I can ask Dad if I can crash with him for a few days."

"Do you have a car?"

"No, I haven't really needed one in a year."

"Call Lawrence," I said. "Tell him to bring you to Old Wooden Bridge Guest Cottages, just before the bridge to No Name Key. I'll pick you up at their marina in an hour. You're welcome to stay here on the island until we leave for DC. I've got plenty of room."

"You'd do that?"

"Hell, I'll put you to work if it makes you feel better."

He laughed and said, "Yeah, I'd like that."

"See you in an hour," I said and ended the call.

"Williams?" Deuce asked.

"Yeah, his boss fired him when he gave notice. He can stay in the bunkhouse with Jeremy and Tony."

"Who is this guy?" Tony asked.

"A Marine I'm trying to help get back on his feet," I said. "Got a raw deal from our friend Jason Smith a couple of years ago."

"Well, any friend of yours," Tony said, lifting his beer.

Thirty minutes later, I was skimming across the shallows between Annette Key and the northern tip of Big Pine Key, dodging the really skinny water along The Grasses. Another five minutes later, I was entering the marina at the Guest Cottages. I didn't see Lawrence's big black Ford in the parking lot, so I tied off and walked up to the boat ramp on Bogie Drive. I didn't have to wait long before Lawrence pulled over to the curb, with his window down. As Jared opened the passenger door to get out, I slipped Lawrence a couple of twenties.

"Evenin', Cap'n," Lawrence said.

"This guy give you any trouble, Lawrence?"

He laughed and said, "Nutin I couldn't handle, sar."

"I appreciate this, Gunny," Jared said as he came around the hood, pulling his wallet out.

"The fare's covered," I said. "You ever swing a hammer?"

"Sure. You building something?"

"I have a few projects going on. You can work it off. Boats over at the dock there." Then I turned to Lawrence, shook his hand and thanked him.

Jared and I walked over to the dock and stepped into my skiff. "Where do you live exactly?" he asked.

"A little island ten miles north of here," I replied. "You'll make eleven people on the island now, might be a

few more later on. Hope you don't mind sharing a bunkhouse with a couple of Squids."

I started the outboard and idled out into Bogie Channel and turned north under the bridge. Once clear of the bridge, I brought the Maverick up on plane and threaded my way back home, arriving there twenty minutes later. I clicked the unlock button on the key fob, and the east side door started opening slowly and the light inside came on. I turned the skiff around and backed it under the house, between the Grady and the *Cazador*.

"Damn!" Jared exclaimed. "All these boats yours?"

"All but the Grady-White there. It belongs to my island caretakers. The Cigarette and the Winter here were confiscated in a drug bust."

"Confiscated? So how is it you have them?"

"I work for the government sometimes. Most of the people here tonight do also. I'll make a deal with you. Give me a week of hard work and I'll pay you a thousand dollars. That should tide you over until you get to Lejeune."

"A thousand bucks? Hell, who do I have to kill?"

CHAPTER TWELVE:

Camaraderie

Jared and I walked across the clearing toward the tables on the north side of the island. The others were still sitting around drinking beer, but someone had started a campfire at the northeast side of the clearing. Probably to keep the mosquitoes away.

"You own this whole island?" Jared asked.

"Yeah," I replied. "I bought it about six years ago and have been improving it ever since. That little house to the west is my caretakers' home. That's where you'll be working. First thing in the morning, we're going to pick up appliances and fixtures."

As we approached the group, Deuce stood up and came out to meet us. "Hi, Jared. I'm Deuce Livingston. I'm a friend of your dad's."

The two shook hands, then Deuce turned to me. "We're going to have visitors in about twenty minutes. Tony, Carl, and Jeremy are lighting three more fires."

Signal fires, I thought. So the chopper could see which way the wind was blowing in the dark. "We'll need a couple of bright flashlights," I said.

"Already got 'em," Deuce replied as two whooshing sounds came from the southeast and southwest sides of the clearing at nearly the same time. Seconds later, a third fire roared to life on the northwest side. "Tony and Jeremy have them. Wind's out of the east."

"This is a freaking LZ!" Jared exclaimed.

"Yeah," I replied. "Looks like we're going to have a party tonight. Come on over to the tables and I'll introduce you to the others."

We walked over to where the others were, as Tony and Dawson joined us. I said, "Everyone, this is Marine Corporal Jared Williams. Jared, you already met Commander Livingston. This is his fiancée, Coast Guard Petty Officer Julie Thurman. These two guys are Navy Special Warfare Operator Tony Jacobs and Coast Guard Petty Officer Jeremy Dawson. That's my caretaker, Carl Trent and this is Cindy Saturday."

"Nice to meet you all," he said, shaking hands all around. Then he asked me, "I thought you said eleven?"

"Carl's wife is putting their kids to bed and Chyrel Koshinski, our CIA tech guru, is monitoring communications in the bunkhouse."

"You're all military and government?"

"Not me and Charlie," Carl said. "We just look after things."

"There's beer in the cooler," I said. "And probably some stone crab claws in the pot on the stove over there. Help yourself." I could hear the whumping sound of an ap-

proaching helicopter. "Tony, you and Jeremy come with me."

The three of us walked over to the east side of the clearing, where I stood close to the tree line. I positioned Tony and Jeremy about ten feet from me at angles, so their flashlights wouldn't blind me.

The chopper flew over slowly, coming out of the northeast. He noticed our fires and turned west, moving out over the water. Then he turned and came back over the trees on the west side and I said, "Hit the lights." Both flashlights came on, illuminating me clearly for the pilot to see. I spread my arms wide, then moved my forearms up and back out to the side, signaling him forward. When he was nearly over the center, I stopped, keeping both arms fully extended out to my sides and he came to a hover. I then moved my arms downward and he began descending. When he made contact with the ground, I brought my arms all the way down and crossed them, then signaled him to cut the engine.

As the rotor blades started to slow, I heard some familiar voices. The three of us walked toward the chopper and Deuce joined us, with Jared. Deuce made the introductions this time. "Guys, this is Corporal Jared Williams. Jared, meet fellow Marines Staff Sergeant Scott Grayson and Sergeant Jeremiah Simpson. These other two are Special Warfare Operator First Class Donnie Hinkle and Special Warfare Operator Third Class Glenn Mitchel."

Jared shook hands with the four men and Hinkle, the Australian, said, "Another bloody Jarhead?"

"Go put your gear in the bunkhouse, Hinkle," I said, "before I thump your ass."

Chyrel came out of the newly redesigned bunkhouse as we all walked over to the tables and I introduced her to Jeremy. "Deuce, the Colonel said for the chopper to spend the night and go back tomorrow. A storm is approaching Homestead. I checked it out, it won't bother us here."

Tony and Dawson doused the two southern fires and Carl doused the one on the west side of the bunkhouses. I had them gather more firewood for the last fire, to ward off mosquitoes. Carl went to the western bunkhouse to turn in, and Deuce and Julie headed to the main house.

Before he left, Deuce said, "Wake me about zero two hundred."

"I will," I said. "We'll let the others get some rest. Tomorrow you can assign watches."

The chopper pilot said he had a hammock he was going to string up in the back of the chopper and headed that way.

"I think I'll turn in, also," Cindy said. "Will there be a chance to do some fishing in the morning?"

"Sure," I said. "I don't see why not."

"Good night, then," she said and headed to the *Revenge*. I walked with her, so I could get a few cases of beer from the pantry under the house. "Some of your friends look pretty scary," she said. "Is there anything I should know about?"

"Scary to the wrong people," I said. "These are the good guys. You can sleep sound tonight. You've never been safer in your life."

I carried three cases of beer back to the group of men standing and sitting around the fire. As I walked past the door to the house, Deuce stepped out and handed me a thermos and a mug.

"See you at zero two hundred," he said and went back inside.

When I got back to the group, Chyrel said she was going back inside to monitor the storm and would turn in soon. Carl brought out a second large cooler full of ice, anticipating we might need it, and I put the warm Red Stripe bottles in it. The other one still held a case and I carried it over to the fire. Ice was a luxury out here, but Carl had a small chest freezer we used to keep ice in and little else.

"Beer light's lit, gentlemen," I said.

I knew what would happen next as everyone reached into the cooler. It happens all over the world, whenever military people meet up.

"So, Jared," Grayson said. "What's your MOS?"

"Was," he corrected. "Maybe again soon. I was oh three seventeen. You?"

MOS is the acronym for Military Occupational Specialty. Almost always the first question two military people ask when they meet. That, and 'Where are you from?'

Grayson and Simpson looked over at me, then back at Jared. "Sniper, huh? Germ and me are eighty twenty-four, Combat Divers. The two Squids there are SEAL snipers. Jacobs is a SEAL EOD specialist and Dawson is Coast Guard Maritime Enforcement, same as Julie. Where'd you serve?"

"Lejeune mostly," he replied. "Did two tours in Iraq. What about the Commander and you, Jesse?"

"Same as you," I replied.

"You going to join our little club here, mate?" Hinkle asked. "Seems we're already a mite heavy on long guns."

"He's going back to the Corps," I said. "For now, anyway."

"What about that other lady, Cindy?" Jared asked.

"Noncombatant," I said. "She's here on vacation from Oregon to do some fishing."

"So all you guys are some kind of special team with the government?"

"Department of Homeland Security," Mitchel said.

"Caribbean Counterterrorism Command," Simpson added. "Deuce is the team leader. He used to be Tony's SEAL Team CO. His boss is an Army Colonel. The Colonel's boss is the Secretary of Homeland Security, who answers to the President."

"Tight chain of command. Wait, terrorists in the Caribbean?" Jared asked.

"It's a growing threat," Simpson said. "That's why our team was created."

"So, the Commander is okay with first names?"

Tony took that one, knowing Deuce longer than anyone here. "When we're around other officers we call him Commander, but when he's with the team, he prefers Deuce. Real name's Russell Livingston, Junior."

"Deuce," Jared said. "I get it."

"Best officer I've ever known. He was just a Lieutenant when I met him. One of those officers that never had a problem learning from their noncoms. We had a Master Chief that took Deuce under his wing and brought out the natural leader. Always look for those kind of officers."

"You have any confirms while you were in Iraq?" Hinkle asked.

Jared looked at me and I nodded slightly. "Yeah," he said. "Eight on my first tour and four on my second."

"Blimey! What range, mate?"

"Nothing really long," he said. "About a thousand yards was the longest. Most were under six hundred."

"Damn," said Grayson. "That's near as long as the Gunny's shot in the Mog."

"Mogadishu?" Jared asked.

"Yeah," I said. "Ancient history."

"Maybe," Simpson said. "But it's still talked about today, thirteen years later. The Gunny here made a twelve-hundred-yard shot at a moving target. A warlord that was beating a kid. Stuff of legend."

"How come you got out, Jared?" Grayson asked.

That was the million-dollar question. I knew it would come up and wondered how Jared would handle it. He'd just lost the only person he could talk to about his demons. Now he was sitting by a fire in the middle of nowhere with seven others who each had their own demons to wrestle. In my experience, warriors were more at ease talking about their psychological problems around others that had the same.

He looked around the fire at the six men looking at him, firelight playing across their features. Then he looked at me. I could see the panic and fear in his eyes. I reached into the cooler and handed him another beer. He opened it and took a long pull on the bottle, then stared into the fire as his story came out in hushed sort of anguish. "I was on my second tour and just a few months away from reenlisting. Me and my spotter found a high-value target north of Ashraf, the Nine of Diamonds. This was almost two years ago. It was a pretty easy shot, a bit long at a lit-

tle over nine hundred yards and slightly downhill, but the air was dry and no wind at all."

Hinkle and Mitchel nodded, affirming that while it was a long shot, it was under ideal weather conditions. "The target was stationary. Sitting in a chair, reading. We got confirmation of identity and clearance to engage. A second after the round left the muzzle, his kid stepped in front of him. She was only eight years old." He said the next part with up, defiant. "I was accused of killing her intentionally by some CIA spook and got a dishonorable."

"Damn," Tony said. The others just stared at Jared.

After a moment, Hinkle, who was sitting closest to Jared, reached over and put a firm hand on the younger man's shoulder. "Not your fault, mate. Sometimes shit just happens."

There was a chorus of agreements and Hinkle added, "We look through that spyglass and we see everything. We can count the nose hairs sticking out of a bloke's nostrils. But it's tunnel vision, mate. We have the power of life and death over the dinks in the reticles. It's something we all have to carry. We can help ya carry it, mate."

Tony sat down cross-legged on the ground. "My second tour in Afghanistan," he started as he stared into the flames, "a kid walked up to me as I was dismantling an IED. Just came out of nowhere. The IED was already defused anyway, so I guess nobody thought it a problem. The kid had tears running down his cheeks. Couldn't have been more than eight or nine. He held out his hand and he had a grenade in it. I could see that the pin was already pulled. Without saying a word, he just dropped it in the hole with the IED. It was a one-five-five round, HE.

I was wearing an explosive suit and dove across a berm into a hole, while I shouted a warning. The grenade went off, setting off the artillery round. The kid's bloody sandals were left right where he was standing. There wasn't anything else, though. I don't think I'll ever forget the look on that kid's face." Tony looked across the fire at Jared, moisture in both their eyes.

"Your CIA spook brings us full circle, Jared," I said, changing the subject. "All of you are here tonight because of him."

Jared looked up at me quickly, followed by twelve more eyes. I continued, "It's been determined that the guy Jared was talking about used undue political and financial influence to have him court-martialed. He did that because Jared nearly beat him to death for insinuating he killed the girl on purpose. I'm taking Jared to DC to meet with the SecNav and have his dishonorable overturned. It's a done deal. He'll be back in uniform by next Monday. The CIA spook Jared beat up was none other than Jason Smith." As Jared continued to stare at me, all the others started talking at once, asking questions.

"Jared, after his assignment in Ashraf, Smith was tapped to head up and create a special team of highly skilled operators to counter a growing threat in the Caribbean. This team. Last winter he pissed off one too many people with his political ambitions and was replaced by an Army Colonel named Travis Stockwell. It was Stockwell that put the ball in motion to have your dishonorable overturned. With a little prodding from me, Deuce and Owen Tankersley."

"Owen 'They thought I knew where the mines were' Tankersley?" Grayson asked.

"Yeah, he's an old friend," I replied.

"Heavy hitter for an old friend, Gunny," Simpson chimed in with a chuckle. "The only active-duty Medal of Honor recipient in the Corps."

"Smith was transferred to Djibouti," I continued. "In the last twenty-four hours we learned that he'd hired two assassins to kill his wife to get her inheritance three years ago. He hired them again to kill me and Deuce yesterday and this morning. The one that tried yesterday is dead and the one that tried this morning is in Gitmo. Smith disappeared in Djibouti about eight hours ago."

Jared looked around at the group of warriors around him and came to the obvious conclusion. "You think he's coming here?"

"He might. Or he might hire another assassin. When he disappeared, he managed to get over two million dollars from his numbered account in Switzerland."

"Think we should set up a watch?" Hinkle asked.

"No, not tonight. He won't know his second assassin failed yet and it'll take him at least twenty-four hours to get here if he decides to make it personal."

"Why's he want you and the Commander dead?" Jared asked.

A couple of the guys laughed. Grayson said, "The Gunny and Mister Smith were like oil and water from day one."

"Last winter I was captured by a Hezbollah cell on an op in Cuba," Tony said. "If it wasn't for these guys here, especially Deuce and Jesse, Smith would have left me there. He wasn't very happy about their coming back for me, against his orders." Then he chuckled and held up his right hand, where he was missing the first joint of

his index and middle fingers. “Well, they came back for most of me anyway. Hezbollah kept these.”

Just then, the generator started up, startling the four new arrivals and Jared. “Relax, guys,” Tony said. “Just the generator charging the battery packs.”

“You have electricity here?” Hinkle asked.

“Newly installed,” I replied. “Charges a bank of thirty deep-cycle batteries running a large inverter.”

“What do you guys do for fun out here?” Jared asked.

“Mostly work,” I said. “And train. But there’s scuba, snorkeling, and fishing gear. With this many people here, everyone will have to pitch in to bring in enough to eat.”

We talked late into the night, telling sea stories. Hinkle and Mitchel seemed to be opening up more. When I’d first met them they were aloof and didn’t fraternize much with the other members of the team. Jared seemed to relax more as the night wore on. After midnight, Tony and Jeremy said they were going to turn in. The lights from Chyrel’s part of the bunkhouse were out. Jared said he was tired and asked where he’d be bunking.

“Come on,” Tony said. “I’ll show you. There’s six bunks left to choose from.”

After they turned in, Grayson said, “He’s having some problems adjusting, isn’t he?”

“Yeah,” I replied. “Nightmares sometimes. He had a friend in Key West, a Nam Vet that he could talk to. The guy killed himself a couple of days ago.”

“We’ll keep an eye on him, Gunny,” Simpson said.

“Yeah,” added Hinkle. “Bloke needs to have mates he can talk to that understand his fears.”

"Thanks, guys," I said. "I think just being out here, away from Key Weird, will be a help. Especially having a bunch of snake eaters around him."

"Let's turn in, G," Hinkle said to Mitchel. "I think I might want to try some fishing in the morning." Hinkle and Mitchel headed to the bunkhouse.

"You can crash too, Jesse," Grayson said. "Me and Germ will stand your watch. What time did Deuce tell you to wake him?"

I grinned at the big black man. "I said we didn't need a watch tonight."

Grayson was usually a very quiet man, slow to anger. At just under six feet and two hundred forty pounds of solid muscle, he didn't need to get angry to get his point across. Like most Marine Staff NCOs, he led by example.

"Yeah, we heard ya." Simpson grinned. "But we know how Deuce operates and you're cut from the same cloth." Simpson was taller than Grayson but a good forty pounds lighter. His coffee-colored skin and light-colored eyes spoke of mixed ancestry. "Besides, you came out here with three cases of beer and a thermos of coffee. We slept in this morning, Gunny. Go get some rest."

"Are you carrying?"

"Any time we leave Homestead," Grayson replied. "Hatch to hatch. Deuce's orders."

"Thanks," I said. "Wake Deuce at zero two hundred. He's in the main house. Won't take more than a light tap on the door. I'll be up at zero five."

Since there was the chance of rain, I figured I'd forego sleeping on the ground. So I picked up my bedroll and headed for the bunkhouse. A single twelve-volt light mounted to the ceiling was on, when I entered. I dropped

my bedroll on the first bunk by the door, unrolled it, removed the blanket and rolled the mat back up.

"Crashing with the troops, Jesse?" Hinkle asked from his bunk at the far end of the squad bay.

"Might rain tonight," I said by way of reply. "I gave Deuce and Julie the house and Cindy has the boat."

"Seems like a nice lady," Dawson said. "What's her story?"

"She was close to my late wife, back when she lived in Oregon. They started a sort of halfway house for troubled kids there. Taught 'em to fish and camp and stuff. She wants to start one here, too. So I offered to bankroll it."

"You got the coin to do something like that and you sleep on the ground?" Jared asked as he stretched out on the bunk across from Tony.

"Probably slept more nights on the ground or in a boat than in a house. You guys want me to douse this light?"

"Scott and Jeremiah are taking your watch, huh?" Tony said. "Yeah, kill the light."

I switched off the light and lay down on the bunk. I made a mental note to buy a couple more coffeemakers in the morning when we went into town. I was asleep within seconds.

My subconscious registered the sound of Grayson and Simpson quietly entering the bunkhouse, but I remained asleep. The snores of the seven men had no effect on my sleep, either.

I woke up completely aware. I quietly pulled back the blanket and slipped on my tee shirt and worn topsiders, then headed outside. The sun was just starting to tinge the eastern sky a dark purple.

"Coffee?" Deuce asked from the nearest table. I walked over and he poured a mug from a thermos. "I put on another pot."

"I'll pick up a commercial-sized coffeemaker when we go into town today." Pescador came trotting up to us from the direction of the main house. "Hey, boy, where've you been?"

He sat down and looked from me to Deuce, who said, "He stayed in the house last night. Guess he heard the weather report, but nothing came."

We sat and enjoyed our coffee, but all three of us were vigilant. The early morning hours are the best time to attack and both Deuce and I knew it. As the sky to the east lightened, our tension eased. A few minutes later, Jared and Tony came out of the bunkhouse, followed quickly by Hinkle and Mitchel.

"I'll go get some more mugs and refill the thermos," Deuce said, then headed toward the house.

The four men sat down at the table, Jared looking around, seeing the island in the light for the first time. "I don't suppose you have a shower on this island?" he asked.

I grinned. "Two, in fact. There's one up on the deck, fed by a cistern, and another that Carl just installed out on the end of the north dock. Neither is heated, but this time of year the water in the cistern is warm. We bathe in the sea and rinse the salt water off in the shower."

Jared noticed Pescador for the first time, who was now curled up next to the stone barbeque. "Where'd he come from? I don't remember seeing a dog last night."

"That's Pescador," Tony said. The dog lifted his head at the mention of his name. "Jesse found him last fall, after Hurricane Wilma, stranded on an island out here."

"Strange name," Hinkle said. "What's it mean, mate?"

"It's Spanish for fisherman," I said.

Jared looked puzzled and asked, "Why would you call him fisherman?"

I stood up and said, "Follow us and we'll show you." I headed toward the pier, jutting out behind the bunkhouses. Pescador trotted beside me, his tail wagging. The four men followed closely behind us.

When we got to the end of the dock, I looked down at Pescador and asked him, "Fish for breakfast?" He barked once and waited expectantly. "Go get it," I said and he ran back and forth along the tee at the end of the pier, then leaped into the water. Carl had built a small ramp down to the water for him, and a moment later he surfaced with a small snapper firmly in his mouth. He swam over to the ramp and then trotted up it, dropping the snapper at my feet.

"Crikey!" Hinkle exclaimed. "The bloody dog catches fish!"

"Unbelievable," Jared said.

"That's a word I used a lot when we first found him. We tried to find his owner. He's obviously well trained. Never found anyone that claimed him."

Charlie and the kids walked out onto the dock, all wearing bathing suits. The kids quickly went to Pescador and gave him a hug. "Breakfast will be ready in about thirty minutes, Jesse. We're just gonna get cleaned up real quick."

"No hurry, Charlie. You've met most of these guys. This is Dave's son, Jared."

"Pleased to meet you, ma'am," Jared said.

She shook hands with him, then she and the kids grabbed small bars of soap out of a closed box mounted on the end of the pier and jumped into the water. The kids squealed and yelled for Pescador, who was still sitting in front of the snapper, waiting.

"Eat first, then you can play," I said and he tore into the small fish, eating bones and all in just a few bites. When he finished, he ran and leaped into the water. We heard the chopper start up and a few minutes later it lifted above the trees and headed northeast.

"Come on," Tony said, peeling off his tee shirt and kicking off his sneakers. He removed a holstered Sig P226 and placed it on the shirt and shoes. As he grabbed a bar of soap from the box and jumped into the water, the others started peeling off shirts, shoes and side arms. In seconds all seven men were in the water, splashing and carrying on like the kids.

Cindy walked out onto the pier and asked what everyone was doing. "Bathing before breakfast," I said. "I was waiting for you to finish so I could grab a shower and some clean clothes from the boat."

I left her there to watch the action in the water and headed to the *Revenge* for a quick shower. Twenty minutes later, wearing clean shorts and a *Rusty Anchor* tee shirt, I went back down to the tables. The others were filing into the bunkhouse to change into dry clothes after rinsing off. Charlie and the kids must already have gone in the other bunkhouse.

Julie and Deuce joined me at the table. "What's the plan for the day?" Julie asked.

"Me, Tony, and Carl are going to the Home Depot to pick up the appliances for Carl's house. Dawson said he was going to do some more planting and Hinkle will probably take the others out fishing."

Chyrel joined us and said, "The Colonel's on video for you, Deuce."

Chyrel sat down with Julie and Cindy while Deuce and I headed into the bunkhouse. Deuce sat down at the desk facing the open laptop and said, "Good morning, Colonel."

"Are you ever gonna just call me Travis, Deuce?" he asked.

"What's up, Travis?" I asked.

"Hi, Jesse. Look, I'm sending Brent over to Miami's ICE office. Smith used to give instruction on disguise in his early years with the CIA, and Brent was in one of his classes. He has some ideas to give ICE, should Smith try to re-enter the States." Brent Shepherd is part of Deuce's team and came from the CIA. He speaks several languages and is the team's resident disguise specialist.

"Anything you can share?" Deuce asked.

"He said Smith put a lot of stock in prosthetics."

"You mean like fake legs?" I asked.

"No, like fake scars, moles, or other deformities. Anything that draws your attention away from the face. Brent said that Smith always taught that if you could draw people's attention to something else, they rarely remembered the face."

"Anything else?" Deuce asked.

"Yeah," Stockwell replied. "I think it'd be a good idea if the two of you split up. Just in case."

"I was thinking the same thing," I said. "Deuce and Julie have things to do in Marathon to get ready for Sunday, anyway."

Deuce looked up and asked, "What things?"

"Trust me, Deuce," Stockwell said. "She'll have a whole lot for you to do." I just grinned and nodded my agreement.

"Alright," Deuce said.

"And take a couple men with you," Stockwell added.

"I don't think that's really necessary, Colonel."

"Then consider it an order, Commander," Stockwell said with a sideways grin as the screen went blank.

I laughed and said, "I'm really starting to like that guy."

"Stuff it, Jesse."

"Besides, I know Tony wants to visit with Rufus and enjoy some more of his cooking. Take him and Grayson."

"Grayson?"

"Yeah," I said. "He can't possibly get enough calories up here eating fish. A guy that big needs beef."

When we went back outside, Tony, Jared, and Grayson were sitting at one table while the women were still talking excitedly at the other, apparently about the upcoming wedding. That reminded me of something.

"Deuce, come with me," I said. We walked across the clearing to the main house and went inside. I went into the bedroom, opened the bottom drawer of my small dresser and took out a small box. I carried it into the living room, where Deuce waited.

Handing him the box, I said, "I'm sure Rusty wants you guys to have these, but he'd never ask for them back."

He opened the little box and looked up in surprise. “These are the rings he gave you and Alex.”

“Yeah,” I said as he started to protest. “He shouldn’t have. They should be worn by you and Julie.”

He closed the box and extended his hand. “Thanks, man.”

“Don’t mention it,” I said, taking his hand. “Now, let’s get some breakfast so you and Julie can head off to pick out napkins and flowers and shit.”

Joining the group outside, which now included everyone but Trent’s kids and Pescador, we sat down to a breakfast of eggs, bacon, and pancakes. When Deuce showed Julie what I’d given them, she came over and gave me a huge hug.

After breakfast we split up. Cindy went fishing with Charlie in the Grady, while Hinkle, Mitchel, and Simpson took their snorkeling gear and borrowed spearguns from the gear locker under the house, then headed out to the southern pier to spearfish in Harbor Channel.

“Scott, you and Tony want to go to Marathon with me and Julie?” Deuce asked.

“Will there be meat?” he asked, causing Deuce and me to laugh.

“Yeah,” Tony answered. “Wait till you try old Rufus’s cooking.” Turning to Julie he asked, “Think he’ll have some of that bacon fish?”

She laughed and said, “If he doesn’t, Tony, we’ll go spearfishing and get you some.” When I first met Deuce, Tony, and Art, they were looking for me to take them to a reef to spread Deuce’s dad’s ashes. I’d recommended they try Rufus’s blackened hogfish and jokingly said it tasted just like bacon.

"Jared, how about you give Carl a hand with whatever he's got going on this morning?" I said. "Dawson and I can go to Big Pine to pick up the appliances."

"Sure thing," he said.

"We didn't know how many people were going to be here when Charlie bought groceries," Carl said, handing me a piece of paper. "She made this list for whoever went into town next, and here's the keys to my pickup at Wooden Bridge Marina. It's parked in front of Skeeter's barge."

Dawson and I took my skiff, and he waited at the dock while I went to the grocery store to fill Charlie's order. On the way, I called Doc to tell him we would be going to DC to meet with the President early on Saturday.

When I called Jackie to tell her, I managed to catch her between rounds. "About time you called," she said.

"Sorry, we've been real busy on the island. Are you busy Saturday?"

"My CO already told me. What's this about?"

"All I know is that the FBI wants to interview each of us and the President requested we come to the White House."

"Have you made airline reservations yet?" she asked.

"Better than that," I replied. "Stockwell is sending a Gulfstream. We'll leave at zero seven hundred and be at Andrews in three hours."

"Isn't Deuce and Julie's wedding on Sunday?"

"Stockwell assured us that we'll be back by sunset."

She had to go, so we said goodbye and I went into the grocery store. Charlie's list was long, as feeding twelve people takes a lot. It took me an hour to find everything and when I got back to the dock at Wooden Bridge, Daw-

son, the Home Depot truck driver, and his helper were just finishing loading the last of the appliances. When I saw the commercial-sized coffeemaker was when I realized I'd forgotten to pick one up. As usual, Charlie and Carl were a step ahead of me. Charlie didn't cut corners, just like I'd told her not to. Everything was top-of-the-line equipment and fixtures, from the double gas oven to the bathroom sink.

What I hadn't expected to see were fruit trees. There were two apple trees, five orange trees, three papaya trees, three banana trees, and my own favorite, two mango trees. They were large, some already bearing fruit, and each one was in its own thirty-gallon bucket. I hadn't even thought of fruit trees, but was very glad to see that either Carl or Charlie had.

It took another ten minutes to move the boxes of groceries from the back of Trent's pickup to the barge. I planned to take the barge all the way around to the north side of the island to make it easier to move the heavy equipment ashore. It only drew about eighteen inches of water, and with the heavy stuff loaded to the rear of amidships, the square bow could be nosed right up to the beach, next to the pier.

The barge only had an old fifty-horse Evinrude outboard, but it started instantly. It took well over an hour to get back to the island and docked on the north side, me piloting the barge and Dawson in the skiff. It was nearly noon when we started unloading. Charlie took charge, directing where everything was to be taken. With all of us working, we had it unloaded in an hour. Trent had everything ready in his house to hook the equipment up

and he and Jared started working on that, with Simpson helping.

Dawson and I worked on the aquaculture system, planting more and more seeds and small plants in places that Charlie had already marked. We worked straight through lunch and it was a blessing when Charlie brought us sandwiches. Hinkle and Mitchel had the hardest job. Digging the holes for the trees.

"I put stakes in the ground where the fruit trees will go," she'd told them. "Some by the main house, some by our house and some on the ends of the bunkhouses."

"You think they'll grow alright in this soil?" I asked.

"The only ones I'll have to baby will be the apple trees, but I love fresh apples. The others are native to sandy and salty soil. We can water them daily from the crawfish tank."

"You're the boss," I said and she smiled.

Dawson and I went back to work and by midafternoon had everything planted in the aquaculture system. Jared and Simpson joined us, helping to move the big trees to their spots and put them in the holes. By supper we had all fifteen trees planted and supported.

While we ate burgers from the grill, I set up a watch assignment. With six of us, we'd each be on ninety-minute rotations through the night, starting at twenty-one hundred. Each man coming off watch would remain outside as a quick reaction force during the next man's watch before turning in. That would give us one man alert and ready, and another man on hand until dawn.

Just after sunset, my satphone chirped. It was Deuce.

"Hey," I said. "How's the napkin selection going?"

"Stockwell was right about that," he replied. "She has a list of things we need to do in the next three days. Stockwell called."

I could tell by his voice it wasn't a social call. "What's the news?"

"Brent spent the day with ICE agents in Miami, reformatting their facial recognition software. Smith came through customs in La Guardia early this morning. Backtracking from there, they found that he flew from Saudi Arabia, to Turkmenistan, to Switzerland, to New York."

"He gained a lot of frequent flyer points. Did we have anyone at the bank in Switzerland?"

"Yeah, CIA. But they must have missed him. He made a wire transfer from a bank in the Caymans. Just over five million dollars. His disguise was just like Brent said it would be. A long scar on his cheek and something in his mouth to change his jaw line."

"Where'd he go from New York?" I asked, already knowing the answer.

"Rented a van from Enterprise about zero seven thirty. One way to Miami."

I thought about it a moment and said, "That's over twelve hundred miles of driving. What time did he leave the car rental?"

I could hear paper rustling. "He left there at zero eight hundred. Driving straight through with minimal stops, he could make it to Miami by noon tomorrow."

"He won't drive straight through. Not after a seven-thousand-mile flight over eight time zones," I said. "He won't make Miami until tomorrow night. How many days did he rent the van for?"

"It doesn't say."

"We need to find out," I said. "And why a van?"

There was a moment of silence, then Deuce said, "I need to find out how long he rented it for. I'll call you back."

Chyrel was listening to my one-sided conversation. "Did Deuce say what time he rented the van?"

"Yeah, zero seven thirty this morning."

"I'll get right on it," she said as she headed toward the bunkhouse.

"Hey," I called after her. When she turned around I said, "Let's have another look at that list of Stolski's associates, too." She gave me a thumbs up and disappeared into the bunkhouse.

"Whatcha thinkin', mate?" Hinkle asked.

"Why would a person rent a van and not a car?"

"To move a lot of people or stuff," Mitchel said. "But, if he bugged out of Djibouti in a hurry, he wouldn't be carrying a whole lot of luggage."

"He plans to pick something or someone up along the way," Jared said.

"I'm not likin' where you're thinkin', mate," Hinkle said.

"Me neither," I said as Chyrel came back out of the bunkhouse with a folder.

"He rented the van until next Monday," she said. "Not a passenger van either. A cargo van."

I flipped open the file, while the others looked over my shoulder. I scanned down the first page, then the second. On the third page, I found him. Joshua Lothrop. A bomb maker. Last known address was Baltimore.

Just then my phone chirped again. I answered it and said, "He has it until Monday right."

"Chyrel," Deuce said. "Figured she'd hack it faster than I could call and get it. Yeah, Monday."

"And it wasn't a passenger van, Deuce. It's a cargo van. Something more, on Stolski's list of associates is a guy in Baltimore by the name of Joshua Lothrop, a former explosives expert with the CIA, now a freelance bomb maker."

"Cargo van," he said, thinking out loud. "Bomb maker. Miami. Monday." I let him come to it and didn't say anything. Then in a whisper he asked, "The wedding?"

"Julies there with you?"

"Yeah."

"Okay, listen. Strategically, it'd be a great choke point. He knows the date and place of the wedding. He blames you and maybe me. Plus he can take out everyone else involved. He knows the whole team, including Stockwell, will be there."

"I need to get back up there," he said. "We need to get proactive and find him. We only have three days."

"Wait till morning," I said. "Nothing we can do tonight. I'll get with Stockwell, email him the information we have and bring him up to speed."

We said goodbye and I turned to Chyrel. "Get the Colonel on video conference and email him the information on the van and Lothrop. I'll be there in just a second."

She headed to the bunkhouse and I turned to Cindy next. "Sorry to ruin your fishing adventure, but we're going to be busy for the next few days."

"Is it safe here?" she asked in a very worried tone.

"Safer here than anywhere else," I said. "We'll have two men on watch all night."

Next I turned to Jared and said, "You're now on the team, temporarily. You okay with that?"

"Aye aye, Gunny!" he said a little too enthusiastically.

"Good. Come with me."

We walked across the clearing up the rear steps to the main house and down to the docks. "Come aboard," I said. "There's a few things we might need."

We went up through the salon and down to the forward stateroom. I knelt down and punched in the code to unlock the bunk and raised it up. I pulled out three boxes and handed them one by one to Jared. Then I pulled out one of the larger fly rod cases and lowered the bunk.

"You familiar with the Sig P226?" I asked.

"Yeah, Dad owns one and I've fired it many times."

I took one of the cases and opened it. Inside were a pair of holstered Sigs, four magazines, and a box of ammo. "Load those mags," I said, handing them to him along with one of the Sigs. I opened the fly rod case, pulled out my M40-A3 and attached the night scope to the rail. "I know you're familiar with this," I said.

"Damn straight. What the hell else do you have in there?"

"Just a few toys," I replied with a grin.

"What's in the other boxes?"

"Pulsar Edge headsets."

"Night vision?" he asked.

"Yeah, they come in real handy for night fishing."

As we walked back across the clearing, Jared said, "Thanks again for letting me stay here. It's good to be able to hang out with others, well, like me."

I glanced at him in the gathering gloom. He seemed a lot more relaxed than the other times I'd seen him in Key West. "Any problem sleeping last night?"

We walked a bit before he answered. "I've had a recurring dream just about every night. The nights I don't have that one, there's several others with the same theme. Bad dreams. I wake up in a sweat every night. But last night was the first good night's sleep I've had in two years. Why do you suppose that is?"

"Could just be the salt air. My guess is you're just more comfortable. Like you said, being around others like yourself, guys that have been fighting their own demons, it's good. Opening up and facing your own fears is better. That's what you and Pop did, right?"

He just nodded as we joined the others. I left him and the boxes on the table and went to the bunkhouse. "He'll be on in just a second," Chyrel said. "He was at a dinner party and had to find a quiet spot."

I sat down in front of the laptop and waited. A moment later, a screen opened and Stockwell's image appeared. "I just read the emails that Chyrel sent, Jesse. Where's Deuce?"

"He and Julie had some errands, but will be back here in the morning," I replied.

"Good. I agree with your assessment and I'll have the Feebs put out an APB on the van and check out Lothrop's place in Baltimore. I'll call you on your satphone within the hour."

I went back outside to the tables and less than an hour later, after most everyone had turned in, my phone chirped. It was Stockwell. "The Special Agent in Charge in Baltimore just called me," he said. "They raided Lo-

throp's house and took him into custody. When he realized he might be charged as a terrorist he sang like the proverbial canary."

"Smith was already gone, I assume?"

"Long gone. Lothrop admitted that he made a bomb for him, but said he had no idea it was for a domestic target. Smith arrived a little after zero nine hundred and left within a half hour."

"Tony's here with me, Colonel. I'm going to put you on speaker. What kind of bomb is it?"

"A really nasty one. Twelve pounds of homemade semtex, with no detection taggant added. It's a triangular-shaped charge roughly four inches on all three sides and two feet long. The semtex is inside a small drum twelve inches around and two feet tall. The rest of the space is filled with small finish nails, like those used in cabinet making."

Tony let out a low whistle and turned to Chyrel. "Do you have a calculator?" While she went to her gear box he asked Stockwell, "Did Lothrop say what type of semtex he made? There's a number of versions."

Chyrel handed him a calculator and he started working numbers quickly. Before Stockwell could find the answer in the fax from the SAIC, Tony said, "Never mind, Colonel. From the dimensions and weight, it's semtex ten. Pretty much what's manufactured today."

"Yeah, here it is," Stockwell said. "You're right, he said he manufactured it identical to semtex ten."

Tony continued as he worked the calculator again, "Without that taggant added it'll be hard for dogs to detect it. Semtex ten has an explosion heat of five thousand and thirty kilojoules per kilogram and a detonation ve-

locity of seventy-three hundred meters per second. Twelve pounds of that shit is equal to about twenty million foot-pounds of force. That can completely vaporize a concrete structure. A drum that size is about eleven gallons, minus the semtex, so you're looking at about a hundred pounds of flechettes. That'll kill anyone standing within two hundred feet. The whole thing is going to weigh at least a hundred and fifteen pounds. Not something you can throw."

"Not something you need a cargo van to haul either," I said.

"At least we know what it is and we know what he's driving," Stockwell said. "I'm sure the van will be found before he can get there. But I'm going to go ahead and mobilize the team. We're all coming Sunday anyway. Expect more people there by zero nine hundred and a detail will accompany you to DC on Saturday."

The screen went blank, so Tony and I joined Hinkle and Mitchel at the other table. They had the first watch. Hinkle already had the night vision headsets out of the box and was checking the battery levels.

The night was uneventful, as I figured it would be. The next morning, Deuce arrived early without Julie. She had a few things to do and would come up later in the day. I told Cindy she should probably head down to Marathon for the time being. I gave her the phone number for Pam Lamarre, the manager of the State Bank of the Florida Keys and a close friend. I'd instructed Pam months ago to form a board of trustees to take care of a large sum of money and create a college fund for the kids of local watermen. They'd also started work on finding the right lo-

cation for Alex and Cindy's school, with the help of some local real estate people.

At zero nine hundred, the now familiar 'whump whump' of a heavy chopper was heard approaching from the northeast. Ten minutes later, the Air Force TH-1 Iroquois helicopter had landed, disgorged eight more guests and taken off. This was just about everyone on Deuce's team, including Art and Kumar, who had just returned from Djibouti.

With this many people on the island, housing was becoming a bit of a problem. The Trents' house was almost complete, but still had a lot of finish work to be done. Trent took charge and as it turned out, a number of people on the team had some construction experience. Several members of the team were women, something I'd not taken into consideration when I built the bunkhouses. Not counting the Trents, Deuce, and Julie, we now had thirteen men and three women to house. I insisted Deuce and Julie stay in the main house.

Carl came up with a simple plan. The partition he'd put in the eastern bunkhouse to separate Chyrel's comm center from the living quarters would be moved so that the comm center would also include the first set of bunks on either side, nearest the office area. An added benefit was that I could put my hammock back outside. The eastern bunkhouse would then have room for the three women, Chyrel and two Miami Dade Police Officers, Charity Styles and Sherri Fallon. Charity is a martial arts expert and Sherri is an armorer.

That left eight bunks in the eastern bunkhouse. I assigned those to the four senior members of the team, something military people are used to. Scott Bond is a

Navy SEAL Lieutenant, and dive supervisor. Andrew Bourke is a Coast Guard Senior Chief Petty Officer and, like Julie and Dawson, a Maritime Enforcement Officer. Kumar, being an Army Sergeant First Class, made three and I made four. That left the western bunkhouse, with its twelve bunks for the remaining nine men.

By noon, the finishing touches were being put on the Trents' house and they started moving in. With everyone pitching in, it didn't take long and by midafternoon everyone had stowed their gear in their assigned places.

Everyone had brought their own side arms and Bond also brought earwigs for the whole team. We could now put two men on duty throughout the night who could be in constant communication with one another.

We sat down that evening to a meal of baked lasagna, fresh-baked bread and early broccoli from the aquaculture system. It was our first harvest and though there wasn't much of it, everyone got a small amount from the near fully grown plants we started.

Over supper, Art asked, "Do you really think you can grow enough to feed this many people?"

"Not right away," Trent responded. "But in a few more months we will."

Everyone pitched in and helped clean up after we ate. Then we broke up into smaller groups clustered around two campfires at opposite corners of the clearing. Jared and I wound up sitting with Deuce, Tony, Kumar, and Charity at the table. I dropped some fish in a bowl for Pescador and he waited for me to tell him to eat, as always.

"How'd you find Djibouti?" I asked Kumar with a grin.

"Went to the Red Sea and turned right," he joked right back. Then in a serious tone, he added, "It's changed since I was there last time. Ever been there?"

"Embassy duty in eighty-four," I replied. "When were you there?"

"About the same time. The people are poorer now. Poverty has a stranglehold on the whole region. Well, except for the politicians. They seem to be doing okay."

"So many people in such a desolate land," Tony said, shaking his head.

We were silent a moment, then Charity asked Jared if he was part of the team. "He is for the next couple of days," I said. "Then he's reenlisting in the Corps."

Once more, the same question is always asked. "What did you do in the Marines?" she asked.

"Infantry, ma'am," he replied and immediately his choice in terms. She was only a couple of years older than him. "Sorry, it's a habit. I'm a sniper. What did you do before joining this team?"

"Long story short, six years ago, I swam on the Olympic team," she responded. "After 9/11, I joined the Army, finished college, and flew a medevac chopper in Afghanistan. I was only there four months when my chopper was shot out of the sky and I was captured by the Taliban. I managed to get away a few days later and then spent six months in a hospital and another six in rehab before I was discharged. After I recovered, I joined Miami PD. I've been training in mixed martial arts since I was a kid and became an instructor with the force until I was asked to join this team."

"I never knew you were a prisoner of the Taliban," Kumar said softly.

"That's what the rehab was for. To learn to deal with the psychological trauma and learn to talk about it."

"Did they..." Jared started to ask.

"Rape me?" she said offhandedly. "Yes, several times a day, twenty-nine times in all. I learned to use that in martial arts. Trust me, if you get in the ring with me, padding or not, you will be bruised." She was grinning when she said this.

"Damn," Jared whispered. "Some of what I've learned here in the last two days makes what I experienced seem trivial."

"There's nothing trivial about what we've all experienced," Kumar said. "Everyone deals with psychological trauma in their own way. Some seek the counsel of a psychiatrist, others seek the counsel of their peers." Then with a chuckle and nodding toward Charity, he added, "And some kick the ever-living shit out of their sparring partners. How do you handle it, Jared?"

Just like the night before, Jared's eyes at first showed panic. Then he regained his composure and said, "I had a friend in Key West, a Nam Vet, and we talked. He died a few days ago."

"I'm sorry to hear that," Charity said. "You're not alone, though. There's lots of others that you can talk to about your experiences. Having been there, I wouldn't suggest psychiatry. Damn shrinks might have tons of diplomas, but they've never been in the shit. Group sessions, or like with your friend, one on one, is a lot more helpful. At least it has been for me."

"Thanks, ma'am, er, Charity."

Deuce stood up and said, “Julie should be out of the shower, I’m going to hit the rack. Did you already assign watch, Jesse?”

“Yeah,” I replied. “Everything’s covered.”

“And I’m not on it?”

“You will be tomorrow if you want,” I said. “We have more than enough people here now.”

“Good night, then,” he said and started across the clearing.

“Think I’ll turn in too,” Kumar said. “I have the midnight watch.”

“Me too,” I said. Then to Jared and Charity I said, “Don’t you kids stay up to late.”

As Kumar and I entered the bunkhouse, he asked, “Did you know about her being captured by the Taliban?”

“Yeah,” I said. “I was helping Julie with her boat boarding course outline the other day and read over everyone’s bios.”

“You put those two together on purpose, didn’t you?”

I nodded. “They’re both athletes, close in age, and they both could use a friend. I hope Jared can come to grips with what happened to him. Charity just might be the one that can help him.”

“You Jarheads aren’t as dumb as most would think,” he said with a grin, then turned to head for his bunk.

“Night, Kumar,” I said as I got ready to hit the rack. I stripped off my tee shirt, tucked my holstered Sig under the pillow, and slipped out of my deck shoes. Pescador made two turns on his poncho liner by my bunk and then plopped down. Laying back on the bunk, I was soon fast asleep.

Two hours later, the sound of the door opening woke me. "Tony's still on watch," Dawson whispered when I sat up. "Which bunk's Kumar's?"

"Go ahead and hit the rack, Jeremy. I'll wake him."

"No need," Kumar whispered.

I slipped into my boat shoes, pulled on my tee shirt from earlier, and took the night vision headset Dawson handed me. After my watch, I planned to get a hot shower aboard the *Revenge*. *Rank has its privileges*, I thought. Kumar and I slipped quietly through the door so as not to disturb Bond and Bourke. They'd have watch tomorrow night.

Outside, I unholstered my Sig, removed the magazine and ratcheted the slide, ensuring there wasn't a round in the chamber. I thumbed the decocker and heard the satisfying metallic click of the hammer dropping, but felt it to be sure, before reinserting the magazine and reholstering it. I put on the night vision headset Dawson had given me and stuck the earwig in and turned it on. I could see Tony headed toward us across the clearing. "You hear me okay, Tony?" I asked.

"Loud and clear," he replied.

"Same here," Kumar said.

When Kumar got the other headset from Tony, we split up and headed in opposite directions around the small two-acre clearing. "Wouldn't it be better if we were outside the tree line?" Kumar asked over the earwig.

"The only places you can walk without getting wet are in front of Carl's house and near the north pier," I replied. "With night vision, you can look through most of the mangroves to the water. Anyone trying to get through

will make noise. Pescador will pick up on that, if we miss it."

We walked the perimeter of the clearing from the northern pier to the main house and back again. I'd set up each watch for two hours, so as not to tire the team out. With eighteen team members on the island, we had more than enough to cover the night hours and alternate nights.

At zero one hundred I heard the sound of an outboard to the south. It wasn't unusual to hear boats out here at night, though. This one was moving slowly north, threading the narrow channel west of Howe Key.

"Sounds like a boat approaching," Kumar said.

"Not unusual up here. Late-night fishermen, sometimes drug runners who get lost."

A few minutes later, the boat slowed as it neared the entrance to my channel. Not good. "Kumar, head for the steps."

"Roger that."

A moment later, the outboard shut off. Pescador and I ran straight across the clearing and met Kumar at the bottom of the steps.

"Wait here and keep your eyes peeled to the north and watch Pescador," I whispered. "It might be a diversion." Then I pointed to the north end of the island and said to Pescador, "Watch the pier." He took off like he'd been shot from a cannon. I didn't have to watch to know he'd stop at the foot of the pier and sit down. I'd come to learn that he'd been very well trained to do a lot of things, and every day, it seemed, I discovered something new.

I went quietly up the steps and was halfway across the deck when I heard the unmistakable sound of a pole be-

ing taken out of its rack and then heard a huffing noise as someone stepped up onto a poling platform.

I stayed close to the wall of the house and drew my Sig. When I got to the door, it cracked open and I could see Deuce's silhouette standing just inside the door.

"Heard it approaching," he whispered. "Waited till I heard the deck planks creak."

"Someone in a flats boat at the entrance to the channel. They're poling this way."

"Take the lead," he said. "I can't see shit, but I have your big spotlight, if needed."

"Just let me know before you turn it on."

I edged to the corner of the house and Deuce crouched down and moved quickly to the far rail under the branches of the mangroves. From there, he moved along the railing to the corner. From where I stood, I could see the boat. A man was standing on the poling platform about halfway up my channel. Another man was sitting sideways on the casting platform near the bow.

"Deuce," I barely whispered as I removed the headset. "Hit the light, about halfway down the channel."

The super bright spotlight hit the water about ten feet in front of the boat and angled up, illuminating it in its blinding light. "That's far enough!" I shouted.

The man on the front screamed and lunged backward, falling off the casting platform into the boat. But it sounded like a woman's scream. The man on the poling platform dropped the pole and raised both hands high above his head.

"Jesse," he said. "It's me, Doc."

Once we got Doc and Nikki's skiff tied up to the south pier, we went up to the deck. I told Kumar everything was alright and I'd be back down in a few minutes.

"What the hell are you doing coming up here in the middle of the night, Doc?" I asked. "You came within a hair's breadth of getting shot. Both of you."

"Wouldn't be the first time today," Nikki said.

We sat down at the table on the rear deck and I asked, "What do you mean, not the first time?"

"Some guy took a shot at me this afternoon," Doc said. "While we were riding on the bike."

"Did you see who it was?" Deuce asked.

"I got a look at him," Nikki said. "Not much of one, but if I ever see him again, I'll know him."

"We spent the whole afternoon with the Key West Police," Doc said. "They were no help at all. Chalked it up to a rival biker gang. Hell, the closest thing to a gang we ride with is American Legion Riders and Patriot Guard."

"Bob thought it might have to do with what happened last Sunday out on the boat," Nikki said. "So we decided to come here. Even knowing where this place is, it still took us hours to find it."

Julie brought some coffee out and I headed back down to join Kumar, while Deuce brought them up to speed on the events since last weekend. I told Doc that he and Nikki could take the guest cabin on the *Revenge*. At the end of our watch, we woke Art Newman and Ralph Goodman for the next watch and filled them in on the new arrivals. Then I went up and joined Deuce and the others on the deck.

"I have an idea," I said.

"Yeah?" Deuce asked.

"Nikki said she'd recognize the guy if she ever saw him again, right? So far the whole cast of characters Smith has written into his little murder and espionage novel have come from Stolski's list of contacts. If Doc and Nikki's shooter isn't Smith himself, she might be able to pick him out of the bio pictures Chyrel has in the office."

"You're right, Jesse," Deuce said.

"Want me to go down and wake her up?" Julie asked.

"Yeah, none of us are going to be able to get to sleep until we know."

Julie started down the back steps but I stopped her. "Hang on, let me tell Art and Ralph you're coming. Oh, and have Chyrel print a picture of Smith, too."

I switched on my earwig and waited for it to boot up. Art and Goodman were talking about Jared and Charity. I said, "You guys know that anyone who turns on their earwig can hear you, right?"

"Sorry, Jesse," Art said. "What's up?"

"Julie's coming across the clearing to wake up Chyrel."

"She's already up. That's who we were talking to. Her and Charity."

"What's up, Jesse?" Chyrel asked.

"Julie's coming to pick up that list of Stolski's contacts. Could you also print a picture of Smith and put that with it?"

"Sure thing. I'll have it ready when she gets here."

I switched off the mic function but left the receiver on and said to Julie, "Go ahead, she's already up."

I sat down next to Deuce, across from Doc and Nikki. Although I'm not an eavesdropper by nature, I was curious. And I had warned them that others could hear. So, while we waited for Julie and drank coffee I listened in to

the conversation between our two watchers and the two women in the bunkhouse. Apparently, Jared and Charity had stayed up quite late and had gone out onto the pier to talk in private. She was curious to know more about him and had wakened Chyrel to tap into Art and Goodman's coms to ask them if they knew anything about him.

"What are you grinning about?" Doc asked.

"Huh?" I said. "Oh, nothing. Planted a seed earlier today and was just thinking about the roots that are starting to spread."

"You're taking that aquaculture stuff a little too serious, man," Deuce said.

Julie came up the steps and handed Deuce the file from Chyrel. I lit a tiki torch that was mounted at the corner of the rail to give more light.

Deuce opened the file and took a picture of Smith out, turned it around and showed it to Nikki. "This is Jason Smith."

"No, definitely not. Too old."

He took out the five pages of Stolski's known associates and placed them in front of Nikki. "Each of these pages has four or five short bios of guys that might be involved, along with a picture of each. Take a look and see if your shooter might be one of them."

She studied the pictures of each person carefully, skipping those that were ethnically disqualified. The shooter was white. On page four she stopped and pointed at a picture. "This is him."

"You're sure?" Deuce asked.

"Absolutely. It's him. Who is he?"

Deuce looked at the page and read the bio. "His name's Dimitri Darchevsky. A Russian national raised in Cali-

fornia since he was a toddler. He was recruited into the CIA out of UC, Berkeley, where he was a liberal arts major. He speaks English with a West Coast surfer accent and Russian with a Ukrainian accent. Posted in Kiev for a year with an embassy clerk's cover ID and went by the name Don Darnell, but he was actually a deep-cover operative. Left the CIA at the same time Stolski did and went into private security for a few Hollywood elites."

"The Agency seems to have a pretty high turnover rate with their spooks," I said.

"Not uncommon," Deuce said. "They're hired with a three-year obligation and a lot of them see that they can make more money outside the Agency with what they learn. Trouble is, it takes a lot more than three years to learn good tradecraft."

"So, if Darchevsky does security work for the stars, he's probably a high-dollar player. I don't see Alec Baldwin letting one of his security guys take time off just any old time."

"You're right. He'd have to be head of security and be able to turn things over to a subordinate for a few days, or low-level muscle that can quit without notice for a more lucrative offer. My guess is the former. He wouldn't be able to do that very often and still find work."

The conversation was still going on in my other ear and I switched the mic back on. "Chyrel, if you're not too tired, can you dig up everything you can on Dimitri Darchevsky?"

"Sure, Jesse," she said. "I'll have Char bring it up. She wants to talk to you, anyway."

"Thanks," I said, wondering what that was about. I switched the earwig completely off.

"If your Jason Smith hired this guy," Doc said, "why us? I never met the guy."

Deuce thought about it for a moment and frowned. "I really don't know. Maybe just to send a message. Maybe he has no idea we're on to him. By now he's bound to know his first assassin is dead. But there's no way he knows the second guy was caught and is in Gitmo being interrogated."

"You mean there was another attempt on the President?"

"We don't think the President was the target at all," I said. "We are. Me and Deuce. Maybe the whole team. Smith was pretty pissed that we went ahead into Cuba to get Tony out."

"Coming up!" Charity called from the bottom of the steps.

"At the table, Charity," Deuce said.

She quickly mounted the steps and handed Deuce another file, this one much thicker. "Got a minute, Jesse?" she asked.

"Yeah, guess I need another cup of joe and it looks like Deuce has some reading to do. Let's go inside."

We went inside the house and I poured another cup of coffee. "Care for a cup?" I asked.

"Sure, I'm not tired anyway. Black, please."

I got another mug, poured her a cup and carried it over to the little table in the corner. "Have a seat," I said.

"This is a nice little place here. Julie said you built it completely by yourself?"

"Every board, nail, and screw." I waited to let her gather her thoughts while I sipped my coffee.

"What do you know about Jared?" she finally asked.

"Quite a lot. Anything in particular you want to know?"

"He told me a lot about his time in the Marines, but I think he might have been a bit humble."

"Wouldn't surprise me," I said. "His former Battalion Sergeant Major is a good friend of mine. I asked him what kind of Marine he was and he said he was one of the best, an 'outstanding young leader,' he said. Otherwise, I wouldn't be going to bat for him. He got a raw deal and that's being fixed. My friend says he has a great future in the Corps."

"Do you know anything about his private life?"

"His dad's a good friend and a straight-up guy. His mom's a churchgoer and his brother's a Marine. A friend in Key West that used to work with him called him a 'mother hen' to his coworkers."

"Never married? Girlfriend?"

I smiled. The seed had taken root. "So, your interest is more than just as a possible team member, or about his problems with the past?"

"We sat out on the pier until just a little while ago watching the stars and talking. He opened up about what happened. That's a terrible guilt to have to carry around. I felt a connection, I guess."

A connection? Suddenly what happened with Doc and Nikki made me realize something. "Charity, I just thought of something and I need to talk to Deuce right now." Before she could say anything more, I jumped up and was out the door, pulling out my phone.

"Deuce," I said, crossing the deck. "Jackie lives in Key West."

I started to pull up her number but Julie stopped me. "You're only going to scare her, Jesse." Then she turned to

Deuce and said, "Do you think the Colonel can have the Shore Patrol from the station send someone over to her house, before Jesse scares the daylights out of her?"

"Good idea," Deuce said and pulled his own phone out. "Jesse, wait until we have security outside her house." I'm not what you'd call a real patient man. Charity came out of the house and sensed something was going on as I paced the deck.

Deuce punched a couple of buttons on his phone and after a second he said, "Sorry to wake you, Colonel. There's been a development." He told him what had happened with Doc and Nikki, gave him the short version on Darchevsky and relayed my concern about Jackie. Then he ended the call.

"He said he'll contact the station's CO and have Shore Patrol send two officers over. When they're outside, they'll call me direct. He said the safest thing to do would be for them to escort her to the Air Station and we can pick her up in the morning."

"Morning, hell," I said. "When I know she's safe, I'm taking the Cigarette to pick her up tonight."

Julie got up and came over to me. "Calm down, Jesse. Going down there in the middle of the night isn't smart and you know it. She'll be safe at the station and besides, even in the Cigarette it would take you nearly two hours to get there and back. And that's only if you don't hit something or run aground."

I paced some more. After several excruciating minutes, Deuce's phone chirped. He answered it, listened for a minute and said, "Okay, sit tight." Then looking up to me he said, "Go ahead and call her, they're parked outside the house and everything's quiet."

I pulled up her number and hit send. After the third ring she answered groggily. "Jackie, it's me, Jesse."

"Timezit," she mumbled.

I looked at my watch and said, "It's zero three hundred. Something's happened."

She was instantly awake, "What's wrong?"

"Someone took a shot at Doc Talbot and his wife. The shooter missed, but he's been identified as an associate of the man who tried to kill us out on the boat the other day."

"Oh my. Where are you?"

"I'm on the island. Look, there's a Shore Patrol car outside your house. I think you should go with them to the Air Station and stay there tonight. I'll pick you up in the morning."

There was a moment of silence and some rustling noise. "Yeah, I see them. It'll take me a minute to get dressed."

"Call me back when you're in the car, okay."

"Are you sure this is necessary?"

"The guy's a former CIA deep-cover operative and a Russian national. He's dangerous."

"Okay," she said. "I'll call you in a few minutes."

I ended the call and told Deuce, "Tell them she'll be out in five minutes."

He relayed the message and ended the call. Deuce handed me the complete file on Darchevsky and I sat down under the torch to read it while we waited. Some parts of it were redacted, even with Chyrel's ability to get information. He wasn't a simple flunky like the other two had been. This guy was the real deal, responsible for

at least five assassinations in Western Europe. He was probably the leader of the three-man team.

As if reading my thoughts, Deuce said, "My guess is that the other two guys worked for Darchevsky. Smith might have put them together, but this guy's the boss."

"Yeah, that was what I was thinking, too," I said. "We need to get this guy off the streets. Did Stockwell say anything about alerting local law enforcement?"

"He said for me to use my best judgment. I'll go down and have Chyrel put an APB out on him for all of south Florida."

Five minutes went by, then ten. Finally my phone chirped. When I answered it, Jackie was breathing hard and said in a rushed voice, "Jesse, there was a shooting. I'm fine, but one of the officers was hit. He'll probably be alright, I'm taking him into emergency surgery now. I can't talk, but I'll call you when I come out." The call ended.

"What's going on?" Charity asked. My face must have shown my reaction to the call.

"One of the officers was shot," I said. "Jackie's taking him into surgery now." First Deuce and me, then Doc and Nikki, and now Jackie. I felt a surge of anger rushing up from my gut. The slow burn turned white hot and my mind began moving faster, planning out the next series of events. I'd felt this way under fire in Somalia, Iraq, and Grenada. It sharpened everything. My vision, hearing, and sense of smell all became acute, along with my ability to think far ahead.

CHAPTER THIRTEEN: Invasion of Key West

I looked at my watch. It was almost zero four hundred. Time to sound reveille. "Deuce, I think it's time we stop letting Smith take the lead."

He stood up and I could see an equally forceful resolve in his eyes. "Charity," he said. "Go down and let Chyrel know I need a video comm link to Stockwell and ask him to patch in the Secretary and the head of the FBI. And tell Art to sound reveille in the bunkhouses, but be quiet so as not to disturb the Trents."

As she turned and headed down the steps, I said, "Deuce, we only have tomorrow to find this guy. Well, that's today, actually."

"I know," he said. "The good thing is, on Fridays everyone is coming into the Keys. We can have the Sheriff set up a roadblock in Key Largo to check out anyone going north and disguise it as a sobriety checkpoint."

"Doc," I said. "You and Nikki go down and crash in the boat. You can get at least a couple of hours sleep. Nothing's going to happen until sunrise."

Doc started to protest, but I insisted. Once they left, the three of us headed down to the bunkhouses. Tony and Sherri were already outside and Deuce motioned for him to join us. I stopped at the tables and lit the six torches around them before following Deuce into the women's quarters.

"The Colonel and Director Mueller are online," Chyrel said. "Secretary Chertoff will be on any second."

Deuce sat down in front of the laptop and said, "Good morning, Colonel. Good morning, Director. Sorry to bother you so early, but we've had two developments in the last hour that you both should be aware of."

Just as he finished speaking, a third window opened and Chertoff said gruffly, "What's this all about?"

"We've had two serious developments, sir," Deuce repeated.

Stockwell and Mueller both greeted the Secretary, and Deuce continued, "Yesterday afternoon in Key West an unknown assailant fired two shots at one of our team and his wife. He missed, but Talbot's wife got a good look at him and identified Dimitri Darchevsky as the shooter. You should all have his bio on your screen."

"You said two developments?" Mueller asked.

"Yes sir," Deuce continued, unflustered. "Thirty minutes ago, while two Shore Patrol Officers from NAS Boca Chica were picking up Commander Burdick, who was with us last weekend when the President was attacked, shots were fired, wounding one of the officers. We believe it to be Darchevsky."

"What's the connection?" Chertoff asked.

"We believe Darchevsky was the leader of the two men that attacked the President and tried to attack us here on the island. All three are known associates of Jason Smith and we believe he is en route here with a bomb."

"What kind of bomb?" Chertoff asked.

Deuce motioned Tony over. "Mister Secretary, I'm Special Warfare Officer First Class Anthony Jacobs, EOD. The bomb has been described as a professionally assembled IED, if you will. It contains a shaped charge of semtex inside a small drum filled with nails. The charge alone is enough to completely obliterate a two-thousand-square-foot concrete building. The shape is made to cause maximum casualties in a forty-five-degree arc from the source to a distance of two hundred feet. Anyone inside that arc and distance will certainly be killed. Severe injuries will result out another two hundred feet."

"How can we assist you, Commander?" asked Mueller.

"I'm taking my team proactive, sir. We'd like you to pave the way with local law enforcement for our arrival in Key West at zero seven hundred, put out an APB on both Darchevsky and Smith, and ask the county Sheriff to set up a roadblock for outgoing traffic in Key Largo, disguised as a DUI checkpoint. We're going to find him and apprehend him."

"With the Secretary's permission, I'll get right on it" Mueller replied. "We already have assets in Key West, and I'll have two more agents out of the Miami field office join them. They'll meet you at the Sheriff's office. Anything else?"

"Yes sir," I said. "Can you arrange for two nine-passenger vans to meet us at Boca Chica Marina on board the Air Station? We'll be arriving by boat."

"I'll send the Miami agents down in our two tactical vehicles. They can carry thirteen passengers each. What's your plan, Commander?"

"We believe the attacks on Talbot and Burdick were meant to draw us out, sir."

"By proactive," Stockwell said, "you mean to set yourselves up as targets?"

"Yes, Colonel," Deuce replied. "That's exactly what I mean. This team was assembled to search out and neutralize terrorist threats in the Caribbean. With the attack on the President, and the use of this explosive device, in my opinion this qualifies as a terrorist threat and Key West is pretty much within our prescribed jurisdiction."

Chertoff said, "While your opinion may be open to interpretation, your team is uniquely qualified to conduct just such an operation. You have a green light, Commander."

"Thank you, sir," Deuce said.

"Deuce," Stockwell said. "Be careful. I'll have an open line to both the Secretary and the Director. I'm leaving DC within the hour and will meet you at the Air Station. Keep me updated."

All three screens winked off nearly at once. "Let's saddle up the troops," Deuce said. "Chyrel, activate all personal comm gear with tracking activated and link us all together. Print out twenty copies of Darchevsky's photo. Jesse, I'm putting you in charge of half the team, Kumar the other half. Scott, Julie and I will use the *Revenge* as a command and control center."

We walked outside. The sky was just beginning to lighten to the east. The team was assembled around the tables, including Doc. "Nikki's done in," he said. "She's crashed in the crew cabin."

"And you're not?" I asked.

"No," he replied simply.

"Everyone take a seat," Deuce said from the end of the table.

When everyone was seated, he brought them up to speed on the developments of the previous twelve hours. He broke everyone up into two teams, Alpha and Bravo. I had Doc, Tony, Jared, Charity, Dawson, Grayson, and Simpson in Bravo. Kumar had Art, Sherri, Hinkle, Mitchel, Bourke and Goodman in Alpha.

"Everyone dress in civilian clothes, long pants and DHS windbreakers," Deuce said. "We'll leave here aboard Jesse's boat in one hour and arrive at the marina on the Air Station, where we'll board two FBI tactical vehicles. Scott, you and Julie will stay with me aboard the boat. Your earwigs all have tracking software and from the boat we'll be able to follow each of you."

Chyrel came out and passed out the photos of Darchevsky. "This is Dimitri Darchevsky," Deuce said. "He's a Russian national raised in California. He used to be with the CIA and has been responsible for several assassinations in Eastern Europe. He's considered extremely dangerous. When we get to Key West, both teams will proceed to the Sheriff's Office on Whitehead Street, accompanied by an FBI driver. There you'll meet up with two more FBI Agents and the Watch Commander for the Sheriff's Department. Every law enforcement officer in the Keys has received an APB with Darchevsky's photo,

from the Fish and Game to Shore Patrol and everyone in between. I want you all to spread out through the city on foot and check every hotel, motel, resort, rental house, and flop house on the island."

Hinkle raised his hand and said, "What weapons are we to carry, mate?"

Deuce grinned, "Bring your long gun, Donnie. Jesse, where should they set up?"

"The two tallest structures on the island are the lighthouse and the La Concha. The lighthouse has a clear view all the way up Truman and Whitehead in both directions. The roof of La Concha has a clear view up both Duval and Fleming. These are also the most traveled streets on the island."

"Donnie you take La Concha. Jared, are you comfortable perching in the lighthouse? It'll be eyes only, I'm sure, and you won't have a spotter."

"Yes sir," Jared replied. "Eyes only."

"I can spot for him," Charity said. "I've been working with Julie doing it and we can see more with two pair of eyes up there."

"Okay, we'll have Key West PD provide security on the ground at the lighthouse and on the roof of La Concha. Everyone else will carry side arms only. Concealed. We don't want to upset the civilians. Any questions?"

"If we find him, do we take him down or just alert the locals?" Kumar asked.

"DHS has the lead, with backup from the Feebs and locals. If you spot him and can take him down without risk to any civilians, do it. If there's any risk at all, call for backup. Chyrel has us all on the same comm and

will provide instant location to send the nearest backup. Anything else?"

Nobody said anything more. "Go gear up and be up on the deck in fifteen minutes."

As everyone started toward the bunkhouses, Deuce pulled Jared aside. "Get with Tony, he always carries an extra wind breaker. I'm going out on a limb, but you're officially a part of this team on Jesse's word."

"I'm good, sir," he said. "Being here has been a huge blessing for me, and everyone has been a great help. Thanks for the opportunity."

Deuce and I watched as he walked toward the bunkhouse. "Charity will keep an eye on him, Deuce."

Doc and I headed across the clearing. I needed a quick shower while Doc got the engines started and the boat ready for departure. Ten minutes later, I was dressed and on the bridge. Doc had already woken Nikki, and she'd reluctantly remain on the island until we returned. A few minutes later, the team started boarding by ones and twos. Deuce and Julie were last to board, carrying two briefcases. While my boat's not exactly designed to accommodate eighteen people, we were only going to be aboard for a little over an hour. Deuce, Doc, and Kumar joined me on the bridge as I idled south toward Harbor Channel.

While I switched on the radar, sonar, and VHF radios, Deuce made a comm check to ensure everyone's earwigs were functioning properly and checked with Chyrel to make sure all eighteen identifiers were reporting.

A moment later I brought the *Revenge* up on plane heading northeast toward Harbor Key Bank and the narrow cut to the open Gulf. Sunrise would be in less than a

half hour, but it was already light enough to see the crab trap markers for the cut.

Once in open, deep water, I pushed the throttles to the stops and the big boat surged forward, reaching its top speed of forty-nine knots in just a few seconds. I made a slow, sweeping turn on the flat Gulf water to the southwest and entered the north jetty markers for Northwest Channel as a waypoint on the GPS. The autopilot corrected our heading a few degrees and showed an estimated arrival of thirty-two minutes.

We never slowed down as I made the turn into Northwest Channel. Early-morning boat traffic on a Friday is always very light and in fact we only passed a single fishing boat coming out of the channel before we turned into it. Ten minutes later, I turned due east around Whitehead Spit and skirted the south side of Key West. Somewhere on that island we hoped to find Darchevsky. But it was going to be like looking for a needle in a haystack.

As we approached the two-story-tall light that marked Boca Chica Channel, I slowly brought the *Revenge* down off plane and turned northeast into the channel. Once we were in the marina basin, I reversed the starboard engine, skidding the boat sideways while still moving toward the dock. Standing up and using my back on the wheel, I reversed the port engine and backed the *Revenge* alongside the main dock at the far end, where two large black vehicles sat with revolving blue lights on the roof.

Doc was on the bow and Dawson at the stern and they had us tied off before I even shut down the engines. The Dockmaster started our way, but as soon as he recognized the *Revenge* from the previous weekend and saw

all the black DHS jackets, he quickly returned to the marina office.

I joined Deuce and Kumar and walked toward the vehicles where the two FBI agents waited, a man and a woman. "Looks like the DHS has just invaded the Conch Republic," the man said. "I'm Special Agent Harry Sherman and this is Special Agent Amanda Elson."

"Deuce Livingston, Caribbean Counterterrorism Command," Deuce said, shaking hands with both agents. "These are my team leaders, Kumar Sayef and Jesse McDermitt."

"We were briefed on the manhunt and I was instructed to give your people a ride to the Sheriff's office and basically be at your beck and call."

"We appreciate that," Deuce said, ignoring the sarcasm. The Bureau didn't like being on the following end of any investigation. "Our team is made up primarily of former and current SpecOps people from all branches of the military, police, and intelligence. Any help the Bureau can provide in finding this man will be needed."

A Gulfstream G-5 flew over on approach and I noticed it had DHS markings. "That'll be the Director, Deuce."

Minutes later, a Navy sedan pulled up and Stockwell got out of the passenger side, along with an older man who carried a large case. He looked to be in his sixties but carried himself like a man half his age as the two walked toward us.

"Director Stockwell, these are Special Agents Sherman and Elson," Deuce said. Then turning to me, he said, "Jesse, meet Jim Franklin. He's got some electronics to set up. Would you show him aboard?"

I shook hands with the man and said, "Pleased to finally meet you, Jim. Follow me."

"Likewise, Jesse. Real sorry about what happened last fall. But I was happy to hear one of the guys died slow, choking on his own blood."

Changing the subject, I asked, "What's in the case?"

"Oh, this? Just one of my toys. It's an interface for cell phones. Uses a real sophisticated algorithm to locate a specific cell phone signal, by sort of connecting the dots between one or two other signals. You're heard of the 'Six Degrees of Kevin Bacon'? How any individual in Hollywood is connected through other individuals to the other stars within six steps? This baby does that with phones."

We stepped aboard the *Revenge* and I was pleased to see that Jim was actually wearing sneakers with his business suit. He caught me looking down and said, "Travis insisted. Said you were kind of particular about the decks." I opened the hatch to the salon, and as he entered he let out a low whistle and said, "Yep, I can see why."

"Right over here, Jim," Scott said. "On the end of the settee. Julie and I are set up to monitor everyone's comm and location."

"As I was saying, Jesse," Jim said, placing the case on the counter and opening it, "if I enter two phone numbers in this baby, it'll run through every number both of them called and find any that are in common. Then it'll use that data and locate any phone that was within a meter of any other that was called more than once. That finds any accomplices and any burn phones the target might have. Deuce said you were going to do a manhunt on foot. By the time you guys get spread out, I'll be able to tell you where your target is within two meters."

"That's a cool toy, Jim."

He lifted what looked like a giant laptop computer from the case, gently placed it on the table and looked around. "There's a power strip inside the cabinet, Jim. Hope you find him. It'll make our job a lot easier."

Deuce and Kumar were on the dock as I stepped off the boat. "The other two Feebs are at the Sheriff's office with the Watch Commander," Deuce said. "They'll meet you and Kumar when you get there. Our two shooters with their spotters will be driven to their locations by a pair of Deputies and everyone else will spread out from there. I hope Jim can locate Darchevsky fast. Otherwise the search could take days."

"He seemed to think it wouldn't take long," I said.

"Once you hook up with the Watch Commander, since you know the island, I want you to assign everyone a section. Use the vehicles to move the teams as the two of you see fit. You can split the teams north and south of Truman."

Kumar and I headed toward the parking lot and joined the others, climbing into the two large vans. A few minutes later we were crossing the bridge from Boca Chica to Stock Island and then on into Key West. It only took ten minutes to get to the Sheriff's office and the two vans parked in the main courthouse parking lot. Two men in FBI jackets waited with a uniformed Sheriff's Department Lieutenant.

I climbed out of the passenger seat and told the others to stay close, we'd be leaving in the van in a few minutes. Kumar and I walked over and introduced ourselves to the two agents and the Lieutenant. Four more Deputies stood behind the Lieutenant.

The Lieutenant was a stocky man by the name of Dwayne Breece. "I've been briefed by these two agents and have two squad cars and four Deputies at your disposal. We've called in every available Deputy and they're already out in the streets."

I stepped up a little closer to the Lieutenant and said, "The man we're after is the one your department wrote off as a 'biker gang' shooting yesterday, Lieutenant. The so-called 'biker' that was shot at is one of my men."

"An unfortunate mistake, Gunny. I know Doc very well, but I wasn't on duty at the time of the shooting. The Detective that took his and Nikki's statement has been reprimanded and the report revised."

I studied him closer. His attitude and bearing spoke volumes. "Semper Fi, Eltee."

"Oohrah, Gunny. We're down to a skeleton crew in both our offices here and over on Stock Island. Every available badge from both the Department and Key West PD is out looking and ready to help in any way we can. Sobriety checkpoints are being set up every ten miles all the way to the mainland. A contract killer is something we want off this island even more than you."

"Thanks, Eltee," I said. Then turning to the group I shouted, "Williams, Hinkle, get over here!"

The two men trotted over with their spotters, carrying their rifles in two unmarked fly rod cases I'd given them.

"Go with those Deputies. They'll take you to your nests and act as security while you're there. Let Kumar and me know when you're set up."

The four Deputies walked with them to the squad cars and drove away in opposite directions. The Lieutenant walked with us to the group and handed out street maps

of the island to each person. "Kumar," I said, "take your group in the van down Whitehead here to Southernmost Point. Split up there and start checking restaurants and any places that rent rooms, working your way east and north to Truman. My group will go up to Mallory Square and start working south and east. The island's small, but there's more than three hundred and fifty restaurants and over one hundred and fifty hotels. Use the van to drop a man off every few blocks along South Street and Atlantic Boulevard. We'll do the same on the north side, along Eaton Street. The important thing is to get spread out fast. With so many places to look, we have to count on Jim finding his electronic signature first, then converge on his location."

"Roger that, Gunny," Kumar said. Minutes later the two vans split up, heading north and south on Whitehead to our destinations. Within ten minutes everyone was on foot, working a grid. Chyrel kept us from overlapping and directed each individual.

Within an hour, I was starting to get the overwhelming feeling that there were just too many places to hide. By zero nine thirty, I was certain of it. I was on Eisenhower Drive, near Garrison Bight, and about to enter Harborside Motel when Deuce's voice came over my comm.

"Jesse, Kumar, this is Deuce. Jim has a hit. The target is stationary at the corner of Olivia and Elizabeth Streets."

"I'm nearly a mile away, on the east end of Olivia," I said. "Headed that way."

Deuce's voice came over the comm again. "Jared, about five hundred yards to the northeast of the lighthouse. You should have line of sight. There's a restaurant called Seven Fish. Can you see it?"

"Negative," Jared said. "I can see up Olivia and, counting the intersections, I can see Elizabeth, but the structures on either side are obscured by trees."

"This is Grayson. I'm on Elizabeth, two blocks away."

"Roger, Grayson. Julie says you and Sherri are closest. She's moving north on Elizabeth and Jesse's coming west on Olivia."

Within seconds two more team members were converging on the restaurant from the east and west.

"Target is on the move," Deuce said. "Heading west on Olivia."

I heard Charity say, "It's Darchevsky. No doubt about it. He's wearing tan slacks, a light blue shirt and a dark blue windbreaker. He's walking straight toward us."

"Hold your fire, Jared," I said. "Grayson and Sherri will be turning the corner behind him any second and I'm less than two blocks away." Already breathing hard, I turned up the speed as I passed the cemetery. Halfway down the block between Windsor and Elizabeth, I saw Sherri stop at the corner of the restaurant and peek around.

"This is Fallon," she said. "I have eyes on the subject."

Across from her, Grayson crouched next to a low stone wall and said, "I have eyes on him, too. He's crossing north across Olivia now. Continuing west on the north sidewalk."

"I got him," I said. "Grayson, you and Sherri start down the sidewalks on either side. Quick, but quiet. I'll be in the middle of the street between you in ten seconds."

"This is Williams. I have him ranged and sighted. I'm standing by."

Jared sounded like the consummate professional, no fear or panic in his voice at all. I knew that this was his

element. And I also knew he wouldn't take a shot unless ordered to. He'd finally come to grips with who and what he was and had conquered his demons, if only for a little while. I felt emboldened, knowing that he was perched up there and had our backs.

As I crossed Elizabeth Street, I slowed to a fast walk. I could see Darchevsky now, not even a block ahead. Grayson and Sherri were just a few yards ahead of me and fifty feet behind him. He stopped at the corner of Simonton Street for a second, then crossed over and continued down Olivia, just two blocks from Duval Street. Even though it was still early, I could see that Duval was already active, people crossing in both directions on the sidewalks.

Just then a Key West Police cruiser turned off of Duval onto Olivia. It stopped and the blue lights came on. Darchevsky stopped in his tracks halfway between Simonton and Center Street. I drew my Sig as I came abreast of Grayson and Sherri, and out of the corner of my eye I saw them draw their side arms also.

As Darchevsky started to turn, the three of us stopped and I shouted, "Darchevsky! Don't move! You're under arrest!"

He was next to a long wall with a picket fence on top of it. He moved quickly across the street and behind a parked car. In a split second he rose up and fired two shots. Grayson and I returned fire, as we steadily moved forward.

I heard Sherri call out, "I'm hit."

"Jared, shoot to maim," I shouted. A second later, there was the thunderclap report of my M-40, and Darchevsky

rolled out into the middle of the street, his weapon flying away from him.

I ran to the sidewalk, where Sherri lay on her side. Blood was already spreading across the front and back of her blouse, just above her right hip. I knelt down as she looked up and said, "Guess next week's marathon is out of the question."

I pulled her blouse up, exposing the wounds. It was a through and through, the exit wound slightly larger than the entry. I reached into the pocket of my cargo pants and pulled out two packages of Quikclot and two self-adhesive bandages. "This is going to burn like all hell, kid," I said as I ripped the first package open and poured the granules into the exit wound. I quickly pulled the backing off one of the bandages and pressed it firmly in place as she tried to muffle a scream. Then I ripped open the second package and did the same thing on her belly wound.

"Doc, get over here, riki tik. Sherri's down, but okay."

"Almost there, Gunny," came his reply.

The sound of a siren split the air and the cruiser sped forward, stopping in the intersection of Olivia and Center Street and the cop shut off the siren. Other sirens could be heard seemingly from every direction. Grayson had Darchevsky face down with his knee in the man's lower back. Doc came running up, so I left him to attend to Sherri and went to help Grayson, who already had flex cuffs on Darchevsky's wrists and literally yanked him to his feet with one hand.

He didn't stay on his feet long. As I strode toward him, I unleashed an overhand right that landed squarely on his jaw, dropping him like a bag of concrete. "What part

of 'don't move' did you not understand?" I shouted down at the unconscious man.

I turned to the cop and said, "Get an ambulance here, now! Officer down!"

The cop ran to his patrol car and called it in. Several voices were talking at once over the comm. Suddenly, it all went quiet and Deuce's voice came over it. "Jesse, report."

"Darchevsky's in custody. Unconscious with a superficial wound to his right hand and a broken jaw where he fell. Sherri was hit, but is awake and talking. Ambulance is on the way."

"Roger that. Everyone converge on the corner of Olivia and Center Street. The vans are on the way. Good job, everyone."

The ambulance arrived and though the paramedics disagreed with Doc, saying any gunshot wounds are required to be transported, Doc pulled rank and she stayed. She was up and walking around, but with a slight limp. The bullet had passed through the fleshy part of her waist. Within five minutes, the rest of the team had converged on the scene with Hinkle, Mitchel, Charity and Jared the last to arrive by squad car.

When Darchevsky woke up, he was moved into the first van to arrive and unceremoniously dumped in the back. I noticed that Jared's bullet had entered his right forearm, just below the elbow, and exited near his wrist.

As Jared got out of the squad car, Hinkle was the first to greet him. "Crikey, mate, that's one hell of a shot. That bloke won't ever shoot right-handed again." Several of the others slapped him on the shoulder as he made his way over to Doc and Sherri.

"Sorry I couldn't have prevented that," he said, pointing at her waist.

"Don't be," she said, shaking his hand. "You fired when ordered."

"And not before," I said with a grin as Charity took his hand in hers and led him toward the vans.

"Everyone mount up," Kumar said.

Within seconds, the two vans were leaving the scene, the four Deputies and Key West patrolman left scratching their heads. Ten minutes later, we pulled into the parking lot at the marina and after shaking hands with Special Agents Sherman and Elson, we boarded the *Revenge*. Three Shore Patrol Officers were waiting to take Darchevsky into custody.

Although the shooting took place in Key West, since it was one of the team that was injured, Deuce asked Key West PD to take jurisdiction. Key West was just glad to have him off the island and the case wrapped up.

Stockwell was standing on the bridge with Deuce when I climbed up to start the engines. "How's it feel, Gunny?" Stockwell asked.

"How's what feel, Colonel?"

"Being back in the saddle, doing what you were meant to do, leading troops in the field."

I just shrugged and started the engines. "Didn't really have time to feel anything."

"Great job," he said. "Both of you. Y'all have no idea what this little op meant."

"What do you mean?" Deuce asked.

"DHS isn't a law enforcement entity, you know that. It's the oversight agency of the FBI, CIA and all the other alphabet soup law enforcement agencies. You've just

taken the first step in the Counterterrorism Command becoming a full-fledged arm of law enforcement. Both abroad and domestically."

"So you're saying this was a test?" I asked.

"No, not at all," he replied as he started for the ladder. "I never had any doubt. I'm staying here tonight, since the G-5's already here. See you at oh six hundred." He climbed down and started toward a waiting Navy sedan. On the dock, he turned and said, "Oh, by the way, Doctor Burdick was here about an hour ago. I explained what was going on and she said she needed to get back to her patient anyway. The officer that was shot is in recovery and is expected to be back on duty in a week." Then he got in the car and it drove away.

Doc called up and said, "Ready to cast off?"

"Yeah," I replied. "Then get up here and take her out. I have a phone call to make."

Doc and Dawson cast off the lines and Doc took the *Revenge* out Boca Chica Channel, while I went up to the foredeck to call Jackie. Once again, I caught her between rounds.

"You mad at me?" I asked.

"I was for about a second. The Colonel explained what was going on. Think you'll find him?"

"They should be bringing him into ER in a few minutes. Feel free to slap him around a little, if you want."

"You already got him?" she asked excitedly.

"Yeah, just turned him over to the Shore Patrol and we're about to head back to the island. Want to join us?" I asked, hoping she'd say no, since we were already underway.

"I can't. The officer that was injured stepped in front of me. I'm going to stay here until he wakes up. Go celebrate with your troops."

"Okay, I'll see you at the dock at zero six hundred and I promise I won't be late."

"If you are, I'll kick your ass," she said as she ended the call.

I climbed back up to the bridge and was suddenly very tired. It didn't seem like that long ago when I could go for days with just a couple of hours sleep. Deuce and Julie were on the bridge and as I climbed up, Doc started to get up from the helm. I stopped him and said, "Take us home, Doc." Then I sat down in the second seat, put my feet up on the side console, leaned my head back and fell into a deep sleep.

It felt like it was only a few minutes later when suddenly I woke up. It was dark and quiet. For a second, I had no idea where I was or how I got there. I realized I was sitting on the bridge and the *Revenge* was docked under my house. My neck and knees were stiff and sore as I slowly stood up. Light softly filtered through the cracks around the big double doors in front of the boat and I could faintly hear voices that sounded far off and muffled.

I climbed down from the bridge and stepped over the gunwale to the dock. When I opened the door and went outside, I could tell by the angle of the sun through the trees that it was late afternoon. Looking at my watch, I confirmed that I must have slept the whole way back and at least two hours after Doc had guided the boat under the house.

Stiffly climbing up the steps to the deck, I crossed over to the rear deck and stood there for a minute, taking ev-

erything in. A chopper was sitting in the middle of the clearing and a large bonfire was going at the east side of the bunkhouses. There must have been thirty people standing and sitting around the fire and at the tables. Trent was busy tending the fire in the stone barbeque, and beyond the bunkhouses I could see his kids and Pescador running and jumping off the pier, then climbing up the ramp and doing it again.

Building this place, I'd had Alex in mind, though not really consciously. Before she returned from Oregon when she left two years ago to take care of her sick brother. This was before we'd even gone on our first real date, or even thought about it. I'd felt empty inside after she was killed and now suddenly realized that what I'd built for us, before there even was an us, I'd improved upon for this group, before there even was a group. My little island was now a thriving community of people that cared deeply for one another in a way that many people would never understand.

Looking down on my little island, for the first time in nearly a year, I felt whole again. I felt alive and suddenly I realized that life really is for the living and though I'd sensed it before, I now felt deep down inside that Alex would have wanted me to pick up the pieces, grab life by the horns and live again. I wanted Jackie here and I wanted to tell her how I felt about her. I resolved to do just that, as soon as I saw her in the morning. Right now I wanted to celebrate the success of a mission with my family.

I ran down the steps and nearly sprinted across the yard. Yes, it was a yard, not a clearing or a landing zone. Even if there was a chopper sitting in the middle of it.

"Whoa, mate," Hinkle said. "What's the big hurry?"

"Hand me a beer, Donnie." Then I spied two bottles of Pusser's Navy Rum on the table. "Belay that," I said. "Gimme a damn glass."

A shot glass was produced and Deuce poured me a double. I raised my glass high and said, "Standing up on the deck just a minute ago, I realized why men and women who have been to war yearn to reunite. Not to tell stories or look at old pictures. Not to laugh or weep. Comrades gather because we long to be with those who once acted their best, who suffered and sacrificed, who were stripped raw, right down to their humanity. I didn't pick you. You were delivered here by fate. But I know you in a way I know no others. I have never given anyone such trust. As long as I have memory I will think of you all every day and I'm sure that when I leave this world, my last thought will be of you, my family." A chorus of shouts went up and glasses and bottles were raised high. I tossed down the rum and it seemed to ignite a fire in me.

"That's more words than I've ever heard you say at one time," Stockwell said as he poured me another.

"Hi, Travis. Is this fine Navy rum of your doing?"

"Deuce told me how you seafaring types liked to celebrate, so I thought I'd do what I could to help. Have a nice nap?"

"You must be getting old," a familiar voice said from behind me. "I remember when me and you could go days with no more sleep than what you just had sittin' there under that house."

I spun around and was grabbed in a huge bear hug. When he put me down I said, "Rusty, when did you get here?"

"Julie called when y'all were headed back, so I tossed Rufus the keys and jumped in my skiff. Been here an hour while you been snorin' away in that boat of yours."

We celebrated until sunset, then Stockwell and his pilot took off and headed back to the Air Base. Then we celebrated some more. But not too much. We still had Smith out there somewhere and there was still a watch to be manned. About twenty-two hundred, those who would have watch drifted off to get some sleep before they had to go on duty. An hour later, I decided to turn in myself. Tomorrow would be a long day.

CHAPTER FOURTEEN:

Beltway Blues

I slept soundly in the bunkhouse and woke well before dawn. When I went outside, there were two large carafes on the table, steam rising from both of them, and a tray full of coffee mugs. Rusty was already up and he and Jared were poking the fire, trying to get it going again.

"Charlie makes good coffee," Rusty said. I poured a cup and joined the two men by the fire. "She said she'll have pancakes ready in thirty minutes."

"Where were you last night, Jared?" I asked. "I don't remember seeing you around."

His face colored a bit and he said, "Charity and I borrowed the Grady and went out fishing."

"Fishing, huh? Have any luck?"

He grinned and said, "You might say that."

"This young Devil Dog was telling me how you charged straight down the middle of the street at that assassin," Rusty said.

"Telling sea stories, are we? I walked, not charged. Did he mention that Grayson was right beside me and Sherri was on the other side?"

"How is she?" Jared asked.

"She'll be fine. Doc gave her something for the pain."

As if on cue, Charity and Sherri came out of the bunkhouse, poured coffee for themselves and came over to where we were standing. Charity kissed Jared, causing him to blush again.

"How's your side feeling?" I asked Sherri.

"Kinda numb. Doc said that's to be expected." She hugged me and said, "Thanks for acting so quickly."

One by one, the others started filing out of the bunkhouses. Deuce, Julie, Doc, and Nikki came across the yard and we all sat down at the tables, talking. Minutes later, Carl and Charlie came out of their new house with the kids, all of them carrying stacks of plates, glasses, orange juice, and a huge platter of pancakes.

After breakfast, those that weren't leaving took care of cleaning up, so the rest of us could get ready. At zero five hundred, Deuce, Julie, Doc, Jared, Rusty, and I boarded the *Revenge* and I started the engines. Stockwell insisted that Rusty come along, but didn't say why.

I called Doc up to the bridge and had him take over for a minute so I could talk to Rusty. We went down to the salon and sat down on the settee.

"What's up, bro?" he asked.

Rusty and I have always been able to talk about anything. I'd known him since before Julie was born and we were like brothers.

"I've decided to tell Jackie how I feel and I need you to talk me out of it."

"Talk you out of it? Hell, I been egging you on to do that for months. It's obvious you two like each other. Why the heck should I talk you out of it?"

"What do I have to offer, man? She's a doctor and I'm a boat bum and now I'm hooked up with a bunch of snake eaters and spooks."

"Jesse, you're a boat bum by choice and you don't have to stay hooked up with this bunch. Tell Stockwell you're done. Or not. Jackie's a smart woman and knows what you guys do. You tell her how you feel and let her decide."

"That easy, huh?"

"Sure it is, man. You two are like grunts and grits, made for each other."

"Alright, then. I'll do it."

An hour later we were tied up at the Boca Chica Marina dock. This time the Dockmaster did come out. I paid him a hundred dollars to dock the *Revenge* there for the day and had him fill the tanks. Stockwell was already waiting in the parking lot with Jackie. I started getting butterflies in my stomach when I saw her.

"Good morning, sailor," she said as we walked over. She gave me a warm hug and a kiss, then said, "Good thing you're on time. I just bet the Colonel here how long it'd take me to kick your ass."

"Jared, the SecNav has changed the location where he wants to meet with you," Stockwell said. "After a full review of the statements of everyone involved, he's asked if you'd accompany the rest of this motley crew to the White House and he'll meet you there."

"The White House?"

Stockwell grinned and said, "Yeah, he was sort of ordered to ask you if that would be alright."

"Ordered to? Who outranks the SecNav?" Jared's brow furrowed. "You mean the President?"

"Are all these Jarheads this slow on the uptake, Deuce?"

That caused me to chuckle a little. "Only us infantry, Colonel."

We got in two Navy sedans for the short ride to where the G-5 was sitting on the apron, its engines already running. Five minutes later we were in the air, headed north. Stockwell had rooms reserved for us at the JW Marriot, just across from the Visitors Center, so we could clean up and change before being escorted the two blocks to the White House.

Once we were settled in the plane and reached cruising altitude and the pilot turned off the seat belt sign, I mustered the courage and turned toward Jackie. "I have something to tell you," we both said at the same time and started laughing.

"Ladies first," I said.

"I just received transfer orders," she said. I tried to hide the pain those five words caused and must have succeeded, because she continued excitedly. "It's really thanks to you. The Surgeon General was so impressed with the operation to remove that bullet from your spine, he's recommended me for a neurosurgery internship at Bethesda. How cool is that?"

"That's great," I lied, feeling all the air being sucked out of my balloon. "When will you have to leave?"

"I have until the end of the month to get things settled in Key West and report for duty. It shouldn't even take that long. I have a sister in Orlando that's already agreed to keep my dog and I'll just put my car in storage. What did you want to tell me?"

She was very excited to start this new phase in her career. That was obvious. What did I have to offer to dissuade her? My mind was moving very slow. Fortunately, Rusty overheard our conversation, though he was pretending not to listen.

"Well, you gonna tell her about our partnership?" he blurted out suddenly.

"What partnership?" Jackie asked.

"Jesse's buying half my bar," Rusty said with faked excitement.

"That's great news. Between the two of you I bet you'll have the finest bar and marina in the Keys."

"See, Jesse. That's exactly what I said."

The rest of the flight lasted less than two hours, but it felt like two days. When we landed at Reagan National, a DHS van was waiting and took us to the hotel, where we split up. When I got to my room, I showered, shaved, and got dressed. To meet the President, one would normally wear a coat and tie, neither of which I owned. I wore the closest thing to dress clothes I did own, besides my uniform, a pair of navy trousers and a long-sleeve white shirt. There was a knock on the door.

I opened it and Rusty said, "Glad I'm not the only one not wearing a monkey suit."

"Thanks for what you said on the plane. I felt like a clown."

"Forget it, man," he said. "What are you gonna do now?"

"Do? She's getting transferred. It's the opportunity of a lifetime for her. I'm not going to do anything that might take that away. No way."

"Then suck it up, Marine. Life goes on."

"Want a drink? The minibar is well stocked and it's on the government's nickel."

"Sure," he said. "Why not? Meeting the President is kinda big, I don't mind tellin' ya, I'm as nervous as a long-tailed cat in a room full of rockers."

I opened two mini bottles of Bacardi, poured them into a couple of glasses with some ice and handed one to Rusty. "Is this what they pass off for rum up here?" he asked.

"The power elite up here don't drink rum," I said. "Only fifteen-year-old scotch."

"Another good reason not to leave the Keys," he said as we both tossed down the tasteless clear liquid.

I opened the fridge and tossed him a Coke, taking one for myself. "Can't meet the leader of the free world smelling like a cheap rum factory."

Rusty walked over to the window and looked out over the imposing skyline. "Why do you suppose that Colonel insisted I come along?"

I thought about it for a moment. Rusty had nothing to do with the fishing trip. His only connection to it was his daughter. "Guess we'll find out in about an hour."

There was another knock on the door and when I opened it, Stockwell was standing there in a custom-made suit. He looked at the two of us and said, "They don't sell ties down in the islands?"

"Couldn't really tell ya," Rusty said. "Never shopped for one."

"Let's get going, the van's waiting."

We followed him down the hall, where the others were waiting at the elevators. I just wanted to get this over with and go home. "What's wrong?" Jackie asked.

I wanted to tell her, but couldn't. "I don't like cities. Too many people."

We rode in silence down to the ground floor, walked out through the lobby and got in the same DHS van that had brought us there. A few minutes later we turned west on Constitution Avenue and passed the South Lawn, then turned north on Seventeenth Street for a block, finally turning into a security checkpoint at East Street. The van was checked over by Secret Service Uniformed Division officers, then we proceeded through the barricades and turned left along the west side of the South Lawn and parked in a slot to the north of the West Wing.

"Okay," Stockwell said from the front passenger seat. "We have to go through another security checkpoint, and the Secret Service is very strict on what can be brought inside the White House. Best bet is put your ID in your pocket and leave everything else. No purses, pens, knives, pretty much everything."

As we got out, everyone left their belongings on their seat and we walked to the Lobby Entrance on the north side of the building. We entered the foyer area, with its high ceilings and matching décor on either side, then straight through into the lobby itself, where we were greeted at the registration desk and issued our temporary IDs. The receptionist punched a button on the phone and said that ADD Stockwell and guests had arrived, then asked us to wait. There were matching couches and chairs on either side of the room, with closed doors beyond them. After a few minutes a Secret Service agent came through the door on the right and said, "The President will see you now, Colonel."

We followed him down a long corridor, through an archway, then turned left down another long corridor, where two more Secret Service agents waited at the end. I recognized one from the fishing trip, Paul Bender.

"I see you left your chest on the boat," he said.

"Good to see you again, Bender," I said, ignoring the dig.

"Good to be seen. I never got a chance to thank you, and especially you, Petty Officer Thurman." Julie's cheeks flushed just a little. Then he said into his coat sleeve, "Colonel Stockwell and guests are here."

A moment later, he said, "Follow me, please." We passed through what looked like an extremely thick and heavy archway that probably had steel doors behind hidden recesses, into a small alcove, built at an angle to the corridor. Another agent stood outside an open door, as Bender walked though and stood just inside and off to the side.

"Come in, Colonel," the President said. "All of ya, come on in." He got up from behind his desk and walked around it to greet us. The Oval Office was bigger than I'd imagined, with two large sofas facing one another in the center of a large oval rug that had the Presidential Seal in the middle of it. At one end was the Resolute Desk I remembered seeing pictures of, with a young John Kennedy, Junior under it. In front of the desk were two striped chairs facing a coffee table situated between the sofas. At the other end of the sofas were identical end tables and two more striped chairs angled next to those. He greeted each of us by name and thanked us for coming.

"Everyone have a seat," he said. "I'm really glad you could all make it."

"Mister President," Stockwell said. "This is Julie's father, Rusty Thurman, and Corporal Jared Williams. Secretary Winter asked him to come along."

The President shook hands with Rusty and Jared and said, "Don should be here in a few minutes to speak with you, Corporal. Mister Thurman, you raised a fine young lady here."

"Thank you, sir," Rusty said. "I'm inclined to agree with you."

After we were all seated, the President said, "Now, I know the FBI has some questions for all of you, but rest assured, they're just trying to sort things out for the record. I didn't get a chance to thank you for a great day of fishing, what with all the chaos."

"It was a pleasure having you aboard, sir," I said.

"Laura was really happy when we sat down to supper the next evening. It really surprised her when I told her I'd caught the dorado myself. The second reason I asked you here was to personally thank you, Miss Thurman. It's not going to be Miss much longer, though, is it?"

"No sir, we're getting married tomorrow."

"Congratulations to both of you. I know you probably have a lot of last-minute plans so I won't keep you long."

Just then another door opened. The President said, "Come in, Don. Folks, this is Don Winter, Secretary of the Navy."

We all stood up to shake hands with him and as he moved around the room, the President introduced each of us. He had a fantastic memory, it seemed.

Winter came to Jared last and said, "Son, I've been fully briefed on what happened to you and I wanted you here to apologize in person. Politics has no place on the bat-

tlefield and you were a victim of politics, nothing more. I have a paper in my pocket that once I sign it will change your discharge to honorable. But first, I have one question for you. What do you hope to gain from this?"

"Mister Secretary, sir," Jared said. "If my discharge is changed to honorable, will that mean I can serve again?"

"Yes, it does."

"That's all I'd want to gain, sir. To go back to my comrades and carry the fight to the enemy."

"May I borrow your desk, Mister President?" asked the SecNav.

"Please do," the President responded with a grin.

"Will you all please join me?" he asked as he walked around behind the desk. "Corporal Williams, front and center, please."

He sat down at the desk, pulled a sheet of paper from inside his coat and signed it, then asked the President if he would witness it. Once the President signed it, the SecNav stood and said, "Please raise your right hand and repeat after me, Corporal."

And just like that, Jared was sworn in, with all the rights and privileges that go along with an honorable discharge. The SecNav shook his hand, told him he had a week to report for duty, then thanked the President and left.

"Congratulations, son," said the President. "I bet there's not a lot of noncoms that can say they were sworn in in the Oval Office."

"No, sir. I wouldn't think so," Jared said, beaming.

"Now, one last thing," the President said. "Colonel?"

Stockwell stepped over to the President's side, took out what I knew to be two medal cases and handed them to

the President. “Petty Officer Thurman, I have here two medals that I’m about to give you. The circumstances of how you earned them can’t leave this office, but my signature is on both citations. I understand you were wounded when that rocket exploded?”

“Just a flesh wound, sir. A piece of shrapnel is what Doctor Burdick said.”

He opened one of the cases and turned it around. “This is the Purple Heart, Petty Officer. Given to men and women in the military who are wounded in action.”

“But, sir...” she started to protest.

“Are you about to argue with the President of the United States on what he considers to be an enemy action?” asked Stockwell.

“No, sir,” Julie replied.

He opened the other case and I immediately recognized the Bronze Star with a V affixed to it. “Colonel, will you please read the citation?”

Stockwell opened a file he’d been carrying and read from it, “To all who shall see these presents, greeting. This is to certify that the President of the United States of America, authorized by Executive Order on twenty-four August, 1962, has awarded the Bronze Star Medal to Petty Officer Third Class Juliet Thurman, United States Coast Guard, for exceptional and heroic actions under hostile fire. On four June, 2006, Petty Officer Thurman displayed superb initiative, selfless courage and extreme valor in placing herself between the enemy and her superior officers when under attack by RPG fire. Petty Officer Thurman’s actions bring great credit upon herself and the United States Coast Guard. Given under my hand, George W. Bush, President of the United States of Amer-

ica." Stockwell handed Julie the citation and both boxes. "Congratulations, Petty Officer."

Julie looked at Deuce and he raised both hands. "I didn't know anything about this, I swear."

"You're the first woman in the Coast Guard to be awarded that medal," the President said. "Your quick thinking saved a lot of lives, mine included. I'll never forget that."

We ended our visit with the President and were escorted back out by Agent Bender. "You people be careful down there," he said as we climbed into the van. "Maybe when I retire, I'll come down and visit you."

The drive to Quantico was full of excited talk and went by quickly. The President was true to his word. Our interviews with the FBI only took an hour, as they split us up and we were each interviewed by different agents.

As we left Quantico, Deuce asked Jared, "Since you don't have to report for a week, how about staying on with us for a few days? We'd love to have you at the wedding tomorrow."

"Good idea," I said. "There's still work to do on the island and you could use a stake to hold you over until Uncle Sam gets you back on the payroll."

"Okay," he said. "I've sorta enjoyed being out there on that island."

"So, it's back to you being a hermit?" Jackie asked.

I'd decided I wasn't going to dwell on her leaving. "Hermit?" I said with a grin. "There's almost twenty people on that island. I might have to spend some time in Key West to get away from the crowd."

She smiled and said, "That'd be nice."

Twenty minutes later, we were back aboard the G-5 and taking off. Stockwell motioned for Deuce and me to join him once we were at cruising altitude.

"Smith's still out there," he said. "And he's got to be getting frustrated, losing his hired killers, not to mention the money he's paid them. Have you given any thought to postponing the wedding?"

"Not an option," I said, looking across the cabin at Julie, who was talking to Doc and Jackie. "Besides, the whole team will be there and we'll be armed."

"There's a lot of ways a bomb that small can be used," he said.

"Not really," Deuce said. "I had a long talk with Tony. He studied the transcript of Lothrop's interrogation. He says the shape of the charge will have maximum effect in about a forty-degree arc, maybe less. So it has to actually be aimed. That means being on site to position it properly."

"The wedding is the logical target, though," I said. "He blames you for his fall from stardom and probably me to a lesser extent. Taking us both out, along with his replacement and most of the team, will be justifiable to a narcissist like him."

"Working on your Psych PhD?" Stockwell asked.

"If you'd met him, you'd know," I said. "The man thinks the whole world revolves around him."

"Okay, but I'm going to request the Sheriff have two Deputies stopping everyone coming in the driveway to the *Rusty Anchor*."

"Better add a third on a boat at the end of the canal," I said. "A lot of people will come by boat."

"Going to a wedding by boat?"

"It's a drinking island with a fishing problem. Rusty's having an open bar."

We discussed other security options, but the simple fact that there would be almost two dozen armed SpecOps people at the wedding meant very little in the way of further security would be needed.

We landed at NAS Boca Chica two hours later. Stockwell said he had some meetings up at Homestead for the afternoon, but would be at Marathon early the next morning. He arranged for Shore Patrol to take Jackie home to get a few things before returning to the base. Until Smith was located, it was best for her, Doc, and Nikki not to stay at home. Rather than stay on base she asked if we'd wait for her to pick up a few things and go back to the island with us. The Shore Patrol took Doc, Nikki, and Jackie to their homes so they could get what they needed for an extended stay on the island. Thirty minutes later, we were idling out of the marina and headed home.

News of Julie's awards and Jared's reenlistment arrived ahead of us and everyone was excited for them. Chyrel pulled Deuce and me aside once we tied up the *Revenge*. "I have some good news," she said with a knowing smile.

"Smith was in a car wreck?" Deuce asked.

"Not quite that good. He deposited the money he withdrew in Switzerland into a numbered account in the Caymans."

"How could he do that?" I asked. "He'd have to take it there, wouldn't he?"

"Not necessarily," she replied. "Most major offshore banks have branch offices in Miami. He went to a branch office there."

"Is that supposition?" Deuce asked. "Maybe he flew down there."

"Nope," she said. "His numbered account in the Caymans was one of the ones he did all those fancy transfers into. I've been monitoring all of them for activity. When I saw the deposit was made at the Miami branch, I hacked into their security system. Got him on video entering and leaving."

"Great work," Deuce said.

"I could transfer it out of the account if you want to mess with him a little."

"No. Just keep monitoring it. He doesn't know we know."

There was a lot to be done at the *Anchor*, so Rusty left soon after we arrived. Tony, Grayson, and Simpson went with him to help out and keep an eye on things there. We had an early supper, assigned watch, and turned in early. Tomorrow promised to be a long day.

Jackie and I took the forward stateroom and Doc and Nikki took the guest cabin. I figured this might be the last night I'd see Jackie for a while, maybe forever.

"You've been pretty quiet all day," she said. "Is something bothering you?"

"You mean besides a maniac with a bomb who keeps sending hired guns after Deuce?"

"Deuce and you, remember."

"Well, that and you're going away. Tomorrow might be the last time we see each other."

"I doubt that," she said. "Key West is my home now. This internship will last a year, but I'll be coming back down here quite a bit. I only accepted it with the condition I be reassigned to Boca Chica when I'm finished."

Still, I knew how fate sometimes threw a monkey wrench into anyone's plans. I decided then and there not to tell her how I felt until I knew she would be returning. "That's good to know."

"Mind if I get a shower?" she asked rather seductively.

"Mind if I join you?"

She smiled and disappeared into the head.

CHAPTER FIFTEEN:

The Wedding Cake

We awoke very early. Earlier than we needed to. Jackie had an idea on how to kill some time, though. An hour later we showered again and dressed. I could smell coffee coming from the galley. I poured two cups and sat down on the settee, where Jackie joined me a moment later.

When Doc and Nikki came up to join us, I made omelets for the four of us. It was zero five hundred and the others should be stirring soon. Doc and I had work to do before we departed. The engines had been neglected for the last couple of weeks and we needed to replace air, oil, and fuel filters and clean the water intake screens. While we were busy the women went up to the main house to see if Julie needed anything.

Deuce joined us, sort of. While the engine room on the *Revenge* is accommodating, it's not the *Queen Mary*. Doc and I took up about all the available space, so Deuce

crouched in the hatchway. "Anything I can help you guys with?"

"Just about done," Doc said.

"Another cup of coffee wouldn't hurt," I said, handing my mug across the starboard engine.

A minute later, Deuce handed me a fresh cup as I was reinstalling the now clean water intake strainer. "We should be ready to go in twenty minutes," I said.

"I'm still wondering if it's a good idea to go ahead with the wedding," Deuce finally blurted out. "If anyone got hurt, I'd never be able to live with it."

Doc glanced up from where he was replacing the port engine air filter. "Cancel on the day of the wedding, dude? Only if you want to stay single forever. Don't worry about it, we got your back."

"What Doc said, Deuce. We know that's when he's going to try again, we know what he's going to use and we know the approximate size and shape. Plus, and this is the important part, he doesn't know we're on to him yet."

"Besides," Doc added, "Tony's at the *Anchor*, knows what to look for, and will turn the whole property upside down to make sure it's not there."

We finished up and joined Deuce in the cockpit. "I need another shower," I said. "We're going to need to take more than one boat to get everyone to Marathon. Doc, will you let Trent know to get the Grady ready?"

"I'll let him know," Deuce said. "Doc looks like he needs to clean up, too."

While I was showering, Jackie came into the head and said, "Julie has asked me to be her maid of honor."

"Really?" I said, rinsing the shampoo from my hair. "I didn't know you two were that close."

"We're not, really. I mean we're friends and we talk sometimes. I don't think she has a lot of female friends."

I pondered that a second and said, "Now that you mention it, she doesn't. Hand me a towel?"

I dried off and got dressed again in clean jeans and a button-down gray shirt. Deuce and Julie had already decided that everyone should dress Keys formal, which meant no swimwear.

When Jackie and I climbed up to the bridge, some of the others came through the door and climbed aboard. I pushed the button on two key fobs and the doors slowly started to swing open. I started the engines and let them idle for a few minutes. Trent started the engine on the Grady and soon we had everyone aboard the two boats. Pescador sat on the dock by the cockpit looking up at me. Deuce and Julie had joined us on the bridge and I turned and asked, "Was he invited, Julie?"

She looked down at Pescador and said, "Yes, maybe his invitation got lost in the mail." He started wagging his big tail.

"Well," I said, "if you were invited, it'd be rude not to attend."

He leaped into the cockpit, then made his way along the starboard rail to the foredeck. "That's everyone, Carl. Go ahead and take the lead."

I suddenly had the thought that this would be the first time the island was completely uninhabited in a few months. Deuce must have had the same thought. "You think everything will be safe with nobody here?"

I looked over at him as I shifted the engines into forward. "I was just thinking the same thing. I'll make sure

to have the guys sweep the island when we get back, just in case."

We idled out into Harbor Channel and turned northeast toward Harbor Key. Fifteen minutes later, we were heading south in Rocky Channel toward the Bahia Honda marker lights. Turning southeast at Teakettle Key we crossed under the Seven Mile Bridge at Moser Channel and made a slow, sweeping turn to the east before lining up on Rusty's channel.

Minutes later, we were tied up at the *Anchor*. Rusty and Grayson came down to the dock as the whole team climbed up to meet them. "Welcome home," Rusty said. "We got everything about set up here."

"Where's Tony?" I asked.

"Inspecting a shipment of clams that just came in," Rusty replied. "He's looked over my whole property, even my damn underwear drawer."

We all walked toward the bar. "Everything's secure, Deuce," Grayson said.

"Thanks, Scott. And thanks for helping out here."

"Don't mention it. Anything for that old guy's cooking. Tony was right. Best food I ever had."

Jackie went with Julie to Rusty's house and I headed toward the bar with several others. When we were inside I noticed Cindy sitting at the bar, rolling silverware in blue linen napkins. "Hi, Cindy," I said. "I didn't know you were going to be here."

"Julie invited me a couple days ago."

"How'd it go at the bank?"

"Pam's great. In fact, everyone has been so helpful. She introduced me to several local business people, who are

on the board of trustees. She told me that you had everything all set up months ago."

"Not me, her," I replied. "I just got the ball rolling. Were you able to find a place?"

"Narrowed it down to two choices today. If you're not busy tomorrow, maybe you can help me decide?"

"No, I don't have anything scheduled," I said. "What's the two places?"

She told me about a property on Grassy Key, just east of Marathon, and another property on northern Big Pine Key. I was familiar with the one on Grassy, but there's so much vacant property on Big Pine, I wasn't sure from her description.

"We'll go out and look at them both tomorrow. I'm going to stay here tonight. What's your fiancé going to think about you splitting your time between two extreme corners of the country?"

"Hans?" she asked. "He's been really supportive."

"He's German?"

"His father was. His mother's Cuban. His real name is Johannes Schmidt."

Johannes Schmidt? Why did the name sound familiar? "You said he worked for the government?"

"A low-level clerk at the embassy in Eritrea. It's a tiny country in north Africa."

"On the southern Red Sea, south of Sudan," I said. And north of Djibouti, I thought. Johannes Schmidt.

"You know it?"

"Never been there, but I've heard of it. Excuse me, I need to check on something."

I looked around the bar and didn't see Chyrel. I walked over to where Dawson and Sherri were sitting. "Either of you see where Chyrel went?"

"I saw her heading out to the deck with Jared and Charity," Sherri said.

"Thanks," I said and headed out the back door. Chyrel, Jared, and Charity were sitting at a table talking to Dan Sullivan.

"Hey, Jesse," Dan said. "How ya been?"

"Doing well, buddy. You playing the after-party?"

"Sure am," he said. "How about a little sparring tomorrow?"

"Sorry, I have to go look at some property. Maybe you could talk Charity here into taking you on," I said with a grin.

He looked at her and said, "You're a fighter?"

She nodded and said, "Mixed martial arts, a little Krav Maga."

"MMA I've heard of," he said. "What's Krav Maga?"

"Probably better you don't know," I said. "But since I know you'll pry, it's Hebrew. Means contact combat. You'd be wise to pad up." I turned to Chyrel and asked, "Did you bring your laptop?"

She rolled her eyes and I said, "Forget I asked. I need you to check something out for me. Meet me on the boat in a few minutes." I left and went to find Deuce.

Minutes later we entered the salon and Chyrel had her laptop powered up at the settee. "Okay, who do you want me to hack?"

"The CIA," I said.

"Are you nuts?" Deuce said. "Their security is the best in the world."

"Not really," Chyrel said. "I've hacked in before."

"You have? When?"

"Just playing around to see if I could. No big deal. What do you want to know?"

"First I want to see Smith's unredacted file. Then check embassy employee records in Eritrea for a low-level clerk by the name of Johannes Schmidt."

"Who's he?" Deuce asked.

"Let's go outside and let Chyrel work," I said.

I poured two cups of coffee and the two of us climbed up to the bridge. "Okay, spill," Deuce said. "Hacking the CIA is dangerous. Even for someone with her skills."

"Let me ask you something. If you married a woman knowing she was going to inherit a lot of money with the plan to murder her later and you were able to pull it off, would you stop there?"

"I'm not sure I follow you."

"Just a hunch. We've been going on the assumption that Smith is after you. Retribution for ruining his career. What if we've been wrong all along?"

"Now you've lost me completely. Who's this Schmidt character?"

"Cindy's fiancé. She just told me he's a low-level clerk in Eritrea. Know where that is?"

"In the Horn of Africa, on the Red Sea. It's rumored the government has ties to al-Shabab."

"Yeah, it borders Djibouti," I said.

Deuce thought for a moment, then I saw the light come on. "Johannes Schmidt. Jason Smith? Man, that's a reach."

"Think about it under this light, Deuce. I changed my will a few months ago, before Smith was sent to Djibouti. If anything were to happen to me, the bulk of Alex's

estate would go into the trust I set up for the fly fishing school for kids, with Cindy as the executor."

"And?"

"Assume for a minute that Schmidt is Smith. He marries Cindy and I'm suddenly dead. He'd be married to the woman who is executor of a seven-million-dollar trust. What if he pulled a 'Downeger'?"

"Like when he murdered his first wife? Hmm, I see where you're going. It's still a reach, though. The money would be tied up in the trust. He couldn't get his hands on it."

"No, but he could convince Cindy and the trustees to invest part of it. He could set up a shell investment company," I said, guiding him.

"But, how's he know you made Cindy your executor?"

"He's not without resources."

We heard the salon door open and Chyrel called up, "Got something."

We went down to the salon and sat down on either side of her as she pulled up Smith's file. "I was able to get in and out undetected. I couldn't download his file, but I was able to copy it and move it through several offices within the Agency, before siphoning it out through the FBI."

It took us twenty minutes to skim through the file. The only connection we found was that he was fluent in German and Spanish. "You didn't find anyone named Johannes Schmidt working at the embassy in Eritrea, did you?" I asked.

"Yeah, I did. But you're not going to like it."

She opened another file. It was on Johannes Schmidt, but he wasn't a low-level clerk. That was just his cover. Schmidt was a deep-cover operative for the CIA.

"Shit," said Deuce. "Got a picture?"

"Yeah, that's the part you're not gonna like." She hit a few keys and Smith's picture came up, with Schmidt's name under it.

"Double shit," I said.

"Okay, so maybe it wasn't a reach," Deuce said. "But hey, let's look at the bright side. I'm not his target."

"Screw you," I said. "What do we do with this information?"

"Chyrel," Deuce said, "How deep is this cover?"

"What do you mean?"

"If Johannes Schmidt were to disappear from the Eritrea embassy, would his ID be good enough to set himself up somewhere in the States, like Oregon?"

"CIA fake IDs are the best there are," she said. "Yeah, he could start over in the States with it, but it'd be flagged by the Agency if he disappeared and he wouldn't be able to enter the country with it."

"Getting a fake Social Security number using his cover ID wouldn't be a problem for him," Deuce said. "And getting into the country with another fake ID wouldn't be either."

"Should we tell Cindy?" I asked.

"There's no need to right now," Deuce replied. "If and when we catch him, maybe then. If he disappears completely, well, she wouldn't be the first woman jilted at the altar. Better that than knowing your fiancé is a wanted murderer."

"No word of this leaves here," I said.

"Word of what?" Chyrel asked.

We went back out to the deck and sat down with Jared and Charity. Several of the others were scattered around at the tables, along with quite a few of the local fishing crowd.

"How long have you and Julie been dating?" Jared asked.

"We only met about eight months ago," Deuce replied. "But it feels like we've known each other forever." Jared and Charity looked at each other and shared a not-so-secret smile.

"Only another hour of bachelorhood," I said, looking at my watch. "I'm going to go check on some things."

I left them there and walked around the side of the bar, then down by the docks. I scanned all the boats tied up there and saw that all but a couple of skiffs in the small-boat area were familiar. The ones I didn't recognize had a couple inches of water in the bottom from the last rain, so they had been here for a couple of days. I walked to the south end of the dock and down the crushed-shell road that paralleled the canal down to the boat launch. A Fish and Wildlife boat was anchored at the entrance to the canal now. I recognized the young man on the boat and waved. He gave me a thumbs up that everything would be okay there.

I walked around the east side of the property, surveying everything. I knew Tony and Grayson had already done this, but they weren't familiar with the property and might have missed something. When I got to the shell driveway, I continued out to the road. Two Monroe County Sheriff squad cars were parked on either side of

the entrance, facing in opposite directions so both the driver's doors were inboard.

A FedEx truck pulled in and both Deputies got out and stopped him. I walked up to the truck as one of the Deputies asked what he was doing here.

The driver thumbed through an electronic device and said, "I have an express delivery for an Anthony Jacobs."

"I'll take it," I said.

"Are you Anthony Jacobs?"

"No, but he works for me," I lied.

"Sorry, sir, but I have to get him to sign for it."

"How big is it?" I asked.

He glanced down at his device and said, "Forty-eight inches long, by six inches wide and two inches thick. Weighs eight pounds."

"Shipped from?"

"Raleigh, North Carolina."

"It's alright, Deputies," I said, grinning. Then to the driver, "Follow me." I walked back down the driveway to the parking lot. I saw Tony talking to Simpson at the door to the bar and called him over.

He trotted up as the FedEx guy parked and went into the back of the truck. "Man says he's got a delivery for you, Tony."

"I thought it wasn't going to get here in time," he said with a huge grin. "It's my Winchester."

The driver stepped down from the truck with the package and asked for Tony's ID, which he showed. Tony signed for the package and said, "I gotta get this wrapped." He turned and ran toward Rufus's little shack on the back of the property.

I walked around to the far side of the canal. There's a trail through the woods there and I remembered back to when Alex and I used to run together. We had a three-mile loop that started and ended running through these woods. The woods were so thick it was out of the question for anyone to get through them, but the trail was a different story.

When I reached the other side of the woods, there was another Monroe Deputy parked there at the end of Sombrero Beach Road. I smiled inwardly. Stockwell had all the bases covered. Walking back to the *Anchor*, I thought about the size and shape of the bomb. Not very concealable and too heavy for one man to move easily.

When I got back through the woods more people had arrived. By both car and boat. The Deputies and Marine Patrol I knew to be locals who would probably recognize everyone in attendance. I started to relax. A little. Most of the team had congregated in the parking lot and I joined them.

"It's almost time to start," Grayson said. "We were discussing if maybe some of us ought to sort of stand around the fringes, instead of all sitting together."

"Everyone's armed?"

"Yeah," replied Grayson.

"Not me," Chyrel said. "I'm not very good with a gun."

"I'll work on that with you this week," I said. "I think it'd be a good idea if five or six were scattered around the area. Pick the best five shooters, Scott."

"Well, two will be standing at the altar, you and Deuce. After y'all would be Donnie, Glenn, Germ, Sherri, and me. We'll spread around the back of where everyone's sitting."

"Everyone else," I said, "should be on the groom's side, toward the rear."

We split up then and I headed into the bar, where I was sure Deuce and Rusty would be. Sure enough, they were at the bar with two shot glasses in front of them. Rusty produced a third and poured two fingers of Pusser's rum in each.

"Son," Rusty said, "Julie's my only child. Her momma died giving her to me. She's so much like her momma. There's no greater gift I could give a man and no better man than the one I give her to. You take real good care of her."

"I will, sir," Deuce said respectfully.

"A shame your dad couldn't be here today," I said, lifting my glass. "To Russ Livingston."

We tossed back the rum and Rusty said, "Okay, that's it. Julie'll kick both our asses if you're drunk."

"I think it's about time we get out there," I said.

"Yeah," Rusty said. "I'll go check on Julie."

Deuce and I walked out the back door of the bar and around the side to the altar that my former First Mate, Jimmy Saunders, had built. Most of the guests were seated, and Dan sat on a stool by the wall, playing softly on his guitar.

Deuce and I were met at the altar by the Reverend Douglas Bader of Conch Unity Church. Rusty took Julie there when she was little, though neither had been in a couple of years.

"Good to see you again, Jesse," the Reverend said. "Be nice to see you in my church one of these days."

"One of these days, Reverend," I said. "This is Deuce, I mean Russell Livingston. He's the groom."

"You're a lucky man, Deuce," he said. "Julie's a fine young woman. Do you prefer Russell?"

"Deuce is fine, Reverend. But Julie doesn't like it, so make it Russell during the ceremony."

He laughed and said, "Yes, even as a little girl she detested schoolyard nicknames. You have the rings?"

"I have hers," Deuce said. "Julie has mine."

"That's perfect," he said. Then he looked over the guests and said, "Quite an assortment of guests. Your side seems to be mostly rough-looking men."

"We're military, sir," Deuce offered. It seemed to satisfy the Reverend.

Just then, Jimmy's girlfriend, Angie, came around the corner of the bar and said something to Dan. He wound up the tune he was playing, turned his amp up a little and started the Bridal Chorus. Everyone stood up and waited. After a few seconds, Jackie came around the side of the bar. She'd changed into designer jeans and a light blue blouse with a ruffled neckline and was carrying a light blue bouquet of hibiscus. She had her hair pulled back in a loose ponytail.

Once she joined us at the altar, Dan started playing the Wedding March and Rusty came around the corner, with Julie on his arm. Deuce inhaled sharply. Rusty had changed, too. He was wearing black trousers and a light blue long-sleeve dress shirt. Both obviously brand new. Julie was dressed in a simple white dress that I recognized from long ago.

I whispered to Deuce, "That's the dress Julie's mom wore when she and Rusty were married."

Gone was the little girl that I'd watched grow up. Gone was the tomboy, besting all the boys in high school at

fishing. Gone was the second best flats guide in the Keys. Gone was the Coast Guard SpecOps Petty Officer. In place was a beautiful woman, her dark auburn hair styled in a simple way, with a narrow headband of small light blue flowers and a simple short white veil.

"Wow," Deuce whispered.

Rusty and Julie walked slowly between the rows of guests and up to the altar. Dan ended the March as Rusty gave her a hug, took her hand and placed it in Deuce's, then took a seat in the front.

"Please be seated," said the Reverend. "My friends, we're gathered here in the eyes of God to join this man and this woman in holy matrimony. Who gives this woman?"

Rusty stood up and with a tear in his eye and a choke in his voice said, "Her mother and I do."

The Reverend continued, "In the Book of Genesis it says, 'It is not good for man to be alone. I will make a helper suitable for him.' I've known this woman most of her life and know that she is more than up to the task. Russell and Julie, as you prepare to take these vows, give careful thought and prayer, for as you make them you are making an exclusive commitment one to the other for as long as you both shall live. Your love for each other should never be diminished by difficult circumstances, and it is to endure until death parts you. Hand in hand you enter marriage, hand in hand you step out in faith. The hand you freely give to each other, is both the strongest and the most tender part of your body. The wedding ring is a symbol of eternity, it is without end. It is an outward sign of an inward and spiritual bond which unites two hearts in endless love. And now as a token of your

love and of your deep desire to be forever united in heart and soul, you, Russell, may place a ring on the finger of your bride."

Deuce turned to me and I reached into my pocket and handed the ring to him. As he slid it onto her finger, he said, "Julie, I give you this ring as a symbol of my love and faithfulness to you."

The Reverend said, "By the same token, Julie, you may place a ring on the finger of your groom."

Julie turned to Jackie, who handed Deuce's ring to her. As she slid it on his finger she said, "I give you this ring as a symbol of my love and faithfulness to you, also."

They both turned to the Reverend. "The ring is the symbol of the commitment which binds these two together. There are two rings because there are two people, each to make a contribution to the life of the other, and to their new life together. Let us pray."

He bowed his head and continued, "Bless, O Lord, the giving of these rings. That they who wear them may abide together in your peace and grow in one another's eyes. Amen."

"For as much as Russell and Julie have consented together in holy wedlock, and have witnessed the same before God and these witnesses, and thereto have pledged their faithfulness each to the other, and have pledged the same by the giving and receiving each of a ring, by the authority vested in me as a minister of the Gospel, and according to the laws of the state of Florida, I pronounce that they are husband and wife together, in the name of the Father, and of the Son, and of the Holy Spirit. Those that God has joined together, let no man put asunder. Russell, you may kiss your bride."

Deuce lifted Julie's veil and kissed her as everyone began to cheer. I noticed that Rusty was weeping openly, but quickly pulled a handkerchief from his pocket and wiped his eyes. Deuce and Julie started back down the aisle as the guests tossed bird seed over them. Jackie and I followed, along with Rusty.

"The bar's open!" Rusty yelled.

Halfway down the aisle, I noticed a white van turning around in the parking lot and backing up to the congregation. It had a mural on the side of a huge wedding cake and the name *Creations by Rebecca* on both sides and the back doors. It came to a stop just ten feet from the back of the chairs, and the driver got out and opened the back doors. The driver was an older man, with gray hair in a ponytail. When he stepped away from the doors, I saw a huge wedding cake. It had four layers, the top one about twelve inches around and each lower one a few inches larger. It was over two feet tall and was sitting on a pallet four feet square.

Twelve inches around? Two feet tall? "Deuce!" I shouted. "The cake!"

Suddenly, all the team members drew their side arms and almost twenty guns were pointed at the driver. Tony was the first one at the back of the van. He produced a long Ka-Bar knife and gently pushed it into the top layer. It only went in less than half an inch. "Solid," he said.

"Where'd this come from?" Grayson asked the driver threateningly.

"A guy in Miami paid me two hundred dollars to deliver it," he replied. "Said his regular driver was sick. And I'd get another two hundred if I was exactly on time."

"Get everyone out of here," Tony said as he began to very carefully cut away the outer cake from the small barrel hidden inside that contained the bomb.

The team quickly moved all the guests through the parking lot and up the driveway. I stood next to Tony with Jared. Deuce came quickly over. "Get the hell out of here, Deuce," I said.

"I'm not going—"

I cut him off. "Dammit, Deuce, you have more than yourself to worry about. Go!"

He reluctantly left, but didn't go far. "How can I help?" I asked Tony.

"Almost got it cleared away. Looking for a deton—oh shit." He looked up at me. "No time to defuse it. The timer's down to thirty-five seconds."

"Can we carry it to the water?"

Tony looked toward the turning basin at the end of the canal, fifty yards away. "No time," he said.

"I'll drive it off the boat ramp, then," I said and started quickly toward the front of the van.

Suddenly, the engine roared to life and the van lurched forward, then turned sharply onto the crushed-shell road heading toward the boat ramp. Jared was behind the wheel.

The van increased speed, crunching over several chairs and speeding down the shell road. "Jared!" Charity yelled as she ran up beside me.

Roaring down the road, the heavy van rocked from side to side in the ruts. Tony, Charity, and I ran after it. He never slowed down. In fact, he drove even faster. The van reached the ramp and swerved sharply to the left toward a shell mound at the concrete sea wall. It hit the

mound and flew over the low wall, somersaulting and hitting the water almost vertically, nose down. When the grill hit, the van immediately flipped end for end and splashed into the water on its roof.

There was a sudden whoosh and a giant fireball erupted, blowing the sides out of the van. Black smoke billowed in a mushroom cloud above it. The flames quickly went out as the van sank in the eight-foot-deep water.

I ran faster, pulling away from Tony and Charity. Reaching the sea wall, I didn't hesitate, but dove headlong into the water, which now had a layer of flames from the ruptured gas tank. The water was clear, and I swam under the flames to the overturned van. I got to the driver's door and tried to open it. It was jammed. I started to swim to the other side. The windshield was gone, so I swam through it.

I found Jared's body floating against the floor of the van. There was no chance he was alive. One of the slats from the pallet was sticking out of both his chest and back. I grabbed his shirt collar and hauled him out the open side door and swam as hard as I could to get clear of the burning gasoline. Finally, I surfaced twenty feet away on the ramp itself, gasping for air.

I heard sirens in the distance and could hear people shouting and splashing down the ramp. There was nothing anyone could do. Jared was dead. Smith had been unsuccessful at ruining his career in the Corps, but killed him in the end. Standing in the waist-deep water, with Jared's body floating face up, the plank sticking grotesquely out of his chest, I swore I'd find Smith and kill him with my own bare hands.

EPILOGUE

Jared's funeral was held three days later and was attended by hundreds of people, including Colonel Stockwell, Tom Broderick, Tank Tankersley, and Tex Latimore. He was buried right next to his friend, Pop. All the military members of the team attended in uniform. Stockwell stopped in Jacksonville, North Carolina, and picked up Tom, Tank, and Tex, along with an Honor Detail of seven riflemen and a bugler, handpicked by Tank, himself. Deuce and I folded Jared's flag and I presented it to Dave. As I knelt before him and his wife and gave the standard grateful nation speech, I whispered in Dave's ear, "I *will* find him."

Stockwell ordered the whole team to take a month off after the funeral. The next day, Deuce and Julie reluctantly left in their Whitby ketch to honeymoon in the Caribbean. Charity had a meltdown after the bombing, but was able to be at the funeral. She and Sherri went up to Miami together immediately afterwards.

Deuce and I decided we had to tell Cindy about Smith. She didn't take it well, refused to believe us at first. Finally we showed her the redacted portion of his file, the news clipping of his wife's murder, and the video of Kyle Parker's interrogation, where he admitted being hired by Smith to kill his wife. She took it hard and left the next day for Oregon.

I told Chyrel to take Franklin's phone trace equipment home with her and to keep tabs on Smith's account in the Caymans. If anything happened, I wanted her to call me immediately. I spent the next three days on the island, working with Trent to get all the little details finished on the bunkhouses and their house.

On the fourth day, Chyrel called. "He's in Belize. He just withdrew ten thousand dollars at the Cayman Bank branch in Belize City."

"Can you freeze his assets?"

"What agency do you want it to show freezing it?"

"Make it the CIA," I said. "He's bound to know they're looking for him and might not be aware that everyone else is on to him yet. Any luck with Franklin's phone gizmo?"

"Actually, yeah. Smith has three burn phones that he's used on occasion. I had to keep the Director up to speed on what I was doing, sorry. Each person he called using the burn phones has been picked up and is being held with no contact to the outside world."

"So, the Colonel knows what we're doing?"

"He surmises," she replied and ended the call.

I already had the *Revenge* outfitted with provisions to last a month and reinstalled the bladder fuel cells. I left before dawn the next morning, not telling anyone.

It was over seven hundred miles to Belize City and I had to stop in Cozumel to refuel. I arrived in Belize early the next morning and cleared customs. Chyrel gave me an address of a cantina where his primary phone had been every day for three days and I went straight there.

I showed Smith's picture to a pretty bartender there and with a polite smile I asked, "*Has visto mi amigo, señorita?*"

She smiled back and said, "*Sí, señor*. Meester Herrero come here three days. Nice man, Meester Herrero. Not so handsome as you, *señor*."

Not very original, I thought. Herrero is Spanish for steelworker, or Smith. I ordered a cold Belikin and took a seat by the door, in the shadows. The bartender came over and asked if I wanted to see a menu.

"*Huevos, salchichas, tomate y sopaipillas, por favor.*"

She smiled seductively and said, "You have been to our country before, no?"

"A few times," I replied.

She turned and went to place my order. She was wearing a pleated flower-print skirt and a white blouse hanging off of her left shoulder. Easy to see why Smith kept coming back.

A few minutes later, she brought my eggs and sausage, with tomatoes and fry jacks on the side. I ate hungrily, then sat back and waited. I didn't have to wait long. My satphone chirped an incoming message. It was from Chyrel and read, "Puerto Cortez, Honduras."

I left a twenty on the table and walked out the door. The next five days, he stayed just ahead of me. It seemed like he knew I was arriving and left just before I got there. I went a hundred and twenty miles south to Honduras,

then to Puerto Cabezas, Nicaragua, then almost six hundred miles to Port Morant, Jamaica. With only ten grand to his name and no access to his fortune, he would run out of money soon.

It was late afternoon when I pulled up to the docks in Port Morant and got another text from Chyrel. "Tried to access account. Moving northeast now."

I fueled up and left Jamaica astern, heading toward the Windward Passage, a very busy shipping lane between Haiti and Cuba. Two hours later I received another text, "Cockburn Town." I plotted the distance to the capital city of the Turks and Caicos on Grand Turk Island. Over four hundred miles. I'd have to stay awake through the night, going through Windward Passage.

I made Cockburn Town at zero two hundred and anchored in the shallow water on the west side of the island. I decided I'd catch a few hours of sleep and also avoid the overtime charge for customs.

I awoke at zero six hundred and called the Harbor Master on channel sixteen. He directed me to the pleasure craft fuel dock on North Creek and said I could remain tied up there for twelve hours. I assured him I'd be long gone before then.

I fueled up, paid the entry fee and cleared customs, then started walking toward the Hispanic side of town. The official language of the Turks and Caicos is English, but there's a lot of people that speak Creole and Spanish. By now, I'd gotten used to the kind of places Smith preferred. Little out-of-the-way cantinas for drinking and tiny restaurants where the tourists don't go for eating. He looked Hispanic and spoke fluent Spanish.

I'd been just far enough behind him that I hadn't seen what kind of boat he was using and so far, Chyrel hadn't dug up anything. She hadn't texted me that he was on the move again, so I was pretty sure he was still here. Somewhere.

I came to a small cantina set back down a narrow alley. The interior was dark, but the music coming from a radio and the pot of coffee on the burner told me they were open. I walked over to the bar and took a seat on a stool at the end. A moment later a large black man came out of the back.

"*Qué quieres?*" he asked with more of a growl than a voice.

I looked him straight in the eye as I slid Smith's picture slowly across the bar, with a twenty on top of it. "*Café y información.*"

He poured a cup and set it in front of me, then picked up the bill and the picture. He looked at it for only a second and said, "*Sí*, he was here last night. A man running."

"Any idea where he's staying?"

"He is running from you, no? *Estás con la policía?*"

I picked up the cup and took a drink of the thick, dark coffee before answering. "No, I'm not a cop."

A grin slowly came to his face. "I tink dis man might find big trouble today. Yes, I know where he stay." I slid another twenty across the bar, but kept my hand on it. "He here *ayer por la noche*. Had drinks and ask about a cheap hotel. I send him to my cousin, she have rooms for rent."

"*Donde está la casa de su prima?*" I asked. He studied me for a moment, wondering how much a threat I might be to anyone other than Smith. "I want only the man."

"Down the alley, *señor. Casa roja a la derecha.*"

I removed my hand from the bill and picked up my coffee. I swallowed the last of it and said, "*Gracias.*"

I left the bar and continued down the alley, looking for a red house on the right side. I found it five doors down. A sign in the window said in Spanish and English there were rooms available.

As I walked up the steps the door suddenly flew open. Smith stood there with a Beretta 9mm pointing at my face. "So, you came to me," he said. "Makes things a lot easier." I stood unyielding and said nothing. "No last words? How'd you find me?"

"Wasn't hard. Your skills have dulled since you left the field. We've been on to you for over two weeks. You left a trail a kid could follow."

"Move. Down the steps and toward the end of the alley." I turned around and slowly walked down the steps and turned right. The end of the alley. "So, you think you know all about me, huh?"

"We know about Charlotte Downeger and your plans to do the same with Cindy Saturday," I said. I sensed him stop in his tracks. I continued walking. "We know about Stolski, Parker, and Darchevsky. Two are dead, one's in Gitmo."

"Keep moving," he said. "Go through the gate on the right."

I pushed the gate open, noting a slight movement behind it. I continued walking. "We know about your Cayman account, too."

That was a distraction. "It was you that froze my account?"

"Well, Chyrel, actually."

"I should have known," he said as he followed me through the gate. "That's far enough. Turn around. I want to see your eyes when I kill you."

I turned slowly. "Sure, I want to watch you die anyway."

When I was facing him, he had a puzzled look on his face. He had the gun and was beyond my reach. In a flash, a leg shot up, kicking the gun from his hand. Then another foot flew to the back of his head, connecting squarely with the fragile vertebrae there. He went instantly down to his knees and fell forward onto his chest, his arms unable to break his fall. In an instant his attacker was on his back, pulling his head up by the hair.

I knelt down in front of him and said, "Jared Williams's dishonorable was overturned and he reenlisted. Then you killed him with that bomb. But before he died, he at least had a chance to know love. Do you remember Charity Styles?"

In the next instant, Charity grabbed him under the chin and yanked his head sideways, pushing his head downward with her other hand. The sudden wrenching motion severed his spinal cord. His lifeless eyes looked up at her.

"Let's go home, kid," I said and picked up his Beretta.

THE END

If you'd like to receive my twice a month newsletter for specials, book recommendations, and updates on coming books, please sign up on my website:

WWW.WAYNESTINNETT.COM

THE CHARITY STYLES CARIBBEAN THRILLER SERIES

Merciless Charity
Ruthless Charity (Summer, 2016)
Heartless Charity (Winter, 2017)

THE JESSE MCDERMITT CARIBBEAN ADVENTURE SERIES

Fallen Out
Fallen Palm
Fallen Hunter
Fallen Pride
Fallen Mangrove
Fallen King
Fallen Honor
Fallen Tide
Fallen Angel
Fallen Hero (Fall, 2016)

The Gaspar's Revenge Ship's Store is now open. There you can purchase all kinds of swag related to my books.
WWW.GASPARS-REVENGE.COM

Made in the USA
Columbia, SC
17 February 2018